Please turn to the
a special afterwor
the Re

Praise for Mary Daheim and her Emma Lord mysteries

THE ALPINE ADVOCATE

"An intriguing mystery novel."
—M. K. Wren

THE ALPINE BETRAYAL

"Editor-publisher Emma Lord finds out that running a small-town newspaper is worse than nutty—it's downright dangerous. Readers will take great pleasure in Mary Daheim's new mystery."
—Carolyn G. Hart

THE ALPINE CHRISTMAS

"If you like cozy mysteries, you need to try Daheim's Alpine series. . . . Recommended."
—*The Snooper*

Please turn the page for more reviews. . . .

THE ALPINE DECOY

"[A] fabulous series . . . Fine examples of the traditional, domestic mystery."

—*Mystery Lovers Bookshop News*

THE ALPINE FURY

"An excellent small-town background, a smoothly readable style, a sufficiently complex plot involving a local family bank, and some well-realized characters."

—*Ellery Queen's Mystery Magazine*

THE ALPINE GAMBLE

"Scintillating. If you haven't visited Alpine yet, it would be a good gamble to give this one a try."

—*The Armchair Detective*

THE ALPINE ICON

"Very funny."

—*The Seattle Times*

THE ALPINE JOURNEY

"Seattle super mystery writer Mary Daheim is back again in *The Alpine Journey*, a very compelling tenth entry in the wonderful Emma Lord series. . . . A dark and complicated plot is a great addition to this winning series."

—*Mystery Scene*

THE ALPINE KINDRED

"Witty one-liners and amusing characterizations."

—*Publishers Weekly*

THE ALPINE LEGACY

"Daheim writes . . . with dry wit, a butter-smooth style and obvious wicked enjoyment. . . . Kick off your shoes by the fire and get cozy with the latest by Mary Daheim."

—*Portland Oregonian*

THE ALPINE MENACE

"This is good, solid storytelling—marvelous escapist entertainment."

—*Tacoma News Tribune*

By Mary Daheim
Published by Ballantine Books:

THE ALPINE ADVOCATE
THE ALPINE BETRAYAL
THE ALPINE CHRISTMAS
THE ALPINE DECOY
THE ALPINE ESCAPE
THE ALPINE FURY
THE ALPINE GAMBLE
THE ALPINE HERO
THE ALPINE ICON
THE ALPINE JOURNEY
THE ALPINE NEMESIS

THE ALPINE NEMESIS

Mary Daheim

FAWCETT BOOKS • NEW YORK

A Fawcett Book
Published by The Ballantine Publishing Group

www.ballantinebooks.com

ISBN 0-345-42125-6

Manufactured in the United States of America

First Edition: October 2001

10 9 8 7 6 5 4 3

Chapter One

I HATE THE term *scoop*. I don't know its derivation in newspaper terms, but I hate it anyway. What I hate even more is having it done to me and *The Alpine Advocate*. But two months ago that's what happened for the first time in my career as an editor and publisher.

Spencer Fleetwood, owner and operator of my nemesis, radio station KSKY, managed to scoop me on a story about a missing snowboarder on Mount Baldy. I've never liked Spence, as he calls himself, probably because he's so full of himself. And, to be candid, because he's provided the *Advocate* with the only serious competition I've ever faced. Furthermore, I think his radio station with its weak little signal and prepackaged DJs is just one step up from shouting through a megaphone on a soapbox in Old Mill Park.

But he beat me on the snowboarder story, and I'm still mad. It started with the "exclusive report" of the missing snowboarder. I'm still not certain how Spence got the so-called scoop, but it was probably from one of the park rangers. In the past, they've always come to me first with any breaking news. I suspect Spence was hanging on to a barstool at the Venison Inn when one of the rangers came off duty and the story fell into his lap before he fell onto the floor.

"You're being unfair," Leo Walsh, my ad manager, declared for about the fiftieth time in the ten weeks that had passed since the snowboarder's disappearance. "Drop it. That's the only story he's beat you on since he started up the station last summer. Face it, the *Advocate*'s a weekly. With daily radio competition, you're bound to get beat now and then."

I shook a finger in Leo's weathered face. "Don't patronize me! Don't humor me!"

"Hey!" Leo batted my hand away and scowled. "Don't wag your finger at me!"

I stared into Leo's green eyes. He was wearing the look that he usually reserved for advertisers who were late with their payments. It was also a look he'd probably used in years gone by for his ex-wife, the publishers who had canned him, and the bartenders who'd refused him a last drink before closing time.

I backed off. "Okay," I said crossly. "I'm sorry. But you, of all people on the staff, know what a pain in the butt this Fleetwood is. You've had to hustle twice as hard since he got here just to keep us faintly in the black."

The hard-edged glint faded from Leo's eyes as he perched on the edge of his desk and lighted a cigarette. "Get used to it," Leo said, squinting through a cloud of smoke. "He's been around for a while. Besides, I thought you'd be in a better mood these days since your knight in shining armor showed up."

I thought I detected bitterness in Leo's tone, but maybe I was flattering myself. "I was glad Tom visited me, of course," I said in an uncharacteristically formal tone. "I hadn't seen him in over a year." More like two, I thought with a pang, but managed to keep my head up and my gaze steady.

Leo burst out laughing. "Come on, Emma, you practically hyperventilated the day he got here. How many times did you walk into the wall? Four?"

"Twice," I said sharply. "But that was because the

phone rang the first time, and the second time Vida screamed."

"The mouse," Leo said, looking amused. My House and Home editor, Vida Runkel, was afraid of neither man nor beast—except for mice. "The mouse was more afraid of the Duchess," Leo asserted, using the nickname Vida loathed. "I thought she was faking it. The next day I figured she'd show up with stuffed mice all over one of her damned hats."

"Even Vida is occasionally vulnerable," I said, though her armor was as solid as that of anybody I'd ever met.

Leo and I seemed to have reached neutral territory. I smiled and went over to the coffee urn to fill my Seattle Mariners mug, a gift from my onetime lover, Sheriff Milo Dodge. I was stirring in a teaspoon of sugar when my only reporter, Scott Chamoud, came through the door.

"Hey, what's up?" Scott inquired, dumping a dark green backpack on his desk by the coffee urn. "Is this Monday, or am I in a fog?"

My smile turned wry. "Both, maybe."

Scott gave me his killer grin. "I did have a good weekend, now that I think about it."

Scott, who is so tall, dark and handsome that he's a cliché, had fallen in love with a local lass. Frankly, his choices were limited in Alpine, with its slightly more than three thousand population. I'd figured Scott, at twenty-six, would probably fall for a student from the community college. Instead he had succumbed to the charms of one of the instructors, the thirty-something Tamara Rostova, whose dark beauty rivaled his own.

"Sheesh," Leo exclaimed, stubbing out his cigarette, "love is in the Alpine air. I feel lonesome."

The smile I gave Leo probably conveyed more amusement than pity. "You don't seem to be looking very hard since you broke up with Delphine Corson."

"Delphine?" Vida stood in the doorway, majestic as

ever in a hat with tulips plastered all over its straw brim. "What about Delphine? Did she break her engagement to Spike Canby?"

Leo gave Vida a wry glance. "Spike left town when the construction crew headed for a job in Everett. Ergo, down at the flower shop, Delphine's run out of daisies to pull apart for 'He loves me, he loves me not.' "

Scott was looking puzzled. "Sometimes I feel like I miss things around here. Is that because I wasn't born in Skykomish County?"

"Exactly," Vida declared, with a bob of the tulips. "You can't possibly know everyone's background unless you were born and raised here."

Leo, Scott, and I exchanged bemused expressions. None of us could claim to be a native, and even I, with the longest tenure—over a decade—in Alpine, was still frequently treated as an outsider. To balance off our staff, the two other locals—besides Vida, of course—came into the editorial office. Kip MacDuff, who ran the backshop, and Ginny Erlandson, our business manager and receptionist, both looked fresh-faced and eager on this Monday morning in June. Kip and Ginny were both redheads, but no relation unless Vida knew a long-ago secret she had never shared with me.

Ginny's face fell when she approached the coffee urn. "Where are the pastries?" she asked forlornly.

Scott slapped a hand to his forehead. "I forgot! Darn, I'll run down to the Upper Crust Bakery right now." He was out the door before anyone could say "bear claw."

"Scott's in love," I said.

Kip lifted his eyebrows. "That college teacher? She's hot."

"Kip!" Vida sounded severe. "That's no way to speak of a young lady."

Kip barely managed a contrite expression. He had known Vida since he was a baby; like most of Alpine's younger generation, he had often been scolded by her. Vida was either related to half the under-forty set or had baby-sat for their parents. They all knew better than to talk back. And that included the older generation.

"Scott's serious about Tammy," Ginny declared, putting lo-cal sweetener into her coffee. "I hope he's not in over his head."

"He's fine," Leo asserted. "He's a city boy, originally."

Vida's head whipped around so fast that her hat almost flew off. "So?"

Leo shrugged. "I mean that Tamara Rostova strikes me as more worldly than most of . . . the few girls Scott's dated since he came to work for the *Advocate*." My ad manager recovered quickly from what I'm sure was an Alpine gaffe. "But Scott's reasonably sophisticated, so the age difference doesn't matter much."

Vida snorted, then started to launch into a diatribe, which was cut short by the arrival of Al Driggers, the local undertaker. "Death news," Al intoned, looking as gaunt and gray as some of the corpses he embalmed. "The first one since mid-April." Death was bad for most people, but good for Al. The profit motive, of course.

Vida practically jumped out of her seat. "Who?" she demanded.

"Oscar Nyquist," Al responded. "He died this morning at five-oh-five. Heart attack."

"Oscar!" Vida yanked off her glasses and blinked several times at Al. "Goodness, he must have been over ninety. I should have known. I'd heard that he'd been shopping for caskets."

"Ninety-two come August twenty-first," Al responded, handing Vida the notice. "Yes, he selected one that was top of the line, what I call Celestial Blue, both inside and out. Very comfortable. Oscar couldn't take his eyes off it. Strange, in a way—I thought he'd live to be a hundred. Oh, well. You never know."

Oscar owned the local movie theatre, the Whistling Marmot. He was a widower, but had extended family in Skykomish County. Vida pounced on the funeral date.

"Saturday?" She was aghast. "At two o'clock? There are four weddings scheduled that afternoon. Then, in the evening, there's the Alpine High School graduation. Whatever were you thinking of, Al?"

From the expression on Al's long face, he hadn't been thinking as hard as Vida. "Well . . . the family wanted it then. I would've suggested an earlier time, but some of the relatives have to come from out of town. Oscar wanted to be buried with his parents, in Oppdal, Norway."

"Ridiculous," Vida declared. "His wife's buried right here in Alpine. Where did he get such a silly idea? And what's that got to do with when the funeral is held? The out-of-towners could come Friday and stay overnight. You won't have half the turnout for Oscar you'd have if the funeral were at ten, or even on Friday. What's wrong with Friday?"

Al considered his answer. "The out-of-towners," he finally said, in his deliberate manner. "They couldn't make it."

"Pooh." Vida waved a dismissive hand and put her glasses back on. "They could if they tried. You should have insisted on a better time. As it is, many people will be torn between attending the funeral and the weddings. Of course there will be better food at the bridal receptions. But you really can't cut one short to run off to the other. Think of the emotional mood swing required. This could start some feuds."

I stifled my comments. Strife in Alpine wasn't caused by ethnic antagonism, deep-seated religious convictions, or political boundaries. The so-called feuds, and there were many, grew out of a slight at not receiving a baby shower invitation, being snubbed in the parking lot at the Alpine Mall, or not getting your regular barstool at the Icicle Creek Tavern.

"By the way," Al said as he backed away from Vida's desk, "I got a call from the parents of that snowboarder who went missing on Mount Baldy back at the end of March."

My hackles rose and I frowned at Al. "His parents? I didn't think they were around here. But then, I didn't get first crack at the story."

As was his habit, Al rubbed his index finger along the side of his nose. "I heard you were upset." He shot me a sheepish, sidelong glance. "I'm sorry."

"Why are you apologizing?" I snapped. "It wasn't your fault that Spencer Fleetwood got the scoop. Unless," I went on, taking a step toward Al, "you were the one who told him about that snowboarder in the first place."

"Me?" Al actually jumped. "How could I? Why would I? I heard about it on . . . the . . . radio." He gulped the last words.

"So did everybody else," I retorted. Al wasn't getting off to a good start this Monday morning, at least not in the *Advocate*'s editorial office. Of course he'd had one good thing happen to him already—Oscar Nyquist had died. Not so good for Oscar, though. Leo, who had sat down at his computer, looked up. "Don't get Emma started, Al. That snowboarder story still hurts."

I nodded three times, with emphasis. "Why did his parents call you? Where are they? What did they want?"

Al managed a feeble smile, which was about all he could muster on any given occasion, unbridled mirth not being part of his undertaker's professional mien. "They live back in New York—not the city, but someplace else with a funny name, like something Chinese. Anyway, they wanted to know if there had been any further word about their son—Brian Conley, that's his name—and if not, could we arrange some kind of memorial for him, maybe up on the mountain."

Vida was still looking severe. "What's wrong with them? Wouldn't they think that if Brian's body had been found, they would have been notified as next of kin? By the way, the town is Penn Yan, and I believe the name is Welsh. When we ran the story, it reminded me of Tom Murphy. He came from there."

Tom Murphy had been an early Alpine settler who had worked for Carl Clemans's sawmill. Tom had come west in search of Yukon gold, but not having found any, he discovered instead a young woman in Seattle who became his wife. Although the couple had lived in Alpine well before Vida's time, she had the Murphys cataloged along with every other soul who had ever set foot on the steep face of Tonga Ridge.

"Yes," Al said sofly. "Anyway, I told them I'd be glad to hold a ceremony on Baldy, though I couldn't promise that it would be exactly where Brian was . . . lost. Indeed, if we knew that, we'd know where to find the remains and could have a proper service. Though," he continued, growing thoughtful, "I haven't prepared a frozen corpse for burial in years. My father was very gifted at that—but he had more practice. In those days when the timber industry flourished, loggers got caught in avalanches and trapped under trees. Not to mention careless climbers falling into crevasses. It's not like it used to be." He shook his head sadly.

"Come, come, Al," Vida clucked. "Most of the people who fell into those crevasses were never retrieved. I can think of four different men who are still up on Baldy and Tonga Ridge."

"True," Al allowed. "Perhaps Brian Conley will still be found now that the spring thaw is under way. His parents also wanted to know if we had a Catholic priest here. I assured them that we did."

"You'd think," Vida said, speaking less severely now, "that they'd want to wait a bit. The spring runoff started only a few weeks ago."

"They don't have mountains like the Cascades in Penn Yan," Leo put in. "Their idea of a mountain back there is only slightly larger than an anthill."

"What can you expect?" Vida remarked. "New York!" She shook her head.

Al was retreating toward the door. He was about to leave when Scott came in, waving a white bakery bag. "Hey, we got lucky. I managed to buy the last of the sugar doughnuts. Hi, Al. What's up?"

"A funeral," Al said, unable to keep the satisfaction out of his voice. "Oscar Nyquist. It should be an impressive event. Oscar wasn't one to go second-class." Al made his farewell, with the hint of a spring in his quiet tread.

Snatching up a doughnut, I headed for my office cubbyhole. We had two days until deadline. The thought of getting scooped rankled particularly on this newsless Monday morning. The last big story in the county had been the unfortunate Brian Conley. He had been reported missing on a Tuesday afternoon, and whoever leaked the item had given it not to us—we'd easily have made our five o'clock deadline—but to KSKY. Our lead articles since then had featured the usual traffic accidents, wrangling at the county commissioners' meetings, and the April start-up date of a new bridge over Burl Creek by the college. I wished no one ill, but I could have used something juicy.

Frankly, this week's issue was painfully dull. We had a big school-end section to fill, and except for the related stories, nothing much of interest. The front page would carry the main articles on the high school and community college commencements, along with the announcement of Oscar Nyquist's death. But there was no lead, nothing to grab the reader. I felt as if I were publishing a shopper, not a newspaper.

I scanned the wire services to see if there were any items with a local tie-in. A fatality accident had occurred this morning outside of Monroe on the dangerous stretch of road known as the Highway to Heaven. Too far from Alpine, and the victim was from Yakima. There was talk of resuming logging operations in central Oregon. Right industry, wrong state. A break-in had occurred at the naval station in Everett. No one from town currently worked there; the commute was too difficult in the winter. I was reminded of my former reporter, Carla Steinmetz Talliaferro, who had once solved the problem of a slow Tuesday by filling up three inches on the front page with a piece that began, "There was no news to report this week from the Snoqualmie National Forest ranger station. . . ." And then proceeded to try to explain why.

Half an hour later, Mayor Fuzzy Baugh showed up, looking pleased with himself.

"Emma, how about a big front-page story?" he asked with the faint Louisiana drawl that still lingered in his voice.

My heart leaped. "Really? What's going on?"

Fuzzy, who has been Alpine's mayor since before I moved to town, eased himself into one of the visitor's chairs. "Tell me, darlin', what's the thing you'd most like to see as a civic improvement in this fine city?"

"Well . . ." I considered the dozens of editorials I'd written over the years, calling for more street repairs, sewer improvements, funding for the library, a bigger budget for the sheriff, trying to get the three old farts who made up the county commissioners to stay awake at the monthly meetings and actually accomplish something. "Schools," I finally said. "I think it's time we tried to pass another levy. The K-12 teachers haven't had a real raise in four years."

Fuzzy nodded slowly. "My, yes, that's an outstanding plan. But I'm thinking of an even more pressing need. Now, Emma, you've heard the complaints about Alpine's great lack."

"Lack of what?" I had no idea what Fuzzy was talking about.

Fuzzy put both freckled hands on my desk and leaned forward in the chair. "A public toilet, that's what."

"A . . . public toilet?" I repeated stupidly.

Fuzzy nodded some more. "I can see your headline now: 'Mayor Brings Relief to Alpine Voters.' I mean Alpine *residents*," he hastily corrected himself.

To be fair, there had been criticism over the years because the town didn't provide public toilets, not even in Old Mill Park. Originally there had been two privies in the park, but they'd had to be moved every autumn and new holes had needed to be dug. Some four or five years earlier, there had been an early frost, right after Labor Day. Since Alpine is three thousand feet above sea level, the ground had remained solid until April. The city council got into a squabble over the placement of the new privies, and didn't resolve the matter until late September, when it was again too late to dig. Somehow, the whole issue got tabled, leaving the public stranded.

Milo and his deputies were forced to cite individuals who relieved themselves in public. And, because of my policy of printing the names and charges of everyone on the police blotter, I became the butt, so to speak, of the irate citizens who had not enjoyed seeing themselves charged with PIP, or Peeing/Pooping in Public.

"You see, Emma," Fuzzy went on, "Granite Falls is putting in a public toilet. If they can do it, so can we."

Granite Falls was another former logging town, north of us on the Mountain Loop Highway. Whatever was good for Granite Falls apparently was good for Alpine. Fuzzy wasn't going to be outdone.

"When?" I inquired. "It's already June."

"Before the summer solstice parade, June twenty-first," the mayor replied, looking pleased with himself. "There's enough money in the parks department budget to put in two toilets. Nothing fancy, of course, just the basics."

"That's great, Fuzzy," I said, trying to show enthusiasm. "Can you give me the details?"

"I'll have somebody from city hall drop off that information this afternoon," Fuzzy said, getting to his feet and brushing at the temples of his dyed auburn hair. "Work should start in a few days. You'll want some pictures in progress, I imagine."

"Definitely," I replied, keeping a straight face.

"Wonderful." Fuzzy rapped on my desk, an apparent sign of jubilation. "I kind of thought that since this was my idea it would be nice to name the rest rooms after me. What do you think of running a contest to see who can come up with the best name? The winner could have the privilege of inaugurating the toilets."

After more than ten years in Alpine, I know there is no such thing as a really terrible idea. "Why not?" I said. "Make up the rules, send them along with the other information."

"I've got a really good photo of the toilets in a catalog," Fuzzy said. "Can you scan them into the newspaper?"

"Why not?" I repeated. Why not have a contest for the biggest hind end in Skykomish County? The candidates were too numerous to mention. I felt as if I were drowning in a sea of . . . something or other.

A proposed toilet was not a lead story, not even for the *Advocate*. I cudgeled my brain for other ideas. Maybe I could use the phone call to Al Driggers from Brian Conley's parents:

CLOSURE SOUGHT BY MISSING SNOWBOARDER'S FAMILY

I sighed, even as I jotted down the possible headline. To refresh my memory, I pulled out the binder that contained the issues for the first quarter of the year. There was the first snowboarder story, telling our readers—after they'd already been informed by KSKY—that a twenty-five-year-old Seattle man named Brian Conley had been missing for four days on the north slope of Tonga Ridge. A week later, the follow-up story reported that Brian still hadn't been found. We had received a black-and-white photo of him from his girlfriend, and I'd run it on the front page just below the fold. I stared at the one-column cut. Brian looked younger than twenty-five, but perhaps the picture had been taken a couple of years earlier. He had a pleasant if undistinguished face. The description that had been given to the authorities listed Brian as five-ten, a hundred and sixty-five pounds, with blue eyes, dark brown hair worn short, and a small scar on the back of his right hand. I stared some more at the photo. He looked like the kind of person I'd inferred from the way his girlfriend had talked about him: ordinary, average, nice. Not the sort of person whose life should be cut off by a tragic accident. I shook my head and closed the bound volume.

If I planned to write another story I'd have to call the Conleys back in Penn Yan. Without much enthusiasm, I dialed Al's number at the funeral home. His gusty, lusty wife, Janet, answered.

"I'm filling in this morning," she announced. "Cammy Olson is in bed with a bad case of postcoital sex."

"The result or the cause thereof?" I inquired, laughing at Janet's typically ribald remark.

"Actually," Janet replied, "she's got chicken pox. At twenty-two, isn't she a little old for that?"

"Not really," I said. "The problem is, the older you

are, the harder the case. I expect she's miserable." Maybe this was my lead story:

SPOTTED WOMAN STALKS ALPINE

Maybe not.

"The younger generation," Janet said scornfully. "She'll be out for at least a week. Between her and Al's new assistant, Dan Peebles, I should quit at Sky Travel and work at the mortuary full time. The only problem is, I get free trips at the travel agency. At the funeral home, people go, but they don't come back. Until this morning, they haven't even been going. It's all these hardy Scandinavians—they live forever."

Janet had found the Conleys' number, and two minutes later I was speaking to Mrs. Conley. She seemed a bit confused about who I was and why I was calling, but finally she figured it out.

"It's a terrible thing, not knowing," Mrs. Conley declared. "My husband and I should have come out when we learned that Brian was missing. But we kept waiting and hoping . . ." Her voice trailed away. I felt like a ghoul, knowing that I had upset her, aware that I had made dozens of such calls to bereaved relatives and friends. I hated this part of the job, but it was necessary.

I spoke up in an attempt to rescue her from the awkward moment. "A friend reported him missing, as I recall."

"Yes." There was an audible sniff at the other end of the line. "Gina, his girlfriend. We met her once, they came to visit last summer. She's very sweet. But by the time she notified the authorities, Brian had been gone overnight. Still, we thought maybe he'd just been hurt or gotten lost or . . ." Again Mrs. Conley's voice faded.

"Brian was alone, as I recall," I said, racing to the rescue one more time.

"Yes." Another sniff. "I guess so. Though we'd spoken with him a few days earlier, and I thought he mentioned something about going with a friend. But Gina wasn't sure, so maybe he changed his mind. Oh, Ms. Lord, you can't imagine what it's like to lose a son!"

I could, but I didn't want to. "I have a son about the same age as Brian," I said. "He's my only child. Do you have other children?"

"Yes," Mrs. Conley said, her voice somewhat stronger. "Two girls and two boys besides Brian. They're a comfort, but they can't make up for losing him. He was the baby of the family, and very special. Brian was such a passionate young man, always caught up in this cause and that. Do you think we're foolish to want to conduct some sort of service on that mountain where he was lost?"

"No," I answered slowly. "If it would help you deal with your loss, it isn't foolishness."

"That's so," Mrs. Conley said vaguely. "You have a priest in Alpine?"

"Yes, Father Dennis Kelly," I said. "He's very spiritual, very intelligent." And his sermons are about as inspiring as legal notices. "Did you plan to come out soon?"

Mrs. Conley said that she and her husband hadn't made up their minds, they'd just come up with the idea of a mountainside service a couple of days ago. Their pastor in Penn Yan had celebrated a memorial Mass just two weeks earlier. Maybe they shouldn't spend the money on travel. Maybe they really were being foolish. Maybe Brian wasn't dead after all.

I pounced on that remark. "What do you mean?" Besides the hope of the hopeless, I thought.

Mrs. Conley didn't respond right away. When she did, her voice had taken on a wary note. "You never know. About disappearances, I mean." She began speaking more rapidly. "Amnesia, for instance. Someone here in Penn Yan had amnesia and went missing for over two years. His son-in-law ran into him at a service station in Albany where he was pumping gas. Imagine—the poor man was an attorney with a very profitable practice."

I made encouraging noises, then politely extricated myself from the conversation. There was no news here, and even if the Conleys did come to Alpine, the story wouldn't rate more than four inches. The missing snowboarder was a dead end.

How could I have been so wrong?

Chapter Two

When I arrived at my little log house, I was still lacking a decent front-page story. I'd spent two hours on the phone, checking with the city, county, state, and federal agencies to see if any of them had generated a smidgen of local news other than toilets. They hadn't. Fiscal reports, that was the thing, they said, coming July first. Wow.

The mail was all catalogs and circulars and a couple of bills. There were no messages on the answering machine. I wished I were back in St. Paul with Adam. I'd visited him in February and we'd spent some wonderful hours together, walking the snow-covered grounds of the seminary where he was studying to be a priest. Leaving winter behind on the return trip, I took a detour to Arizona to see my brother, Ben. I enjoyed the sun in Tuba City for two days before I started griping about the heat. My brother had laughed at me. At his mission church in Mississippi and now tending his flock in Arizona, he had grown accustomed to hot weather, both humid and dry. I preferred the cold damp of Alpine. Ben thought I was nuts.

Then Tom Cavanaugh showed up the week before Easter. He'd been promising to come for over a year, and I'd almost given up on him. It wouldn't have been the first time that the father of my son had broken a promise. Our entire off-and-on-again relationship of almost thirty years had been full of them.

But he finally arrived, and he spent over a week with me in the log house that now felt empty and desolate. Ironically, I'd used up most of my vacation time visiting Ben and Adam. I suppose that, deep down, I didn't believe Tom would ever come to Alpine. But he had, and he'd talked of marriage. His mentally unbalanced wife, Sandra, had been dead for over three years, and his daughter, who—like me—had given birth to a child out of wedlock, was finally capable of taking care of the baby and herself. It helped, of course, that Tom could afford a nanny, a maid, a gardener, and for all I knew a clutch of liveried footmen in his San Francisco mansion.

So now I was pondering the possibility of finally marrying The Love of My Life. Vida was all for it. She became unwontedly starry-eyed whenever I mentioned Tom—or Tommy, as she insisted on calling him. Vida hadn't carried the scenario through to its logical conclusion: I'd have to sell the *Advocate* and move to San Francisco. It was not a prospect that thrilled me, though that of being Tom's wife did.

Thus, I poured a hefty bourbon and water—and pondered. For a month now, pondering had taken up most of my spare time. Tom had even offered to buy the *Advocate* from me and add it to his string of small dailies and weeklies. But I hated abandoning the paper; maybe I hated more the idea of surrendering my hard-won independence.

Half an hour later, I was pondering what to cook for dinner. Nothing that I had on hand appealed to me. Risking frostbite, I reached far back into the freezer compartment, hoping to find some hidden shrimp. Curry seemed tempting, and Alpine was short of ethnic restaurants.

There was no shrimp, so I took out a chicken breast and was defrosting it in the microwave when I heard a series of distant cracking sounds. One, two. I hesitated with my finger on the timer and listened again. Sometimes the power lines that marched down through the Skykomish River valley made that kind of sound. Three, four. The noise was muffled. I waited for a full minute, but all was quiet. My faint hope dwindled; apparently, nothing had exploded to give me a lead story.

I was frying the chicken when I heard a far-off siren. Experience has taught me to differentiate among the various emergency vehicles. This was Milo Dodge's British police horn, a rare bit of whimsy for the usually practical sheriff. A little over a year ago, he had found the item in a catalog and ordered it through Harvey's Hardware and Sporting Goods. I guess he wanted to pretend he worked for Scotland Yard. The siren was used on his private vehicle, a red Grand Cherokee Chief. Now my interest was piqued. What had brought the sheriff out after his official shift was over?

I dialed Vida's number. "Did you hear those noises a few minutes ago?" I asked.

"No," Vida replied. "Roger has the TV on. It's a trifle loud."

Roger was Vida's odious grandson. His parents had taken an off-season vacation trip to Hawaii and he was staying with Vida. Roger was sixteen, and learning to drive. I was certain that he'd soon replace Durwood Parker as Alpine's worst menace behind the wheel.

"Did you hear Milo's siren?" I inquired further.

"No." Vida sounded vexed. "Roger, dear, could you lower the volume just a teensy bit?" she asked, away from the phone. There was a pause. The volume remained at full decibel. "Roger? Roger!"

At last the little creep responded, though not without complaint. Vida spoke again into the receiver. "What is it? I didn't hear anything."

"I'm not sure," I replied. "I thought it came from over your way."

"I'm sorry," Vida said. "I've no idea. Should I call Billy?"

Bill Blatt was Vida's nephew and one of Milo's deputies. "Yes, if you get a chance. It may have been the power lines. You know how they snap sometimes."

"Yes, that could be it," Vida agreed, "though it usually happens in the winter cold. I must dash, Emma. I'm making Roger some lovely pudding."

The description was dubious, I thought. Vida's collection of House and Home–page recipes over the years overflowed from the bottom drawer of her desk. They were, as is said, enough to choke a horse—which is also an apt description of her cooking. But pudding from a box might not be ruined: I envisioned a huge vat of it, with Roger plunged facedown, only his feet showing above the creamy chocolate rim.

For once, Vida had proved a washout as the source of all knowledge. I still wondered what Milo was up to. The siren had definitely been off to the east, no doubt starting from the sheriff's home in the Icicle Creek development. After dinner, I'd call him to see if there was any news, even the slightest of stories to put on page one.

It was exactly seven o'clock when I finished my meager dinner and dialed the sheriff's number. He answered on the fourth ring, out of breath.

"Dodge here," he said, sounding official.

"Lord here," I said. "Were you running to catch the phone or chasing a perp?"

"I was in the can," Milo growled. "Why does the phone always ring when I'm in the can?"

I chuckled, not because I was amused, but because after more than two long, awkward years, the sheriff and I seemed to have picked up the pieces of our friendship. After our breakup, his rebound romance with the much younger Jeannie Clay hadn't panned out. Milo had recently taken up with a widow, Tara Peebles, the mother of Al Driggers's new assistant. Tara was much closer to the sheriff's age, and a relative newcomer to Alpine. Milo hadn't seemed to resent Tom's visit. Maybe he figured we deserved each other—if we ever got to that point.

"I heard your British inspector's horn," I said, cradling the cordless phone against my shoulder while I loaded the dishwasher.

"You did," Milo replied. "Somebody up on Second Hill called to say there was a commotion at the O'Neill place."

My spirits rose a trifle. "Was there?"

"Nope. Everything was quiet when I pulled up."

"Oh." I tried to hide my disappointment. "I thought I heard something that sounded like gunshots."

"Probably," Milo said in his laconic manner. "The O'Neills are always taking potshots at birds and stray cats and whatever else wanders onto their property. They already put about twenty bullet holes in that new arterial stop sign by the Icicle Creek turnoff."

"Were they sober when you got there?"

"Are they ever?" Milo snorted. "I didn't bother to knock. The last thing I need at the end of a workday is a false alarm and getting cussed out by those wild Irishmen."

The infamous O'Neills were a clan of freelance gyppo loggers, forced to find work outside of Alpine since the decline of the local timber industry. The father, Paddy, had died the previous winter, and his remains had been sent back to the old sod in County Armagh. His three sons, though into middle age, still considered themselves lusty lads and beer-loving brawlers. The O'Neills' ongoing feud with Cap Hartquist and his two "boys" had long been a source of amusement—and occasionally terror—for Alpine residents. Thirty years ago, more or less, Cap's pet goat had been run over by Paddy O'Neill, igniting the war between the two families. I suppose it was wishful thinking, but I'd hoped that Paddy's demise might signal a truce. As far as I knew, the Dove of Peace had yet to fly.

"I don't suppose you could discover a crime between now and five o'clock tomorrow," I said wistfully.

"How come?" Milo asked with genuine puzzlement. Even after more than ten years of observing me as editor and publisher of *The Alpine Advocate*, the sheriff never seemed to understand my need for news.

"Never mind." I sighed, then had a small idea. "What about equipment? Anything new?"

"Equipment?" Milo paused. "Hell, no, we're lucky to afford pencils with the county budget so tight."

"Programs? Why don't you come up with some new programs to fight crime?"

"Like what?" Milo responded. "Starting a curfew now that school's out?"

"That's good," I enthused. "Are you really considering it?"

"No," he replied. "I just thought of it now. It's pretty dumb."

"Why? The kids are always at loose ends in the summer. With the college students around now, there aren't enough jobs for the teenagers." I was gaining momentum. It wasn't the best idea I'd ever heard, but I rather liked Milo's brainstorm. "How much vandalism do you have to contend with between Memorial Day and Labor Day? How many drunken parties? How many drug busts up in the woods?"

"Jesus," Milo muttered. "You're serious."

"Why not? I've had worse ideas."

"When?"

"Ohhh . . . never mind." I lost patience and promptly dropped a glass on the kitchen floor. Luckily, it was plastic, and bounced harmlessly in the direction of the stove.

Milo's recalcitrance and the newly hatched idea made me thoughtful. If I was out of big black headlines, I was also suffering from a paucity of ideas for the editorial page. Maybe I'd write an editorial for this week, suggesting a curfew. If nothing else, it would fill up space and annoy Milo.

I used my laptop to type up the two-column, six-inch argument for a ten o'clock curfew. The older folks would like the idea; the younger set didn't read the paper. Or much else, I thought with deep, dark disapproval.

"A curfew, huh?" Leo said the next morning when I told him about the editorial. "How's Dodge supposed to enforce that one?"

"He can't," Vida put in. "He doesn't have enough deputies. Of course, he might be able to get some volunteers. Concerned parents. Teachers. The clergy."

I gave a slight nod. It was possible. Volunteers weren't always hard to find in a small town. When you don't have your social calendar filled with opera, theatre, sporting events, and coming up with a name for Mayor Baugh's toilets, you have time to spare.

Scott was showing me his story on the upcoming high school commencement when we first heard the sirens.

"News?" I said, perking up a bit.

"Car accident," Leo said, barely intelligible with a pencil in his teeth.

That was often the case when we heard multiple sirens. The sheriff, the medics, the fire department. Scott was tied up on the phone, so I rushed outside to take a peek.

I couldn't see anything unusual, but the sirens were close by. I walked down to the corner and looked around the intersection of Fourth and Front. A half-dozen other people had stopped in their tracks, looking like bloodhounds on the scent.

The sirens stopped. Harvey Adcock, of Harvey's Hardware, had just come out of the Venison Inn. "Emma," he called, "where are they?"

"Not far," I shouted back. "Maybe Railroad Avenue or River Road." I nodded to the north where the streets paralleled Front on one side and the Skykomish River on the other. "I don't see any smoke," I added as Harvey strolled in my direction.

"It must be a wreck," Harvey said. "Maybe somebody drove into the Sky. Remember that guy from Sultan a couple of years ago? Of course, he was very drunk."

"It happened after dark," I said, as Harvey and I wandered down Fourth toward Railroad Avenue. "Two in the morning, as I recall. He was darned lucky that some of the other tavern habitués drove by about then." That was a story, even if it had happened on a Saturday night and we couldn't run it until Wednesday. But there had been no Spencer Fleetwood, no KSKY to scoop us then. The item took up an inch and a half in the *Seattle Times* and the *Post-Intelligencer*, but we got all the details, including the rescue by a trio of men who had been either brave enough or drunk enough to risk their own skins in the high, fast, icy waters of the Skykomish River.

At the next intersection, Harvey waved an arm toward his right. "I think the sirens stopped down there."

"I agree," I said, but our line of sight was blocked by some Burlington-Northern freight cars pulled off onto a siding.

We crossed the street and then the railroad tracks. Sure enough, Milo's Grand Cherokee, an official sheriff's car, and the medics' van were pulled up two blocks away, outside of Alpine Meats.

"It's not a fire," Harvey said in his deliberate manner. "Even if we couldn't see any smoke, we'd have smelled meat burning. Maybe it's some electrical problem, though.

I always worry about that at the hardware store. I really should update the wiring." He chuckled wryly. "You'd think a hardware owner would have all those bases covered, wouldn't you?"

I smiled, but my attention was on Alpine Meats. Harvey was right—nothing looked out of order. Upon closer inspection, the emergency vehicles were empty and no one was milling around outside except for a dozen curiosity seekers, including the Nordby brothers, who owned the local General Motors dealership. They exchanged greetings with Harvey while I proceeded up to the meat warehouse's entrance on River Road.

Milo Dodge and Barney Amundson, the owner of Alpine Meats, came outside. Barney, who is a big bull of a man, looked blotchy in the face, as if he'd been crying. I couldn't see Milo's expression under the regulation Smokey the Bear hat, but his usual loping stride seemed hobbled.

Barney leaned against the sheriff's Grand Cherokee, took out a red-and-white handkerchief, and mopped his brow. Milo noticed me and lifted one long arm in greeting.

"You heard?" he called across the twenty feet of parking lot that separated us.

"Heard what?" I asked, moving swiftly to join him.

The sheriff removed his hat and rubbed at his graying sandy hair. "Jesus," he breathed. "It's the worst thing I ever saw."

"What?" I demanded, realizing that Milo was unusually pale. I heard another siren; it sounded like the ambulance.

Milo gestured in the direction of the building with his elbow. "The O'Neills. Stubby, Rusty, and Dusty. They're all in there, dead."

"*What?*" The word was torn from my throat. Barney

jumped, then started crying again. The medics, one of whom was Barney's cousin, Del, hovered over him, asking questions.

Milo took me by the arm, though from his stricken expression I couldn't tell if he was comforting me or steadying himself. "They've all been shot. I don't know how the hell they ended up in the walk-in locker. Barney swears he doesn't know, either. He found them this morning. Jesus, it's the damnedest thing I ever saw."

"I'll get Scott over here," I mumbled, grappling in my handbag for the cell phone. "Are the O'Neills still in there?" I couldn't take it in. It was a nightmare. The morning sun seemed to fade in and out; the sound of the nearby river was a roar in my ears. I leaned against Milo. "God," I whispered. "God."

The ambulance had pulled in next to the medics' van. Milo went over to talk to the drivers while I composed myself and keyed Scott's number into the cell phone. The connection snapped, crackled, and popped, as it sometimes does with interference from the surrounding mountains and cross-state power lines. Scott, however, got the drift and said he'd be right over with his camera. I rang off just as two of Milo's deputies, Jack Mullins and Dwight Gould, came out of the warehouse.

"Dustin's coming to take the official photos," Milo said, referring to yet another deputy. "It doesn't look like they were killed in the warehouse," he added, directing his comments to the ambulance men. "But we can't move the bodies until Dustin has finished up."Maybe I should call in the state's homicide unit. This is one hell of a thing."

The medics had taken Barney's vital signs. After a few words with the sheriff, they got into their vehicle and slowly drove away. Apparently, Barney had rejected further medical attention. The O'Neills were beyond help. Their deaths were beyond belief. Like Milo, I'd never encountered such a massacre, not even in my Big City days on *The Oregonian* in Portland.

"The Hartquists?" I said to Milo.

The sheriff put his hat back on. "They're my first choice as suspects. This has to be the ruckus up at the O'Neill place last night." He turned to Dwight and Jack. "Get out to the Hartquist house. Take Sam Heppner and Bill Blatt along, even if you have to roust them out of bed," Milo ordered, referring to his other deputies. "You're going to have to take it easy. If those damned Hartquists did this, they're probably not in a good mood."

"What about the rest of the O'Neills?" I asked. "Have you told the wives yet?"

Milo shook his head. "I haven't had time. Anyway, I don't think there's anybody else up at their place on Second Hill. Both of the wives are long gone."

I'd heard that Rusty's wife had left him at least a year earlier, though she'd done that before and eventually had returned. Dusty had never married. "I didn't know Mrs. Stubby took off," I said, never able to keep the O'Neill scions or their wives straight. "When was that?"

"Lona left last summer with their daughter Meara when she went off to have her baby," Milo replied, the recitation of facts steadying his nerves. "They never came back."

Not everybody sent Vida a copy of their travel itinerary. Especially not when a fifteen-year-old like Meara has gotten knocked up and isn't sure who to call Daddy.

I'd taken my notebook out of my handbag and was making notes. "What time did Barney find the bodies?"

"About half an hour after he opened up this morning," Milo said. "Eight-thirty, let's say. He's pretty rattled."

I glanced at Barney; he was talking to Dustin Fong, who had just arrived. A moment later, Spencer Fleetwood roared up in his blue BMW. I grimaced as he emerged from the car, dressed in his uniform of tailored slacks, cashmere sweater, glittering gold chain, and Gucci sunglasses. He always wore the sunglasses, even when the rain was coming down in buckets.

"Damn!" I swore under my breath. "He's going to beat me on this story, too!"

Milo gave me a wry look, then walked over to Dustin. I ignored Spencer as I headed into the warehouse. Inspecting dead bodies repulsed me, but not as much as facing off with my archrival. I was trying to figure out where the walk-in was when I sensed someone behind me. Giving a start, I whirled around. It was Scott Chamoud, carrying his camera.

"What's happening?" he asked, looking bewildered. "Did you say there were a bunch of dead O'Neills in a freezer?"

"That's pretty much it," I said, catching sight of a heavy-duty door open down the corridor that led from Barney's small office. "Three of them, stacked up like sides of beef." I sounded crass, but it was the only way I could cope with the enormity of the crime.

"Wow." Scott breathed the word. "How did they get dead?"

"Shot, according to the sheriff," I responded, my steps heavy as I approached the open door.

"Who shot them?"

"I don't know," I said, feeling a blast of cold air from the walk-in. "The Hartquists, maybe."

"Wow."

Taking a deep breath, I steeled myself to look inside. There actually were sides of beef—pork, too, and maybe lamb. Outside of the Grocery Basket's meat department, I wasn't used to identifying cuts of flesh. But I had no trouble recognizing the three O'Neills. They were lying on top of each other, their clothing stained with blood, their limbs at awkward angles.

"I've seen them," I said in a choked voice. "I'm through here." God help me, I was afraid I was going to be sick.

"You sure you want pictures?" Scott asked, his own voice none too steady.

"Yes," I replied thickly, propping myself up against the wall in the corridor. "Don't touch them, don't move anything. It's a crime scene. Dustin still has to take the official photos."

"Got it," Scott called back.

I took some deep breaths, then made sure my knees wouldn't buckle. Scott let out a strange, strangled cry.

"What is it?" I asked.

Scott came out of the walk-in, his usual olive skin a sickly gray. "How many O'Neills?"

"What?" It took a couple of seconds for the question to sink into my brain. "Oh—the three sons."

Scott put a hand to his head. "Then something's wrong. I counted eight feet."

"No! Count again!"

"I don't need to," Scott asserted. "You'd better tell the sheriff."

I forced myself to move. Scott had to be wrong. Like a zombie, I made my way out of the warehouse. The sunshine suddenly seemed so bright that I wished I was wearing Spencer's expensive shades.

"Milo," I called in a thin, wavering voice. "Milo?"

The sheriff, along with Dustin Fong, was coming toward me. I stumbled forward and put both hands on Milo's chest. "Did you know—" I stopped, my throat constricted. He stared at me as if I'd lost my mind. "There's another body in there, under the pile."

Milo kept staring at me, then let out a string of obscenities. He moved away so fast that I almost pitched forward. After staggering a bit, I caught sight of something that brought me to my senses: Spencer Fleetwood was holding a microphone and interviewing Barney Amundson. I got so mad that a wild idea hit me.

"Scott!" I called to my reporter, who was taking some exterior shots. "Finish up, take the film to Buddy Bayard's studio, and hurry back to the office."

"What about that other—" he began, but I waved a frantic arm for him to be quiet and go. Then I marched back into the warehouse. Milo and Dustin were standing by the corpses; both still looked upset.

"Who's under there?" I demanded.

"We're just going to see," Milo said. "Dustin's taken all the pictures we need."

"Then get on with it," I snapped.

Slowly, Milo turned around to look at me. "What's the rush? The paper doesn't come out until tomorrow, right?"

"Wrong," I shot back. "This paper comes out immediately. I'm going to do a special edition. This is the biggest news to hit Alpine since I've been here, and I'm not going to let that jerk Spencer Fleetwood beat me by more than a few minutes."

"Hunh." Milo looked bemused.

"That's cool," Dustin said, giving me his slightly diffident smile. "You mean, like the old movies, where the kid on the corner yells, 'Extra, extra!'?"

"Exactly," I said, "though I don't think I'll ask Kip MacDuff to do that. Now come on, let's see Corpse Number Four."

Milo gave me a disapproving glance. "Hey, how did you get so bloodthirsty all of a sudden? I thought you were going to pass out on me a few minutes ago."

"Competition has that effect on me," I replied, still struggling against nausea. "I've turned into a hard-hearted ghoul."

"Okay," Milo said with a sigh. "We'll need a tarp or something for the bodies."

"Don't you have one?" I asked, fighting down bile.

"Yeah," Milo replied, looking toward the outer office, "but it's tacked up to the ceiling in my office. The damned roof leaked when we had that big rain last week. Ah—there's some heavy-duty plastic in the corner. Dustin?"

The deputy fetched the large roll of plastic and a pair of shears. For all my bravado, I winced as I watched the sheriff and his deputy carefully remove Rusty, mercifully placing him facedown near haunches of pork. Stubby and Dusty were intertwined. Rigor had set in, which made the extrication doubly difficult. It appeared that all three brothers had been shot in the head and the chest.

"What the hell . . . ?" Milo was bending down over the fourth and final body.

From the angle at which I was standing, all I could see were a pair of high-tech outdoor shoes and black pants. "Who is it?" I asked, wondering if I dared take a closer look.

"I don't know," Milo said. "How about you, Dustman?"

Dustin also bent down. "Gee . . . he does look kind of familiar, but I can't place him."

Reluctantly, I inched closer. It was the face of a young man, bruised and discolored. He was wearing a blue and black parka, and his matted hair was brown. I'd like to say he looked peaceful, but he didn't. Frankly, he appeared to have been in pain when he died.

I kept staring, forcing myself not to cringe. Like Dustin, I thought there was something familiar about him. His eyes were closed, his mouth was slightly open. He was clean-shaven, with a broad face and a short chin. In death he looked painfully young, though I guessed him to be in his late twenties.

"Well?" Milo said.

The face metamorphosed not into a real live person, but a black-and-white photograph. "My God," I whispered, "it's Brian Conley!"

Chapter Three

"By God," Milo said softly, "you're right! Those pictures we got from his family or whoever—the ones we posted after he went missing. I remember now."

"Me, too," Dustin agreed. "I knew I'd seen that face somewhere."

Milo stood up, his expression utterly bewildered. "How the hell did he get in here?"

I wanted to know the same thing, of course. But I felt the pressure of time. "Check, see if you can tell how he died."

"Exposure, probably," Milo said, shaking his head over and over. "We'll have to get Doc Dewey to take a look. Dustin, give him a call. If he's not in the O.R., I'd like him to come over pronto."

Dustin started out of the locker, but I grabbed his arm. "Do me a huge favor, please?" I gave him my best middle-aged vamp look, which was undoubtedly hampered by my queasy stomach. "Don't mention this to anybody outside, especially not to Spencer Fleetwood."

Earning my endless gratitude, Dustin grinned and nodded. "Got it. He's kind of a dork, isn't he, Ms. Lord?"

"That describes him," I called after Dustin as he left. "And after all this time, you'd better start calling me Emma." I turned to Milo, who was studying the late Brian Conley. "How do we keep Fleetwood out of here?"

"We can't," the sheriff replied, looking me straight in the eye. "How many times have you told me that the press—and the public—has a right to know?"

"Damn." Milo was right. It was an old argument, which I'd often used on him to elicit information for the paper. "Maybe Fleetwood's squeamish."

"Could be," Milo allowed, and continued to cautiously poke and prod the body. "Hey!" he exclaimed, his voice low. "Look at this."

I looked, though I didn't really want to. My stomach was still threatening to rebel, but I fought back the urge to be sick. Milo had turned Brian over onto his side. The back of the dead man's parka had been slashed, and a crusty dark stain spread over the blue Gor-Tex fabric. Getting down on his hands and knees, the sheriff scrutinized what appeared to be a wound.

"Knife, I'd guess," he finally said, getting on his feet again. "Doc Dewey will know."

"Call me," I said, backpedaling out of the locker. "I'm going to the office and get this extra edition off the drawing board."

I saw Milo's hat nod before I turned around and scooted through Barney Amundson's office. Outside, Spence, as I supposed I ought to call him since everybody else did, was still talking to Barney. I moved furtively across the parking lot, hoping my nemesis wouldn't see me.

But he did. "Emma!" he shouted in that mellifluous radio voice. "Big news, huh?"

I winced, then faced Spence. "How's Barney doing?" I asked, sounding sour.

Spence put a hand on Barney's shoulder. "He'll be fine. Quite a shock, though. I haven't come across anything like this since Chicago."

I didn't respond to his allusion. Spence would have everyone believe that he'd covered not only Al Capone, but the Hindenburg crash, the Battle of Britain, Jack Ruby shooting Lee Harvey Oswald, and Marilyn Monroe's wedding to Joe DiMaggio. "You'll make the ten o'clock news, I imagine," I remarked, trying not to be annoyed by his customary supercilious attitude toward me and the rest of Alpine.

Spence glanced at his watch, which I'd been told was a Rolex. "Can do. But I'd better get going. Got Tim Rafferty and a couple of students from the college on the air right now. See you in the funny papers, Emma."

"Ha, ha," I said, looking in my handbag for my own watch, the band of which I'd broken two weeks earlier and hadn't gotten around to replacing. It was nine-forty. I stuffed the watch down into the deep bottom of my purse—and stabbed myself in the hand.

I let out a little yip, but no one noticed. Annoyed, I dug around in my purse for the offending object. It was a corkscrew that Tom and I had taken on a picnic to Deception Falls. The damage to my hand was minimal, but the awful idea I got from the corkscrew was as brilliant as it was sinister.

Milo hadn't come out of the warehouse yet. Barney and Spence were still chatting. The ambulance drivers were talking to each other. The rest of the crowd, maybe close to forty people, milled around, shaking their heads and staring at the building's entrance. Word was spreading fast, as it always did on Alpine's grapevine. But the locals were convinced that any event was real only by reading about it in print. Or hearing it on the blasted radio.

I was unobserved, so I went over to Spence's BMW, quietly opened the door on the driver's side, inserted the corkscrew into the ignition, and turned it with all my might. The sound of wrenching metal was faint, but the damage was sufficient. Spence wouldn't make a hasty getaway.

I practically ran all the way back to the office. Scott was busy at the word processor, Vida and Leo were having a heated exchange, and Kip and Ginny were huddled together by the coffeemaker.

"The O'Neills! And that snowboarder!" Vida cried. "I must go over there at once."

"No, you mustn't," I said. "Didn't Scott tell you we were putting out a special edition?"

"Yes," Vida began, "but—"

"No buts," I interrupted. "Start writing up a background piece on the O'Neills. Leo, can you throw in a couple of ads from the school's-out edition? We'll only go two pages, but we can't fill them up with copy. Scott, whatever you're doing, stop. I'll take the lead story—you do the one on Conley from the files. Let's go, I want this on the street in an hour."

Scott seemed excited, Leo was shaking his head, and Vida looked dismayed. "Really, now!" she exclaimed. "Are you sure this is wise?"

"Vida." I turned my most severe expression on her. My House and Home editor often has a problem remembering who is the boss, and not without good reason. Vida's older and wiser, and I'm inclined to defer to her, but not this morning when the news and my temper were at the boiling point. "Don't you think we owe this to ourselves?" I asked in a solemn voice.

She whipped off her glasses and punished her eyes with the heels of her hands. "Ooooh . . . I don't know. It seems so . . . peculiar."

I leaned on her desk. "Do you want the *Advocate* to get beat on the biggest story that's come along in the past ten years? Spence is already bragging that he's covered this kind of wholesale mayhem in other places. So he makes it sound like nothing to him, but it's something to us because this isn't Chicago or New York or L.A."

Vida's chin shot up. "It certainly isn't," she agreed. "This is Alpine."

Fighting words to Vida. She put her glasses firmly in place and turned to her battered typewriter. "Paddy O'Neill arrived in Skykomish County in nineteen thirty-six. He was fifteen years old, and had ridden a freight train from the Twin Cities," she said aloud, and then went silent as the rattle of her two-fingered typing filled the office.

I went into my cubbyhole to begin the lead story. I wished I'd spoken to Barney Amundson, but the risk had been too great. Spence had monopolized him, and I didn't want to lie to Barney about the other body. He'd find out soon enough. I supposed that he'd start crying all over again.

I didn't have time for tears. At ten-twenty, I'd finished the story, except for a couple of gaps I needed to have Milo fill in. I'd asked Ginny to listen to KSKY on the hour. She came into my office to tell me that the warehouse bodies hadn't made the news.

"One of those college kids read the stories," Ginny said. "They sounded like the same ones I heard when I was driving to work at eight o'clock."

I heaved an enormous sigh of relief. In the newsroom, I discovered that Vida had dug out the history of Alpine Meats, Leo had found photos, if not very good ones, of all the O'Neills, and Scott had pulled the picture of Brian Conley that we'd run when he'd been reported missing. Ordinarily, Scott isn't the fastest guy at the word processor, but he'd outdone himself. Pushing his hard copy at me, he raced off to Buddy Bayard's studio to retrieve the photos he'd taken earlier.

My phone rang and I raced into my cubbyhole to pick it up. Thank God, it was Milo.

"Looks like a stab wound to Doc Dewey," the sheriff informed me. "A hunting or fishing knife, he figures. The guy's been dead for a long time, probably since he disappeared on Tonga Ridge."

"You mean he was murdered, too?" I said.

"What'd you think?" Milo said dryly. "He stabbed himself in the back?"

"No, no, of course not," I responded. "It's just that . . . well, it wasn't the Hartquists who killed him, right?"

"I wouldn't think so."

"What about them? Have you heard anything from the deputies?"

"Jack phoned in a few minutes ago," Milo replied. "The Hartquists are holed up out at what's left of their place on the Burl Creek Road."

Milo referred to the Hartquist house that had been partially burned more than a year before in yet another incident involving their feud with the O'Neills. At the time, I'd thought the two-story frame structure was a total loss, but they'd patched it up and stayed put.

"You mean it's a siege?"

"Let's put it like this," Milo said. "My guys are outside and the Hartquists are inside. Call it what you want."

I called it tricky, not just for Milo and his men, but for me. "Is an arrest imminent?"

"Hell, no," Milo said. "Do the usual—'persons of interest' or whatever. We want their cooperation. Et cetera."

"I know the drill." I sighed. "Okay, call me if you find out anything new." I started to sign off, then remembered to ask Milo about Spence. "Did he fly off with his hot scoop?" I asked innocently.

"Skunk Nordby had to give him a lift," Milo said. "I guess some kid jimmied his ignition when nobody was looking. I've told Spence to lock up that fancy piece of automobile when he parks it. But he thinks Alpine is safe compared to the city. Maybe he'll learn that there are troublemakers even around here."

I didn't remind Milo that finding four bodies in a meat locker indicated that we had more than just troublemakers in Alpine. "Have you called the state in?"

"I contacted them, but they're tied up on some other stuff in Seattle and Tacoma," Milo said, sounding disgusted. "Us little guys don't count for much in their scheme of things. They'll get back to me."

"You can handle this," I said, wanting to give Milo's ego a boost. Having punctured his self-esteem when we broke up, I owed it to him.

"Hunh," Milo responded. "Let's hope."

By ten thirty-five we had all our copy, photos, and ads ready to go. Kip, who had already contacted our carriers, took over in the backshop. The first copies of the special edition would be on the streets by eleven. I felt vindicated as a journalist.

But I felt horrible as a person. The sick feeling I'd had since seeing the bodies inside the meat locker washed over me again. Having used up my adrenaline rush along with every ounce of energy and determination, I caved in. My head touched the desk; my knees turned to jelly. It was all I could do to move far enough to throw up in my wastebasket.

As usual, the door to the cubbyhole was open, but my staff members didn't notice. Vida was on the phone, no doubt making contact with her myriad sources, many of whom were related to her by blood or marriage. Scott had left to see what was going on with the sheriff and the Hartquists. Leo had gone off to soothe the advertisers he'd pulled from the regular Wednesday edition and put in the special issue. Ginny was in the front at the reception desk. Kip was readying the paper for distribution.

I threw up again, laid my head back down on the desk and panted. It was Kip MacDuff who found me still lying there several minutes later.

"Hey, what's wrong?" he asked in alarm. "Emma?"

Slowly, I raised my head. "I'm okay," I said, and knew that the shaky voice, green face, and glazed eyes told Kip otherwise. "Can you grab me some paper towels from the newsroom?"

"You don't look okay," he said, stating the obvious. "Are you sick?"

"I was," I said, glancing in distaste at the wastebasket.

"Oh, boy," Kip said softly. "Be right back!"

Vida had just hung up the phone. "What on earth's the matter?" she demanded.

"Emma's sick," Kip replied, ripping off a half-dozen or more towels and racing back into my office.

Vida was on his heels. "Good heavens!" she cried. "Emma, do you need a doctor?"

Feebly, I shook my head. "No, it's just shock." I took the paper towels from Kip and wiped my face. "I'm better now. I just have to sit for a minute."

"Let me empty that," Vida said, grabbing the wastebasket and marching off to the rest room next door to my cubbyhole.

"You sure you're okay?" Kip asked.

"I will be. Honest." I attempted a smile that must have been a pathetic imitation. "Is the paper out?"

Kip nodded, beaming. "That's what I came to tell you. I got hold of six of our carriers. They're already headed out, with two of them covering downtown. The rest are going door to door to the residential customers. I'll take the van and do the routes outside of town."

"Wonderful, Kip," I said, my smile growing stronger. "Go ahead. I'll be fine."

Kip left and Vida returned. "My word," she said, sitting down in one of the chairs and studying me closely. "You're so pale. Maybe you should go home to rest."

"I can't," I said. "I've got to keep on this story. It's huge."

"Scott and I can manage," Vida declared.

I shook my head. "No. It's a matter of personal pride—professional pride, too. Besides, how could I miss out on something like this?" Like this terrible tragedy, I thought, with four people dead, and three more possibly headed for prison. Alas, the catastrophes of others are a boon to those of us in the media. There were times when I hated my job, yet some part of me thrived on disaster. My evil side, I often thought, but salved my conscience by telling myself I was only human.

I made a pit stop to repair my makeup and brush my hair. I looked god-awful. My short brown hair was sticking up in several directions, my skin was sallow, my eyes had developed dark circles under them, my usually trim figure slumped.

To hell with it, I thought, closing my handbag with a defiant gesture. I was after a big story, and looks didn't count.

In the reception area, Ginny was on the phone. She paused, put her hand over the receiver, and looked up at me. "They're ringing off the hook. I haven't put anybody through because I knew you were all tied up. What's this business about Mayor Baugh and a toilet?"

"It'll keep," I said. "Thanks, Ginny." I dashed out through the front door, then realized I didn't know where Milo was. He could have called from anywhere, including en route to the Hartquists' on the Burl Creek Road.

On Front Street, all of Alpine appeared to be congregating in little knots of threes and fours. Some people were heading for Alpine Meats. Many were already holding copies of the *Advocate*. I tried to stifle a triumphant smile as I turned toward the sheriff's headquarters a block away.

Several people attempted to waylay me, including Father Dennis Kelly from St. Mildred's.

"Is it true?" he asked, his earnest cocoa-brown face full of concern. "All three of the O'Neills?"

"I'm afraid so," I said as a half-dozen others pressed around us. I pointed to the newspaper that my pastor held in his hands. "It's all in there, so far as anyone knows at this point."

"And that poor snowboarder?" Father Den shook his head. "It seems like yesterday that I celebrated the Requiem Mass for Paddy O'Neill."

I had seldom seen any of the O'Neills inside of St. Mildred's. But they were Catholics, and entitled to burial from the church. "This will be a triple for you, Father," I said ruefully.

Den nodded slowly. "I assume the boys didn't ever mention being shipped to Ireland like their father. They weren't born there. Do you realize there've been two funerals in town during the past six months involving bodies being sent over there?"

I had, in fact, forgotten that Liam Rafferty also had requested that his remains be buried in Ireland. "That is unusual," I remarked, trying to break away tactfully. "But both Liam and Paddy had come from Ireland. I suppose it made sense to them."

A slight smile touched Father Den's mouth. "I may be a Kelly, but I doubt that most of my ancestors came from there. More likely, the name came from one of my great-great-grandfather's plantation owners."

I smiled at Den. "You don't want to be buried in Africa, I take it?"

"I don't even want to go to Africa," he replied. "I have no missionary zeal."

I smiled some more, waved, and hurried on down the street. Another gaggle of Alpiners called out to me; I waved and smiled at them, too. The special edition was out, I wasn't really in a rush, but I didn't want to spend the rest of the day fielding questions. Everything I knew so far was in the *Advocate*'s extra edition.

Milo's Grand Cherokee was nowhere in sight. In fact, the sheriff's department looked empty except for Toni Andreas, the receptionist. She was on the phone, and looking uncharacteristically agitated. I had to wait for her through three calls, all of them seemingly related to the warehouse bodies.

"That's it," Toni declared, yanking the headset from her ears. "I'm not answering any more phones for a while unless they're 911 calls. Beth Rafferty's on break." Beth was the sister of Tim Rafferty, who tended bar and who occasionally used his people skills filling in at KSKY. Like most bartenders, he was better at listening than talking.

"Where is everybody else?" I asked Toni.

She rubbed at her forehead, as if to erase the tension. "Boss man is still at Alpine Meats," she said. "So's Dustin Fong. But the rest of them are out at the Hartquist place. I guess those creeps won't come out of their crappy old house. Listen."

Toni turned up the volume on the link between her console and whichever deputy had the radio on at the other end. At first, I heard only static, but then Jack Mullins's nasal voice came through:

". . . riot gear on . . . Hell no, you know better than . . . Then get it out, Sam . . . Dodge is still at . . ."

Another voice, probably Dwight Gould's, cut in over Jack's. Dwight was speaking through a bullhorn, demanding that the Hartquists come out before the police had to come in after them.

I turned to Toni. "Have they issued an ultimatum before this?"

Toni's pretty face had assumed its usual phlegmatic expression. "I think so. I've been on the phone so much that I haven't actually noticed."

I started for the door. "I'm going out there. If Scott Chamoud shows up, let him know where I am and tell him to bring his camera."

Toni's dark eyes widened. "Scott? Sure, I'll tell him . . . Is it true he's seeing that teacher at the college?"

"I think so," I hedged, not wanting to get caught up in the romantic rumor mill. "Bye, Toni. Thanks."

Front Street was still a gathering place for some of the locals, though I suspected that most of them had headed over to Alpine Meats. I nodded to various little groups as I hurried by, then got into my car, and headed out onto Alpine Way.

Most of the emergency vehicles I had seen at the warehouse were now lining the dirt track that led from the Burl Creek Road to the Hartquist property. I was reminded of a similar scene over a year ago when the Hartquists had kidnapped Meara O'Neill and held her captive on the second floor of the old house. Even as Milo and his deputies tried to get the Hartquists to come out and bring Meara with them, the resourceful teenager set fire to the upstairs. Her father and one of her uncles had shown up. Rudy Hartquist accidentally shot Milo in the foot, and Meara managed to jump out of a window. It had been quite a night.

The charred skeletons of two huge cedar trees stood like ugly sentries in front of the house. At least two of the windows had been replaced with cardboard, and the exterior paint was still scorched. I marveled that the old man and his two sons had stayed on. But then I guessed that the Hartquists didn't watch Martha Stewart on TV.

I pulled up behind the medic van. I could see Bill Blatt

and Sam Heppner getting something out of the trunk of their squad car. Jack Mullins, wearing riot gear, was positioned behind a Douglas fir. Dwight Gould's outline was barely visible toward the back of the house. He still held the bullhorn and was shielding himself with a stand of young vine maples. The scene was deceptively calm. The only sounds were the chattering of chipmunks and the breeze moving softly through the cottonwood trees.

Cautiously, I edged around the fire truck and moved in Jack's direction. He saw me and made a scooting motion with the hand that didn't hold his Glock pistol.

"Get back," he ordered. "These goofballs may shoot at anything that moves."

"Have they shot at you yet?" I asked, retreating a few steps.

"Nope," Jack replied, keeping his eyes on the house. "But they may. They sure as hell aren't coming out."

"Are you sure they're in there?"

Jack nodded. "They gave us a bunch of bullshit when we got here. They claim Cap is real sick. That's crap; yesterday afternoon Cap was cited for grabbing Betsy O'Toole's ass in the produce aisle at the Grocery Basket."

"Again?" I said.

Jack's eyes never left the house. "Cap loves to prowl that aisle because you have to bend over to get the dried fruits and stuff. Still, you'd think he'd have more sense than to play grab-ass with the store owner's wife."

Sam Heppner and Bill Blatt appeared, also dressed in riot gear. Dwight was on the bullhorn.

"This is your last warning," he shouted. "I'm counting to ten. Come out with your hands up. If you don't, we're coming in with tear gas."

"Screw 'em," Jack growled after a full minute had passed. "Let's go!"

Bill and Sam had their gas masks on and the canisters

ready. They separated, with Bill headed for what was left of the front porch and Sam going around to the rear. I backed off, just in case the deputies aimed the tear gas in the wrong direction. After all, they hadn't had much experience with flushing out dangerous suspects.

Bill disappeared inside; I assumed Sam had gone in the back door. Nothing happened for what seemed like at least a minute or two. Then, to my amazement, I saw two figures on the roof. They had a rope, which they flung out at a thirty-foot hemlock near the house. It took three tries, but they finally got it around the tree trunk. A third figure appeared; I recognized Cap Hartquist. In a matter of seconds, they were all on the rope, shinnying down the hemlock.

Jack Mullins swore, a stream of obscenities I'd never heard him use before. "Loggers!" he yelled at the end. "Wouldn't you know it?"

Dwight Gould had rushed over to the hemlock, his gun aimed up into the heavy branches. "They're not going far," he shouted as Jack rushed to join him.

As it turned out, the Hartquists went fast, if not far. They were burly, and the rope snapped just past the halfway point. Rudy Hartquist landed first, then Ozzie, and finally Cap—all three cursing and screaming.

Jack and Dwight had the trio covered. The medics and firefighters moved cautiously toward the men on the ground just as Sam and Bill emerged from the house. As they removed their masks, both men looked bewildered until they saw the little crowd by the hemlock.

"So that's how they got out," Sam muttered in disgust.

Jack was informing the Hartquists that they were wanted for questioning in the multiple slayings discovered that morning at Alpine Meats. The suspects said nothing. They were rolling around on the ground, checking their various body parts for damage.

Scott Chamoud pulled up just then. "Quick," I called to him. "Get some pictures."

Scott stared, shook his head in wonder, and advanced on the Hartquists. So did the medics. I hurriedly jotted down some notes. Until this moment, I'd been too mesmerized by the action to ply my trade.

One of the medics announced that the trio should be checked out at the hospital before they were taken in to headquarters. Jack scowled and mumbled something to the effect that those "damned Scandahoovians are too damned tough to get hurt by falling out of a damned tree."

The medics, however, persisted. They volunteered to help the Hartquists, but the offer was rejected.

"How many times do ya t'ink I fall outta one of dem t'ings?" Cap growled in his ragged old voice.

Scott had finished one roll of film and was putting another into his camera. "This is pretty cool," he said, his dark eyes sparkling with excitement. "You don't know what to expect around here, do you, Emma?"

"That's right," I said dryly. "This town is full of surprises." Many of them bad, I thought.

The deputies had patted down the Hartquists and were herding them into the two squad cars just as Milo drove up. "Okay," he called to his men, "we've got probable cause. Haul them in while I look for weapons."

"You ain't got nutting," Cap shouted as Bill Blatt shoved the old man into the backseat of the car. "You need a goddamned varrant!"

"Like hell I do," Milo retorted. "You're lucky we're not arresting you on the spot. You kill four people, you pay."

Cap twisted around in Bill's grasp. "Four? You can't count, you big galoot! If ve killed anybody, it vas self-defense, and it vas only t'ree of 'em."

Milo stared at Cap. I stared at Milo. Scott stared at me.

"What does he mean by that?" Scott whispered.

"It means," I said slowly, "that what I suspected all along may be true. Somebody besides the Hartquists killed Brian Conley."

Chapter Four

THE MILL WHISTLE went off at precisely noon, just as we arrived at the sheriff's office. There were five hours to go before our regular Tuesday deadline. After Scott had taken down the entries in the police log—including Cap Hartquist's citation for groping Betsy O'Toole—I sent him off with a list of other stories to cover. Including, of course, Mayor Baugh's toilets. Meanwhile, I would stay on top of the developing homicide investigation.

Milo had shown up with the Hartquist arsenal, which consisted of a half-dozen handguns and almost twice as many rifles. The weapons had been hidden in various parts of the property—a fruit cupboard, an old icebox, the bathroom medicine cabinet, a fishing basket, a carton marked RAT TRAPS. Meanwhile, Dwight Gould had joined Dustin Fong up at the O'Neill place on Second Hill, collecting whatever evidence that could be found. No doubt there was a collection of guns there, too.

I was trying to organize my notes when Vida tromped into the sheriff's reception area.

"Well!" she exclaimed. "This has been quite a morning! Now tell me what I've missed. It's not quite fair that I've been relegated to the office for most of this."

Bill Blatt was standing behind the curving reception desk, filling out some forms. "Bill," I said, "can you bring your aunt up to speed on what's happened? It would be better coming from you. You're official."

Bill's pink complexion darkened slightly. I knew he didn't want to be put on the spot, but better him than me. Kinship means so much to Vida, I thought, somewhat gleefully. Nor did I see why Bill should be let off the hook.

While Vida sucked in all the details like a high-powered vacuum cleaner, I asked Jack Mullins how the interrogation was going.

"They confessed," Jack said with his mischievous grin. "But they swear it was self-defense. Given all the other hostilities between them and the O'Neills, they might be right."

"But doesn't it appear that the Hartquists went to the O'Neill place?" I pointed out. "Isn't that where the shots were heard last night?"

"That doesn't mean that Cap and the boys went there to kill the O'Neills," Jack answered, growing serious. "The O'Neills are as well armed as the Hartquists. Those crazy Irishmen might have fired first."

It was certainly a possibility, though the shootings had appeared to be virtual assassinations. I said as much, then added that I found Cap's denial of the Conley killing credible.

"Me, too," Jack agreed. "That poor guy has been dead for quite a while. But the Hartquists swear they didn't put Conley in the meat locker. In fact, they insist he wasn't there when they dumped off the O'Neills."

"When was that?" I asked.

"Last night," Jack said. "Around eight."

"Why? I mean, why put them in the locker?"

Jack shook his head. "They couldn't get hold of Al Driggers. Nobody was at the funeral home last night. The Hartquists didn't want the bodies to spoil. Don't try to make sense of it, Emma. They're all nuts."

But I had to make sense of it. It wasn't just my own curiosity about what makes human beings tick, but my obligation to the public. I was attempting to find some kind of logic in what had happened when Vida plucked me by the sleeve of my cotton shirt.

"The Conleys," she said. "Have they been notified?"

"Oh!" I'd forgotten about Brian's parents. "I don't think Milo's had time. Go ahead, I just spoke with Mrs. Conley yesterday, so it's not as if we're butting in. And let his girlfriend, Gina Whatever-her-name-is, know, too."

Already armed with the numbers, Vida commandeered a phone from her nephew just as Milo came out of the interrogation room. "Jeez," he uttered with a shake of his head. "It's like interviewing monkeys at the zoo."

"What now?" I asked.

"They're sticking to their story," Milo said, pouring himself a mug of what I've always considered the world's worst coffee. "The Hartquists swear they just happened to be driving by the O'Neill place last night when Stubby opened fire on them with a .22. They claim they kept going in their pickup, but had a flat about twenty yards down the road. They were afraid to stop to change the tire, so they went back to the O'Neill place, where Ozzie took out his gun and warned Stubby that if he shot at them again, they'd start shooting back. Stubby fired a second time, and the war was on."

"Do you believe them?" I inquired.

"No," Milo replied, lighting a cigarette in front of the No Smoking sign on the wall. "If that many shots had been fired, everybody within half a mile would've been on the alert. How many shots did you hear?"

I thought back to the previous evening. "Three," I responded. "Maybe four. But not a fusillade."

"That's what I figured," Milo said. "I didn't hear the shots at all, though I'm farther away. Besides, I went up there after the complaints about the noises came in, and I didn't see any sign of trouble. Everything was quiet."

"What about the wounds?" I asked. "Were the O'Neills shot with rifles?"

"Rusty was," Milo replied, "but at fairly close range. Stubby and Dusty were killed with handguns, also up close."

I was surprised. "So maybe the O'Neills weren't even armed?"

"It's possible," Milo said. "It seems they were caught off guard."

"But the Hartquists say otherwise," I remarked. They would, of course. "What else did they say?"

"Not much," Milo responded with a sour look. "At least not much that makes sense. Cap claims they threw the bodies in the pickup, tossed a tarp over them, and drove around trying to figure out what to do next."

"Why didn't they call Al Driggers?" I asked.

Milo gulped more coffee before replying. "Who knows? They say they drove by the funeral home and didn't see anybody around. So they got the bright idea of taking the bodies to the meat locker. They broke in, dumped Stubby, Rusty, and Dusty into the walk-in, and took off. They meant to call Al this morning, but they forgot." Milo rolled his eyes.

"Gosh," Scott said, "that's pretty incredible."

"You bet," Milo said. "But then the Hartquists are a pretty incredible bunch of jackasses."

"So you've officially charged them with multiple homicide?" I asked.

Milo nodded. "We had to charge all of them, since they insist they don't know who shot who. And now they want a lawyer."

"Court-appointed?"

"No. Somebody named Svensen from Snohomish," Milo said. "He's some old coot Cap knows from way back when."

"What about Brian Conley?" I asked.

Milo shrugged. "Doc figures he's been dead since March, about the time he was reported missing. I suppose he riled one of those mountain men up on the Ridge, and got himself stabbed to death. It happens."

Unfortunately, Milo was right. Mountain men, hermits, recluses—they sought refuge from civilization in the vast forests of the Cascades, living in shacks, huts, abandoned cabins, and whatever other shelter they could find. Intruders, even innocent passersby, were met with hostility and occasionally death. Milo's predecessor, Eeeny Moroni, had told of finding human skulls decorating the fireplace mantel of one such hermit. Perhaps Brian Conley had been foolish enough to say a simple hello to a man who didn't want to socialize.

"You'll investigate, though," I remarked.

Milo stubbed his cigarette out in a metal ashtray. "Sure. But I don't expect to find out much, not after all this time."

I didn't blame the sheriff for his lack of enthusiasm. The trail was cold, in more ways than one.

"Goodness," said Vida, who had just gotten off the phone. "How very odd."

I turned in her direction. "What's that?"

"The Conleys were stunned, then relieved," she said, looking puzzled. "I reached the girlfriend at work. Gina—Gina Ancich. After becoming semihysterical, she told me that Brian had always wanted his body buried in Ireland. What is all this silliness with being buried abroad? First Oscar Nyquist, now this Brian Conley. Tut!"

"Roots," Toni Andreas put in. "People want to be connected with their past. One of my uncles was buried in the old country last year, one of those Greek isles. He'd retired to Arizona, but he missed the water and wanted to be buried by the sea."

Vida looked askance. "It's absurd. I can't imagine being buried anywhere but here. The Alpine Cemetery is such a lovely place, up on the hill, above the river, the mountains around it, looking out over the town."

Vida, no doubt, expected to be able to see the local goings-on even when she was six feet under. "Are the Conleys coming out?" I asked, wanting to change the subject.

"Yes." Vida adjusted her cartwheel straw hat with its pink and blue streamers. "They don't know exactly when. They have to make the travel arrangements. I gave them Father Kelly's number at the rectory in case they want to have a service here."

"They told me they did," I noted.

"They may have changed their minds," Vida said, coming from behind the counter and into the reception area. "In fact, I got the impression that they planned to bury Brian in Penn Yan." She frowned. "How odd. Perhaps they didn't know of their son's request."

That was the least of my worries. I still needed to sort through the details of the Hartquist arrests. After Vida went on her way, I asked Milo when the arraignment would be held.

"As soon as that attorney from Snohomish gets up here," the sheriff replied. "First, though, I'm going to have lunch. You want to come along, Emma?"

I hesitated. But after my earlier stomach bout, I felt as if I were running on empty. "Sure," I said. "You can tell me what I may have missed so far."

We went across the street to the Burger Barn, where Milo was besieged with curious customers. He held up his big hands and announced he wasn't going to say anything until he'd downed a cheeseburger, fries, and three cups of coffee. Everyone looked disappointed, but they honored the sheriff's pronouncement.

"I can't make mistakes on this story," I said after we'd placed our orders. "What about the rest of the O'Neills? Has anybody tracked them down?"

Toni Andreas had been given that task, Milo said. "The only ones that I know of around here are Mickey, Rusty's son, and Kathleen and Margaret, Stubby's daughters by his first wife. Mickey works for Blackwell Timber, so he's probably in the woods. Kathleen—Kathy, I guess—is living with some guy out by the fish hatchery. I'm not sure where Margaret—Peggy, she's called—is, but Toni said she saw her the other day at the Alpine Mall."

"You don't know where Lona and Meara are?" I asked.

Milo shook his head. "I heard they moved to Everett or Marysville before Meara had the baby. Did anybody ever say who the father was?"

"Not that I heard," I said as our waitress delivered coffee for Milo and a Pepsi for me. "What about Brian? Who put his body in the locker? You may be able to find that much out anyway."

"Maybe." Milo sipped his coffee. "If the Hartquists are telling the truth, then Conley was put there after they dumped the O'Neills. It could be—they broke into the place, they admit it. But what are the chances of anybody knowing that the bodies were there?"

"What," I said wryly, "are the chances of somebody else in Alpine driving around with another spare body? And how come Brian was in relatively good shape?"

"Doc figures he'd been under the snow where the animals couldn't get to him." Milo began rearranging the salt and pepper shakers—an old habit of his. "Brian was still partially frozen inside."

I was startled. "So he'd been found very recently?"

"Probably sometime yesterday afternoon," Milo said.

I was thoughtful for a few moments, right up until Ed

Bronsky banged into our booth. "Hey, hey, hey!" my former ad manager bellowed. "Caught you just in time, Emma. Hi there, Dodge. How's it going?" Ed didn't pause for an answer. "Got room on the front page?" he said to me. "I got a big one."

Yes, you do, Ed, I thought, and it's your big fat ego. "Why do you ask?"

"Six weeks from Saturday," Ed responded, beaming all over himself. "That's when *Mr. Pig* debuts on national television."

I managed not to groan aloud. *Mr. Pig* was a cable TV program loosely based on Ed's self-published rags-to-riches autobiography, *Mr. Ed.* I never really wanted to know how or why, but the book had been sold to a Hollywood producer who had turned the characters into an animated cartoon about a family of pigs.

"I don't know if I can get it on page one," I said. "It looks like we're going to be pretty full tomorrow. Did you see the special edition today?"

"Special edition?" Ed's round face was mystified. "Is that what everybody was standing around reading? I thought it was some flyer for the summer solstice."

If a nuclear device exploded in the middle of Front Street, Ed was so self-absorbed that he wouldn't notice until he looked in the mirror and saw that he glowed in the dark.

Milo was regarding Ed with a wry expression. "We had some excitement around here," the sheriff said in that lazy drawl he reserved for the very young and the very stupid. "The Hartquists knocked off the O'Neills and dumped them in Barney Amundson's meat locker."

Ed evinced mild surprise. "Really? That's a shame."

"They found the missing snowboarder in there, too," I put in, "but the Hartquists claim they didn't kill him."

"No kidding," Ed said, squeezing his bulk next to me

in the booth. "Gee, that would have been good for my book and the TV series. I keep thinking I should do a sequel. I'll try to remember that. You ordered yet?"

We said we had. In fact, the waitress was on her way with our meal. Ed glanced at my burger and Milo's cheeseburger. "How about a couple of those and the super basket of fries, sweetheart?" he said to the waitress. Ever since Ed had sold his book to TV he called every female whose name eluded him "sweetheart." I guess he thought it made him sound like Hollywood.

"You know," Ed said, putting both elbows on the table and forcing me even further into the corner, "I was thinking. The summer solstice deal is coming up pretty quick, and it might be smart of me to enter myself as a float."

I couldn't help it—I was drinking my Pepsi, I choked, and I spewed soda all over Milo's shirt. The sheriff jumped a bit, brushed himself off, but didn't take his eyes off Ed. "How do you mean, a float?" Milo asked with a perfectly straight face.

"You know," Ed said eagerly as he accepted a cup of coffee from our waitress, "as a promotional tool for the TV series. Shirley and the kids and I could ride on it, maybe decorate it like a farm. A little silo, a barn, a pigsty. Have it pulled by a tractor. We could borrow one from the Overholts or one of the other farmers around here. Then," Ed continued, gathering momentum even as he swiped four of my French fries, "we could maybe dress up like pigs."

Who needs to dress up? I thought nastily. Ed, Shirley, and their brood were porcine by nature.

"I still belong to the chamber of commerce," Ed went on. "I mean, how could I not? Between all my experience in advertising and now in high finance, it wouldn't be right to quit."

"Certainly not," I intoned, not daring to look at Milo, who I knew was trying as hard as I was to contain hoots of laughter. In my own case, the events of the morning had shredded my emotions. I felt positively giddy. Ed had been the most morose, the laziest, the least creative advertising manager imaginable. I'd been on the verge of firing him several times after I bought the *Advocate* from Marius Vandeventer. But I always felt sorry for Ed. He had a growing family to support—growing in all sorts of directions. As for his involvement with "high finance," the large inheritance he'd received from an aunt was, fortunately, managed by a professional in Everett. Ed didn't have to lift a pudgy finger.

"You'd better get on with it for the parade," Milo commented. "Scooter Hutchins is the chairman this year."

"I know," Ed said in a tone that indicated he knew just about everything. "Scooter's good people. He won't mind an addition to the spectacle."

Scooter probably wouldn't, since the so-called spectacle consisted mainly of a couple of logging rigs, an old flatbed truck carrying the county commissioners, the high school band, Miss Alpine in a borrowed Corvette from the Nordby brothers' dealership, a U.S. Postal Service van, a half-dozen pickups decorated with plastic flowers and palm leaves, Mayor Baugh riding in his 1990 Cadillac convertible, and a lot of people wearing balloon animals on their heads.

Ed's cheeseburger and hamburger arrived. He looked dismayed. "Sweetheart," he said in a plaintive voice to the waitress, "I ordered a couple of each of these."

"Oh." The young woman's blue eyes widened. "Sorry," she murmured, and skittered back to the kitchen.

Milo took advantage of Ed's filling his face to return to the subject of the homicides. "So Conley's girlfriend will be in town tomorrow?"

"That's what Vida told me," I said.

"I don't suppose she'd have any ideas about somebody who might want to whack her boyfriend."

"Other than a recluse?" I shrugged. "Doubtful. Do you remember where he worked?"

"The Irish consulate in Seattle," Milo replied. "I think the girlfriend works there, too."

"Poor guy," I said, trying to ignore the chomping and slurping noises Ed was making next to me. "I got the impression Brian was by himself. That's always foolish in the mountains."

"The forest rangers around here are recommending that anybody going hiking or cross-country skiing or whatever should take along a cell phone," Milo said, finishing his meal and lighting a cigarette. "You never know what's going to happen: a sudden storm, an avalanche, a bear—or just plain falling down and breaking a leg."

"Did Doc notice any broken bones on Brian?" I inquired, wishing as I often did that I hadn't quit smoking. Again.

Milo shook his head. "He hadn't done a complete autopsy," he explained as the waitress refilled his coffee mug.

"Say," Ed interrupted, hamburger juice running down his chin, "I'll take the rest of my order to go, okay, sweetheart? I'll pick it up at the counter." He turned from the waitress to look at each of us. "I've got to run if I want to catch Scooter. I can eat in the Mercedes."

Ed could eat inside an erupting volcano. I'd seen the interior of Ed's luxury car—Shirley had a Mercedes, too—and it was littered with fast-food wrappers, paper bags, and empty soda cans.

"See you later, Ed," I said as our uninvited companion grunted his way out of the booth and waddled over to the service counter where his order to go was waiting.

"Ed," Milo sighed. "Ed."

"I think I liked him better when he was morose," I said as the waitress returned with our bill.

"My treat this time," Milo said, picking up the small slip of paper. He glanced at it, stared, then called to the waitress who was across the aisle waiting on an elderly couple I didn't recognize. "Hey, this must be the wrong bill. It's for over forty bucks."

The waitress came to the booth and scrutinized the tab. "No," she said slowly, "this is right." She gestured at the departing bulk of Ed Bronsky, who had just gone out the door. "For all of three of you, it comes to—"

"Never mind." Milo sighed, then added, "Ed."

Vida supplied me with some fragmentary quotes from both the Conleys and Gina Ancich that I could use in my lead story. Scott had reinterviewed Wes Amundson, who was Barney's younger brother and, by coincidence, the park ranger who had been our source when Brian had disappeared.

Wes, a taller, leaner version of Barney, stopped in to see me after talking to Scott. He was on duty, and the rain that had started during the noon hour dampened his regulation brown shirt.

"That's something about that Conley," he said. "Who the heck do you think found him and brought him down here?"

"I was hoping you'd have a clue," I replied. "Apparently it happened yesterday. Have you got anybody on the list of people who went up Tonga Ridge?"

Wes's craggy face, which always looked as if it needed a shave, grew blank. "Just a couple from California. You know how it is—hikers are supposed to sign in at the ranger station this time of year, but often as not, they don't. The locals never do, unless it's dead of winter. Besides, it's early in the season. Some of the lakes up there are still snowed in and will be for a couple of weeks at least."

I nodded. "How's Barney doing? I really never got a chance to talk to him this morning." An oversight, certainly, but Spence had monopolized the warehouse owner.

"He's okay," Wes responded. "The new doctor checked him out. Barney's had some trouble with high blood pressure, you know."

The new doctor was a young man from Hawaii named Elvis Sung. He had studied medicine at UCLA, completed his residency in San Diego, and interned in Santa Barbara. Having declared himself sick of sun, Dr. Sung had accepted a position in Alpine. So far, there had been no complaints, either from his new patients or from him. He seemed very competent, and, for the most part, it had been a damp, cool spring.

"As I recall, Brian Conley didn't go near the ski lodge," I remarked.

"No," Wes replied. "He took the trail from the Icicle Creek ranger station."

"No one in town remembered seeing him," I said. "His SUV was left in the ranger station's parking lot, but Milo never found anything of interest inside."

"I was with the sheriff when he checked it out," Wes said, standing up and going over to my U.S. Forest Service map on the far wall. "I'd sure like to know where Conley was found. We combed that whole area for him back in March," he said, making a sweeping gesture with his hand."

"You're certain he went in by himself?" I asked.

"He signed in alone," Wes said. "But you never know. People are darned funny. Sometimes one will register and the other one will say to heck with it."

"Especially," I remarked, "if they don't want anyone to know they've gone with someone else."

Wes gave me a wry grin. "You mean like somebody else's wife or girlfriend?"

"Like that," I said.

But I was thinking more along the lines of a killer.

Chapter Five

GINNY ERLANDSON HAD been so busy out front that she hadn't had a chance to tell me about Spencer Fleetwood's news broadcasts. "You really should turn on the radio," she urged in her most serious manner. "Spence is doing on-the-spot coverage all over town. He's hardly played any music at all."

"Damn," I breathed, and glared at my little portable radio. I'd received it as a high school graduation gift. It had been a friend to me at night while I was studying for college exams, a comfort while I awaited the birth of Adam, a source of calm enjoyment on warm summer evenings when it brought me baseball games from faraway places such as Cleveland, Chicago, and New York. Though it was often full of static, and sometimes faded in and out, I relied on my little radio for companionship. But lately it had betrayed me. I might not receive the Seattle or Everett stations loud and clear, but I could always get KSKY.

"I'll listen in," I said, and thanked Ginny for the suggestion.

The station was on a commercial break, with Spence using a high-pitched, racketing voice to extol the wonders of the hottest new releases at Platters in the Sky. He did most of the local commercials himself, though occasionally he used Tim Rafferty or a college student to lend some variety.

Spence came on live, dropping down a few decibels and sounding deadly earnest. "I'm reporting directly from Alpine Memorial Hospital," he intoned, "where I'm speaking with Debbie Murchison, registered nurse. What's the latest on the autopsy of Brian Conley's body, Nurse Murchison?"

"Dr. Dewey just finished," Debbie said in her youthful voice. "He went to lunch, so I haven't had a chance to speak with him. I think he's at the Venison Inn."

There was a scant second of dead air, apparently while Spence considered his options. "Then that's where KSKY is headed. Thank you, Nurse Murchison. Now for a word from one of our fine sponsors."

I called Milo. "What did Doc say about the autopsy?" I asked. "I hear he's all done."

"I've got it right here," Milo replied. "Doc dropped it off on his way to lunch. There's not much of interest, all the usual gobbledygook. Conley probably died about three hours after his last meal, so he wasn't up on the ridge for very long before he met somebody with a knife."

"The stab wound was the cause of death?" I asked.

"Right," Milo said. "Two stab wounds, in fact. The body was probably hidden someplace, in a cave, maybe. There were bits of evergreen needles and dirt and other debris you'd find in a sheltered place. I'm guessing that he wasn't up that far on the mountain. Of course, snowboarders don't go up too high as a rule."

"But high enough that he got frozen in later, right?"

"Right. We had that big storm in March, remember?"

I did remember. Alpine had gotten over a foot of snow, and I was sure that all my bulbs were dead before they could even peek out of the ground. "What about the snowboard itself?" I inquired.

"No sign of it," Milo replied. "No sign of a tussle, either. Conley must have been taken by surprise."

"Are you suggesting he knew his killer?" I asked.

"No," Milo responded. "Just that he didn't expect to be attacked. He was stabbed in the back, remember? There could be two scenarios: He was talking to somebody, turned around, and the killer struck. Or it's possible that he never saw his murderer. Somebody could have sneaked up behind him. Conley was wearing earmuffs, so he might not have heard someone approach. Either way, there wasn't a struggle."

"Poor guy." I sighed. "Out for a nice day in the mountains—it was fairly nice that weekend, as I recall—and he ends up dead."

"I know." Milo sounded solemn. "I wish I knew why."

"And who," I noted.

"Definitely who," Milo said, suddenly sounding tired. "It's a tough one. By the way, Doc's sending the body over to Driggers Funeral Home. Al came down with the flu this morning, but his assistant Dan Peebles is in charge for now."

I couldn't resist asking, "And how is Dan's mother?"

"Tara?" Milo's tone lightened. "Good. We're thinking of driving over to Lake Chelan weekend after next."

"That sounds like a good idea," I said. "You should have good weather over there." June could be wet and chilly on the western slope of the Cascades, but sun and warm weather were almost guaranteed on the other side of the pass. And I meant what I said to Milo—I wished him nothing but the best with Tara Peebles. She seemed like a nice, sensible woman, a widow who had been left to raise two sons, Dan and Don. Last winter they'd moved to Alpine from Seattle, fed up with traffic and soaring real estate prices. Dan was the elder of the two boys; Don was in the navy, fortuitously posted to the naval station in Everett. Tara had found part-time work at Mountain View Gardens, the local nursery. Milo said she had a green thumb.

After hanging up, I mused briefly on the renewed friendship between Milo and me. It had been a tough two years, first with Milo angry and hurt by our breakup, then with my resentment of his romance with Jeannie Clay, who was young enough to be his daughter. Now Milo had Tara, and I had Tom. If I wanted him.

Which I did, I always had. I was still attending the University of Washington when I met Tom. He was an editor on the city desk at the *Seattle Times*, and I was an intern. We had fallen hopelessly in love, and I had gotten pregnant with Adam. But there was an obstacle—Tom's emotionally fragile wife, who was also expecting a child. My lover's decision to stay with Sandra Cavanaugh was both admirable and awful. Some might laud Tom as a hero, others would damn him as a heel. At the time, I chose the latter point of view. I quit the university and moved to the Mississippi delta town where my brother, Ben, was serving in the home missions. Adam was born there, and I moved back to the West Coast, enrolling at the University of Oregon to finish my degree. I had no contact with Tom Cavanaugh for eighteen years. It was my choice. He had abandoned me, and I refused to let him see the son I had borne him.

Then one day, after I had been in Alpine about a year, Tom showed up. Nothing had changed between us. Love doesn't go away, it merely gets shoved into the back of our emotional closets. Tom finally met Adam, and somewhat to my surprise, the two of them hit it off. Somewhat to my resentment, too: I thought I had done an excellent job of being two parents. But Adam wanted, needed, a father. Uncle Ben was a fair substitute, but he was rarely around for his nephew.

Tom and I saw each other off and on over the next few years, but he remained loyal to Sandra. Oh, he made the occasional promise to leave her, but though she was unstable, her sensibilities were extraordinary. Just when I'd get my hopes up, Sandra would suffer a downturn. Filled with guilt, Tom would go back on his word to me. I expected it; I got used to it. So when Sandra overdosed, intentionally or accidentally, I finally glimpsed a future for Tom and me. I realized my reaction was callous, but my evil side kept whispering that Sandra had brought it on herself. She had been raised in wealth and luxury; she was spoiled and selfish. I always wondered if she'd married Tom with the intention of being a wife and mother. It seemed that a husband and children were merely adjuncts to her persona. The symptoms of mental problems struck me as attention-getting devices. She hadn't wanted to share the limelight, and eventually, she paid for her self-absorption with her life. I may have been uncharitable, but I truly believed that Sandra had a destructive personality. Maybe such a thing emanates from self-hatred more than self-love, yet the result is often the same, ending in self-destruction.

But after Sandra's death, my long-awaited future was delayed by the birth of Tom's daughter's illegitimate child. My child's birth hadn't delayed anything as far as Tom was concerned. I had been alone, two thousand miles away in Mississippi. Tom and Sandra had been together in Seattle when their son was born a month after Adam.

Now circumstances seemed to have changed. Tom appeared unencumbered. He'd asked me to marry him. I'd said yes—and then suffered qualms that didn't make much sense. Having waited most of my adult life for Tom Cavanaugh, suddenly I wasn't sure of what I wanted.

It wasn't that I didn't want Tom. It wasn't that I would hate to move away. It was losing *The Alpine Advocate* that disturbed me. Maybe I'd married the newspaper instead of Tom. Maybe my commitment to my career was greater than my commitment to marriage. Maybe I was as crazy as Sandra Cavanaugh.

The phone rang, rousing me from my reverie. It was Milo, saying that Cap Hartquist's attorney, Alfred Svensen, couldn't make it up to Alpine today. His bunions were acting up, and he was unable to drive. The arraignment would take place tomorrow.

I added that sentence to my story and uttered a sigh of relief. The paper was almost ready to go to bed.

I came out into the newsroom, where Kip MacDuff was talking to Leo Walsh. "Is everybody finished?" I asked.

Scott said he had to go over his copy one more time. Leo made a thumbs-up gesture. Vida, however, was frowning.

"In all this excitement," she said, "I didn't get enough items for 'Scene.' "

Scene Around Town was Vida's pet, a three-inch front-page column made up of gossipy little items. It was, along with the obituaries—when we had any—the best-read part of the paper.

"Didn't you get enough stuff with half the town out on Front Street, jabbering about the murders?" Leo asked.

"I can't use those items individually," Vida retorted. "All I'd have is a list of names."

Kip snapped his fingers. "I saw Ryan O'Toole driving a really hot Acura Integra last night. It's red and it has tinted windows, sun roof, the whole bit. I think it's his first car."

Vida made a face. "Jake and Betsy ought to know better than to buy a teenager a car like that. He'll get into a wreck, mark my words. And, I might add, they wouldn't be able to afford such things if they didn't overcharge for their meat and produce at the Grocery Basket."

Vida would, however, use the item. She typed it up

swiftly. "Well? Who else has something? I need two more."

Scott handed me his hard copy, then turned to Vida. "I saw two real cute little kids pulling each other in a wagon on my way home from work, but I didn't recognize them."

"Where were they?" Vida asked.

"Ah . . ." Scott looked up at the newsroom's low ceiling. "On Spruce, between Third and Fourth."

"How old?" Vida persisted.

"Four and six, maybe?" Scott gave Vida a sheepish look. "The older one was a boy, the younger one was a girl. Both fair-haired."

"The Burleson children," Vida said. "Axel and Dagmar. The family moved here from Grotto two months ago. Their parents are renting but have been looking for a house to buy." She rattled out the item on her upright. "Well? One more. Emma?"

I felt as if I were being called on in school. I didn't know the answer, which made me cringe a bit. Before I could admit my ignorance, Ginny came through the door on her way to the rest room.

"Toilets!" I cried, startling Ginny and causing the rest of the staff to stare at me. "Fuzzy Baugh and his toilets. I forgot to write it up as an article. He never dropped off the details."

"Typical of Fuzzy," Vida remarked. "Such a dunderhead. What was he doing with his toilets? Though I certainly hate to ask."

I explained about Fuzzy's great innovation for Alpine. Vida nodded. "Since he's been remiss in supplying additional information, I'll put it in Scene. It'll serve him right to have only the briefest of mentions of his toilets since he's been so careless."

I also remembered to give Vida Ed's plan to ride in the

summer solstice parade. Vida looked traumatized; she announced for perhaps the four hundredth time that Ed was the biggest ninny she'd ever met. Which was saying something, considering how many people Vida considered ninnies.

We were done for the day. I felt euphoric. I shouldn't have. Four dead bodies were the source of my elation. Instead I should have been wreathed in sorrow. But beating Spencer Fleetwood on the homicide story was a professional coup. It was an unhappy fact of life that big news was often bad news.

Kip was in the backshop; the paper had gone to press. I was gathering up my things in preparation for going home when the phone rang. I figured it was Fuzzy Baugh, finally delivering the details for his rest room story. Too bad, Fuzzy, I thought, you're too late.

But it wasn't the mayor. "This is Mae Conley in Penn Yan," Brian's mother said, her voice tremulous. "Ms. Lord?"

"Yes," I replied, trying to keep the surprise out of my voice. "I'm sorry if the discovery of Brian's body upset you."

"Well . . . it did and it didn't," Mrs. Conley said. "I mean, Pat—my husband—says we should be relieved. Maybe he's right, I don't know. Anyway, we're having Brian shipped to Penn Yan. We have a family plot here."

"Yes," I said. "It would only be painful for you to make the trip all the way to Washington State. Expensive, too."

"My, yes," Mae Conley agreed. "Funerals are expensive enough, particularly when they're so unexpected. Thank heavens Brian had life insurance."

"Yes," I repeated, not sure what else I could say. Mrs. Conley's remark struck me as rather inappropriate.

"Thank you and Mrs. Bunkel for keeping us informed," Mrs. Conley went on. "We appreciate the kindness."

"Of course." It was pointless to correct Mrs. Conley. Vida needn't know she'd been misnamed. Over the years, Vida had been referred to as Mrs. Rumple, Mrs. Kunkel, Mrs. Fungus, and—my personal favorite—Mrs. Rumpus. "We'll keep you in our thoughts and prayers," I said to Mrs. Conley.

"How nice." She thanked me again and rang off.

With a shake of my head, I turned out the lights and headed into the soft spring rain. My Lexus was parked on the diagonal in my usual spot at the curb. Even after more than a year, I felt a slight pang of guilt when I got into the expensive car. I was buying it from Tom for fifty dollars a month. He had been with me in Alpine when my precious though aging Jaguar had been wrecked by vandals. He'd wanted to give me the car as a gift, but I'd refused the offer. I wasn't a kept woman, and I didn't want to feel like one.

As soon as I got behind the wheel, I flipped on the radio. The five o'clock news had finished, and Spence—or a computer—was playing a trio of oldies-but-goodies. They would probably last until I got home. Old songs they might be, but after two of them, I realized I'd hated them thirty years ago and I hated them now. No more so-called goodies for me, I decided, and reached for the on-off button.

Before I could hit it, the music stopped, and Spence's voice filled the car.

"In a startling new development in the Alpine Meats tragedy, KSKY has just learned the identity of the person who found Brian Conley's body on Tonga Ridge. Live and direct from our studio, here is KSKY's Tim Rafferty to tell us exactly how the gruesome discovery was made."

Damn. I couldn't believe it. I'd been scooped again. But the worst was yet to come:

"This is Tim Rafferty reporting for radio station KSKY in Alpine. This has been a very difficult day for me, both as a lifelong resident of the town and as a radio personality."

Personality? The only personality Tim had developed over the years had been by tending bar in various local watering holes. He could listen, I'd give him that much, but so could a cedar stump.

"After some serious conversations with Spencer Fleetwood, the owner and the voice of KSKY, I came to the conclusion that I had to take a bold step and acknowledge that I was the person who found the late Brian Conley on Tonga Ridge."

Double damn. Was it true? Or was this some publicity stunt on Spencer's part? I wouldn't put it past him.

"After work yesterday—Monday—I went for a hike with my girlfriend, Tiffany Eriks. We took off about six o'clock on the Icicle Creek trail and then cut off on the spur to Spark Plug Lake. We got to Little Plug Lake first, and decided to rest for a while. There was still snow on the ground in most places and the sun had gone behind the clouds. Sure enough, it started to rain."

I had reached my house, where I pulled into the carport and remained riveted to the radio.

"It came down pretty hard, so we looked for some shelter and found a place under a ledge about ten yards from Little Plug." Tim paused, apparently for dramatic effect. "That's when we found Brian Conley." Another pause. "Naturally, we were shocked. We didn't know for sure who it was, but I guessed that maybe it was the missing snowboarder. It kept on raining for at least a half hour, which meant that it was getting darker up on the Ridge—darker than it usually does this time of year. Finally, it let up and we decided to get Conley out of there.

Between the two of us—and I have to thank Tiffany for being so brave and strong—we got the body back down to the ranger station. Nobody was around, so we put it—him—in my Jeep and started for town. We were coming down Second Hill when we saw a pickup ahead of us. Whoever was driving was kind of erratic. We were curious, so we followed them."

Until those last words, I'd believed Tim Rafferty. But his tale had taken a suspicious turn.

"The rain let up when we turned off Highway 187 onto Railroad Avenue," Tim continued. "But the Amtrak passenger train was coming through town, heading east. The red lights were flashing, so we prepared to stop. But the driver of the pickup gunned the engine and sailed right over the tracks. The train barely missed them. It really jarred me to see something like that, especially when we had a dead body in the Jeep. I was pretty shaken up by then." A pause for breath. "Anyway, Tiffany and I figured we'd lost whoever we'd been following, but after the train had gone by, we had to turn left anyway, and sure enough, the pickup had stopped at Alpine Meats."

He paused again. "I'll continue with my story after this word from one of our sponsors. To my amazement, the commercial featured Alpine Meats, a cheery little jingle that went something like, "Fresh meat / is good to eat / when you look for treats / try our special Alpine Meats." End of jingle, followed by Spence doing the straight lines: "Our butchers keep our locker full of fine cuts for every taste bud, with deliveries made daily. So when you think meat, you know what brand to eat. That's Alpine Meats, wholesalers to your favorite store, special discounts for bulk buyers."

While I reeled a bit in the driver's seat, Tim took up his tale:

"It was almost dark by then, going on nine o'clock. Tiffany and I parked by the Nordby Brothers used car lot half a block away. We still weren't sure who was in the pickup, even after two of the men got out. They had some kind of tool, a crowbar, I think, and they used it to break into Alpine Meats. Then we saw the men start hauling big bundles out of the back of the pickup. When they moved away from the truck, we saw—to our horror—that they were people. Tiffany wanted to leave, and I couldn't blame her. This was turning into the scariest night of our lives. We were utterly paralyzed while we watched the two men carry the dead bodies—they seemed to be dead bodies because they were limp and didn't move—into the meat warehouse. The third man stayed in the truck the whole time. The whole thing didn't take more than five minutes, though it seemed like forever. After they drove away, Tiffany and I just sat there for I don't know how long, still unable to move or speak."

Pause. Muffled clearing of throat away from the microphone. I wished I had a cigarette.

"We panicked," Tim declared in a heavy voice. "It was the wrong thing to do, but our nerves were shot. We took Brian Conley's body out of the Jeep and carried it into the warehouse. Then we saw those other bodies in the meat locker. We recognized the O'Neills. It was a terrible sight. We left Brian Conley's body there, knowing it would be found with the others. Then we went home and collapsed. I must apologize to the citizenry of Alpine, to Brian Conley's family, and to the owner of radio station KSKY, my good buddy, Spencer Fleetwood. Maybe I behaved in a cowardly fashion, but for any of you out there in radioland who have ever come across a corpse, you know how disturbing that can be."

Yeah, right, all six people in Skykomish County who happened to have stumbled over a body. Tim sounded like an idiot. More alarming, he sounded like a liar.

"So thanks for listening," Tim concluded. "And thanks to Spencer Fleetwood for allowing me to get this off my chest over the air. Tiffany thanks you, too. This is Tim Rafferty, live and direct from the studios of KSKY."

I waited to see how Spence would follow up this startling story. But after a canned commercial for Safeway, Spence merely thanked Tim for his heartrending revelation and added, "Remember, you heard the news first on KSKY—every day, every hour, every minute of late-breaking local, national, and international events."

As soon as I got in the house, I called Milo at his office. He was still there, as I had hoped he would be.

"Did you hear Tim Rafferty on the radio just now?" I asked, slightly breathless.

"No," Milo replied. "When do I have time to listen to the radio around here?"

"Tim says he found Brian Conley up on the Ridge," I said.

"What?"

"You heard me. Tim also said he was so panicked that he put Brian in the meat locker with the O'Neills. Whom, I might add, he had followed down from Second Hill."

"The O'Neills drove to Alpine Meats?" Milo sounded bewildered.

"No, no," I clarified. "The Hartquists were driving the O'Neills. At least I guess it was the Hartquists. I don't think Tim ever identified them on the air."

"Sweet Christ." Milo went silent for a moment. "This was on the radio just now?"

"Yes," I responded. "I sat out in the car to listen to the end of it. I came in and called you right away."

"Damn." Milo sounded angry. "I'd better get over to KSKY right now. I'll have to call Tara and tell her I'll be late. She's making me her special veal dish tonight."

"Yum," I said. "Will you let me know what you find out from Tim?"

Chapter Six

I SAT BY the phone. I was in a quandary. If Tim Rafferty had worked for anyone in the world except Spencer Fleetwood, I would have been off like a shot to interview him. But I wasn't going to show up at KSKY like some poor beggar asking for alms. I'd have to rely on Milo for now, and catch Tim later, away from the station. Since going to work for Spence, Tim only moonlighted occasionally at the Venison Inn. I wasn't sure how he got by, because I was convinced that Spence paid him in gift certificates and coupons from the local merchants who advertised on the radio station. Then again, I'd heard that Tim was e-trading on the Internet, so maybe he was cleaning up in the stock market.

I had to alert my staff, however. I called Scott first, but he wasn't home yet. Perhaps he was romancing Tamara Rostova. Then I phoned Vida, not because she was second in importance, but because I knew the call to her would take some time.

Vida claims she never listens to KSKY, but I know better. She would never reject a news source, even from an archrival. There isn't much that Vida misses, but just in case, she tunes in to Spence's station. This is a fact, because at least twice she has caught him in mistakes. Unable to contain her glee, Vida had to pass these erroneous bits of news on to me.

"I heard all but the very start," Vida said in an excited voice. "What did I miss?"

"Not much," I replied, propping the phone between my chin and shoulder as I reached for the bourbon bottle. "Tim Rafferty was just setting the scene."

"Ridiculous," Vida huffed. "How could Tim and Tiffany have found that body? It's too much of a coincidence."

"I thought so at first," I said, plunking ice cubes into a glass, "but then I visualized the scene. The rain starts pouring down, they seek shelter, and who knows what they were really doing under that ledge?"

"True," Vida responded, then switched to a tone of reproach. "Is that ice I hear?"

"Yes," I said, knowing what was coming next. Vida was antialcohol, except on those very rare occasions when she felt it absolutely necessary to have a drink, usually a Tom Collins.

"Are you making an adult beverage?" she demanded, still in that critical tone.

"Yes."

"Are you drinking alone?"

"Vida," I said with a big sigh, "you know perfectly well that I often have a drink after I get home from work. Usually, I am alone at that time. Do you really think I'm becoming a hopeless sot?"

"It can sneak up on you," Vida said. "Look at Ernest's brother, Edwin. And Elmo Runkel. Not to mention his father, Rufus, in his later years."

As far as I could tell, all of the Runkel men had been raging drunkards. Except, perhaps, for Vida's late husband, Ernest. Either he hadn't dared to take a drink, or he was very good at keeping secrets, even from his wife.

"I'm merely thinking of your welfare, Emma," Vida said, then paused and turned away from the phone.

"You're back, Roger dear. Did you get the ice cream that Grandmums forgot?"

I heard a grunt in the background, apparently signifying that Roger had indeed brought home the gallon or tub or truckload of ice cream his fat stomach desired.

"But it's the rest of the story that bothers me," I said, giving Roger the heave-ho from my mind's eye. "Maybe I can buy the part about following the Hartquists down from Second Hill. Maybe I believe that they got as far as Alpine Meats. But why sit around and watch what they were up to? And especially, why decide to dump poor Brian in with the O'Neills?"

"Exactly," Vida said. "It doesn't make sense. If I had a corpse in the back of my car, I wouldn't want to sightsee. I'd go directly to . . . Roger dear, don't pour out so much of that chocolate syrup. And really, you might consider taking the ice cream out of the carton first. Yes," she went on, now speaking into the phone again, "I'd go to the sheriff straightaway."

I'd gone back into the living room with my drink, and plopped onto the sofa. "There's something else that bothers me, now that I think about it. If Tim and Tiffany took Brian to the walk-in after the Hartquists were there, why was he—Brian—on the bottom instead of on top?"

"An excellent point," Vida said. "Does Milo know all this?"

"Yes, I told him," I replied. "I made him late for dinner at Tara Peebles's house."

"That's too bad," Vida said absently, then added, "I certainly hope this isn't some sort of hoax."

"I wondered, too," I said. "But it wouldn't explain the body."

"No," Vida agreed. "It'll certainly be interesting to find out what Milo learns when he interrogates Tim Rafferty. I've had one question to put to that young man for quite a while."

"Which is what?" I asked.

"Why doesn't he marry Tiffany Eriks? They've been going together for years."

That wasn't a bad question, but not exactly Milo's line of inquiry.

I'd just finished my dinner of pasta, prawns, and a green salad when I heard someone at the door. It was a few minutes after seven o'clock and still broad daylight. Through the peephole, I could see Milo gazing up into the roof that covered my small front porch.

"What's up?" I asked, letting him in.

"That damned Rafferty," Milo cursed. "Screwing around with a crime scene. Not once but twice. I'd like to kick him from here to Everett."

It took me a moment to understand what Milo was talking about. "Oh—you mean at the meat warehouse and up on the Ridge."

"Right." Milo sat down heavily in the armchair that matched my sofa. "I've got him and Jack and Dwight on their way up there to comb the place under the ledge where the body was found. The rain's stopped; they'll have daylight for a couple of hours."

"Do you think Tim's lying?" I asked.

"About what?" Milo removed his hat and punched in the high crown. "Finding Conley or the rest of it?" He took a pack of cigarettes out of his pocket and proceeded to light up.

It was apparent that Milo was settling in. "Do you want a drink?" I inquired.

"Sounds good," Milo replied, finding the ashtray I kept in the drawer of the side table next to the chair.

"What happened to your dinner date?" I asked, halfway to the kitchen.

"Tara had to go into Seattle with Dan," Milo said. "They're taking Conley's body to the airport."

"Tonight?" I was surprised.

"They had to catch a certain flight," Milo responded, "and the sooner the better. Even Conley won't keep forever, unless we put him back in the meat locker."

I supposed that was true enough. I put several ice cubes in a glass and poured out a measure of Scotch for the sheriff. "So you haven't eaten, I take it?"

Milo accepted the drink with a grateful look. "No. I'll stop at the Venison Inn on my way back to the office. I've got to stick around there to see if Jack and Dwight come up with anything from the Ridge."

"Anything new on the Hartquists?" I asked, sitting back down on the sofa.

Milo shook his head. "Just what you'd expect. A lot of cussing and complaining from their jail cells. Protests of innocence. The usual crap."

"What's the charge?"

"Rosie's thinking second-degree homicide for all three Hartquists," Milo said, referring to our relatively new prosecuting attorney, Rosemary Bourgette.

"That sounds about right," I remarked, "unless it was a gangland-style killing."

Milo wrinkled his long face at me. "The Hartquists aren't the Norwegian Mafia."

"You know what I mean," I responded, getting on my feet again. "Wasn't at least one of them shot in the back of the head?"

"Right," Milo allowed. "The other two were shot in the chest. That doesn't necessarily mean they were assassinated. Hey, where are you going?" he asked as I started toward the kitchen.

"To feed you and freshen my drink," I replied. "Want to join me?"

"Come on, Emma," Milo protested, though he was already out of the chair, "you don't have to do that."

"I know I don't," I said, searching the freezer for a

steak. "But you've had a long, hard day, and you're not finished yet."

"You've had a tough day yourself," Milo said, leaning against the kitchen counter. "Want a cigarette?"

"Of course I do," I replied crossly, "but I'm not going to have one. T-bone or rib steak?"

Milo shrugged. "Whatever's easier."

I put the T-bone in the microwave to thaw. "You went out to KSKY?"

Milo sat down at the kitchen table. "I listened to a transcript of Tim's statement first. Then I questioned both him and Fleetwood."

I readied a large potato to zap in the microwave when the steak came out. "Did Tim omit anything on the radio?"

"Not really. He was more specific about the details, but it didn't tell me much."

Steak out; potato in. "Did Tim explain why Brian Conley was on the bottom of the pile?"

"He said he couldn't remember much about being in the warehouse. It was all a daze. Oh," Milo added in a disinterested manner, "Tim mentioned the meat. You know, pork chops, lamb steaks, pigs' feet. He said he'd never seen so much meat, especially whole carcasses."

Milo's chunk of meat was sizzling in the skillet. "Do you believe him?"

"I don't know what to think," Milo answered slowly. "Put yourself in Tim's place. He's out for a nice spring evening with his girlfriend. They go up on the Ridge—it's not really that much of a hike to Spark Plug Lake, not for folks who've been raised around here—and they get caught in the rain. They go under a ledge to keep dry, and they find a corpse. That'd shake up most people, and if I remember right, Tiffany's the hysterical type. For whatever reason, Tim decides not to go for help, but to bring the body down the mountain. Then he spots the pickup on the Icicle Creek Road. Oh . . ." Milo stopped for a moment. "I forgot, Tim didn't mention this on the air, but he said the lights were out on the truck, which made him suspicious."

I was putting a small green salad together—romaine, tomato, scallions, cucumber. "Do you think that's true?"

"It makes sense from the Hartquists' point of view. The bodies were in the back, covered with a tarp. It was dark, and they wouldn't want to be spotted if they could help it. I haven't asked them about this yet, but I will. Anyway, I can see that might be how it was."

I turned the steak over. "So Tim and Tiffany are following a vehicle with no lights. That would arouse curiosity."

"I agree," Milo said. "Say, that smells good. I'm hungrier than I thought."

"It'll be about five more minutes," I said, setting a place at the table. "You insist on medium well when it comes to meat."

"Not too well done," Milo cautioned. "I just don't want it to get up and walk out the door."

"What about Spence?" I inquired. "Was he preening all over the place?"

Milo grimaced. "Well . . . not exactly. I mean, there's nobody around to preen for at the station."

"You didn't get any hint that this was a publicity stunt?"

Milo shook his head. "No. How could it be?"

"I'm not sure," I admitted.

"You and Spence may wind up killing each other one of these days," Milo said with a crooked grin. "I take it you don't much like competition."

"Mainly, it's cut into our revenue," I replied, removing the baked potato from the microwave. "Oh, I realize that when you put out a weekly, you're going to get scooped. But it's the big stories—like Brian Conley disappearing in the first place—that really bother me.

And now this—Tim's confession. It certainly makes me suspicious that he also happens to work for Spencer Fleetwood."

Milo nodded slowly. "I can see that. You're not hurting for money at the paper, are you?"

I sighed. "We've never had a big profit margin. Spence cutting into it doesn't help. But with Kip MacDuff using the backshop for commercial jobs, we'll get by. I'd just hate to see some of the national advertisers drop us in favor of KSKY. You know, like Safeway and Starbucks and UPS. That would really hurt."

"I kind of like the music he plays," Milo remarked in what I took to be a teasing manner.

I put the steak and microwaved potato on Milo's plate, then handed him the salad. "I don't. I'd forgotten how many of those songs from way back when were god-awful."

"Better than that junk the kids listen to now," Milo declared, slicing open his potato.

"I'm not entirely sure," I said, sitting down at the table across from the sheriff. "The lyrics are better today. They're more innovative, more realistic."

Milo's only response was a grunt. I sipped my drink and watched him eat. With the kitchen full of cooking smells and the crows cawing out in the cedar trees and the soft twilight at the windows, a familiar sense of comfort swept over me. For a long time, I thought I'd lost it, that friendship could never resume where desire had intervened. But this was a different kind of intimacy than the merging of bodies, and I cherished what Milo and I had managed to salvage between us.

"So tell me about Tara," I said. "I've met her a couple of times, but I don't really know her."

"Nice woman," Milo said, putting what looked like about a quarter of a pound of butter on his potato. "Tara lost her husband two years ago to cancer. She was raised in Montana on a sheep ranch. She met her husband in the Peace Corps in . . . I forget—one of those countries in Africa they keep renaming. Anyway, they settled in San Francisco." He paused to eat a forkful of salad. "Her husband, Charlie, was in the banking business. He got transferred north to Seattle after a couple of years. Then, after Charlie died, Tara decided she'd had enough of city living, so she moved up here."

"I can see that, since she was raised in the wide open spaces of Montana," I remarked. "All that big sky. Tell me, how does a young man decide to become an undertaker? I've always wondered about that. In Al Driggers's case, he inherited the business. But what about Dan Peebles?"

Milo didn't answer until he'd chewed and swallowed a large chunk of steak. "I don't really know. I gather that both boys—Don's the other one—were a handful growing up. Charlie worked long hours and traveled quite a bit. After their father died, the boys seemed to drift. Tara talked Don into joining the navy, but I'm not sure how Dan ended up in the funeral business. He's got an A.A. degree from one of the community colleges in Seattle. Maybe he's just filling up time."

"And graves," I said.

"Right," said Milo.

Tim Rafferty worked the morning shift at KSKY, and I wasn't going near the place. I'd wait to catch him after work. He and Tiffany had moved in together a year or so ago. I planned to give them both a call in the mid-afternoon.

"Such a rush," Vida remarked that morning. "I don't understand why Brian Conley had to be shipped out of here as if he had to keep an appointment."

"Vida," I said with a smile, "you resent anybody who leaves Alpine, even if they happen to be dead."

"It's unseemly," she declared. "I'm calling Al Driggers to find out what all the hurry was about."

Hoping that Al had recovered sufficiently from the flu to deal with Vida, I went back into my cubbyhole to handle the first phone calls of the day. Several pertained to Tim Rafferty's confession, as I knew they would. Others either complimented me or complained about the special edition that had come out the previous day. Those in favor felt that we'd done an outstanding job of keeping Alpiners apprised of local news. The critics didn't understand why we couldn't have gotten the Rafferty story into the Tuesday Extra. At least two people griped that the *Advocate* had never come out on a Tuesday, and now their whole week was out of sync. Another crank insisted that Vida couldn't spell "toilett."

Just after eleven, Toni Andreas called to say that Alfred Svensen, known familiarly as Sven, was in town and that the arraignment would take place at the courthouse before noon. I debated whether to send Scott or to go myself. But Scott was at the sheriff's office, trying to get Jack Mullins to tell him what kind of evidence had been found at either the Hartquist or the O'Neill property. Jack, naturally, was playing it close to his chest.

Vida had finally gotten in touch with Janet Driggers. "That makes sense," she said as I came into the newsroom to get a coffee refill. "Janet says Al still isn't feeling well, and with Oscar Nyquist's service coming up Saturday morning, they thought it best to dispatch Brian Conley as soon as possible. Oscar should have a very large turnout."

I agreed, though I didn't see how the number of mourners would increase Al and Dan's workload. Vida announced that she was going with me to the arraignment.

"I wouldn't miss it for the world," she avowed.

We arrived at the brown brick courthouse at eleven-thirty. The old-fashioned rotunda with its WPA murals of loggers, miners, and railroad workers was crowded with curiosity seekers.

"My, my," Vida murmured. "The Hartquists have certainly drawn a crowd."

Most of those who milled about on the worn mosaic tile floor greeted Vida like the old friend or relative that she was. I left her to work her way through the gathering and headed straight for the courtroom. It was a drab place, with fir-paneled walls, a bank of vertical windows on the street side, and the hardest wooden benches this side of the pews at St. Mildred's.

Our superior court judge of long standing had become incapacitated the previous autumn, and in his stead was a fortyish woman originally from Monroe. Marsha Foster-Klein was her name, and a brisk demeanor was her game. She was already in her place when I slipped onto the high-backed bench that was reserved for the press. Marsha, who wore her pale blonde hair in a Dutch bob, was giving hell to a teenaged D.U.I. I didn't recognize. In a county as small as SkyCo, the judge was forced to handle everything but speeding tickets. I was informed by the bailiff that Judge Marsha had already handed down the ruling on Doc Dewey's postmortem of Brian Conley: death by foul play, by a person unknown. That came as no surprise.

Hearing a commotion nearby, I turned, half expecting to see Vida shaking off overly inquisitive pests. Instead, I spotted Spencer Fleetwood, Gucci shades in place and wired for sound.

"This is Spencer Fleetwood, live and direct from the Skykomish County courthouse," I heard him intone in his mellifluous voice. "We're here reporting for radio station KSKY. Judge Marsha Foster-Klein is already on the bench, dispensing her own particular brand of rough justice."

"If I ever see you so much as looking at another half-rack of Coors," Judge Marsha berated the young man before her, "I'll run over you myself. License suspended for six months, thirty days in jail, eighty hours of community service." She banged her gavel. I wondered that wood chips didn't fly. "Get out of this courtroom, and don't let me ever see you in here again."

The dejected perp shuffled off, apparently into the arms of his obese mother who had been sitting in the front row. Spence kept up his commentary with the microphone.

Vida finally appeared, her floral bonnet askew. "Goodness, people are snoopy! Why do they think I always know everything that's happening?"

The answer was as obvious to me as it should have been to Vida, so I said nothing. The courtroom was filling up. Judge Marsha was listening to a divorce proceeding involving an adulterous relationship, spousal abuse, and the question of which party would be awarded custody of a ferret named Yvonne.

"Tomlinson," Vida said in her stage whisper. "They live out by the fish hatchery. She's from Startup, he moved here from Tacoma to work for the park service. Or was it the forest service? Dear me, I forget."

The divorce was swiftly granted, the ferret was given to the wife. Or ex-wife, as she had become.

The judge stared at Spence, who was still crooning into his microphone. "There will be no recordings or broadcasts from my courtroom, Mr. Fleetwood. Tune yourself off or I'll turn you out."

Spence offered the judge his most ingratiating smile. "Sorry, Your Honor, I was only setting the stage for my later newscast. You know, atmosphere, live and direct."

"I don't know," Judge Marsha snapped. "The only thing around here that's live and direct is justice. Take a seat, Mr. Fleetwood, and make sure you've got your little black gadget turned off."

Still jaunty, Spence complied. I couldn't help but grin at Marsha Foster-Klein. She had made herself a candidate for my next new best friend.

A side door opened, and sherrif's deputy Sam Heppner entered behind the three Hartquists and Sven Svensen. Sam nudged the senior Hartquist, apparently reminding him to remove his wrinkled snap-brim cap, which I gathered was his signature piece of apparel. The sons also doffed theirs. Cap Hartquist busily scratched at his rear end; his offspring followed suit.

The voices in the courtroom grew hushed. Cap, though gnarled and slightly stooped with age, looked like his usual pugnacious self. There was a contemptuous expression on his weather-beaten face as his beady-eyed gaze swept over the gathering. Ozzie, the elder and the larger of the two brothers, swaggered behind their father, while Rudy attempted to joke with the dour Sam Heppner.

"Showing off," Vida murmured. "Typical."

Moving with the aid of a walker was Sven Svensen, whom I judged to be about Cap's age, but not in nearly as robust shape. Sven had once been a large man, or so his loose-fitting dark blue suit indicated, but he had apparently shriveled with age or illness, perhaps both. He wore an obvious toupee and there was a straw boater in the basket of his walker.

"Good heavens," Vida gasped, "Sven Svensen! I remember him from my youth. I thought he'd been dead for years. Do you think he'll live through the trial?"

Sam Heppner, Rudy Hartquist, Judge Marsha, and the entire front row of spectators stared at Vida. Sven Svensen, however, did not. That was when I noticed his hearing aids.

Rosemary Bourgette was already in the courtroom. She was a pretty, dark-haired woman in her thirties from a large family who belonged to St. Mildred's parish. The judge ordered the group to approach the bench. As the formalities began, I saw Milo lope through the double doors at the back of the courtroom. He looked unusually grim.

"How do your clients plead?" Judge Marsha demanded after the charge of second-degree homicide had been read for all three defendants.

Sven appeared oblivious. The judge repeated her query. Sven leaned forward with one hand on his walker, the other cupping his right ear. "Eh?"

With an impatient sigh, Judge Marsha again asked for the plea. Sven gazed at each of his clients in turn. Before he could speak, Cap's ragged voice rumbled through the courtroom:

"Not guilty, goddamn it!"

"Not guilty, goddamn it!" echoed his sons.

"Watch your language in my courtroom," Judge Marsha shot back, and pounded her gavel.

"Vell, ve're not," Cap retorted in a testy tone. "Ve vas shot at first, pygolly."

"Not guilty, Your Honor," Sven finally said as if he hadn't heard a word of the exchange.

"Very well." Judge Marsha seemed faintly relieved. "Bail is set at one hundred thousand dollars apiece. The trial date will be scheduled for . . ." She paused to glance at what I assumed was her court calendar. "—Monday, June twenty-first."

Rosemary Bourgette lifted a hand. "I don't believe that these defendants should remain at large. There is the risk of flight, Your Honor. The accused are well-versed in the wilderness areas of the Pacific Northwest, including British Columbia."

"Flight?" Cap shouted. "I never been in no damned airplane! Vhere vould ve go? Ain't no place for us but Alpine."

"Mr. Hartquist," Judge Marsha said in a firm voice, "I told you to watch your language. One more outburst of profanity and I'll cite you for contempt." She turned to the bailiff. "Get these people out of here before I lose my judicial composure."

The three Hartquists were hustled out through the side door while the spectators began to chuckle and buzz. Judge Marsha announced the noon recess. Once again, Vida was besieged by at least a dozen people who apparently thought she knew more than the judge, the attorneys, or the accused.

I slipped away and managed to catch Milo as he was crossing through the rotunda.

"What do you think?" I asked. "Is it safe to let the Hartquists out on bail?"

"How the hell should I know?" Milo grumbled. "At least I wouldn't have to listen to them bitching and cussing in the county jail."

"Is there anything new you can tell me?" I inquired, hurrying to keep up with the sheriff's long, loping strides.

Milo fended off a couple of people who had questions for him, then scowled at me as we reached the street. "What do you need to know now? You don't have a paper coming out until next week."

"What's wrong?" I asked. "You're not in a very good mood."

"That's not news," Milo responded, jaywalking across Front Street.

Someone in a blue Honda honked at the sheriff and me. A tourist, no doubt, who didn't know or care what Milo's uniform represented.

"It's kind of news," I said, remaining patient. "You've been in a good mood lately. Didn't Tara come back from the airport?"

"I don't know," Milo muttered. "I haven't had time to find out."

We crossed Second Street—legally—and headed down the half-block to the sheriff's office.

"How about lunch?" I asked in my brightest voice.

"I'll have Toni pick up something for me," Milo said, his face now clouded with what I perceived as distress. "I've got work to do."

I started to speak, to prod Milo further, but I knew that in his present state of mind he wasn't going to tell me anything. Parting company with him at his office, I walked on to the *Advocate*.

Now I felt as upset as Milo looked.

But I didn't know why.

Chapter Seven

THE REST OF Wednesday was relatively calm, except for the usual complaints about the weekly edition of the newspaper and a couple of nutcases insisting they'd seen Brian Conley alive and well over the Memorial Day weekend. Then there was Mayor Baugh, unable to comprehend why we hadn't run his public rest room story as a feature on page one. I let Vida field that one, but I got stuck with Ed Bronsky.

"The Mr. Pig float isn't a Scene item," he complained over the phone. "That's big stuff, with at least a twenty-four-point headline. How many other people in this town have ever had a TV series based on them?"

Ed actually had a point, but I wasn't giving in. "You were only in the planning stage when I spoke with you," I countered. "You hadn't talked to Scooter Hutchins yet. When it's firmed up, we'll do a full-blown story."

"It is firmed up," Ed asserted. "I met with Scooter right after I saw you and Dodge at lunch."

"But you didn't let me know," I argued. "Hey, Ed, I'm not a mind reader."

There was a brief silence at the other end of the line. "So when's the summer solstice preview coming out?"

"Next week," I replied. "The solstice is the weekend of the twentieth."

"Right." Ed hesitated again. "What's your front-page pix?"

"The Solstice Queen candidates," I said. "We do it every year."

"Stale," Ed proclaimed. "Ever since we ditched Loggeramma—five, six years ago—it's been the same old thing. You need something new. How about my float?"

Again, Ed surprised me. He had a viable idea. I, too, had grown weary of the five overly made up princesses in their prom dresses and tiaras, grinning like they had wedges stuck between their cheeks. If nothing else, Ed and Company might provide some comic relief.

"Will you be ready by Monday or Tuesday?" I inquired. "I'd prefer Monday, just in case."

"Sure," Ed responded. "Why not? We've already got the float planned out. We'll start putting it together this afternoon."

"It's a deal," I said, then added, "I noticed the other day that you're three months behind on your subscription payment. Are you thinking of canceling the *Advocate*?"

"What?" Ed sounded taken aback. "No, of course not. I must have forgotten to write a check when I paid for my *Wall Street Journal* subscription." His voice turned a trifle sly. "I was thinking—as a former staff member, how come I don't get a free subscription to the *Advocate*?"

"Because that isn't our policy," I said. "If it had been, we'd have done it when you quit five years ago."

"Oh." Ed sounded disappointed. "Okay, I'll have the check for you when we do the photo shoot."

"Good. Remember, three months." I rang off just as Ginny hurried into my office.

"Line two," she said, pointing at my phone. "It's that Mrs. Conley, calling from back east. She sounds upset."

I punched the red button on my phone. "Mrs. Conley? This is Emma Lord."

"Thank goodness," she said in a distraught voice. "Maybe you can help me."

"With what?" I asked as Ginny exited my cubbyhole.

"Well . . ." Mae Conley's voice was shaky. "The flight bringing Brian's body to New York and then on to Corning-Elmira was due in this morning around eleven. The coffin was to be picked up by our local funeral home and driven here to Penn Yan. But Mr. Barnes—the funeral director—went to the airport, and poor Brian wasn't on the connecting flight."

I frowned. "Did you check with JFK?"

"Yes, we even checked with La Guardia," Mrs. Conley replied, her voice gaining strength as she dealt with practical matters. "It was JFK where the flight from Seattle landed. The coffin was definitely on the plane. But they had no record of it being sent on to Elmira-Corning or Ithaca, the other nearest airport."

Surely the airline and the airport couldn't lose a coffin. On the other hand, they probably could. Brian seemed capable of getting lost both alive and dead.

"I trust they'll keep looking," I said.

"Yes, they assured us they'd check it out," Mrs. Conley responded. "But I thought perhaps you might have some information at your end."

"No," I said, "I'm afraid not. Did you call the funeral home here?"

"I did," she said, "but they could tell me nothing other than that they were certain that Brian had been sent on the right flight. And of course the people at JFK said he'd arrived. I just thought that—" Her voice broke. "You've been so . . . helpful, and maybe . . . you might have heard . . . something at your end."

Alas, I couldn't help. As I hung up the phone, I envisioned the chaotic scene at a busy airport such as JFK in New York. It was probably a wonder that they didn't misplace jumbo jets, let alone a coffin. If he still hadn't been found by our next deadline, I'd turn the latest Brian Conley misfortune into a story.

Around three, I called Tim Rafferty at his apartment in the Pines Villa. Tiffany answered in her little-girl voice.

"Tim's on the computer right now," she said. "I never interrupt him."

"Okay," I replied, trying to sound agreeable. "What's the rest of his afternoon like? Would he be available, say, around four-thirty?"

"I'll have to check," Tiffany said in a tone so solemn I thought she might be referring to Bill Gates. "I'll call back as soon as I find out."

Twerps, I thought. Tim had spent most of his adult life tending bar; Tiffany had worked as a waitress. But now that Tim had started e-trading on the Net, neither of them had a full-time job anymore. Unless you counted Tim's stints at KSKY, which I didn't. As far as I was concerned, Tim playing broadcaster was just an extension of his duties behind the bar. Except that behind the mike, he got to do all the talking instead of most of the listening.

Kip MacDuff came in with a question about the flyers we were printing for the summer solstice. He took one look at my annoyed expression and asked what was wrong.

"Nothing, really," I said, forcing a smile. "I was just wondering if I'm the real fool for not getting involved in stock trading on the Internet."

"Well," Kip said slowly, perching on the edge of my desk, "some people really clean up that way. I'm kind of leery, though. You can also get burned real bad."

"Tim Rafferty seems to have a knack for it."

"Tim?" Kip laughed and shook his head. "The one thing Tim was really good at when we were in high school was math. Not that that has much to do with e-trading. I mean, you have to know how to invest. I think there's a lot of luck, too, though serious investors thoroughly research the companies. Somehow, I don't see Tim doing that."

"I don't either."

"Still . . ." Kip shuffled the poster mock-ups in his freckled hands. "I wouldn't mind having him show me the ropes. Just to get a feel for what it's like to trade on-line."

"Have you asked him?"

Kip nodded. "A couple of times. He sort of put me off. I guess he doesn't want to give away any trade secrets."

I reached for the poster mock-ups, which were so detailed that they looked almost like the finished product. "Nice," I commented. "As usual, Kip. Say, don't tell me you've got money to spare on investments, with what I pay you?"

Kip's eyes scoured my cubbyhole's low, slanting roof. "Oh—I've got a little nest egg."

It was possible, given Kip's organizational skills and talent for cost cutting. I really didn't know what we'd have done without him while we made the transition from old-fashioned typesetting to computer. He had started out as one of our carriers, before I bought the *Advocate*. After he got his driver's license, he'd been put in charge of carting the paper down to Monroe to be run off on a press that published several weeklies and shoppers. He'd helped with our limited backshop work for several years, but when I made the move to computers, I discovered that he was an in-house gold mine. If I ever sold out, it would be to Kip. It was a good thing he had his little nest egg. He might need it one of these days, if I ever made up my mind about marrying Tom.

Mayor Baugh stopped by with the details on his rest room project. He hoped to have the toilets installed at Old Mill Park by the nineteenth, in time for the solstice festival. He was still miffed that we hadn't made his momentous idea a page-one story.

Right after he departed on a sea of umbrage, Janet Driggers called from the funeral home. "Here's a hot story for you: not only is Cammy Olson recovering from the chicken pox, but Al's feeling better. Maybe I can go back to work at Sky Travel tomorrow. Jeez, why do men have to suffer so when they get sick? You'd think Al had caught plague."

"It's either that or the wounded bear syndrome," I said. "You know, where the guy goes off into a coat closet and doesn't come out until he's healed."

"Men." The word sounded like it left a bad taste in Janet's mouth. "The only thing worse is women. Say, did you know that Gina Ancich, Brian Conley's girlfriend, is in town?"

I was surprised. "What for?"

"She came to the funeral home this morning with some friend of Conley's," Janet said. "His name's Nolan Curry, and I guess he worked at the Irish consulate with Brian. But here's the kicker—would you believe Gina's a receptionist for an old-line Seattle funeral home? We've dealt with them a few times, but I don't think Al or I ever talked to Gina."

"So why did Gina come if the body's been shipped to New York?" I asked.

"They want to make a pilgrimage," Janet said with what sounded like disgust. "They're not going back for the memorial in Penn Yan, so they wanted to do something here, where Brian died."

"You mean on Tonga Ridge?"

"Wherever." I could visualize Janet shrugging her shoulders. "I sent Gina and Nolan to the ranger station. Wes Amundson can tell them where to find the spot. Frankly, I think they're being ghoulish."

It seemed an odd comment from a woman whose husband was in a rather ghoulish—if necessary—business. But Janet often blurted out whatever was in her head. At least she hadn't expressed a desire to get in the sack with Nolan Curry.

"I'd like to interview them," I said. "Will they check back with you?"

"I doubt it," Janet replied. "For all I know, they may have come and gone. It wouldn't take them more than a couple of hours to go up to Tonga Ridge and come back. Plus do whatever they were going to do when they got there. Like screw, maybe. Hey—isn't that what you figure Tim and Tiffany were doing under that ledge when they found Brian?"

"Maybe," I allowed. "It'd kill time."

"That's funny," Janet said, and laughed.

I didn't exactly agree. But I suppose in Janet and Al's business you had to be able to look Death in the eye and laugh.

I checked with Wes Amundson at the ranger station. He said he hadn't seen Gina Ancich and Nolan Curry since they headed up Tonga Ridge a little after one o'clock.

"They promised to come by on their way back," Wes said, "but you know how people are."

"Is their car still in the parking lot?" I asked.

Wes didn't answer right away. I assumed that he hadn't bothered to check and had gone to the window. "Yeah, it's here. Maybe they're holding a service or something."

"That'd make sense," I replied. "If you see them, would you please have them give me a call? Just in case they come down after five, I'll leave my home number, too."

By four twenty-five, I hadn't heard back from Wes or from Brian's mourners. And Tiffany still hadn't returned my call. I dialed the number again and got a busy signal. Genius that Tim was, he apparently hadn't figured out how to use an answering machine. Ten minutes later, I told my staff that I was leaving early. I didn't say why, because I knew that Vida would want to tag along. She didn't ask, because she was on the phone with Roger, who wanted to do something she didn't think he should do. Like placing land mines along Front Street, maybe.

The Pines Villa Apartments were on Alpine Way, only a few blocks from my own house on Fir Street. Carla Steinmetz Talliaferro had lived there before she got married. The complex was comparatively modern, at least for Alpine. It had lost the distinction of being the newest apartment building in town since construction had begun on Clemans Manor, just west of Old Mill Park.

Pines Villa had a security system. According to the call boxes, T. Rafferty and T. Eriks lived on the second floor. I punched the button and waited.

"Yes?" It was Tiffany, sounding wary.

"Emma Lord," I said, my mouth close to the wire mesh box. "May I come up?"

She didn't answer right away. "This isn't a good time," she finally said. "Tim's still tied up."

"When is a good time?" I asked, no longer patient.

"Um . . . tomorrow, maybe? Can you call first? Afternoons are best."

I knew that, since Tim was usually on the air in the mornings. "Okay," I said, still irritated. "But I'd rather not be put off again."

"I'll let him know," Tiffany said, her little-girl voice indifferent.

"Please do," I said, "or I'll turn his next stint on KSKY into a call-in program."

"Huh?"

I didn't reply, but turned away and stomped off to my car. For a change of pace, I decided to pick up Chinese food at the mall, just a couple of blocks north on Alpine Way. To my knowledge, no Chinese people had ever lived in Alpine, unless you counted Dustin Fong and the recent arrival of a half-dozen community college students who had all been born in the United States. It was the Japanese and the Koreans—then spelled "Coreans"—

who had built the railroads and dug the gold and silver mines in the area a century ago. For some reason, the Chinese had been prevented by law from working on the railroads during the period that the Great Northern tracks had been laid through Stevens Pass. Thus, Alpine had never had any authentic Chinese cuisine. I was stuck with the take-out place in the mall, run by a Norwegian and a German. The Mexican restaurant next door was no better; it was owned by a Dane.

I made do with chicken chow mein, pork fried rice, and a couple of limp-looking egg rolls. I'd just sat down on the sofa to watch a Mariner away game while I ate when the phone rang.

The voice was oh-so-familiar; the question was not. "Are you ready to set the date?"

"Tom!" I gasped like a nincompoop. "Hi."

I could hear his laughter roll over the fiber-optic cables or bounce off the microwave towers or whatever the hell phone calls did these days. "Since when did I start scaring you?" he asked.

"You didn't," I said, hitting the mute button just as the Mariners grounded into a double play to end the inning. "I thought you were in New York at that publishers' meeting."

"I am," Tom replied, still sounding amused. "But I'm supposed to fly back to San Francisco tomorrow morning. I thought it might be more fun to fly into Sea-Tac instead. That is, if you could put me up in Alpine for a few days."

"Of course." I knew I sounded slightly breathless, which annoyed me. I couldn't help but resent the fact that Tom Cavanaugh still had the power to turn me into a moonstruck teenager.

"Okay," he said. "But how about my first question?"

"Ahhh . . . Well . . ." I swallowed hard. "I still haven't

come to a final decision. This has turned into a really wild week."

"I haven't talked to you for over two weeks," Tom said, now solemn. "How wild can all that time actually have been?"

"Oh, Tom . . ." I sat up straighter on the sofa. It wasn't fair to keep putting him off month after month. Except that he'd put me off year after year. Maybe the perverse streak in my nature was exacting revenge. "If you come to Alpine, I'll have my answer. I promise."

"Okay." His tone had lightened again. "I'll see you tomorrow night. I think there's a direct morning flight out of here at nine. I should get into Sea-Tac around noon your time. There are a couple of people I need to see in Seattle, so don't wait dinner."

"I'll keep the welcome mat warm," I said.

"Good." He lowered his voice to a deep purr. "And anything else you've got, too. It may be June, but it's chilly without you."

It was less than an hour later that my son called. Adam sounded so serious that at first I thought something was wrong. Now that he was less than a year away from being ordained a priest, I was accustomed to a more reflective son, a more contemplative son, a multidimensional son. But Adam had retained much of his easygoing personality and sharpened his already keen sense of humor.

"Are you okay?" I asked, using that time-honored phrase of frightened mothers everywhere.

"I'm fine," Adam replied. "Are you?"

"Yes, yes, I'm fine, too. But you sound so serious. I thought something was the matter with you."

"Not with me, Mom," Adam said, and a hint of irony surfaced in his voice. "I hear Dad's coming to see you again."

"He told you?" I asked, characteristically resentful of the confidences shared between father and son.

"I just got off the phone with him," Adam replied. "Hey—are you going to give him an answer or what?"

"I told him I would," I said, suddenly on the defensive.

"When?"

"When he gets here," I replied. "Tomorrow night."

"You sure you aren't still waffling?" Adam sounded suspicious.

I didn't, couldn't, answer right away. "This is a very difficult decision for me, Adam. Surely you can understand that."

"I do," my son responded in a more sympathetic voice. "But it has to be made, Mom. You can't keep Dad dangling forever."

As he did with me? But I didn't say it out loud. It sounded spiteful, and in fact, it was.

"I know." I sighed. "You realize it means giving up the paper, leaving Alpine, moving to San Francisco. That's a huge change."

"You're afraid you'll lose your identity," Adam said flatly.

"Yes."

"That's selfish. If you marry Dad, you'll bring what you are to the union. It's you he loves, not the wife he wants to mold you into. Why does that scare you?"

"Adam, you sound like some kind of goofy counselor," I said with a shaky little laugh.

"Counseling is what I intend to specialize in as a priest," he said, quite serious. "Remember all those psych courses I took when I was in college?"

"Yes." I heaved another sigh. "When did you make that decision?"

"About a month ago," Adam answered.

"You have no experience with marriage, you weren't even raised in a two-parent home," I countered. "I don't get it."

"I didn't think you would," he said in a tone that just

might have held a note of sarcasm. "Hey, Mom," he went on, suddenly sounding more like himself, "you've managed to steer this conversation off course. It's probably none of my business, except that I'd like to see my parents grow old together. I'd like to have parents who live together. I'd like to have married parents show up for my ordination next spring. Okay?"

I bristled a bit. "Are you ashamed of us?"

"No," Adam responded wearily. "Of course not. But I honestly believe you'd both be happier with each other. You've never shown much interest in marrying anybody else, and Dad hasn't even dated since Sandra died. Imagine the pressure that's been put on him by friends and associates to take out this widow or that divorcée. Give the guy a break, okay, Mom?"

"You're trying to make up my mind for me," I complained.

"No," Adam asserted. "I'm trying to get you to make up your mind. As I said, it's not fair to Dad to keep him hanging."

That much was true. "Honestly, I told Tom I'd give him an answer when he got here. I just don't know what it is yet. I think I'll know what to say when I see him."

There was a pause at the other end. "Okay, that sounds fair enough. I'll pray on it. I'll send you ESP messages. I'll poke pins in a voodoo doll if it helps."

"Thanks," I said. "And don't think I am not appreciative of your efforts on my behalf. It's just that as your mother, I'm not used to you giving me advice. That's probably a normal reaction for—" I stopped as my doorbell sounded. "I've got company. Can I call you back?"

"Not tonight," Adam said. "I've got contemplative prayer at seven. Then some of the other guys and I are going out to drink the taverns of St. Paul dry before it's lights out time. Call me when you've given Dad your answer."

"I will," I promised, already at the door. "I love you, even if you think you're smarter than I am."

"But you're older," Adam said. "Love you. Bye."

I didn't recognize the young woman and the young man standing on the porch, looking faintly nervous. Taking a chance that they weren't criminals or Jehovah's Witnesses, I opened the door.

"Ms. Lord?" the young woman said.

"Yes." The identity of my callers dawned on me. "You're Gina Ancich?"

The young woman with the short jet-black hair and the large blue eyes looked surprised. "Yes. How did you know?"

I put out my hand. "Newspaper instincts," I said. "This must be Nolan Curry."

"That's right," Nolan said, his smile revealing a slightly chipped front tooth. "We're Brian Conley's friends. We heard you wanted to see us."

"I do. Come in." My eyes drifted to the half-eaten Chinese food on the coffee table. "Sit down," I said, turning off the TV and gathering up what was left of my meal. "May I get you something?"

"We're fine, thanks," Gina replied, then held up a slim hand. "Oh, we've interrupted your dinner. Please go ahead."

"That's okay." I headed for the kitchen. "I can warm it up later." Instead, I dumped everything that was left—except for the fortune cookie—in the garbage, then returned to the living room.

Gina had sat down in the armchair; Nolan had taken the other side chair. I resumed my seat on the sofa.

"As Wes Amundson may have explained, I own the local newspaper. I thought it might be appropriate to interview you about Brian. Do you mind?"

Gina exchanged a quick glance with Nolan. "No, that's not a problem. I'm sort of over the real grief stage.

I mean, when Brian wasn't found after the first week, I pretty much gave up hope."

"But," I put in, "you still wanted to honor him."

Gina looked blank, her long, dark eyelashes batting up and down as she blinked at me several times. "You mean his memory?"

"I mean going up to Tonga Ridge today," I said.

"Oh." Again, she glanced at Nolan. "To see where he died. And leave some flowers. What else could we do?"

I turned to Nolan. "You worked with Brian, I understand."

Nolan nodded. He had an angular yet boyish face, with unruly red hair falling over his high forehead. "We were best friends. We worked together at the consulate for four years."

"I don't suppose," I said gently, "that either of you would know of anyone who might want to kill Brian."

Gina's pale face lost what little color it possessed. "Oh, no. The police asked me that on the phone. Brian was such a wonderful guy. Whoever did it must have been crazy."

That was probably true, if the mountain-man theory was right. "I understand that Brian wanted to be buried in Ireland," I said. "But his parents apparently changed their minds."

"Did they?" Gina looked vague. "Yes, I guess they did. I talked to Mae Conley Monday night, but she was totally out of it."

I turned again to Nolan Curry. "Why do you think Brian said he wanted to be buried abroad?"

"Well . . ." Nolan's hazel eyes darted around the living room. "A joke, maybe. I mean, you don't expect to die when you're only twenty-eight, right? And he worked for the Irish consulate, so maybe he just thought it'd be cool to say something like that. The Irish—the ones born over there—are kind of sentimental."

"Have you ever thought about such a thing?" I asked.

Nolan looked startled. "Me? You mean, dying?"

"I meant being buried in Ireland," I said. "Because you work for the Irish consulate."

Nolan's Adam's apple bobbed up and down as he laughed nervously. "Heck, no. I'm only twenty-six."

I tried to keep a straight face. My line of inquiry seemed to be going nowhere. I wasn't sure where to take the conversation, but I gave it a try. "What do you do at the consulate, Nolan? I didn't realize that foreign missions hired Americans."

"Sometimes they do," Nolan responded. "Usually, the jobs are mostly clerical. You know, checking visas, green cards, all that stuff. But sometimes both Brian and I would get to help out a tourist who was stranded or had gotten into some kind of trouble."

"What kind of trouble?" I asked.

Nolan shrugged. "A car accident, a robbery victim, whatever."

"No big crimes?" I inquired, keeping my voice light.

Nolan's eyes wandered to the Monet print above the sofa. "Not really."

"But occasionally?" I persisted.

His gaze shifted back to me. "Getting drunk, that kind of stuff. You know how the Irish like their dram. Once in a while, they don't know the local rules about drinking. It's no big deal. And anyway, it's not fair to make Irish people sound like all they do is drink. That's wrong."

"An unfortunate stereotype," I allowed, then addressed my next question to Gina. "How long had you gone with Brian?"

"Um . . . close to two years," she replied, still sounding vague. "I'd known him for a while before that."

"Did he often go snowboarding alone?" I inquired.

"Sometimes," she said. "I don't snowboard." She looked at Nolan. "You went with him a few times."

"Up at Snoqualmie," Nolan said. "Never around here. Brian liked the Stevens Pass area for snowboarding. He said there was more variety, plenty of steeps along with some more mellow runs."

They both seemed so oblivious that I decided it wouldn't hurt to ask a few more questions. Gina and Nolan didn't strike me as easily offended, or even as being curious about my motives. "Who else went with Brian?"

Another exchange of glances. Were they cueing each other, or did they need constant support?

"Howie?" Gina suggested.

"I think so," Nolan replied.

"Who's Howie?" I asked.

"Howie Schramm," Nolan said. "He works for an import-export firm in the same building the consulate is in."

"What about T. C.?" Gina inquired of Nolan.

"Top Cat?" Nolan grinned. "He's the one who taught Brian how to snowboard when we were on vacation at Lake Tahoe. I don't think he's been around lately."

My line of inquiry wasn't going anywhere. Again, I gazed at Gina. "You're certain that Brian came here by himself?"

"I think so," Gina answered slowly.

"You're not certain, then."

"Well . . ." Gina brushed at her round chin. "He mentioned he might go with somebody else, but he didn't say who. I just figured he'd gone alone."

Her Royal Vagueness was driving me crazy. Nolan Curry wasn't much better.

"At least," I said, trying not to sound too sarcastic, "you're sure that Brian was murdered."

Looks were exchanged. Gina blinked several times at Nolan. "That's what the sheriff said, wasn't it?"

"That's what you said he said," Nolan replied.

I'd run out of queries. On the other hand, they had

seemed to run out of answers first. We made more small talk and then they left, about five minutes later. I went out to the kitchen to finish cleaning up. The fortune cookie still lay on the counter. I broke it open and started to munch on it while I read the message on the blue strip of paper: *Beware of lying eyes.*

That seemed like good advice. But whose eyes were lying?

Chapter Eight

AFTER FORTIFYING MYSELF with three cups of strong, decent coffee Thursday morning, I called on Milo Dodge.

"Java?" he offered, holding up his own mug, which no doubt contained the usual vile brew.

"No, thanks," I replied cheerfully. "I just finished a cup. Are you in a better mood this morning?"

Milo frowned at me. "Better than what?"

"Better than yesterday," I said, still cheerful. "After the arraignment, you were kind of grumpy."

"Oh." Milo sipped from his mug. "I guess so. You seem pretty chipper this morning."

My smile seemed to freeze. "Tom's coming tonight."

"So soon?" Milo looked surprised. "Wasn't he here just a few weeks ago?"

"It was at Easter," I said. "Two months ago. I told him this time I'd let him know if I intended to marry him."

Milo grimaced. "Do you?"

For a moment, the short space between us seemed like a bottomless chasm, full of memories and deep feelings, of hope and despair, of love and hostility. None of it had anything to do with Tom. All of it had something to do with Milo. And with me. For that one startling moment, it occurred to me that if I jumped across that chasm, I'd land in the safety net that was Milo. But that wasn't a solution, it was an escape.

My smile dissolved. "Oh, Milo," I wailed, "I don't know what to do!"

Milo carefully set his mug down on the desk. "I don't blame you. It's one hell of a decision."

I rarely cry, and I didn't then. Shoring up my composure, I tried to find my smile again. "Isn't it stupid? For almost thirty years, I've wanted to marry Tom. Now, when I have the chance, I don't know what I want."

Milo shrugged. "That's not so strange. If Tom agreed to move here, you'd know what to say, wouldn't you?"

"Yes."

He shrugged again. "Then there's your answer. What difference does it make if he lives in San Francisco or Alpine? He always seems to be on the road."

Dear, good, practical Milo. "We've discussed it," I said, "but it always sounds as if Tom wants to live in San Francisco. He's not a small-town sort of guy."

"It wouldn't kill him," Milo said in his laconic fashion. "He'd still be traveling to big cities for meetings and whatever else he does there. I thought he liked to fish."

In Milo's world, if you fished, you could live on Jupiter if there was a good river with some nice riffles. "Tom used to fish, when he still lived in Seattle. He was into a lot of outdoor sports when I first met him, but I don't think he's had much leisure time in recent years."

"He'd probably like getting back to the great outdoors," Milo said with the confidence of a man who believed that fishing in particular could cure just about any malady. Wading into the river, casting the line, waiting—to fishermen like Milo, fishing was a state of grace, a sense of wholeness, of trust, of peace. "Cavanaugh could make up for lost time. Hit the ball in his court, Emma. Why should you take on the whole burden of the decision making?"

Milo was right. He'd made me feel better. I could

have kissed him, but it probably wouldn't have been appropriate.

"Thanks," I said, genuinely grateful. "You have common sense. Even Vida should acknowledge that. You know how much weight good sense carries with her."

"Oh, I sure do." Milo allowed himself a small grin. "So what's up besides the most important decision of your life?"

"Nothing," I said, "except I was worried about you yesterday. You seemed upset."

"Well," Milo began, taking a roll of breath mints out of his shirt pocket and offering one to me, "I was."

I accepted the mint and popped it in my mouth. "About Tara?"

He shook his head. "No, she called this morning. It was pretty late by the time she and Dan got Brian's body to the airport night before last, so they decided to stay over. She's fine. I'm having dinner there tomorrow."

"So what was the problem?" I persisted.

The sheriff grimaced. "I can't tell you."

I leaned back in the chair. "Milo . . ."

"Don't give me the evil eye," he said with a wave of his hand. "This isn't one of those public record deals where I have to tell you. Believe me, it's better that you don't know for now."

I wasn't giving up. "Has it something to do with Brian Conley?"

"No."

"The Hartquists?"

Milo hesitated. "No."

"The O'Neills?"

"Stop asking."

"So it *is* the O'Neills," I said. "But not the Hartquists?"

"I said not the Hartquists," Milo replied, sounding impatient.

I thought for a few moments. "The O'Neills were up to something. What was it?"

Milo threw his arms up in the air. "I'm not going to tell you. Got that?"

I folded my arms across my chest. "I'll trade you for it. Brian Conley's body has gone missing at JFK in New York."

Milo didn't change expressions. "That's not my jurisdiction."

"But it is your homicide," I persisted. "Don't you care?"

The sheriff sighed. "Yes, I care." He made a note on a legal-sized yellow tablet. "How did you find out?"

"Why should I tell you?"

"Because you're a good citizen."

I thought it over. I *was* a good citizen. Slim chance it might be, but it was possible that the missing coffin could be some sort of bizarre lead in the homicide case.

"Brian's mother told me," I finally said.

"I'll check it out. But," he went on, "it's probably just some screwup at the airport."

"Probably," I admitted. "But isn't it worth something in terms of a trade?"

Milo shook his head. "Nope."

"Okay, let's try this one," I said, determined not to let him off the hook. "What if I told you I had a nice chat last night with Gina Ancich and Nolan Curry?"

Milo evinced mild surprise. "They were in town? How come?"

"Apparently to honor Brian," I said. "They went up to Tonga Ridge and left some flowers."

"How did they stop to see you?" Milo asked, clearly miffed.

"I'm not going to tell you," I said, and gave Milo a superior look.

Milo chomped down so hard on his mint that I heard it crack. "Come on, Emma, don't get ornery."

"I'm not being any more ornery than you are," I declared smugly.

The sheriff expelled a big sigh. "Okay, I don't give a damn what they said. I already talked to them both on the phone. They sounded like a couple of nitwits."

I couldn't argue the point. "Do you think it's an act?"

"No. They're like a bunch of these kids in their twenties," Milo said. "They're self-absorbed and not tuned in to the rest of the world. How did Gina seem? Upset?"

"Not really. She said she'd gotten over her grief when Brian wasn't found right away."

"That figures," Milo said with disgust. "These kids don't have any attention span, either. She's probably got a new guy already. Maybe this Curry she came up here with. What do you think?"

"I think I already told you too much," I declared. "I'm leaving now. Goodbye, Milo."

"Don't go away mad," Milo called after me.

"I'm not," I said, and turned in the doorway. "I have other resources to find out what the O'Neills were up to." I gave the sheriff my cheesiest smile. "Vida. And her dear nephew, Billy Blatt."

"He wouldn't say anything," Milo retorted. "Not this time."

"Every time," I said and walked away.

Upon my return to the office, the O'Neills were already the topic of conversation. Vida was in a snit, expounding on what she deemed were the crudities of an Irish wake.

"Imagine!" she exclaimed to Leo and to me as I came through the door. "It's archaic. How could Betsy and Jake O'Toole stoop to such a thing?"

"Hey," Leo said, holding up his hands as if to ward off

an imminent physical attack from Vida, who was pacing the newsroom. "I'm just the messenger. When I went to see about next week's ad for the Grocery Basket, Jake told me they were hosting the wake tonight. It can't be held at the O'Neill place, because it's a dump. It's also a crime scene."

"Still?" I said. "That's interesting. Given the circumstances of the O'Neill murders, I would've thought that Milo would be finished there by now."

"Guess not," Leo said with a shrug, then turned to Vida. "I'm going to the wake. Why don't I pick you up around seven-forty, Duchess?"

Vida, who was standing at her desk, shot Leo a look that would have withered most people. "Don't call me Duchess. You know how I despise that nickname. And what makes you think I'd attend such a tawdry affair?"

Leo raised his unruly eyebrows in an expression of utter innocence. "Isn't it a House and Home item? Don't you always cover big funerals and other death-related shindigs?"

Vida made a sour face. "Yes, yes, of course I do. But this seems like a most distasteful event. Still . . ." She gave me a quick glance. "I suppose you feel I ought to attend, don't you, Emma?"

I nodded solemnly. "Yes, I think you should. If it's any reassurance, I don't believe mourners drink at the wake. It's only after the funeral that they . . . um . . . celebrate the life of the deceased. Or lives, in this case." I had to turn away; I was about to burst into laughter.

"Very well." Vida took a deep breath, as if she were ready to march into battle. "I can drive myself," she said to Leo. "The O'Tooles live very near my home. But thank you for the offer."

"If you need moral support," Leo said, "I'll be there. Of course, you could ask Buck to go along."

Buck was Buck Bardeen, a retired air force colonel and Vida's longtime companion. She hadn't mentioned him much lately, and I sensed that Leo was angling for information.

"I shan't bother Buck," Vida declared. "And I still don't understand why Jake and Betsy are hosting this wake. They weren't close to the O'Neills in any way."

"The surviving relatives asked them to do it," Leo replied, sitting back down at his desk. "Most of them don't live around here anymore and the O'Tooles have a house big enough to accommodate the ritual. Besides, Jake's Irish."

"That's not much of a reason," Vida muttered, picking up her purse and putting on a green hip-length cardigan sweater with big orange patch pockets. "I must dash. I interview the summer solstice princesses today. But first, I'm off to see my nephew Billy at the sheriff's office. Perhaps I'll treat him to lunch."

Leo's gaze followed Vida until she closed the door behind her. "What's up with the Duchess and the Colonel? She hasn't talked about him much lately."

"I know," I said. "For a while there, I thought they were getting . . . how shall I put it?" I couldn't find the right word. *Serious* didn't work; neither did *involved*. As ever, Vida didn't fit into a mold.

Leo looked bemused. "Did her late husband actually get killed going over Deception Falls in a barrel?"

"Not exactly," I replied. "Ernest was about to make the attempt, but after he got inside the barrel and before he could be placed in the water, a truck backed over him. Or so I've been told."

Leo choked on the coffee he'd been sipping. "Holy Mother!" he cried between gasps for breath. "You're kidding!"

"No. That's the story."

Shaking his head and still chuckling, Leo seemed incredulous. "Are you sure the Duchess didn't run over him herself?"

"Leo," I said in a chiding voice, "from what I've heard, Ernest was an exemplary man. By the way, how come you're going to the O'Neill wake this evening?"

Recovering from amusement, Leo tipped his head to one side. "Oh . . . Irish solidarity, I guess. I haven't been to a wake since my father died almost twenty years ago."

"You haven't been to Mass very often, either," I remarked.

"Hey, I go at Christmas and Easter," he retorted.

"A C-and-Eer," I said, heading to my office. "You're going to hell, Leo."

My ad manager uttered a snort. "I've already been there."

In the early afternoon, I consulted with Scott Chamoud about the O'Neill and Conley murders. We had agreed that I would write the lead stories on both investigations, and he'd do all the interviews and sidebars.

"Where do we go from here?" Scott asked. "We can't do much about the Hartquist-O'Neill angle until the trial, and so far, Conley's homicide seems to have come to a dead end. So to speak." He flashed me that fabulous grin with all those wonderful perfect white teeth.

"There are some leads we could follow up," I said, behaving like the virtuous middle-aged professional woman that I am instead of catapulting across my desk and landing in Scott's lap. "Dodge isn't telling everything he knows. For example, the O'Neill house is still a crime scene. Why?"

Scott shrugged. "Maybe because it's so trashed? I've driven by there several times, and that place is even more of a dump than the Hartquist house, fire notwithstanding."

"So maybe we should take a look," I suggested, glancing at my watch. "It's one-thirty. Have you got time to drive up there with me and bring a camera?"

Scott did, so we headed for Second Hill, out Front Street to Highway 187—otherwise known as the Icicle Creek Road—then took the jog onto the gravel track that had always been known as Disappointment Avenue. It had been given the name some ninety years earlier by disgruntled miners who hadn't found their pot of gold on First and Second Hills. The road was a dead end in more ways than one.

We wound among tall evergreens and arches of vine maples. It was a gloomy ride, with overcast skies and the thick foliage shading our uphill climb. A broken gate marked the entrance to the O'Neill property. Sure enough, there was crime scene tape strung across it.

"Dare we?" Scott inquired, looking slightly apprehensive.

"We leave my car here," I said. "We walk. If we get caught, we say we're lost."

I reminded myself that this was Scott's initial involvement with a multiple homicide. His dark eyes sparkled, like those of a little boy who had been given his first fielder's glove. But he had some reservations.

"Should we have waited until after dark?" he asked, lowering his voice as if Milo might be lurking in the jumble of blackberry bushes that all but engulfed the broken fence.

"It's okay," I assured him. "I don't see anyone around. If Jack Mullins or one of the other deputies shows up, we can handle it." Fleetingly, I thought of Vida's "handling" of her nephew, Bill Blatt. I was sure that her lunch treat would include more grilling than what was going on in the restaurant's kitchen.

The O'Neill house had been built on a steep slope, with two and a half stories. What I assumed was the basement had boarded-up windows in front but was below ground level in back. The whole thing was a boxy affair, with an ancient tin roof and a crooked tile chimney. Indeed, the whole house looked crooked. But then the O'Neills had always been a little crooked, too.

We trudged through the tall grass, rampant clover, and various weeds, including nettles and a sinister stand of devil's club. Three pitiful fruit trees whose branches were full of caterpillar nests stood to the right of the house. The entire place was littered with beer and liquor bottles, empty tin cans, old newspapers, articles of clothing, including at least a dozen unmatched socks, and an ancient icebox.

"I guess," Scott said as he picked his way through the debris, "that the sheriff didn't bag this stuff as evidence."

"Maybe that's why it's still a crime scene," I said, then stepped into a hole and almost turned my ankle. "Drat," I muttered, "this place is a regular obstacle course. Maybe the sheriff means to sort through this junk later."

Scott began taking pictures—of the house, the surroundings, and a close-up of the icebox. "This place definitely lacks a woman's touch," he remarked as we moved closer to the front door.

"The old man was widowed several years ago," I said, "not long after I moved to Alpine. Dusty—he's the one who never married—was still living at home." I winced as I noted at least two broken windows and several missing shingles. The gutters sagged and moss covered large patches of the house's exterior. "Anyway, Dusty stayed on after his father died, and Rusty and Stubby were in and out, depending upon whose wife had left him and for how long."

We were on the wooden porch, where the boards creaked beneath our weight. It was a marvel that the O'Neills hadn't fallen through at some point. None of them were small, though age and ill health had wasted Paddy O'Neill before his death.

Removing a roll of film from his camera, Scott indicated the front door, which had been padlocked by the sheriff. A boldly lettered sign read:

CRIME SCENE—KEEP OUT
BY ORDER OF THE SKYKOMISH COUNTY
SHERIFF'S DEPARTMENT

"Now what?" Scott inquired.

We checked the basement door, which was just around the corner from the front porch. It, too, was padlocked, and it bore a similar sign. So did the back door. A window at the rear of the house had recently been boarded up, perhaps by the sheriff.

"Damn," I breathed, gazing at a couple of the other windows, which were intact. "I wonder if Milo would bust me for breaking and entering."

"He might," Scott said in a worried tone. "Wouldn't it be illegal?"

I nodded, then studied the padlock on the back door. "The wood's so rotten that if we leaned on it . . . ?" My voice trailed away.

"Gee, Emma," Scott said, frowning, "I don't think that's a good idea."

"Scott," I began in a cynical tone, "how do you think Pulitzer Prizes are won? Not by the faint of heart." I leaned my one hundred and twenty pounds against the door frame and pushed. The wood creaked; the hinges groaned. "Your turn," I said to Scott.

My reporter looked dubious. "Is that an order?" he asked, then gave a start as we heard a rustling noise nearby.

Anxiously, I turned toward the source of the sound, some salal bushes at the corner of the house. A squirrel emerged and scooted through the grass, pausing once to sniff at an empty whiskey bottle.

"Maybe he wants a stiff drink," I remarked, then gazed at our surroundings. An old shed had collapsed about twenty yards away, its dilapidated roof covered with berry vines and morning glory. There was a surprisingly tidy woodpile, a bale of rusted barbed wire, the transmission from a car, and various other objects, including the ubiquitous bottles and cans. The brick chimney of the nearest neighbor could be seen through the cottonwood trees.

I nodded at Scott. "Go for it," I said. If nothing else, it would serve Milo right for keeping secrets.

Scott gave me one last look, his dark eyes sparkling. Maybe he realized this was his first big adventure in journalism. With boyish enthusiasm, he slammed his shoulder into the door, which cracked in three places, all on the horizontal. But the hinges and the lock had broken. We ducked under the chain with the padlock and went inside.

The house was a mess. No doubt it had been that way before the sheriff and his deputies tossed it, but we could barely get through without stepping on all manner of objects, including a stuffed leprechaun.

"This looks hopeless," Scott said as we picked our way through the living room, which had three TV sets, all old, all smudged with dust and grime. "What are we looking for?"

"Who knows?" I made a face. "Whatever was here—if anything but junk was ever here—has probably been removed by the sheriff."

"Then why are we here?" Scott asked plaintivly.

I uttered a big sigh as we started upstairs. "I don't know. That is," I said, stumbling on the uneven wooden steps, "sometimes things are overlooked by the law enforcement officials."

"Clues?" Scott said behind me.

I gave a small laugh that sounded more like a snort. "Well . . . maybe. Imagination isn't Milo's strong suit. He solves crimes strictly by the book. None of his deputies is particularly imaginative, either, except maybe Dustin Fong. But Dustin's the youngest of the crew, so he may feel out of line if he makes what seems like a far-out suggestion."

The small bedrooms—there were four of them—were remarkably spare and comparatively tidy. Each contained a crucifix, and a black-beaded rosary lay on one of the dressers.

But the drawers and tiny closets had all been searched. We trooped back downstairs and found the entrance to the basement. A single bare bulb illuminated the rickety steps, with only another bulb hanging from a beam in the middle of a dirt-covered area.

There were tools, some of which were so old that they might have fetched a good price at an antiques show. I smiled when I saw that the O'Neills' fishing equipment had been left unmolested. The same would not have been true for their hunting weapons, since they were nowhere in sight. It was possible that their last prey had been the Hartquists.

Several wooden and cardboard boxes had been opened, revealing nothing of much interest except old books, dirty magazines, worn-out clothes, and—touchingly—what might have been Mrs. O'Neill's wedding dress and veil. The tattered muslin gown had once been white, but was now brown with age; much of the veil had rotted away, but a small satin-covered bandeau still sported tiny artificial rosebuds. Gently, I refolded the ensemble and tucked it inside one of the boxes, then closed the lid.

"Hey," Scott said, speaking from a semidark corner, "this looks suspicious."

He was pointing at the bare floor. "I don't see anything," I said, moving toward him.

"That's the point," he responded. "Something's been moved from here. A couple of somethings, like cartons, maybe."

I peered down at the dirt. Sure enough, there was an impression, three feet wide and maybe ten feet long. A small ridge of dirt rose a little past the middle, as if two items had sat side by side.

"Milo," I breathed. "He took whatever was there."

Scott held out his hand. "I'll bet this was part of whatever the sheriff removed."

I stared at Scott's palm, where a frayed piece of black leather strap with part of a buckle reposed. "From a trunk?" I said.

"That's what it looks like."

My eyes returned to the bare patch on the dirt floor. "Two trunks. They must have been filled with something heavy or they wouldn't have made that much of an impression."

Scott fingered the bit of leather. "Do you suppose those were the trunks that Paddy brought over from the old country?"

"Possibly," I said in a vague voice.

"Just think," Scott mused, "I'll bet the old boy brought everything he owned in those trunks. That's what my grandfather did when he came to the United States. Except he had only one trunk, and it was cardboard."

I smiled at Scott as I started for the stairs. "I'm not as interested in what Paddy O'Neill brought from Ireland sixty-odd years ago. What I'd like to know is what his sons had in those trunks up until the sheriff took them away."

"Guns, maybe," Scott said as we climbed the rickety steps to the main floor.

"Maybe," I allowed. "Then again, maybe not."

The larger trunk, if that is what it was, must be about six feet long. I wondered if it had held a body.

Chapter Nine

We left the O'Neill house just before it started to rain. Scott was doing an interview with the community college registrar about the upcoming commencement ceremony, so I made a detour out Tonga Road and onto the campus. He said he'd get a ride back to the office. No doubt, I thought, from Tamara Rostova, his current inamorata. She had nice teeth, too.

Vida was at her desk when I returned at exactly three o'clock. She was drumming her nails and looking vexed. "Dick Bourgette is behind schedule on those homes he's building out near Cass Pond," she said. "I think that's news, but it's not my department."

Dick was the prosecuting attorney's father. He had spent many years in the construction business, but only recently had begun building single-family dwellings in and around Alpine.

"What's the problem?" I asked.

"Plumbing," Vida said. "He can't get the hardware from his supplier. I didn't talk to him, however. I heard this from Erin Burleson."

"An impeccable source?" I queried, perching on Leo's desk.

Vida grimaced slightly. "The Burlesons haven't been in Alpine very long, so ordinarily I'd be wary of their information. But in this case, it's a personal matter. They've been renting up on Spruce Street—you may recall that

Scott gave me a Scene item about their kiddies—and just yesterday they put money down on one of Dick Bourgette's houses. Very nice, three bedrooms, two baths, fenced yard, finished basement. Oh, and a fireplace. They were scheduled to move in the first of July." Vida paused for breath while I tried to remain patient. So far, it sounded as if she had another Scene item featuring the Burlesons, rather than a big construction story.

"Then," she continued, with a sly glint in her gray eyes, "just after they got back from Doukas Realty, Sam Heppner and Dustin Fong showed up to tell the Burlesons they had to move out of their rental, at least for a few days. This is Thursday, the motels and even the ski lodge are full for the weekend, so they don't know what to do. I suggested they try the college dorms. Some of the out-of-town students who've finished their final exams are already moving out."

"Hold on," I interrupted. "Why must the Burlesons move in the first place? What's going on with the sheriff and his deputies?"

"Well." She sat back in her chair, hands on hips, bust jutting. "That's the interesting part. I tried to convince my nephew Billy to have lunch with me today, but he couldn't. They're very busy at the sheriff's department, it seems. As well they should be. But what's most intriguing about this whole affair is that the Burlesons have been renting from Stubby and Lona O'Neill."

I stared at Vida. "Should this make sense? It doesn't to me."

"Stubby and Lona lived there together off and on for several years," Vida said slowly. "As you may recall, Lona would periodically throw Stubby out and he'd move back in with Paddy at the family home. But when Meara became pregnant, Lona and she moved away. The house didn't go up for sale, however. They—Lona, actually—rented it instead, first to someone who was working temporarily for the state fish and game department, then this spring to Erin and Andy Burleson."

I nodded, then told Vida about the little adventure Scott and I had had at the O'Neill place on Second Hill.

Vida scowled at me. "You should have waited until I got back. I would gladly have gone with you. You ought to have known that Scott, being young and impressionable, would have had qualms about entering the O'Neill house."

"I wanted to go before the rain started," I said, only half lying. "Besides, I didn't know when you'd be back. I figured you were grilling Bill Blatt."

"I should have been," Vida said ruefully. "I believe he's deliberately avoiding his poor old aunt."

"So," I said, picking up my train of thought, "Milo and his mighty men searched the O'Neill house first. They found what may have been two trunks. Something important must have been in the trunks, because they were confiscated. I'll bet that whatever it was is the big secret Milo's keeping from us."

"How silly," Vida declared. "What could it be? The Hartquists killed the O'Neills. Period. The O'Neills may have fired first—I wouldn't put it past them—but what's so mysterious about that? Unless they were fighting over treasure. Do you suppose," Vida continued, looking owl-eyed behind her big orange-rimmed glasses, "that those trunks or whatever they were had gold bullion in them?"

I hadn't thought of that. "It's possible. Scott thought it was guns. I considered a corpse."

Vida's eyes grew even wider. "Whose?"

I shrugged. "Some Hartquist shirttail relation that old Paddy plugged twenty years ago?"

Vida grimaced. "Again, anything's possible. But we've gone off the track. Why turn the Burlesons out of the house they rented from Lona O'Neill?"

"I wish I knew," I said as Leo came through the door.

"Hey, what's up?" he greeted us.

"We're playing Clue," I replied.

Leo glanced at Vida. "You must be Mrs. Peacock. Emma's definitely Miss Scarlett."

"More like Miss Black and Blue after staggering around the O'Neill place." I turned to Vida. "You have your assignment for the wake this evening. Find out why the Burlesons have to move."

"I'll certainly try," Vida promised with a lift of her chin. "You must get involved, too, Leo."

My ad manager was settling into his chair. "Huh? Doing what?"

Vida began to explain as I went into my cubbyhole. At my desk, I considered calling Milo to see if I could squeeze any information out of him. But maybe that wasn't a good idea just yet. I wondered if, when he discovered that someone had broken into the O'Neill house, he'd figure it was me.

I was still mulling when Scott came into my office. His skin looked slightly flushed and there was a gleam in his eyes.

"I'm back," he announced.

"It looks like you had a successful interview with the registrar," I remarked.

He nodded and looked over in the direction of my Skykomish County map. "Yeah. It was great. I mean," he amended, again meeting my gaze, "I think I got a decent story out of it."

"And you got a lift back to the office," I said with a small smile.

Scott nodded slowly, deeply. "Yes. A lift. Say," he said, pulling himself out of what I assumed was a Tamara-induced stupor, "I don't get it. If the Hartquists admit they shot the O'Neills, what's all this other stuff about?

I'd think that the sheriff would be more interested at this point in figuring out who murdered Brian Conley."

Briefly, I stared at Scott. "Yes, you'd think so."

"I suppose," Scott said in a thoughtful voice, "Dodge could be doing both at the same time."

"Probably," I agreed.

Scott shrugged. "The sheriff knows what he's doing, right?"

"I hope so," I said.

It was still raining when I got home at five-thirty. I'd driven by the sheriff's office, but Milo's Grand Cherokee wasn't parked out front. Maybe he was investigating his cases; maybe he'd gone home.

Shortly after six, Tom phoned from Sea-Tac. His flight had been late getting in, and he didn't expect to finish his dinner engagement until eight-thirty. It would take him another hour and half to get to Alpine.

"Will you wait up?" he asked.

"I'll try," I said in an uncharacteristically coy voice. "Drive safely. It's raining here."

"Here, too," Tom said. "Love you. See you soon."

I purred a bit after I hung up the phone. When I'd finished eating a Stouffer's chicken-noodle casserole and a few fresh strawberries, I wondered how to pass the time for the next four hours. Then it occurred to me that I could attend the O'Neill wake. I'd never been to one before, and even aside from my journalistic interest, it might be possible to interview some of the family members.

I'd go alone, just in case the observance lasted longer than a couple of hours. That way, I could leave on my own and be sure that I arrived home in time to make myself gorgeous for Tom's arrival.

Jake and Betsy O'Toole lived in an old but well-maintained house on Cedar Street. When I arrived just before seven-thirty, I couldn't find a parking place. It looked as if the O'Neills had drawn quite a crowd. I found a spot a block and a half away, ironically, by Driggers Funeral Home. At the corner I met Vida, who was dressed all in black, including her silk toque.

"Did you walk or couldn't you find a parking place, either?" I asked as we passed by John Engstrom Park, with its memorial to one of the original mill's first superintendents.

"I walked," Vida replied tersely. "It's only two blocks. I don't mind a little rain." There was a hard glint in her eyes.

"What's wrong?" I inquired.

"Billy," she responded as we waited for a car to turn the corner before we could proceed. "He's avoiding me. What's wrong with that boy?"

"You mean he wouldn't tell you why the Burlesons have to move out for a few days?"

"Precisely." Vida lowered her voice as we neared the O'Toole house, where other guests were also arriving. "If Lona O'Neill is here for this silly escapade, I intend to corner her. Maybe she knows something. She should, since she rented to the Burlesons and she was married to Stubby."

"I'll see what I can find out, too," I said, noting Al Driggers's hearse, which was parked in front of the O'Tooles'. "Which, I guess, is really why I came."

"I thought Tommy was arriving this evening."

I explained about the delay in Tom's arrival. "I figured I might as well tag along to kill time."

The O'Tooles' living and dining rooms usually provided an airy, bright setting with splashes of chintz and cheerful pillows. Now, in the gathering dusk, it was lighted only by candles, and it fairly bulged with mourners. I wasn't prepared for the three caskets that sat in front of Betsy's breakfront cabinet. In the flickering reflection from the glass that shielded the O'Tooles' best china, I could see the three waxen faces of the O'Neill brothers. I shuddered and clutched at Vida's arm.

"Wouldn't you think it would be a closed-casket ceremony?" I said in her ear.

"No," Vida replied, appearing more curious than moved as she edged through the mourners to reach the coffins. "How can you properly grieve unless you can see the deceased?"

I merely shook my head and hung back. On the French doors that led from the dining room to the hallway, someone had hung photographs with Scotch tape. A rifle-toting Stubby, showing off a big buck with enormous antlers; a teenage Dusty with what I assumed was his first car; a gap-toothed Rusty, no more than six, with five fat rainbow trout hanging from a long twig. Happier times, before hatred and stupidity ruined their lives and laid them out in big steel gray coffins.

I stood back to observe the gathering. While Alpine's population has largely been made up of Scandinavians, there is a sizable Irish minority. Straight off, I recognized Jake's brother, Buzzy, and his wife, Laura; Delia Rafferty, widow of Liam, and mother of Tim and Beth, who stood next to her; the Dugans, the Shaws, the Daleys, the Dunns, Jack and Nina Mullins, and, of course, Leo Walsh. I also noticed that Lona O'Neill was there, accompanied by her daughter Meara, who was carrying a chubby baby about eight months old.

I poked Vida, who had come away from the caskets and was again standing next to me. "Did you ever hear who got Meara pregnant?" I whispered.

"No," Vida replied, obviously anxious to move away from me and begin prying. "I would have told you if I had. Very mysterious."

Seeing Father Dennis Kelly come through the door, I

took a couple of backward steps. Jake O'Toole had hurried over to greet our pastor, so I joined them both at the threshold, where we all exchanged greetings.

"Father," Jake said, "have you ever done one of these before?"

"No," Father Den admitted. "But I looked it up. I don't do much, except lead the mourners in some familiar prayers after we say the rosary."

Betsy also came over to welcome our priest. "This is all Jake's doing," she announced, glaring at her husband. "The big grocer, the big Irishman, the big stoop."

Both Father Den and I were accustomed to the public bickering of the O'Tooles. The wrangling must have suited them; they'd been married for almost twenty years.

"It's a nice gesture," Father Den said in a noncommittal voice. "I'm sure the rest of the O'Neills appreciate it."

"Bull," said Betsy, still glaring at Jake. "The only thing they'd appreciate is if we held the damned thing at the Grocery Basket with a free run at the beer and wine sections."

"Take it easy," Jake said, putting a hand on his wife's arm. "Observe Lona by the caskets. Her bereavement almost prostates her."

I tried not to wince at Jake's overblown and often misused vocabulary, a bad habit he'd acquired after Safeway moved to town and cut into his profits. I figured he believed that big words made him an even bigger businessman. Or something.

I looked in the direction that Jake had indicated. Lona, supported by Dan Peebles, was standing over what I presumed was Stubby's body. She had placed a red and green flannel shirt in her husband's casket. Maybe it had been his favorite garment; maybe she treasured it because he never beat her when he wore it. Lona's plump shoulders shook and she covered her face with a handful of tissues. Jake was right: Her grief seemed genuine.

"The first ex-wife's not here," Betsy said in a dry tone. "She moved to Seattle."

"What about the daughters from that first marriage of Stubby's?" I inquired as Father Den slipped away.

Betsy pointed toward the front door. "Here they come now. The taller one is Kathleen. Margaret's got the spiked hair. That's Rusty's son, Mickey, behind them."

Vaguely, I recognized the threesome. Kathleen—Kathy—was rather plain and bordered on gaunt. Margaret, nicknamed Meg, was the better-looking of the two, despite something of a weight problem and the orange-and-blue spiked hair. Their cousin Mickey was a nondescript lad of twenty—dark hair, dark clothes, dark expression. It was no wonder I'd forgotten there was a male O'Neill to carry on the family name.

"Where's Mickey's mother?" I whispered to Jake as Betsy welcomed the younger O'Neills.

"Dana?" Jake shrugged. "I don't know. She and Rusty never divorced, but the ultimate information I retained said she'd moved to Lynnwood or Mountlake Terrace—one of those suburbs north of Seattle."

By the caskets, Lona's sobs had been joined by those of Meara. "Dana O'Neill was the wife who kept leaving and coming back, right?" I said.

Jake, who was keeping an eye on the growing crowd of mourners as if he expected someone to make off with the Belleek china on the mantel, nodded once. "Dana's been gone for a while this time," he said. "Lona left once or twice before she finally departed the town. I heard she'd filed for divorce but I don't know if it was decreed final by the time Stubby got killed."

"It wasn't." Jack Mullins had come up behind me. "What do you think of our Irish rituals so far, Emma?"

"So far, they're relatively tame."

I'd spoken too soon. The three younger O'Neills and a couple of older people I didn't recognize had joined Lona and Meara at the caskets. Yet another stranger was placing a half-dozen extravagant bouquets behind the trio of gray coffins. Virtually all the mourners were now sobbing, but the worst was yet to come. Within seconds, it did.

The Wailers arrived, three black-clad women who showed up at every funeral, interment, or other grief-related event. Long black coats, voluminous black veils, black cotton stockings, black shoes, black gloves, and black purses made them look like three black crows. Even their faces seemed dark, the wilted veils turning their natural pallor into featureless masks of gray.

As if joined at the hip, they glided together toward the coffins. Jack, who had been joined by his wife, Nina, nudged me. "This is a real bonus. How's Father Den going to say the rosary over the shrieks of the Wailers?"

Apparently, he wasn't. At least not immediately. As if on cue, the three women began to moan and keen. Apparently they struck some atavistic chord in the other mourners. They, too, began to groan and shriek.

Meara's baby joined in, crying and thrashing in his mother's arms. I caught Vida's eye from across the room. She looked as if she were about to commit Alpine's next homicide on the spot.

Father Den was trying to edge his way in front of the caskets. He looked like a slow-motion replay of a running back squirming and twisting his way to the goal line. Dan Peebles tried to run interference for him, but was partially blocked by the large form of Brendan Shaw, whose back was turned and who was apparently trying to sell life insurance to somebody I didn't recognize.

"That's it," Jack declared, and assumed the role of law enforcer without benefit of his official uniform. "Can it,

everybody! Let Father say the prayers. Come on, pipe down, or I'll clear the room."

Everyone but the Wailers complied. The black-clad trio kept up their grieving noises until Vida marched over to confront them. She spoke very softly; I couldn't hear what she told the women. But they stopped and withdrew to the floral stands with their masses of gladioli, roses, and calla lilies.

Father Den announced that those of us who were Catholic were about to say the rosary, I got down on my knees. Luckily, the O'Tooles' carpets were fairly plush. Fingering the mother-of-pearl beads that Adam had given me for Christmas, I made the sign of the cross with the silver crucifix.

Just as we got to the rosary's First Glorious Mystery, someone tapped my shoulder. Awkwardly, I turned around and found myself staring up at Spencer Fleetwood.

"Have I missed anything?" he whispered.

I wanted to say, Yes, you missed finding another corpse. Ha-ha. Instead, I practiced charity and merely shook my head. After all, I was praying.

Unlike some priests I've known, Father Den doesn't race through the decades of the rosary as if he were reading off the entries in the feature race at Emerald Downs. We finished about twenty minutes later, after Den had offered a few prayers for the repose of the O'Neills' souls. The Wailers were poised over the caskets, about to shriek and moan again, but Father Kelly asked for silence as we prayed privately for the dead men and their survivors.

"How long does this stuff take?" Spence whispered as he bent down closer to my ear. For once, he'd dispensed with the designer sunglasses.

I shrugged. Forever, I hoped, despite the growing stiffness in my knees. Maybe Spence would get bored and leave. His mere presence rankled me.

But after no more than five minutes, Father Den announced that the period of reflection and mourning could begin. People got to their feet, half of them moving away from the caskets, the other half moving nearer. A few soft sobs and gentle sniffs could be heard, along with the clearing of throats. Dan Peebles, looking slightly diffident and a trifle flushed, raised his hands.

"This is a quiet time, set aside to remember the loved ones who have passed on," he said in his rather high voice. "We're here to honor the beloved dead and keep their earthly bodies company." He paused to clear his throat. "Our thoughts and remembrances accompany them to their heavenly home. Let us observe these moments in silence."

The Wailers conferred. It seemed that they'd never been to an Irish wake, though I found it hard to believe. Surely they could have tracked one down in Sultan or Skykomish or even Monroe. After further consultation, they left in a sea of black disapproval. Their disappointment was palpable, and I was sure I heard one of them snort in disgust.

Spencer Fleetwood had gone up to the caskets, where he made a show of bowing his head for a few seconds in front of each corpse. Then he began to speak quietly with Kathleen and Mickey O'Neill. It was only then that I realized he was miked up. Not wanting to be outdone, I scanned the premises for Lona O'Neill, but Vida already had her cornered by the buffet in the dining room. Instead, I made a beeline for Meara, who was rocking her baby in her arms and avoiding further communion with the body of her father, Stubby.

"Boy or girl?" I asked in what I hoped was my friendliest voice.

"Boy," Meara replied, not looking up from the baby.

"What's his name?"

"Cornelius," she said. "That was my father's real name."

"I didn't know that," I said. "By the way, I'm sorry about your father's death. And your uncles', too."

Meara gazed at me with eyes the exact shade of blue spruce. "Why?"

"Why?" I was caught off guard. "Because they're dead. You were crying for them just a few minutes ago, weren't you?"

Meara shook her head. She'd let her auburn hair grow out in the year since I'd last seen her in the Hartquist kidnapping incident.

"I wasn't crying for my dad or my uncles," she said.

"Oh?"

The blue-green eyes began to fill up with tears again. Meara jiggled the baby in her arms. "I cried for him," she asserted, brushing her cheek against the baby's tufts of brown hair. "Because he has no father. Even a bad father is better than none at all."

I smiled gently. "I raised my son without a father. He's turned into a wonderful person."

"Your son Adam?" Meara blinked back the tears. "Isn't Adam a priest?"

"Not yet," I said, still smiling. "He'll be ordained next spring."

Meara appeared to mull over my words. Maybe she was thinking that her son could be a priest someday, too.

But that wasn't what was on her mind. "I heard Adam's father is still around. Wasn't he in Alpine a while ago?"

"Ah . . . yes." I felt my smile waver. "But he was gone all the time Adam was growing up."

"That's different," Meara declared, her lower lip thrust out.

"It didn't seem so different at the time," I said quietly.

"One of these days Cornelius's father may come back to you."

Meara, however, shook her head. "He won't. He can't." She took a deep breath and dabbed at her eyes with her sleeve. "Cornelius's father is dead."

Meara O'Neill was sixteen years old, and I scarcely knew her. I had only known her father and her grandfather and her uncles on sight and by reputation. Upon occasion, I had run into her mother, Lona, at the Grocery Basket, Parker's Pharmacy, or St. Mildred's. Meara and I were a full generation apart. I honestly didn't know what to say.

"I'm sorry," I repeated. "I didn't know." Seeing Meara's quizzical expression, I thought perhaps she'd misunderstood me. "That is, after you and your mom left town, I never heard—"

"Excuse me," Meara broke in, drying her eyes once more, "I have to rescue my mother. That awful Mrs. Runkel is talking her ear off."

Sure enough, Lona O'Neill looked as if she was wilting under Vida's interrogation. As Meara and the baby left me, I noticed that Father Den was shaking hands with Jake and Betsy O'Toole. I hurried to the door.

"You're leaving?" I said to Den as he stepped across the threshold.

Den nodded. "I haven't gotten started on my sermon for the weekend," he said. "I don't like to rush through the writing."

Father Kelly didn't like to rush through the delivery, either. His homilies were always intelligent, always spiritually grounded, and always exceedingly dull. At least he gave them in the context of the proper era, unlike our former pastor, Father Fitzgerald, who, in his dotage, harped on the dangers of bathtub gin and flappers in short skirts.

I decided that I was leaving, too. Vida would gather all

the news and gossip available. Besides, I had a question for Dennis Kelly.

"I'm not prying, I hope," I said as we made our way to the sidewalk, "but I was just talking to Meara O'Neill. I didn't realize that the father of her child was dead. Do you know anything about the circumstances?"

A slight frown crossed Father Den's smooth, high forehead. "How do you mean, 'the circumstances'?"

We were heading down the street. Apparently Den had parked his car at quite a distance, too. "For instance, who the father was and how he died. I know this sounds like I'm being a snoop, but it could have a bearing on the O'Neill murder case."

"The Hartquists killed the O'Neills," Den said. "I don't understand why there's any mystery about that."

"I wouldn't think so, either," I said, "but Milo's the one who's being mysterious. He and his deputies found something suspicious at the O'Neill house, and the sheriff refuses to say what it was."

Father Den chuckled. "I can't help you there. Sherrif Dodge doesn't confide in me. As you know, he's not part of my flock."

"But there could be some other factors," I persisted. We had stopped at the corner, and it appeared that we were about to go our separate ways. "There seem to be a lot of dead people tied into the O'Neill clan. I wonder who little Cornelius's father was and how he died."

For the first time since I'd met him, Dennis Kelly didn't look me in the eye. Instead, his gaze roamed in the direction of John Engstrom Park, searching somewhere among the trilliums and rhododendrons and maidenhair ferns. If he was seeking the answer to my question, if he'd in fact found it or already knew it, he wasn't going to tell me.

"I can't help you, Emma," he said, finally looking at

me again. "I'm sorry. Goodnight." With a rueful expression, he turned and walked away.

Father Den had never lied to me. I didn't believe that he was lying to me now. I thought there must be a solid reason why he wasn't telling me the truth.

I had a feeling that it was something I needed to know.

Chapter Ten

My lipstick zigged and my eyeliner zagged as I readied myself for Tom's arrival. The unsteady hand was the result of nerves, a double dose. I honestly still didn't have an answer for Tom, and I was unsettled by Father Den's evasion of my question about the father of Meara O'Neill's baby. Looking in the mirror, I saw that my makeup could qualify me for a spot as a clown in the summer solstice parade. I was about to start over when the doorbell rang.

"Damn!" I gasped, checking my watch. It was only nine o'clock. Surely Tom couldn't be here so soon. Maybe, I thought, as panic set in, his dinner meeting had been canceled.

But when I looked through the peephole, I saw a black silk toque and disorderly gray curls.

"Vida," I said in relief as I let her in, "I thought you were Tom."

"Ha!" she exclaimed, tromping over to the nearest armchair and plopping down. "He won't be here for at least an hour, correct?"

"That's what he told me," I replied. "Hold on, let me get my makeup mirror from the bedroom. Would you like some tea?" I called over my shoulder.

"No, thank you," Vida responded. "I had plenty of tea at the wake. That—and coffee—was all they served. Leo was correct when he informed me that liquor isn't permitted at a wake. Very smart."

Vida's clear, strong voice carried from the living room. I returned with the mirror, a bag of cosmetic puffs, a jar of face cream, and my makeup kit.

"So what happened after I left?" I inquired, plugging the mirror into an outlet by the sofa.

"Not very much," Vida said, making no effort to hide her disappointment. "Apparently, after the prayers are finished, an Irish wake consists primarily of sitting or standing or kneeling around the deceased. There was very little conversation and no food. Now, I don't mean to criticize Jake and Betsy, but they do own a grocery store, and a bit of cake or some nice cookies wouldn't have been amiss."

"What about Lona?" I asked, cleansing my face with cream.

"Lona." Vida spoke the name as if the Widow O'Neill was a millstone. "She's not the brightest person, you know. Lona insisted she had no idea why the Burlesons have been asked to leave the rental house, at least temporarily. I had much better luck with Erin Burleson."

"Erin?" I almost dropped my mascara wand. "Was she there, too?"

Vida shook her head. "No, but it's only a short walk from the O'Tooles' to their place. I caught them just as they were leaving for the college dorms. As I'd suggested, they were able to find lodging there to tide them over until the sheriff is done with the house or their new home is ready, whichever comes first."

"And?"

Vida wore her Cheshire cat expression. "Well, now. I told them I was interested in their house as a possible future rental for one of my nephews who's moving back here from Tacoma. Of course, that's a bit of a fib—Allan only went to Tacoma for an overnight meeting—but

I thought I was acting in a good cause. Anyway, Erin couldn't see the harm, so she let me in. A good thing, too, because Sam Heppner showed up just a few minutes later. But I'm getting ahead of myself."

"Yes, you are, Vida," I agreed. "Let's have it."

"The Burlesons had to leave most of their things behind," Vida said, still taking her time with her tale. "It's not a very large house—I can see why they want to move, I believe Erin may be expecting again, she looks rather round—so it didn't take me long to go through the rooms. Nothing struck me as unusual until I got to the basement. That was where I found the padlocked steel cabinets."

I stared as Vida paused for effect. "What was in them?" I asked.

"I don't know," Vida confessed. "They were padlocked, and not by the Burlesons. Erin informed me that they came with the house and that Lona had said they were for storage and not to be disturbed."

"Describe the cabinets."

"Slightly taller than I am, about six feet, dark gray steel, four in all, a foot and a half wide." Vida stopped, and fretted her upper lip. "They were rather like gym lockers, but no vents. Can you picture them?"

I could. "So Erin and her husband had no idea what was in them?"

"That's right. What's more," Vida continued, "Erin had the impression that Lona didn't know, either."

"Huh?"

Vida nodded solemnly. "Erin said that Lona was rather nervous when she told them about the cabinets. I guess she and Andy thought it was rather odd, and pressed Lona for information. But she—Lona—became all atwitter and said it was just family heirlooms, things that belonged to Stubby and the rest of the O'Neills."

"That doesn't sound right," I remarked.

Vida agreed. "What do you think? The cabinets are what Milo wants out of that house? But why?"

"Well," I said dryly, "because of what's in them. Whatever it is, maybe it's the same thing that was in the chests up at the O'Neill house on Second Hill."

"Possibly," Vida conceded, removing her black cotton gloves and flexing her fingers. "Drugs, perhaps?"

Strangely, that idea hadn't occurred to me. "Maybe. There's been more of a problem with drugs in Alpine since the college opened."

"So far," Vida noted, "the suppliers have been primarily college students. Unfortunately, they sell not only to their peers, but to much younger children, even of grade school age. So horrible, so tragic. It makes me wild." She paused, apparently reining in her wrath. "But none of that means that the O'Neills might have been trafficking in drugs. It's just the sort of thing they might do, though. Ugh."

"Yes," I agreed, feeling a trifle distracted. My ears were pricked up, listening for Tom's arrival. It wasn't yet nine-thirty, but he could be early. "By the way," I said, trying to refocus on the O'Neills, "I spoke with Meara at the wake. She told me that her baby's father is dead."

"Goodness!" Vida exclaimed, then her jaw dropped. "Oh, good grief—you don't think . . ." She stopped and stared at me from behind her glasses.

"Think what?" I was puzzled, then, judging from the dismayed expression on Vida's face, I realized what was going through her nimble mind. "Not . . . one of her uncles?"

Squaring her shoulders, Vida sat up very straight. "Such things happen, loathsome as they may be. On the other hand, the Hartquists are the ones who kidnapped her. The problem there is that they're still alive."

"Meara was pregnant before the kidnapping," I pointed out.

"True," Vida murmured, putting her gloves back on. "Yet it would be more acceptable if the father of her child was a Hartquist, rather than one of her relatives. It's a shame, really, that Rudy or Ozzie wasn't killed in the shoot-out. It would make things so much . . . tidier."

"When's the funeral for the O'Neills?" I asked. "I thought Father Den would announce it at the wake."

"Oh, dear!" Vida shot me a sheepish look as she stood up. "I forgot to tell you. It's a Mass, tomorrow morning, ten o'clock. Father Kelly's secretary called it in to me late this afternoon. The O'Neills apparently want to be buried in Ireland with their father. Dan Peebles said the bodies would be shipped from here tomorrow morning right after the service."

"Another burial abroad?" I said in surprise. "What is this, some new fad? Are we running out of room at the cemetery?"

"Actually, we may be," Vida said as she moved toward the door. "I believe one of the county commissioners mentioned recently that we may have to expand across First Hill Road to some vacant property by the women's shelter."

"I'll have Scott check on that," I remarked as I accompanied Vida to the door. "But I still find all these overseas burials peculiar."

"In a way," Vida allowed. "I must dash. Roger will wonder what's happened to me. I don't like leaving him alone for too long in the evenings. He won't admit it, but I'm sure he gets lonesome."

I was sure that Roger was out in Vida's backyard smoking cigarettes, or even wacky tobacky. "He's old enough to amuse himself," I said, keeping my thoughts to myself.

In the doorway, Vida paused to scrutinize me. "You do look very pretty, Emma. I hope you have a lovely time with Tommy."

"Thanks," I said, and felt my stomach give a lurch of excitement. Or fear.

Whatever the cause, pacing the living room wouldn't help. After Vida had been gone for ten minutes, I stepped outside for a breath of fresh air. And all the better to see Tom's arrival. The rain had almost stopped, and a waning moon was forcing its way through the clouds. Or so it seemed. My brain wasn't working on all cylinders. I felt like a silly fool.

Back inside, I got out two glasses and the bottle of Irish whiskey I'd purchased for Tom earlier. It was precisely ten o'clock. Wandering back into the living room, I checked for any stray dust. Then I searched the carpet for dirt. Finally, I went into the bathroom to make sure my makeup was still in order. It was, but the face that looked back at me seemed pale and just a little frightened.

I *was* frightened. Here was the biggest decision of my life, and my mind still wasn't at peace. Still, Milo had given good advice—let Tom make some of the choices. Our future shouldn't fall only on my shoulders. But what if Tom was unwilling to accept his role? I couldn't bear to contemplate a deadlock.

Giving myself a good shake—without disarranging my short brown curls too much, of course—I set my jaw and stared again into the mirror. That was better. I didn't look quite so much like a deer facing a twelve-gauge shotgun. If only my heart would stop pounding like a jackhammer, I thought, and then realized that the thudding wasn't coming from me, but from the front door.

"Oh, Jeez," I said out loud and raced to the door. I didn't bother to look through the peephole.

"Hi, there," Tom said, grinning at me. "Where were you? I rang about three times. Is the bell broken?"

"Ah . . . no," I said, suddenly short of breath. "I was in the bathroom."

For a long moment, we stared at each other. It was

game time. I felt like a pitcher who hadn't thrown any warm-up tosses, an actress who hadn't memorized her lines. I was suspended in time and space, frozen to the floor.

Tom broke the spell. He came inside, shut the door behind him, and swept me into his arms. "You look terrific," he declared, kissing my forehead, my cheeks, my chin, and finally my lips.

"So do you," I said after a long moment. And he did—the chiseled profile, the silvered brown hair, the keen blue eyes, the perpetual tan. If age had eroded some of his good looks, an air of distinction had compensated. He was as attractive to me now as he'd been when I first met him almost thirty years ago on the copy desk of the *Seattle Times*.

"Would you like a drink?" I asked from the circle of his arms.

"Sure," he replied, holding me close as we headed for the kitchen. "How are you?"

"Nervous," I admitted.

He didn't comment, but asked instead if I'd talked to Adam.

"Yes," I answered, moving away to make our drinks. "The other night. He was kind of rough on his old mother."

Tom gave me a sidelong look and a wry grin. "He's been kind of rough on his old dad, too."

I was surprised. Having seen Tom and Adam together so seldom, I didn't understand the dynamics between them. "How so?"

The grin disappeared. "I guess it was about a year, maybe a little less, after Sandra died that Adam started pressing me to make a serious commitment to you. He had trouble accepting the fact that Kelsey needed me to help with her baby."

I'd had trouble accepting the fact, too. Tom hadn't

seemed half so concerned when I'd had my own child out of wedlock. "You never told me Adam felt that way," I said, trying to push the old resentments aside.

Tom took his drink from me and we returned to the living room. "I didn't see the point. You knew my situation."

We sat down and he put his arm around me. "The baby's walking now," he went on, looking rather proud. "Aidan has Kelsey and Sandra's coloring, but he's got my eyes and mouth."

"Aidan," I said. "That's a wonderful name. Where did Kelsey come up with it?"

"It was my father's name," Tom said, sipping his drink. "You never met my folks, though you must have seen them in church."

One of life's ironies was that my family and the Cavanaughs had been members of the same Seattle parish, though we lived in different neighborhoods. I had seen Tom as an altar boy at St. Benedict's, but the seven years' age difference had kept each of us from noticing the other.

"You said your father had an artificial leg," I said. "I vaguely recall a man who limped, but I honestly don't remember his wife."

Tom smiled softly. "Mom had hair about the color of yours when she was younger. She was about your size, too. But she wasn't someone you'd pick out of a crowd. She'd had a hard life, after losing her first two children."

I'd known that both of Tom's brothers had died, one while being born, the other in a hit-and-run accident, when a drunk plowed into their front yard and ran over the three-year-old. Tom had come along several years later, when his parents were in their forties. Aidan Cavanaugh had died when Tom was a college senior. Tom's mother had passed away some twenty years later. While I had known Tom while Charlotte Cavanaugh was still alive, I wasn't his wife, I was his girlfriend, and not the sort you'd bring home to Mother.

"So Kelsey and little Aidan are getting along on their own?" I ventured.

Tom nodded. "They're living in a condo near the Presidio. Her brother, Graham, is coming up from L.A. for a couple of weeks next month."

"And the sale of your house?"

"I took it off the market."

I craned my neck to look up at him. "Why?"

He kissed my forehead. "Because I'm not sure what's going to happen. With us."

"But I thought you were buying a condo on Nob Hill," I said, feeling a new surge of panic.

"I'm not in any rush." He finished his drink and put both arms around me. "Not about real estate, anyway. I think it's our bedtime."

"I think you're right." I wrapped my arms around his neck. As always, he smelled like pine-scented soap and soft leather. I buried my face in his shoulder and wished all decisions were as simple as this one. "Carry me," I whispered.

He did, with relative ease. In the bedroom, we undressed each other, slowly at first, then with greater urgency. Time and place seemed to dissolve. There were no pressures, no decisions, no panic—only joy. When at last we were spent, Tom held me close and rested his lips against my temple.

"Well?" he breathed. "What's your decision?"

I couldn't believe my own ears. The damned phone rang on the nightstand. I let out a little yelp and Tom laughed.

"Answer it," he said, adding what only a fellow journalist would advise. "It might be breaking news."

As if I wanted to strangle the phone, I gripped the receiver with both hands. But of course it was the caller I wanted to choke.

I all but shouted: "Hello?"

"Emma?" Vida sounded shaken. "Is that you?"

"Yes," I shot back, then lowered my voice. "What's wrong?"

"Roger," she said, her voice still unsteady. "He hasn't come home."

I glanced at the digital clock radio on the nightstand. It was almost eleven-thirty. "He hasn't?" I said stupidly, then added for Tom's benefit, "Roger's been out all evening?"

"Yes," Vida replied. "He left before I went to the wake. He was going to Old Mill Park for a while. Oh, Emma, should I call the sheriff?"

I didn't know what to tell her. Roger was probably horsing around somewhere, doing whatever sixteen-year-olds did on a late-spring evening. Not that that couldn't be bad, especially where Roger was concerned. But Vida wouldn't have been so uncertain if she wasn't truly upset.

Damn the kid, I thought. "Maybe you had better call the sheriff," I finally said. "Whoever is on patrol tonight will probably find him with some other kids. Roger's probably lost track of time. It stays light so late this time of year."

"That's so," Vida allowed. "Very well, I'll do that." She hung up.

"Roger, huh?" Tom said, propping himself up on the pillows. "What is he, fifteen, sixteen?"

I said he'd just turned sixteen.

Tom chuckled and shook his head. "I remember Graham at that age. It's a wonder I didn't get as off-balance as Sandra. Graham got picked up twice for shoplifting and once for an attempted breaking-and-entering. Did you know that?"

"No," I said in a vague sort of voice. I didn't want to think about Tom's son or Vida's grandson. "You asked me a question before the phone rang, remember?"

Tom nodded, his blue eyes keen. "I've been damned curious about your response."

I took a deep breath. "Let me ask you a question first. How do you feel about moving to Alpine?"

Tom's face grew very serious, though he didn't register surprise. "You don't want to give up the *Advocate*, right?"

I tried to keep my gaze steady. "Right."

Tom shrugged his bare shoulders. "I can understand that." He paused while I held my breath. "I suppose I could learn to live in Alpine. You did. So what's your answer?"

My astonishment was so great that I couldn't speak. I just stared at Tom with my mouth open. Then, with enormous effort and tremendous relief, I threw myself against his chest and cried, "Yes!"

We spent the next half hour sitting in bed, drinking more Irish whiskey and making plans. Tom explained how San Francisco didn't hold so much charm for him anymore. It had grown too congested, too crowded, and the grande dame façade was crumbling around the edges.

"Graham plans to stay in L.A. to pursue his acting career," Tom said as the digital clock clicked over to midnight. "Kelsey wants to work with underprivileged children, maybe in San Francisco, maybe somewhere else. She liked New York, but doesn't want to go back. Too many bad memories, involving that idiot who fathered her child." He gave me a sheepish grin. "An idiot like me, only more so."

I smiled at the self-deprecating remark. I could afford to, now. "You must have some bad memories of San

Francisco," I said. "Life there with Sandra wasn't always happy."

"No, it wasn't," Tom said simply. "I don't know how I'll adjust to small-town living, but you did. Anyway, I visit plenty of small towns when I'm out checking on my weeklies."

Setting the date had been easy. I had at first suggested an autumn wedding, but Tom thought it would be a great idea to let Adam marry us. That meant in the spring, following our son's ordination. The idea filled me with pride.

I was still glowing when the phone rang again. This time, I was neither startled nor angry.

"Dwight Gould found Roger," Vida announced. "He's quite safe, but very naughty."

"Where was he?" I asked, relieved for Vida's sake, if not for Roger's.

"Coming down First Hill with two of the Gustavson boys. Cousins, you know. Such little mischief-makers. They'd simply been out strolling around the town. I think I'll put it in next week's Scene."

I pretended to be pleased, though I would have preferred it if Dwight had cuffed the kids and hauled their butts to jail. They could have spent the night in a cell next to the Hartquists. It would have served all of them right.

"See you in the morning, Vida," I said cheerfully.

"Of course," Vida responded, then her tone grew a bit breathless, no doubt with rampant curiosity. "Oh—did Tommy arrive safely?"

I looked down at Tom, whose eyes had closed. He was safe, he was with me, he was mine. "Yes," I said, and bade Vida goodnight.

Chapter Eleven

FRIDAY MORNING, JUNE eleventh. It was no ordinary day; it felt like the first day of my life. Unlike most mornings, I woke up feeling almost alert and definitely happy. I couldn't remember when I didn't pause in full consciousness to enumerate the negative aspects of the coming day. Instead, I gazed down at Tom, who was still asleep. In my bed. Next to me. Where he belonged.

The only drawback was that he felt we ought to keep our engagement quiet for the time being. He had so many loose ends to tie up, the house to sell, the transfer of his business base from San Francisco to Alpine. I wasn't pleased, and we argued a bit. But he was the one making the big sacrifice; I could cut him some slack. After all, any announcement of our plans would put me in the gossip spotlight until the wedding took place. I could do without that added nuisance.

Thus, I composed myself upon entering the *Advocate* office. Since I was almost ten minutes late, my staff had already arrived. Vida wore a quizzical expression, but I tried to ignore it. Leo, Scott, Kip, and Ginny all appeared to take me at poker-face value.

"Sheriff Dodge called first thing," Ginny said. "He wants you to come over to his office."

"Ah! Maybe he's going to open up."

"It's about time," Vida remarked. "You'd better get going."

I intended to, but not without my own brand of coffee in hand. Ten minutes later, I was sitting across the desk from Milo.

"Can you keep a lid on this?" he inquired, looking faintly weary.

"Sure," I said. "Don't I always?"

Milo took a minute to respond. "Yeah, you're usually good about stuff like this. But now that you've got competition, I have to wonder if Spence might goad you into something."

"Are you going to tell Spence what you're going to tell me?" I asked.

Milo winced. "I should."

I leaned forward in the vinyl chair. "Are you?" I demanded.

Milo sighed. "No. But it's not giving him a fair shake. On the other hand, you can't print anything until Wednesday. Unless you put out another one of those special deals."

"I won't," I said. "It's too expensive." Expensive. For the first time, it dawned on me that I could excise expensive from my vocabulary. I certainly wasn't marrying Tom for his money, but it would be nice not to have to pinch every penny.

"What are you grinning about?" Milo asked in his dour fashion.

"Nothing." I couldn't stop grinning.

Milo scowled. "You sure as hell are grinning about something. Don't tell me you really would publish a—" He stopped and slapped his forehead. "Cavanaugh! You said yes!"

"Milo!" I stifled the grin and tried to lie. But I couldn't. "Yes." I grinned again.

"Jesus." Milo shook his head and chuckled. "I'll be damned. Really?"

I nodded vigorously. "Yes, but don't say anything. I haven't even told Vida. In fact, Adam won't know until Tom calls him later today."

"Jesus," Milo repeated, but more softly this time. "When?"

I explained how we were going to wait until Adam could marry us in the spring. "So I'll keep your secret if you keep mine," I concluded. "What's going on?"

Milo lighted a cigarette and took a big swig of coffee before he spoke. "I suppose you and Vida cruised around the O'Neill place recently."

"Actually, no," I replied. "That is," I continued, not wanting to mislead the sheriff at this point, "Vida wasn't with me. It was Scott Chamoud. He takes better pictures."

Somewhat to my surprise, Milo didn't seem annoyed. "We're done with the O'Neill place anyway. The crime scene tape's there just to keep out vandals. What we found up there was what we expected in the way of guns. The O'Neills, like their sworn enemies, the Hartquists, kept a bunch of them—shotguns, handguns, rifles, you name it. But what we didn't expect was an arms cache."

Milo paused to drink more coffee and, I assumed, to get my reaction. "Like what?" I asked, suitably surprised.

"Like two big trunks full of rocket launchers and ammo."

"Good Lord!" I gaped at Milo. "What for?"

"Good question," he responded. "Rocket launchers seem a bit much to aim at the Hartquists." He shot me a shrewd glance. "First thing this morning, we went over to Lona and Stubby O'Neill's house. You know, the one the Burlesons had been renting."

"Yes?"

"Guess what we found there in the basement."

"Nuclear bombs?"

Milo chuckled. "It wouldn't have surprised me. But it was more rocket launchers, stored in steel cases. I'm sure as hell glad that the Burleson kids didn't figure out a way to get inside those things. They might have launched each other into Snohomish County."

I confessed to being mystified. "Did you ask Lona about them?"

"I had her go with Dustin and me this morning," Milo replied. "Lona and Meara and the kid stayed over last night to attend the funeral. She claimed she didn't know anything about the weaponry, that Stubby had brought those cases in just before she moved out and rented the place to the Burlesons. Stubby had warned her that if she ever tried to open the things, he'd bust her chops."

"Had he warned the Burlesons, too?" I inquired, finishing the coffee from the *Advocate*'s pot and hoping Milo wouldn't offer me a refill.

"Lona got the point across," Milo said. "It wasn't a big deal to the Burlesons. They were renters, they didn't care what the owners had stored in the basement. It was the O'Neills' house, after all."

"Why rocket launchers?" I asked, still flummoxed.

Milo shook his head. "I can't answer that. Not now. But we're following up some leads. That's why I don't want this to leak out for a while. These weapons are illegal for civilians and they cost a bundle. Three big questions here—how the hell did the O'Neills get hold of them, where the hell did they get them, and why the hell did they get them?"

"Weird." I fingered Milo's desk as if it were a piano keyboard. It appeared he wouldn't—more likely couldn't—answer all of those questions just now. "Say, did you ever look into the disappearance of Brian Conley's body at JFK?"

"Dwight called back there," Milo replied, putting out his cigarette in a clamshell ashtray. "He got the run-around. Just what you'd expect with those New York types. We'll try again today."

"I should hope so," I said, getting up. "It's your corpse, after all."

The sheriff tipped his head to one side. "Do you really think whoever killed Brian showed up at JFK and snatched the body?"

"No," I replied, "but losing your victim doesn't look too hot on your résumé."

Milo grimaced. "The trail's colder than Tonga Ridge at four thousand feet. According to the girlfriend and the buddy, Conley didn't have an enemy in the world. His coworkers at the consulate couldn't think of any reason why somebody would want to kill him. His parents, especially his mother, have nothing but good things to say about him." Milo held his hands palms up. "It's got to be one of those weirdos in the woods."

I should have been inclined to agree with the sheriff, but something held me back. "Any theories about the O'Neills' weaponry?" I asked, deciding to change the subject.

Milo fingered his coffee mug. "Well . . . if it were anybody but the O'Neills, I'd start sniffing for terrorists. But, like the Hartquists, the O'Neills are—were—just the kind who might want to have an honest-to-God arsenal."

"Have you asked the Hartquists about the rocket launchers?" I inquired.

"The Hartquists?" Milo frowned at me. "Why? To give them ideas in case they ever get out of prison?"

"Oh," I said slowly, getting to my feet, "it was just a thought."

Milo also stood up, then loped around his desk and put an arm around me. "Hey," he said, looking down into my face, "I'm really glad for you."

"Thanks, Milo," I said, turning my cheek for the obligatory kiss of congratulations. "You're still my dearest friend."

Milo, however, didn't kiss me. Instead, he gave my shoulders a squeeze and stepped away. "If . . . if anything ever goes wrong, or you need . . . well, you know . . . I'm still here."

I looked at his long, grave face. Milo was right. He was always there. Like a tree, like a rock, like a friend.

"Yes," I said softly and felt my eyes mist just a bit. "I know."

I'd decided I might as well attend the funeral Mass for the O'Neills. It would save listening to Vida twitter about Catholic oddities and excesses. Before heading to St. Mildred's, I called Tom to see how he was getting along.

"I spent most of the morning on the phone with business arrangements. That was enough to make me feel a need for fresh air. Now I'm cleaning your carport," he informed me. "I found three mouse nests."

"Really?" I wasn't surprised. Field mice often made their home in the woodpile. If they didn't hurt me, I wouldn't hurt them.

"It looks like the grass needs mowing," Tom said. "How do you get the mower to go uphill out back? Or have you got a pet goat around here someplace?"

"It's not easy." I laughed. "Don't knock yourself out. You haven't taken over as lord of the manor yet."

"No, but I need the practice. What are you up to? Any hot news?"

"Yes, in fact," I said, and made him promise not to tell about the discovery of the rocket launchers.

"The O'Neills were probably planning to sell them," Tom said when I'd finished. "They could get a good price from terrorists."

"I wondered about that," I said. "Where would the O'Neills meet up with terrorists?"

"Damned if I know," Tom replied. "The real question is, where did they get the rocket launchers in the first place?"

"Milo's looking into that," I said. "At least, I hope he is."

"No word on your other homicide?" Tom asked.

"Nothing. Milo thinks he's hit the wall on that one."

"Could be." Tom paused. "What do you want me to do with these boxes of old magazines and newspapers at the front of the carport? They're a fire hazard, you know."

"Then throw them out," I responded. "I waited all year for one of the schools or somebody else to have a paper drive and they never did. Too much recycling these days, I guess. Got to run. I'm attending the O'Neill funeral. Care to join me?"

Again, Tom paused. "No, thanks. I need to stick around here and earn my keep. See you this evening."

I could hardly believe it. Tom would be there this evening and tomorrow evening, and then, though he would have to leave for a time, there'd be endless evenings when I would come home to him. I gave myself a little shake.

St. Mildred's was already jammed when I arrived at two minutes to ten. The old white wooden structure is small and modest, but it has a certain charm. At least our pastors haven't modernized the sanctuary. Too many of the new and renovated churches in the area look like bowling alleys or union halls or are otherwise butt-ugly.

I managed to find a seat in the second pew from the back. I was mildly surprised to see Vida in attendance. She was up front and easy to spot with her pigeon hat. I have tried to count how many hats Vida owns, but lost track years ago. Judging from the styles, particularly this one with its three pigeons nestling in powder blue veils around the high crown, she had been acquiring headgear since becoming a grown-up. The pigeons were especially intriguing: They had glass eyes that moved around like a doll's. And, like Vida herself, they seemed not to miss a trick.

Most of the people who had attended the wake were present, plus several others, some of whom I didn't recognize. Noticeably absent were the Wailers. Perhaps they were at home, rehearsing for Oscar Nyquist's funeral on Saturday.

Al Driggers and Dan Peebles were both on hand, not only in their capacity as funeral director and assistant, but as pallbearers. Three caskets required eighteen men, which made for an impressive procession down the center aisle. I noted that Brendan Shaw, Buddy Bayard, Bill Daley, Jack Mullins, Jake and Buzzy O'Toole, and, to my astonishment, Ed Bronsky had been called into service. Ed wasn't Irish, but he was a member of the parish. I figured he'd volunteered because it was good publicity.

Father Kelly gave an adequate homily, considering that the O'Neills weren't regular attendees at Mass and that our pastor didn't know them well, except by reputation, which wasn't very good. Mainly, he spoke of being prepared for death, of not knowing the day or the hour. He did not add that you never could tell when your archrivals were going to show up with their .22s.

The only member of the O'Neill family to give a eulogy was Mickey, Rusty's son. He looked fairly terrified, and I suspected that the ill-fitting brown suit he wore was a castoff from someone else.

"My dad taught me a lot," Mickey began in a quavering voice. "He taught me about logging, and how to work in the woods. I'm proud of that. I'm proud to be a logger, too, like he was. Not everybody gets to be a logger these days, with all the tree-huggers and nature lovers and the rest of those crazy people out there making trouble."

Mickey's voice had gained strength and momentum as he rode his sawhorse from the pulpit. I saw several people nod their heads in agreement, and at least a couple of voices mutter, "Damn straight" and "Right on."

"My dad taught me other stuff, too," Mickey went on. "He taught me about the old country, about how bad the Irish got treated by the English, and how everybody starved during the potato famine. My dad said all those hard times made the Irish tough. We could stand up to anybody. We don't have to take second place to nobody else in the world."

If there'd been a Hartquist among the mourners, Mickey's blue eyes would have pierced flesh. As it was, the morning sun slanted through the stained glass windows and the last of the O'Neill males seemed bathed in a beatific glow.

Of course, it would have helped if he'd had better grammar, I thought, then winced. I was in church, at a funeral, about to receive the grace of the Holy Eucharist. Maybe there was something good in Mickey's recollections, even if his father had been a disreputable man and the son was a potential loser. I despised myself for letting my mind wander, especially to uncharitable thoughts. But then it often did. I prayed for forgiveness. As I concluded my prayer, Mickey was also coming to a conclusion.

"So thanks, Dad, for all you taught me. I wasn't an easy to kid to bring up, like you always said, but I learned something all the same. I'm proud to be Irish and glad I'm your son."

His voice broke on the last phrase, and he put a hand to his eyes as he stepped down from the pulpit. A handful of people in the congregation, most of whom I didn't recognize, shared their remembrances of the O'Neill brothers. These memories consisted mostly of getting wiped out at the Icicle Creek Tavern or smashing heads at Mugs Ahoy. In retrospect, it sounded like a lot of fun. In reality, a couple of people had landed in the hospital, and at least two of the O'Neills had spent the night in jail.

After the service had concluded, I stayed at the rear of the church, waiting for Vida. But, as usual, she was being waylaid by various persons. The caskets had been rolled outside, so I joined the other departing mourners. Three hearses, which I hadn't noticed on my way in, awaited the bodies.

"Al had to borrow a hearse from Sultan and one from Monroe," said Roseanna Bayard, Buddy's wife.

"Al's busy these days," I remarked. "Tomorrow is the Nyquist funeral."

"We'll be busy, too, developing all these photos for you," Roseanna said, as Dan Peebles gave directions to the pallbearers. "Is Vida taking the pictures for both services?"

Watching the first coffin being placed inside the hearse from Driggers Funeral Home, I nodded. "Scott's got his hands full with the upcoming summer solstice preparations, the high school and college graduations, and all the usual end-of-year school stuff. We should have a big issue Wednesday. I hope the advertising can support it."

"You worry too much, Emma." Roseanna gave me her slightly gap-toothed smile, then gestured off to her left. "Or is he the problem?"

I looked in the direction Roseanna had indicated. Spencer Fleetwood was interviewing Mickey O'Neill. "You know darned well he's the problem," I said. "By the way, I appreciate the fact that you and Buddy haven't advertised with him so far."

Roseanna shrugged her plump shoulders. "We don't

need to. Besides, he doesn't give us any business like you do."

"I don't know how he keeps afloat," I said as the Driggers hearse pulled slowly away from the church. "He must have money somewhere in his background."

"You interviewed him for the paper when he got here," Roseanna recalled. "Did he let on about his financial status?"

I made a face. "He gave me a big line about how successful he'd been in radio over the years and how when he hit forty—fifty would be more like it—he wanted to escape the Big City and Big Network rat races. I didn't believe him, but that's as much as he'd tell me."

"Maybe he's a crook," Roseanna said. "You know, one of those radio personalities who took payola."

"Could be," I said, watching the second casket being put into the borrowed hearse from Sultan. "I suppose I could launch an investigation, but I don't have the time or the staff for that."

As Lona and Meara O'Neill got into Al's black Cadillac limousine, Roseanna nudged me. "You heard about the change of plans?"

"What change?" I asked.

"Before Mass," Roseanna said, her voice still low, "Al Driggers announced that the O'Neills would be buried in Alpine after all. I guess the rest of the family nixed the trip to Ireland. It must cost the world to do that. None of them have that kind of money."

"You mean," I asked in surprise, "the hearses are headed for the cemetery right now?"

Roseanna nodded. "Yes. Buddy has to go along as a pallbearer, but I'm going back to the studio. I can't keep the place closed up all morning."

I couldn't afford to linger, either. As soon as the third hearse had pulled out, I got into my car and headed for the *Advocate*. I was distracted, however, and almost ran an arterial stop sign at the Icicle Creek Road and Front Street. Something was bothering me, and for once it had nothing to do with my personal life.

It was those damned weapons, and the concept of terrorists. Mickey O'Neill had bragged about being Irish. No doubt his father, as well as his uncles and grandfather, had instilled Celtic pride in the young man. Was it possible that the O'Neills had been running guns for the IRA?

The suggestion was so ludicrous that I laughed aloud behind the wheel and actually did go right through the yield sign at the pedestrian walk on Front at Fifth. Unfortunately, it was occupied; I managed to scatter Edna Mae Dalrymple, the town librarian and one of my erstwhile bridge partners, Jim Medved, the local veterinarian, and Averill Fairbanks, our resident sighter of UFOs.

"Save the Earthlings!" Averill cried as my bumper missed him by inches. "Death to Uranus!"

"Sorry!" I shouted through the window as the trio collected themselves and staggered toward safety. "I thought this was the landing pad," I added for Averill's benefit. Clinging to a light standard, he glared at me as I drove on.

Back at my desk, I asked Leo to join me. "What do you know about the IRA?" I inquired.

Leo shot me a quizzical look. "They cause trouble," he replied, sitting down in one of my visitor's chairs. "Why would I know anything about it?"

Did he sound defensive? I thought so, and said as much. "Are you a sympathizer?"

Leo laughed. "Hell, no. They're a bunch of hoodlums. The current wrecking crew is actually the Provisional Irish Republican Army. They're from the north, and broke off from the more conciliatory Dublin-based organization thirty years ago. I'll bet at this stage hardly any of them know Ireland's real history. 'Bloody Friday' is just a catchphrase, and Michael Collins is only a name."

"Mickey O'Neill said this morning that his father taught him all about Irish history," I said. "He even mentioned the potato famine."

"Potato famines," Leo corrected me. "There were two, you know. But then you're not Irish."

"No," I said, "I'm not. I'm mostly English and part German."

"Were the Germans the Catholic ancestors?" Leo asked.

I nodded. "I suppose you'd call it English whimsy, but I can't help wondering if the O'Neills had some kind of IRA ties."

Leo looked at me as if I were crazy. "The O'Neills? You're kidding."

I couldn't confide in Leo about the rocket launchers, but I could tell him my suspicions about bodies being shipped abroad to Ireland. "Doesn't that strike you as odd?"

Leo shrugged. "I thought Oscar Nyquist wanted to be buried in Norway. Does that make Oscar a Norwegian terrorist?"

"No, of course not, but—"

Leo held up a hand. "Hold it, Emma. You just said the family had changed their minds about burying the O'Neills in the old sod, right? So how do you explain that?"

I admitted that I couldn't. "But I've heard things over the years," I persisted, "about an Irish network all across the United States and Canada. You know darned well that most of the IRA's arms are shipped out of this country."

"Call them the Provisionals," Leo advised. "For Provisional Irish Republican Army. No, Alpine's never been a hotbed of pro-Irish sentiment."

"Seattle is, though," I noted. "I heard some tales when I was growing up."

Leo shrugged. "Could be. I've never lived there."

My ad manager wasn't being much help, and, to be fair, he was at a disadvantage because I couldn't mention the weapon stash. Of course, I'd told Tom, but that was different. Now that we were engaged, I felt that we two were one. It was a romantic notion to be sure, but also a novel concept. For me, anyway.

Leo wandered back to his desk while I considered my editorial for the coming edition. I'd have to do the obligatory summer solstice piece, urging Alpiners to support and enjoy their annual festival. I should expound on the recent violence between the Hartquists and the O'Neills, but meaningful ideas proved elusive. When I wasn't trying to think of reasons why Brian Conley had been murdered or how the O'Neill clan had acquired serious weaponry, I was envisioning my life with Tom. This particular Friday wasn't lending itself to creativity at the word processor.

Tom called just before noon to tell me that he'd made reservations at Le Gourmand, the French restaurant down the highway. We should celebrate, he said. Besides, he was in the mood for duck.

It crossed my mind that once he was living in Alpine, Tom might be in the mood for many things, of which few were available less than two hours away. All those years he was married to Sandra, I'd had visions of him attending the opera, the theatre, the symphony, and all sorts of Giants and Forty-niners and Warriors games. Yet I knew that as Sandra declined, he socialized very little. His contacts seemed to be all business, with little time or energy left for pleasure. Maybe he wouldn't care that Alpine's extracurricular offerings were limited to high school football, the college's faculty talent show, and the Burl Creek Thimble Club's annual Quiltathon.

Although I didn't write a meaty editorial that afternoon,

I was busy. Civic-minded locals brought in items they wanted in the summer solstice edition, Oscar Nyquist's relatives fed Vida anecdotes about the local movie impresario, and what seemed like a hundred proud parents came by to make sure we carried their offsprings' high school and college achievements.

I got stuck with some of the latter, featuring a Petersen scion who'd been chosen "Most Likely to Become a First-Class Chicken Farmer," a Pidduck lass who'd won the Miss Charm Award, and a cheerful chubster nicknamed "Meringue" who'd chomped his way through the annual pie-eating contest in the high school parking lot. By the time I'd whipped out copy on this trio, I was ready for a break. In fact, I was hungry for a piece of pie, but since it was almost four and I didn't want to spoil my gourmet dinner, I avoided the Upper Crust Bakery and marched to the sheriff's office.

Milo, however, wasn't in.

"He left town," Jack Mullins informed me, the familiar twinkle in his eyes.

"For the weekend?" I asked in surprise.

"No," Jack replied. "He went over to Everett. Strictly work-related. But I doubt he'll be back in the office this afternoon."

"What's he doing in Everett?"

Jack's expression grew furtive. "Can't say. Top secret."

Fleetingly, I considered telling Jack that I knew about the weapons cache. If I did, maybe he'd confide in me about Milo's reason for driving the fifty-odd miles to Everett on a busy June weekend. But I decided not to reveal my covert knowledge. The sheriff might get miffed.

"So what else is new?" I asked Jack. "Anything we should know before the weekend starts?"

Jack shrugged, though he avoided my gaze. "Not much. Commencement weekend, should be the usual wrecks out on the road. All those students and parents taking Highway 2 to get across the state. Pray for sun. Half those people out there don't know how to drive in the rain."

"Speaking of prayer," I said, "what did you think of the tripleheader at St. Mildred's this morning?"

Jack shrugged again. "Kind of a letdown, in a way. But I heard the reception in the church hall was semiwild. It went on until about two-thirty, when Father Den and Jake O'Toole started throwing people out. The last I heard—I'll bet it won't really be the last—the heavy drinkers took off for Mugs Ahoy."

I wasn't surprised. "The taverns and bars should be busy even without the mourners. I understand there aren't any vacancies at the motels and the ski lodge. Many of the parents, mainly of the college kids, have come for the weekend."

"Not to mention Oscar Nyquist's relations," Jack noted. "Some of those Norwegians can outdrink the Irish."

"Have you got extra men on patrol tonight?"

Jack nodded. "Three deputies. Not to mention the emergency personnel on standby. Hell, all the bars have hired extra help, too."

Toni Andreas looked up from her phone console. "Emma, there's a call for you. Do you mind?"

"No," I said, a bit surprised. "Where shall I pick it up?"

Jack pointed to the phone on the other side of the counter. "Can you grab that?"

I took the receiver and said hello. Mae Conley's tearful voice was on the other end of the line. I could barely make out what she was saying:

"Mrs. Lord? I have some awful news."

"About what?" I asked, giving Jack a puzzled glance.

"About Brian." Mrs. Conley paused, sniffled, and

coughed twice. "Excuse me, I'm so upset. Anyway, the airline people found Brian's casket."

It was my turn to pause. "They did? Why is that awful news?"

"Because," Mrs. Conley replied, and now her voice grew stronger, "Brian wasn't in it."

Chapter Twelve

I WASN'T SURE I'd heard correctly. "Did you say Brian was not in the coffin?"

"Yes, that's what I said." Mae Conley now sounded faintly impatient with me. "The coffin was empty."

"I don't understand," I said, grabbing a memo pad and a pen from beside the telephone. "Where was the casket found?"

"At JFK in New York," Mrs. Conley said. "It was in a storage area where it shouldn't have been. My husband and I are going to sue."

I'd hastily scribbled the information about Brian's missing body on a sheet of memo paper and I handed it to Jack Mullins. "Sue? Who would you sue?" I asked, still dismayed.

"Whoever is responsible," Mrs. Conley declared, sorrow and impatience giving way to wrath. "This is an outrage! I suppose we should start with the funeral home in Alpine."

Jack was rolling his eyes. "I'm at the sheriff's office, right now," I said. "I'll let them know what's happened. Is there any possibility of a mistake?"

"Certainly not," she snapped. "Brian was either in the coffin or he wasn't. And he wasn't."

"Have you contacted the police?"

"That's who found the casket in the first place," Mrs.

Conley replied. "My husband had called the authorities in charge of the airport. As usual, the police are baffled."

"I'm terribly sorry," I said, while visions of body snatchers danced through my head. "Is there anything I can do at this end?"

"It seems to me you people in Alpine have done enough already," Mae retorted. "I knew we should have had Gina's funeral home in Seattle handle this. I've been in touch with Brian's coworker at the Irish Consulate, Nolan Curry. Such a kind young man, and such a good friend of Brian's. Helpful, unlike some people," she added with a touch of spite. "Meantime, we'll be in touch with Mr. Driggers or Mr. Peebles, but if you see them, you tell them that we're serious about taking them to court. The airline, too, if we have to, and the cargo people at JFK. This is a disgrace. Where is my poor boy?"

Mrs. Conley's voice broke again, just before she banged the phone down in my ear. Jack was looking bemused. Toni appeared stupefied.

"How," she asked, "could anyone lose a dead body?"

"Good question," Jack said. "But that's New York for you. Maybe poor Conley's in the East River. Isn't that where they put bodies in New York? At least we know what to do with a corpse here in Alpine. We bury it. But in New York, nobody cares about anybody else, nobody knows anything, nobody wants to get involved. Thank God I've never been east of the Idaho state line."

"It's pretty weird, I'll admit," I put in, "but the body could have been removed before it ever left Sea-Tac."

Jack shrugged. "I suppose. Wait till Dodge hears this. He'll pitch a five-star fit. The Conleys may want to sue the county, too."

I kept my own counsel, but I didn't have a great deal of sympathy for Milo. He'd treated the Conley murder as a side issue, insoluble and anonymous. Brian Conley was a stranger; the O'Neills and Hartquists were native sons. While typical of Alpiners, the sheriff's attitude was annoying.

On my way home from work, I swung by Driggers Funeral Home. Dan Peebles met me on tiptoe at the door. I always wondered why undertakers walked so softly. Surely they couldn't be afraid of waking the dead.

"Dan," I said, putting out my hand, "I'm Emma Lord. We haven't officially met until now."

Dan's handshake was firm, though his skin was soft. "Yes, I've seen you around town. You're the newspaper lady, aren't you?"

It was better than being the garbage girl or the waffle woman, I supposed. "I have, in fact, some unsettling news for you and Al," I said. "Is he still around?"

Dan's earnest, round face showed regret. "He's not available right now. He's speaking with some of Oscar Nyquist's relatives from out of town."

We stood in the plush-carpeted foyer. The floor, the walls, the ceiling were all a soft beige. The color was intended to soothe, but it reminded me of human flesh. Imagination can be a frightening thing.

I explained what Mae Conley had told me over the phone. Only the flicker in Dan's blue eyes indicated mild interest. Or perhaps it was discreet alarm.

"That's not our fault," he said staunchly. "The deceased was definitely in that casket. I sealed it myself and drove it into the airport at Sea-Tac."

"Can you prove it in case the Conleys sue you?" I asked.

He blanched. "Well . . . no. That is, once the casket is sealed here, no one opens it until it reaches the funeral director at its final destination."

Final in more ways than one, I thought. "Have you ever heard of such a thing happening before?"

"Well . . ." Dan looked around, as if he expected

somebody to march forward with a Typical Example. "Not firsthand. There are some stories—old ones, I think—about smugglers using caskets to transport all sorts of things, including drugs. But I don't know of specific cases."

I started backing toward the door. "You'll tell Al, of course."

Dan looked offended. "Of course."

Feeling a bit sorry for having upset the young man, I gave him a sympathetic smile. "I'm sure there's some logical explanation."

"Yes," Dan Peebles replied. But he didn't look convinced.

That evening, I relayed all of the day's mysterious adventures to Tom at Le Gourmand. He, however, seemed more interested in truffles and goose liver pâté.

"Dodge is probably right," Tom remarked, signaling the waiter for another glass of a French wine I'd never heard of. "I was here while the search for Conley was going on, remember? The weather was pretty bad, at least at the higher elevations. Which, I assume, is where your weird woodsmen hang out."

"True," I allowed, "but it seems too pat. I mean, with Brian's body disappearing, it strikes me as more complicated than just some nutty recluse ridding himself of an intruder."

"I don't see any connection," Tom said, consulting the menu once again. "Milo probably won't, either. Shall we try the Atlantic scallops in a flaky crust?"

"Sure." I backed off from discussing the Conley investigation. Tom wanted to celebrate, not cerebrate. I hardly blamed him. We were engaged at last. We deserved to put the rest of the world aside for a while.

Before leaving for Le Gourmand, we had called Adam. He was elated at our news. In fact, he had been downright incredulous.

"I was beginning to think it'd never happen," he declared joyfully.

Then Tom had asked if Adam would marry us in the spring. Our son hadn't been able to respond at first. I couldn't recall when Adam had been so overcome with emotion. Maybe it was sixteen years ago when the ten-speed I'd given him for Christmas got stolen on New Year's Eve.

So we spoke of Adam and of our future and of all the things we hadn't dared to mention while our lives were teetering on the balance beam. It was a lovely evening, and it only got better after we returned home.

On Saturday, Tom was still in his handyman mode. After breakfast he started pruning every bush, shrub, tree, and vine that he could reach. By noon, I barely recognized my yard. In fact, there was much more of it, especially out back.

I was admiring his accomplishments when the phone rang. Hurrying into the house, where I'd left the receiver on the kitchen counter, I caught the call just before it trunked over to my answering machine.

"Emma." Vida sounded grave. "I'm calling from the office at Faith Lutheran."

"Yes? Is Oscar's funeral over?"

"Just," Vida replied, her voice muffled. I suspected she was shielding the mouthpiece with her gloved hand. "Emma, I must see you. I'm only going to stay for a short time at the luncheon reception here at the church. I'll take some pictures and then, if I may, I'd like to stop by your house."

It wasn't like Vida to be so mysterious. "Sure," I said. "You're . . . all right, aren't you?"

"In a way," Vida replied cautiously. "Here come a clutch of Gustavsons. I must dash."

By the time I went back outside, Tom was talking to

the Marsdens. They were my nice neighbors; the family on the other side had never been friendly and their kids were noisy pests.

"I'm going to borrow the Marsdens' pickup and haul this yard stuff to the dump," Tom called to me as I waved in my most affable manner. "Where is the dump?"

Viv Marsden gave Tom directions while Val offered to help load the pickup. Apparently Viv's directions were confusing. Her husband broke in while she pointed this way and that.

"Hell, Viv," said Val, "I'll ride with Mr. Cavanaugh. Hell, I'll drive."

"You don't need to," Tom began. "And please call me Tom."

"Sure, Tom, come on," Val said, leaping the three-foot split rail fence between our properties. "Let's get cracking."

I shrugged, smiled at Viv, and went back inside. Tom seemed to be fitting in with his surroundings. Maybe he'd join the Kiwanis or the Rotary Club or the Knights of Columbus. I pictured him running for city council, organizing a drive for the library, volunteering for the United Way of Skykomish County. I smiled again when Tom and Val drove off to the dump some twenty minutes later. They had no sooner departed than Vida arrived. Coming up the front walk, she looked furtive and darted glances in every direction.

"What's wrong?" I asked as she entered the house.

Vida collapsed into one of the armchairs. "Oh, my! Such a time!"

"The funeral?" I inquired, perching on the arm of the sofa.

Vida shook her head, which was adorned with a simple black straw. "No, that was fine. It's not—" She stopped and looked me in the eye. "Would it be terribly cheeky of me to ask for a cup of hot tea?"

"Of course not," I said, getting up again. "If you're in a hurry, I'll microwave it."

"That's good," Vida said, though she usually made quite a production out of tea-brewing. "I'll wait here."

I fixed us mugs of English Breakfast tea, zapped them for ninety seconds, and loaded Vida's with cream and sugar. "Here," I said, handing her the mug before I sat down on the sofa. "Now tell me what's got you in such a dither."

"Oh, Emma." She shook her head several times. "I don't know what to do."

"About what?" I asked, growing more mystified by the second. I'd never seen Vida in such a state.

She took a big sip of tea, followed by a deep breath. "It's Roger. He has Brian Conley's snowboard."

It took a few seconds for me to comprehend what Vida had said. "Brian Conley's snowboard. The item that wasn't found with him. Do you know how Roger happened to get hold of it?"

Vida lifted her chin and gazed at me with steadfast gray eyes. "No."

"Did you ask him?" It was a foolish question on my part. Even with Roger, Vida wouldn't be reluctant to ask.

"Yes," she replied, her lips stiff. "He said he found it, period. He wouldn't say when or where. Indeed, he behaves as if it were some time ago, that he's had it all along."

"I assume you've impressed on him that this is very important," I said, "since the snowboard is part of a homicide investigation."

Vida yanked off the straw hat and glared at me. "Certainly I told him! Do you think I'm a silly old fool? But you know what teenagers are like, especially boys. They don't trust adults, they keep things to themselves, they're borderline antisocial."

It was the nearest I'd ever heard Vida come to criticizing Roger. But she was right. Even Adam had gone through a silent period at about Roger's age.

"So what are you going to do about it?" I asked. "You'll have to tell Milo."

Vida grimaced. "That's what makes it so difficult. I do not want the sheriff browbeating poor Roger. Think how it might scar him emotionally! I don't want the poor boy to spend the rest of his life in fear of the authorities."

I'd also figured that's exactly what would happen to Roger anyway, and with good reason. But I couldn't say so to Vida. Indeed, some of my greatest fantasies involving her grandson had come into focus. Alas, I'd hoped for a more disturbing fate, such as Roger in a striped prison suit, an iron ball shackled to his chubby leg, a round paper hat on his head. And all the while being forced to drink Milo's miserable coffee.

Nonetheless, I regarded Vida with compassion. "Milo will have to know. What do you think, Vida? How long has Roger had the snowboard?"

"I've no idea," she admitted. "Last night I went out in the garden after supper. There's so much weeding and cutting-back to do this time of year. Alongside the fence between the driveway and the house, I saw an object stuck behind the tulips and daffodils. I hadn't noticed it before, perhaps because the bulbs have been in full bloom until the past few days. At first, I didn't know what it was. It looked like a very odd ski." Vida's expression was one of chagrin. "Ernest's father, Rufus Runkel, may have helped start the ski lodge, but I must confess, I've never been an outdoor sportswoman. I removed the thing and kept on working. It was almost dark when I went back inside the house, and I'd become so engrossed in what I was doing—yard work is endless, you know—that I forgot about the object until this morning when I started out for Oscar's funeral. I'd left it lying against the house, you see, and I took another look before I went to the car. This time I noticed that there was a name etched on it. Brian Conley's."

As Vida related her story, I kept moving closer and closer to the edge of the sofa. Aware that I was about to fall on the floor, I scooted back. "What did you do then?" I inquired, breathless.

"I went into the house and woke Roger up. He likes to sleep in, especially on Saturdays." She paused to smile fondly. "I asked if he knew what the object was. Now remember, he was barely awake and not entirely coherent. He finally mumbled that it was a snowboard. I thought as much, since it bore Brian's name, but I wanted to be sure. I asked Roger if he knew where it came from. At first, he buried his head in the pillow—so difficult for youngsters to wake up when they're still growing—but finally he said he'd found it. I pressed him a bit, but he just got cranky and said he didn't remember where or when. Naturally, I'll question him again when I get home, assuming he's up by now."

Since it was one-thirty in the afternoon, I certainly hoped Roger might have hauled his sorry butt out of bed. "He must remember," I pointed out. "Snowboards are expensive. Roger wouldn't forget finding something like that."

Vida didn't comment directly. "It's Milo I'm concerned about. But you're right—he'll have to know, won't he?"

"You of all people know that, Vida."

With effort, she got to her feet. "I dread it, though. Poor Roger. But it's necessary, particularly since Brian Conley's body seems to have disappeared."

I nodded again. "His poor parents need all the help they can get."

As Vida tromped to the door, straw hat in hand and shoulders uncharacteristically slumped, I felt sorry for her. She might be blind when it came to Roger's faults, but I'd never held it against her.

"Have you mentioned this to Buck?" I asked as we reached the porch.

Vida shook her head. "I haven't seen much of Buck this week, what with Roger staying at my house. So awkward, you know."

"Yes, of course."

Vida's eyes suddenly narrowed. "Where's Tommy?"

"At the dump."

"Oh." She stared at me for another long moment. "What's happening with you two? You seem . . . different since he returned."

I feigned surprise. "I'll bring you up to date. In fact, if Roger's parents get in early enough tomorrow, would you and Buck like to come to dinner?"

Vida tipped her head to one side. "Yes, I think that would be nice. I'll let you know as soon as I can. My daughter Amy should call from Sea-Tac when their flight arrives from Hawaii."

"Good," I said.

Vida, however, wasn't about to let my evasion pass by. "You do have news," she declared.

"We'll let you know tomorrow," I said.

It was a measure of Vida's concern for Roger that she surrendered without further probing. It was probably a measure of my devotion to Tom that I didn't tag along to help make Roger talk.

Tom, however, laughed at Vida's conundrum. "It's the first time she's had to make a moral decision about Roger, I'll bet," he said when he returned from the dump and was drinking a glass of red wine at the kitchen table. "Besides, the kid undoubtedly found the snowboard someplace where it had been chucked by somebody else who found it up on the mountain where Brian was lost."

"Probably," I agreed, opening a Pepsi. "Oh, it's not

that Vida thinks Roger was involved. She just doesn't want Milo to give him a bad time."

"I gather," Tom said with an amused look, "that Dodge isn't any fonder of Roger than you are."

"That's right," I said. "Roger is not terribly popular around here with the adult community."

Refreshed, Tom returned to yard duty. Surveying the increasing number of bare spots in the yard, I drove the Lexus to Mountain View Gardens across from the mall. It seemed as if everyone in town had gone garden-crazy. Roseanna Bayard was pushing a trolley filled with begonias and impatiens; Harvey and Darlene Adcock were discussing the merits of various rock garden plants; the Reverend Poole and his wife were picking out marigolds and petunias.

I selected flats of snapdragons, cosmos, dwarf dahlias, and several varieties of daylily. Shoving my trolley up to the counter, I recognized Tara Peebles.

"We've met," I said with a friendly smile. "Sort of, anyway. I'm Emma Lord."

I could see her heavy-lidded hazel eyes look me up and down. The Ex-Squeeze. The One Who Got Away. The Potential Rival.

"That's right," Tara said with a smile almost as friendly as mine. "You run the newspaper."

Tactful, very tactful. I nodded. "I heard you worked part-time at the nursery." Then, boldly, I added, "Milo says you have a green thumb."

Tara laughed, a musical sound. "I love flowers and I like to garden. But believe me, I have my failures just like most people. In fact, I'm still getting used to how short the growing season is at this altitude."

As she spoke, I was sizing her up. Of course. Tara was tall, very slim, sharp-featured, with silver-streaked dark hair. Attractive, I supposed, in a no-nonsense kind of way.

"Everything blooms late in Alpine," I said, "and the first frost can hit in September. But tubers and bulbs winter surprisingly well unless it gets unusually cold for long periods of time." Thus I babbled, while I wondered what Milo saw in her compared to me. At least I had a noticeable bosom.

"So I've learned," Tara responded with a glint of amusement in her eyes. "You've made some good choices, I see."

I'd seen those eyes look beyond and realized that a line was forming. I paid for my purchases, gave Tara another friendly smile, and hauled my flora out to the car. She was sharp in mind as well as features, I decided, and had a sense of humor. Maybe she, too, liked baseball.

I didn't hear from Vida until almost five o'clock that afternoon. When she called, she was steaming.

"Honestly," she declared in her most exasperated tone, "having raised children of his own, you'd think Milo would be more sympathetic. Of course, after his divorce, his wife took the children to live in Bellevue, so I suppose he doesn't have as much experience as you'd think. But still—"

"What happened?" I interrupted. "Where did Roger find the blasted snowboard?"

"Ooooh . . ." I could picture Vida rubbing fiercely at her eyes. "At the O'Neill place. It was right there, all along, in the front yard. If Milo and his idiot deputies—and that includes my nephew Billy—had actually looked for things instead of acting just like men and having whatever it was right under their noses, they would have found it themselves. The snowboard was in a bit of a hole, but it was there just the same."

I recalled stepping in a depression when Scott and I were at the O'Neill house. I'd figured it was a gopher hole. Maybe I would have found the snowboard if I hadn't been more concerned about falling down and embarrassing myself in front of Scott.

"So," I said, keeping an eye on Tom through the kitchen window, "nobody knows how the snowboard got there in the first place."

"Correct." Vida's voice had dropped a notch. "Really, you'd think Roger and his chums put it there, to hear Milo go on."

"I wonder who did," I remarked as Tom turned the soil in a newly cleared patch of earth. "The killer?"

"Well . . ." Vida finally sounded normal. "That's possible, but it's more likely that someone else found it first and tossed it aside later. They probably had no use for a snowboard."

"They cost money," I said. "Whoever found it might have sold it. On the other hand, if they saw Brian Conley's name on the board and made the connection . . . Say, you don't suppose Tim Rafferty and Tiffany Eriks found the snowboard and dumped it off at the O'Neills'?"

Vida considered. "Why?"

I admitted I didn't know. Tim had denied finding the snowboard in the first place. The only reason he might lie about it would be if he himself intended to keep it or sell it. He'd done neither one. And he and Tiffany claimed they had followed the Hartquists from the O'Neill place. There would have been no opportunity to dump the snowboard off on Second Hill.

"It probably has nothing to do with the murder itself," I finally said. "If one of the hermits killed Brian, he might have kept the snowboard, then brought it into town when he was foraging for supplies. They do have to get in touch with civilization eventually."

"Some do," Vida allowed. "There are others who don't. They live off the land. That's why they're in the mountains to begin with."

When I told Tom where the snowboard had been

found by Roger and his friends, he agreed that it was probably a coincidence. "You don't think the O'Neills—or the Hartquists—killed Brian Conley, do you?"

"I don't know what to think," I admitted. "Those two families are so crazy they could have done just about anything. Look what they did to each other."

"But they were in a long-standing feud," Tom pointed out. "Brian Conley was a stranger."

That was true. There was dinner to prepare and the rest of the weekend to enjoy. Tom would leave Monday morning, though he promised to return in a month or so. I wanted to savor my time with him. Unlike his visits in the past, this time I was looking at the future. With Tom. I smiled and took a package of prawns out of the fridge.

Sunday passed quietly. We attended Mass at St. Mildred's, where we were the cause of head-turning and whispered comments. Nor did tawdry gossip matter now. I was going to be married, and I could ignore it. I held my head high; I was soon to become Mrs. Tom Cavanaugh.

Roger's parents arrived on time, thus releasing Vida for our dinner date, and allowing her to bring Buck. Tom had met him once, very briefly. The retired air force colonel was a congenial man, big, bald and, as pilots always are, keen-eyed.

Vida, who gushed over "Tommy," deigned to accept a glass of white wine before dinner. Buck, I noticed with amusement, took his Scotch on the rocks, no water back. Tom made the announcement, proposing a toast.

"To my future bride," he said, lifting his glass.

Vida let out a shriek that could have been heard all the way down at the *Advocate* office. "I knew it, I knew it!" she cried. "Oh, Emma!" She hugged me and sloshed wine on the carpet in the process. "I was certain you were going to announce your engagement! We have to put it on the front page!"

"Hardly," I said, laughing. "It'll go just fine on your page."

But Vida vigorously shook her head. "No, no, no. You're a public figure. Tom is a very important newspaper magnate. It's definitely page one."

I didn't argue then. Buck was pumping Tom's hand and offering him a cigar. I couldn't help but stare: Vida was opposed to any kind of smoking, but especially hated cigars. I wondered if she allowed Buck to smoke inside her house.

"We have some news, too," Vida said, sitting back down and glancing at Buck, who was lighting his cigar after giving me a nod to ask permission.

I'd remained standing, about to check on the progress of my rib roast. "Oh? What is it?"

Buck, in turn, glanced at Vida. "I'm going to move to Alpine," he said. "I'm too far down the highway where I am now. Oh, it's fine this time of year, but in the winter, driving can be treacherous."

Vida's forehead was wrinkled in a frown. "It won't be easy finding a nice place," she said. "We were thinking that perhaps he could buy Lona O'Neill's house if she puts it on the market."

"So Lona won't be coming back to Alpine?" I asked.

"No," Vida responded. "She and Meara like their new place in Everett. Lona has a job at the naval air station now, and Meara is going to get her GED. I gather they have too many unhappy memories of Alpine. So sad, really."

I wasn't sure if Vida meant that their memories were sad or that it was sad that the memories had forced them to leave Alpine. The latter, I suspected. A 7.5 earthquake with its epicenter under Carl Clemans's statue in Old Mill Park wouldn't force Vida to leave her beloved hometown.

The evening had passed pleasantly, however. Buck was

good company; he and Tom talked sports, but veered away from politics. I saw Tom off early Monday morning for his nine-thirty flight to San Francisco. I felt a trifle wistful until he said he might be back the following weekend. Maybe he planned to commute on a regular basis.

After the usual morning get-together with my staff, I forced myself to write a lead editorial. Guns-and-violence was too trite. Besides, if the Hartquists and O'Neills hadn't owned firearms, they would have poured boiling oil on one another or broken out the bows and arrows.

Harping on feuding families—and they were hardly the only ones in a small town like Alpine—would be useless. Feuds provided, among other things, entertainment. If you couldn't go to a professional theatre or an NBA basketball game, you might as well snipe at your relatives. Literally, in some cases.

My head was full of distractions—the Brian Conley murder, the O'Neills and Hartquists, the upcoming trial, and, most of all, Tom. I gazed lovingly at the photograph I'd placed on my desk that morning: It was a picture of Tom and me at Leavenworth two winters ago. He had asked a stranger to take it in front of one of the Bavarian-style buildings. We looked happy, even handsome, standing together by a huge stuffed teddy bear in front of a candy store. I could display the photo now with pride and optimism.

But it didn't inspire an editorial. I was still stumped when Scott Chamoud came into my office. "Let me get this straight," he said, one foot planted in my visitor's chair, the other on the slightly uneven floor. "The O'Neill story is not the lead this week?"

"I'm not sure," I hedged. "The discovery of Brian Conley's snowboard is real news, and so far, Spencer Fleetwood hasn't gotten hold of it."

"He may, though," Scott pointed out. "I mean, Sheriff Dodge can't keep it a secret from him, can he?"

I winced. "He could, but he shouldn't and he probably won't. Let's wait and see what happens."

Scott left, looking unsettled. So was I. It wouldn't do to tell him about the arms cache at the O'Neill rental until I got it cleared through Milo. Abandoning my editorial once more, I decided to go see the sheriff.

On this overcast morning, Milo was standing at the corner, looking uncertain.

"Hey!" I called, hurrying my step. "Wait up!"

"I was thinking of going to the bank," Milo replied as I joined him. "I ran out of money over the weekend."

I crossed Front Street with him, trying to match his long strides. "Did Tara Peebles force you to lavish money on her?" I asked in a teasing tone.

"No," Milo replied as we reached the sidewalk. "My pipes rusted out in the bathroom. I had to get a plumber from Sultan and pay triple time. He's still there this morning. It's a hell of a job. I'd have done it myself, but I've got too damned much on my plate at work."

I stopped at the entrance to the Bank of Alpine. "Can we run the story about the weapons cache this week?"

Milo grimaced. "Hell. I guess so. But keep a lid on it for now, okay? I'm waiting for some official information."

I was puzzled. "From who?"

Milo looked around as if he expected to be overheard. Only Crazy Eights Neffel, Alpine's unofficial loony, was chasing imaginary butterflies across the street in front of Parker's Pharmacy.

Milo looked pained. "I can't say. That's why I don't want you telling anybody about the weapons yet. You haven't, have you?"

Opting for candor, I told Milo that I had passed the information on to Tom. "But Tom knows how to keep a secret. Remember, he's a longtime newspaper person, too."

Milo shrugged, though he kept one eye on Crazy Eights, who had abandoned his butterfly net and was shinnying up a light standard. Our local nut's long, gray beard almost reached his waist, and he was dressed in logger's pants made of canvas (known as tin pants), heavy boots, and bright yellow suspenders over his union suit. One suspender strap had slipped down to his elbow, something of a fashion statement for Crazy Eights.

"You're right," Milo agreed. "Besides, Cavanaugh left town this morning, didn't he?"

"Yes," I said, "but he may be back this weekend."

The sheriff gave me his lopsided grin. "This is new territory for you."

I grinned back. "It sure is. Until now, my life has been on an uncertain course." Alone. "It may take some getting used to. Right now, I'm still riding a cloud of euphoria."

An older-model Chrysler sedan had stopped at the intersection to let a couple of elderly ladies cross the street. Crazy Eights was also coming our way. But he walked directly toward the car, opened the back door, crawled through the backseat, and came out on the other side. The driver, who looked vaguely familiar, cursed and started to roll down his window. Then he recognized Crazy Eights, shrugged, and drove off.

"You forgot your net," Milo called to Crazy Eights, who was on the opposite corner. "It's on the other side of Front, in that concrete sidewalk planter."

"I don't need it," Crazy Eights called back. "There aren't any butterflies around here. Any damned fool should know that." Pityingly, he shook his head and continued on up the hill.

"What about Roger's find?" I asked the sheriff. "Where do you think that snowboard came from?"

If Milo had looked pained a few moments ago, now he appeared downright miserable. "What do you think?"

"I'm asking you."

Milo stepped aside as a woman pushing a stroller exited from the bank. He tipped his regulation hat at her and grimaced at me. "I have to wonder—did the O'Neills kill Brian Conley?"

The thought had briefly crossed my mind. It made some sense. Presumably, Brian had the snowboard with him when he was murdered. Ergo, the O'Neills had stabbed the young man and stolen his snowboard. Then, either not knowing how to use it, or not giving a damn, they had chucked it with the rest of their junk in the front yard of their ramshackle house on Second Hill. It was a logical solution to a thorny problem.

Still, it was unlike Milo to jump to conclusions. "How did you deduce this?" I inquired.

"I was awake half the night," Milo replied. "Mainly, I was worrying about how much the new plumbing was going to cost. But then I got to thinking about Roger and the snowboard. Vida's so damned protective of that kid, and it took about half an hour to get the story out of him. He's not exactly talkative, at least not with adults."

"She thought he'd be scared," I said with a droll expression.

"He wasn't," Milo retorted. "He was kind of surly. But then he's at that age . . . Anyway, along about four in the morning while I was wondering if the shower would work, I had a thought. Maybe it wasn't a coincidence that the snowboard was found on the O'Neill property. You know me, I'm not too keen on coincidences. So the logical explanation was that they put it there. The next question was how did they get hold of it." Milo lifted his hands. "Bingo. Maybe they took it off of Brian Conley. He was probably dead when they did it, which doesn't mean they killed him. But the body was tucked under that ledge. If the killer didn't take the snowboard, then where did it go? My money's on the O'Neills, but we'll never know for sure."

"You keep using the plural for them," I pointed out. "Why not just one O'Neill? I mean, it would appear that there was only one assailant, two stab wounds notwithstanding."

Milo looked skyward where the morning clouds were starting break away. "That's what I mean. We'll never know."

Chapter Thirteen

"WHAT WERE THE O'Neills doing up on Tonga Ridge?" I asked Vida after explaining Milo's theory. "They weren't exactly athletes."

"They fished and hunted," Vida said between sips of hot water.

"But this was the tail end of winter," I countered. "The fishing and hunting seasons weren't over, except for steelhead, and they wouldn't climb up the ridge to fish there."

"True," Vida allowed. "They would fish the Sky or Martin or Beckler Creek. The streams closer to Alpine and the highway." She paused, looking thoughtful. "Still, it makes some queer kind of sense. The O'Neills probably paid no attention to the state regulations regarding seasonal restrictions. They might have been at one of the lakes."

"The lakes up there would have been frozen over." I posed another question. "Motive, then?"

"Orneriness," Vida said. "Wretched people like the O'Neills don't need a motive for violence. Too much liquor or the misinterpretation of a phrase or action can set them off. They're animals."

We were interrupted by the arrival of Scott Chamoud, who wore a big, beautiful grin on his handsome face. "Got a Scene item for you. Mrs. R. and I ran into Grace Grundle on my way to take some summer solstice float pictures. She was going to file a complaint with the sheriff."

"Grace!" Vida spat out the name. "That woman is so addled. What is it now? Something to do with her cat, Doozle?"

"I thought it was Foozle," I put in.

Vida glared at me. "You know better, Emma. What's bothering Grace now?"

"Fumes," Scott replied. "The other night she let Doozle out and there was an odd smell in the air—a stench, Grace called it. Anyway, Doozle got sick after that and she's had to take him to Dr. Medved twice since then."

"Grace and her silly cats," Vida huffed. "It serves her right. I wouldn't give those animals house room, let alone put out money for them." Vida frowned at Scott. "A stench? What kind of stench?"

Scott shrugged. "It was probably from the sawmill. You'd think the cats around here would be used to that smell. It took me a while, but I don't mind it anymore. It only gets bad on certain days and depending on which way the wind is blowing."

"Cats are very stupid animals," Vida asserted. "I'll use the item, however. And bear in mind, Scott, that sawmills can produce some wonderful odors as well. What's lovelier than the smoke from burning wood chips and sawdust?"

"True," Scott said with another grin for Vida, who suddenly wore a peculiar expression. "That's a good smell. Maybe I'll do a feature one of these days about the smells in a logging town. 'Aromas of Alpine.' What do you think, Emma?"

"Not bad," I said, noting that whatever had been bothering Vida seemed to have passed. She was going through her in-basket and seemed unruffled. "How did the float pictures turn out?" I asked my reporter.

Scott winced. "The Old Timers had some bad luck.

Ellsworth Overholt fell off the float and may have broken his kneecap. One of the big logging rigs got a flat. The Miss Alpine float caught fire. I should have some good shots of that."

"Caught fire?" I echoed. "I didn't hear any sirens this morning. What happened?"

"Somebody lighted a cigarette that set off the streamers from the summer solstice pole. They put it out right away, so they didn't call the fire department. But I was able to get some pictures of the guys flailing away with their jackets."

I had to ask: "What about the Mr. Pig float?"

Scott was grinning again. "Ed's not quite ready for prime time. He wants me to come back this afternoon. For one thing, his pig suit isn't finished."

"He needs a suit?" I retorted.

"Ed!" Vida tossed her pencil across the desk. "Such a ninny. Does he really have to disport himself in the parade?"

"Of course," I replied as a harried-looking Al Driggers came through the door.

"Who died?" Vida demanded.

"Nobody," Al groaned. "It's that Mrs. Conley in Penn Yan. She says we lost her son's body."

"Did you?" Vida asked in a stern voice.

"Of course not." Al scowled at Vida. "Have we ever lost a body in seventy years of the Driggers Funeral Home's existence?"

Vida scowled back. "I do recall an incident in forty-nine with DeForest Vance."

Al's pale face took on a spot of color. "Before my time," he murmured.

"Your grandfather," Vida said, retrieving her pencil and pointing it at Al. "DeForest disappeared for two days after he died."

"He was in the wrong compartment," Al asserted.

"My grandfather's eyes were failing. He thought the sign on the drawer said *vacant.*"

Vida harrumphed. "An unfortunate mistake for the rest of the Vance family. Erna Vance lost her mind after that and had to be put in a home."

"My father said Erna was always crazy," Al countered. "Mislaying her husband had nothing to do with it."

"Oh," Vida fumed, "stop it, Al. In any event, that has nothing to do with poor Brian Conley. Do you or do you not have any idea of what might have happened to his body?"

Al's narrow shoulders slumped. "No."

"At least you didn't lose Oscar Nyquist," Vida remarked. "Or did you?"

"No." Al was looking at the floor, as if he were being berated by his second-grade teacher. "We buried Oscar here in Alpine, you know."

"Yes." Vida gave a single nod. "Despite his wish to be buried in Norway."

Al gave a faint nod.

"The family didn't want Oscar to have his way," Vida said. "He usually did. They got back at him, in the end."

Al gave another nod.

"So are the Conleys actually going to sue you?" Vida queried.

Al sighed. "They're threatening to. I don't blame them in a way. It's a terrible thing. But it's not our fault. The . . . mix-up must have occurred at one of the airports, either Sea-Tac or JFK. I've got the Port of Seattle police checking on it at this end, and the Conleys have whoever is in charge of the airport in New York. I'm also in touch with a young man named Nolan Curry at the Irish consulate. He not only worked with Brian but was a close friend. Nolan agrees that it's a real mystery, but that doesn't help me much."

"Body snatchers?" Scott suggested. "That is, people who steal bodies for organ harvesting?"

"No," I said. "They can only do that right after a person dies. Brian had been dead for months."

"That's right," Al agreed, turning to face me. "The reason I came here is because Mrs. Conley said she'd told you she was going to sue. You don't have to put that in the paper, do you, Emma?"

"Not until they actually file a suit," I said, hoping to soothe Al.

He remained glum. "I feel as if the family business is going to be ruined by this horrible incident. Which, as God only knows, isn't our fault."

Vida's expression had softened, no doubt at the thought that a local enterprise could go under because of unexpected forces from the distant east. "You trust that young man you hired?"

"Dan Peebles?" Al looked offended. "Certainly. He had an excellent résumé."

"Curious," Vida murmured.

"What's curious?" Al appeared to be on the defensive.

Vida shrugged. "Being a funeral director. Now, now," she went on, seeing Al bristle, "I don't mean you. Your father and your grandfather were in the business. It was only natural that you should go into it, too. I realize it can be a prosperous enterprise—certainly you never run out of clients—but still, it strikes me as odd."

"It's a service," Al declared, squaring his shoulders. "A much-needed one, I might add. Not to mention the compassion and comfort we can offer to the survivors. A sensitive young man like Dan finds that very appealing. Unlike his brother, he was certainly not cut out for the military."

I was about to make a tactful exit from this seemingly endless discussion when Leo breezed into the office.

"Greetings, all," he said in a rush. "Damn these advertisers! They change their minds every time we have a big issue to fill. I've got to redo half the special section. Whoever told Clancy Barton he knew how to lay out an ad?"

The owner of Barton's Bootery was famous for changing his mind and offering his own not-so-bright ideas. "Good luck," I said to Leo, and with a wave retreated into my cubbyhole. I still had an editorial to write.

Alas, it was an editorial that simply wasn't forming in my mind. What to say about one family wiping out another? Hatred was bad, killing was bad, lack of remorse was bad, too. I could write my arms off to the elbows, but I hadn't a doubt in my mind that if the Hartquists had to do it all over again, they would.

So absorbed in thought was I that the arrival of Tim Rafferty made me jump.

"Hi," he said in a diffident voice. "I hear you've been trying to talk to me."

"For several days," I said, regaining my composure. "Have a seat. What's new with KSKY?"

Tim's sharp, not unattractive features had softened after he turned thirty. There was a slight puffiness around his eyes and mouth, perhaps a result of serving himself one too many beers. Now his face became suspicious.

"Why do you want to know?" he asked.

"Because Spencer Fleetwood is the competition," I said. "Why else?"

Tim, who had sat down, leaned forward on the desk. "You mean you think he sent me here to spy on you?"

"Sure," I responded. "Why not?"

"I stopped by because Tiffany said you'd been looking for me," Tim replied, on the defensive. "Spence can do his own spying. Besides, all he has to do is count advertising inches in the paper."

"True, more or less," I allowed. "But you're right. I wanted to ask about the night you and Tiffany found

Brian Conley. By the way, did you know his body has gone missing?"

Tim's jaw dropped. "You're kidding! How could that happen?"

"Don't ask me," I said. "Ask around. Isn't that part of your job with KSKY?"

Tim shook his head. "No. That's up to Spence. I only do some of the on-air stuff. And maybe get some ads." His suspicious look returned. "How come you're telling me this?"

I shrugged. "It's probably all over town by now. There's no point in keeping it a secret. You're going to beat me on this one no matter how much I keep my mouth shut. However," I added, giving my chair a little twirl, "I'd appreciate it if you'd tell me more about your evening adventures on Tonga Ridge."

Tim raised his hands in a helpless gesture. "I've told everything already. On the air, at that. Man, there's nothing to add."

"What about the snowboard?" I wasn't going to tell Tim that it had been found. Again, the story would probably leak before we went to press, but I wouldn't tip my hand.

"The snowboard?" Tim gazed vaguely around the little room. "Heck if I know. We never saw it. Was it supposed to be there?"

"You'd think so, since Brian Conley was using it when he was killed. You're certain you never saw it when you and Tiffany found him?"

Tim looked me in the eye. "Sure. I snowboard sometimes myself. I'd have noticed. Of course," he added more slowly, "Tiff and I were pretty upset."

I let the comments pass. "What I don't get is why in the world you dumped Conley's body off at the meat locker. That's never made any sense to me."

Tim shrugged. "Panic, I guess. You ever find a dead body?"

I ignored the question. "You said that the funeral home was dark. Why didn't you simply call Al Driggers at home? Or get hold of the sheriff?"

Tim hunched his shoulders and let out a big sigh. "We should have. But like I said, we panicked. It was pretty horrible."

I decided to move on. "Okay, here's another thing that I wondered about—why did you put Brian under the O'Neills?"

Tim looked alarmed. "How do you mean?"

I assumed an air of innocence. "Maybe I'm mistaken. I thought Brian Conley was found under the other bodies."

"Yeah," Tim said hastily, "that must be it. You heard wrong. He wasn't under those other guys. Anyway, it was kind of dark in there. We only turned on one light. I think."

"Is that what you told Sheriff Dodge?"

"I can't remember now," Tim said, appearing confused. "Jeez, it was such a mess. I mean, I really panicked, big-time."

Panic seemed to be Tim Rafferty's middle name. Just to throw him off balance, I tossed out what would seem to him like a random question. "What is your middle name, Tim?"

He looked startled. "What? My middle name? Why do you want to know?"

"Just curious." I was smiling in a playful manner. "What is it?"

Tim grimaced. "It's kind of old-fashioned. I never use it. Why do you want to know so bad?"

"I don't," I responded. "It just popped into my head. You know, one of those odd segues that flit through your mind."

"Then it doesn't matter?" Tim asked. "I mean, if I don't tell you?"

"No." I shook my head. "It came under the heading of 'idle question.' Now tell me what you told the sheriff about putting Brian Conley in the meat locker."

Somewhat to my surprise, Tim relaxed, stretching his legs out to one side of the desk. "Okay, let me try to remember just what I told Dodge." He cleared his throat, more in self-importance than because of nerves, I thought. "The O'Neills were all over the place in that meat locker. Tiff and I hauled Brian in there and . . . well, this sounds crazy, but being panicked and all, we weren't thinking straight. Maybe we did sort of move the other bodies around. To make room, you know. I think Tiff thought Brian looked . . . cold, so we might've sort of arranged the O'Neills around him."

I suppressed my disbelief. I hoped, if this was the same tale that Tim had told Milo, the sheriff had felt the same. The only problem was that I could see no reason for Tim to lie. Nor could I see any reason why he and Tiffany would have taken the time and trouble to "arrange" the bodies in the meat locker. It simply didn't make sense.

I surrendered for the time being. Even if I got Tim to make some kind of revelation on this Monday morning, I wouldn't have an exclusive. As an employee of KSKY, Tim would feel obligated to rush out and tell Spencer Fleetwood whatever he had told me.

"Thanks, Tim," I said. "I just wanted to clear up a couple of points for this week's edition."

"No problem." He got to his feet. "How are you doing with the Conley story?"

I shrugged. "So-so. It's a pretty cold trail, if you'll excuse the pun."

"I guess." Tim made an effort to look pensive, which didn't much suit him. "Spence figures it's one of those unsolved mysteries."

"Yes," I said. "Probably."

Tim Rafferty went on his way. As soon as I was sure he was gone, I called Scott into the office. "I hate to bother you on a trifling matter, but have you gone on your rounds at the courthouse yet?"

"I was just headed that way," Scott replied.

"Do me a favor," I said, feeling a bit silly. "If you have time, that is. Look up Tim Rafferty's birth certificate and find out his middle name."

Scott broke into a grin. "Sleuthing, Ms. Lord?"

"Not really," I answered truthfully. "But Tim wouldn't tell me what his middle name was just now, so it must be something gruesome. If he hadn't been so secretive, I wouldn't give a hoot."

"Will do," Tim responded. "Maybe it's a girlie name." He started to turn around, then swiveled on his heel. "Hey—congratulations. I hear you're getting married."

I beamed at Scott. "Yes, and you'll be invited. Start saving for a lavish gift."

"I'll do that."

This time as he turned to leave, Vida was blocking the door. Scott excused himself and went on his way.

"I've an idea," Vida announced. "I want to do a feature for my page on Lona O'Neill and the other women in the clan. What do you think?"

"What's the hook?"

"Grief." Vida pursed her lips. "Pain. Not merely for the deaths of a husband and two kinsmen, but for what went before. The difficult years, so to speak."

"It sounds a little touchy," I said.

Vida bridled at the comment. "You don't think I could handle it?"

"Of course," I said, though I feared the worst of what we used to call sob sister journalism. "I'm just not sure I see the point."

"The point?" Vida looked at me as if I were the

class idiot. "The point is that this story would be the ultimate in human interest, especially for women. Abuse, estrangement, reconciliation, divorce—the whole gamut of what happens to women who fail to stand up for themselves. Making the wrong choices. Believing that love can endure anything. Three generations of terrible mistakes."

"Three?" I said.

Vida nodded. "Paddy O'Neill's wife, Bridey. Bridget, that is. She followed him over here from Ireland even though he'd run out on her when they were engaged. Still, he married her. But the union wasn't a happy one."

I thought of the faded wedding dress I'd seen in the O'Neills' basement. By the time I arrived in Alpine, Bridey had been dead for over a year and Paddy had already starting slipping into decline. I never knew the senior O'Neills as a couple. Apparently I hadn't missed much in the way of role models for holy matrimony.

I retained my doubts about Vida's proposed article. "It seems just a bit ghoulish, even voyeuristic," I said.

"Nonsense," Vida declared, then quickly turned around. "Jake! Just the person I wanted to see." She rushed into the newsroom, where Jake O'Toole was approaching Leo's desk.

As a precaution, I followed, nodding at Jake while I pretended to check the monitor on Scott's vacant desk. Vida was temporarily deferring to Leo. Evidently Jake was yet another advertiser who wanted to make last-minute changes in his Grocery Basket spread.

"Hey," Jake was saying to my ad manager, "I couldn't help it if Buzzy overordered on the strawberries. My brother's not always the most perspicacious man in town. Anyway, we can't let the berries rot, so we'll have to lower the price by twenty cents a flat."

"Okay," Leo responded, showing a patience with advertisers that always surprised me. "Is that it, now? We've already substituted cantaloupe for Crenshaws and pork shoulder for pork loin. Is it a go?"

"It's fine," Jake said, nodding several times. "Unless the porcini mushrooms don't arrive tomorrow. They can be delicate."

Leo merely nodded. "You know the deadline, Jake."

Jake did. He started to turn away, but Vida tapped him on the shoulder. "Do you have a spare minute?"

Jake gave a start. "What? Oh, Vida! Certainly. I can always spare a woman of quality like yourself precious minutes."

"Indeed," Vida said dryly, gazing at Jake over the rims of her glasses. "Can you tell me how to reach Lona O'Neill?"

Jake rubbed at his high forehead. "She departed town yesterday. I don't have her number on my person, but Betsy has it. She's home this morning, doing her domesticities."

"I'll call her," Vida said, and marched over to her desk. "Thank you, Jake."

Recognizing dismissal, Jake waved a hand and left the office. I gazed at Vida for a moment, but she didn't look up from dialing the phone. The O'Tooles' home number, like at least half of Alpine's residents, was kept in the file that was Vida's brain.

Back in my cubbyhole, I told myself that maybe her feature idea wasn't the worst thing she could write. In fact, it might inspire an idea for my editorial. The Legacy of Violence. I'd have to wait and see how Vida handled it first.

Scott returned just before noon. He poked his head through the door and grinned at me. "No wonder Tim Rafferty didn't want to tell you his middle name."

"What is it?" I inquired.

"Well, maybe it's not all that bad," Scott said, "but I wouldn't brag about it if I were him. It's Cornelius."

That rang a bell. I wondered why.

"Vida," I said as she tied the ribbons of a flowered bonnet under her chin, "where have I heard the name Cornelius lately?"

"Where indeed?" She cocked an eye at me. "Ah! That was Stubby O'Neill's given name. Meara named the baby after him. Why do you ask?"

"No reason, really. It's Tim Rafferty's middle name. He wouldn't tell what it was, so I had Scott check it in the birth records over at the courthouse. Tim must be embarrassed because it's kind of old-fashioned. Frankly, I like it."

"It has a certain dignity," Vida conceded. "Though Stubby suited him much better, especially after he lost two fingers in a logging accident."

Vida started for the door, but I called after her. "One other thing—this sounds silly, but I have to ask. Is Tim Rafferty any relation to the O'Neills? The names are both Irish."

"Heavens, no," Vida responded. "The O'Neills are—were—Irish Catholics." She paused for emphasis, as if all Irish Catholics must be as disreputable as Paddy and his sons. "Tim Rafferty's family are Protestants. Not that they attend regularly, but his parents were married in my church, First Presbyterian. Now I must dash. I'm meeting Kathleen O'Neill at the Burger Barn on her lunch hour. This afternoon I'll try to see Margaret—Peggy, that is—and I suppose I'll have to interview Lona and Meara over the phone."

Leo watched Vida sail out through the door. "That hat," he mused. "Were those real flowers once? Did the Duchess grow them out of the top of her head?"

"No," I laughed, "they're fake." I hesitated, wondering if I should join Vida and Kathleen O'Neill. Unlike Vida, I had qualms about butting in where I wasn't invited.

Scott looked up from photos he'd been studying. "Do you suppose that guys named Cornelius are called Corny?"

"Not if they're big, burly guys with bad tempers," I replied with a smile. "That's a problem Meara O'Neill's baby will have to face later on. Maybe she'll give him a nickname. His initials, for instance."

"Like if Tim used initials, he'd be T. C.," Scott remarked.

"Like that," I said heading back into my cubbyhole. "Except Tim's a good nickname in itself."

My phone rang before I could sit down. I snatched up the receiver, banged into the desk, and half-fell into my chair. "Hel-*lo*?" I yipped at my caller.

"Hel-*lo*, yourself, Sluggly," said my brother Ben. "Did an irate reader just shoot you?"

"Oh, Stench," I cried, using his childhood nickname in exchange. At least neither of us was Corny. "I sort of crashed and burned getting back into my office. What's up?"

"My ire," Ben said, his crackling voice dropping a notch. "What's with you? Have you forgotten I exist just because I'm a man of the cloth?"

"What do you mean?" I asked, frowning.

"What do you think I mean, you little twit. I had to find out about your impending marriage from my nephew. Damn it, Sluggly, why didn't you call me?"

I clapped a hand to my head. "Oh, Ben! I'm so sorry! I was going to call you tonight. So much went on this weekend, and not just with Tom and me. We've got a big story—"

"I don't give a rat's ass about your big story," Ben growled. "Unless it's the one about your wedding. You wait almost thirty years to get married, and then you can't let your only brother know? I'm plenty pissed."

Ben wasn't kidding, and I felt terrible for putting off the phone call. "I don't know what to say. Tom didn't leave until this morning, and I had to start work on my—"

"Don't try to apologize," he said, still angry. "In time, I will forgive you, as my Christian faith dictates. But right now I'd like to strangle you until you turn penitential purple."

"I don't blame you." There was nothing more to say.

"Okay." Ben sounded as if he were getting control of his emotions. "I offer you prayers and congratulations. In fact, I'll say a Mass for you and Tom later this week when I don't feel like kicking your ass from Alpine to Arizona."

"Thanks."

"Are you happy?"

"Delirious. That's probably why my mind is shot." Happiness was new to me; I had to break it in, like a pair of shoes.

A faint chuckle arose from the other end of the line. "Maybe so."

"Ben—are you angry because we asked Adam to celebrate the nuptial Mass?"

"No," Ben replied. "I think it's a wonderful idea."

"The two of you could concelebrate it," I said eagerly. "We should have thought of that before."

"It's better if Adam does it alone," Ben said.

"But he might be nervous. It'll take place right after he's ordained. It'll probably be his first wedding."

"Yours, too," Ben remarked dryly.

"Let's think about it," I urged. "Tom would be happy to have you and Ben perform the ceremony. I'll speak to Adam about it."

"Slow down," Ben cautioned. "You're already running off the tracks. This is a huge change in your life. Now tell me how it came about while I contemplate why I shouldn't be mad anymore."

For the next five minutes, I regaled Ben with how Tom and I had reached a compromise concerning our future living arrangements. I was still waxing eloquent when Ginny Erlandson entered my office and placed a sheaf of bills on the desk. I waved at her, signaling that I'd get to them later. Ginny, however, gave a shake of her head and stood firm.

"Ben," I interrupted, "I may have a crisis looming. Ginny Erlandson won't go away, which means she needs me. Can I call you back tonight?"

"Only if you remember that I exist," Ben retorted. "Anyway, I have to go, too. Even a priest can have the occasional fire to put out, and I see one approaching my humble abode in the person of Ronald Twoblades."

"I'll call. I promise." I hung up and turned to look at Ginny. "What is it? These are the regular bills, right?"

"Yes, but they're due tomorrow, the fifteenth. I need you to initial them so I can get them in the mail before the one o'clock pickup. I should have done it Friday, but I got busy with other things."

"Oh," I said, leafing through the invoices. "I'll do it right now." Swiftly, I initialed the half-dozen bills and handed the sheaf back to Ginny.

"Thanks," she said. "I'm sorry I interrupted your phone call."

"Good," I replied absently, then noticed Ginny's curious expression. "I mean, that's okay, it was a personal call. My brother."

"Father Ben?" Ginny said. "He's a very nice man." She leaned forward and smiled widely. "Oh, Emma, I'm so happy for you. Everybody is, even Leo, though he probably won't admit it."

"Leo?" Come to think of it, Leo hadn't offered his congratulations. "Why not?"

Ginny shrugged, then lowered her voice. "I think he's jealous. Kip and Scott think so, too. I mean, the two of you have gone out sometimes, right?"

"It was never really a romance," I protested. "We were just friends. We still are."

"I may be wrong," Ginny said, but she gave me a knowing little smile. "Thanks for the initials."

"Sure," I said, the little bee in my brain buzzing as it had a few moments ago when I was distracted. Initials. What was it about them that bothered me? Not my own. Then whose?

T. C.—Scott had mentioned that if Tim Rafferty went by his initials, he'd be known as T. C. Where had I heard those initials before? Did it matter?

I was sure that it did, but I couldn't figure out why.

Chapter Fourteen

By three o'clock, I'd finally cranked out an adequate editorial. Somehow I managed to tie together Alpine's history, why we celebrated the summer solstice, the eternal struggle between good and evil, the timber industry, and how every community was a sum of its parts. I'd rambled a bit, made some awkward transitions, and was far too fulsome, but at least the damned thing was finished. My chances for a Pulitzer Prize would have to wait another year.

Vida hadn't returned to the office by four-thirty. I was getting worried. Surely her interviews with Kathleen and Peggy O'Neill couldn't take so long.

Visions of Vida's car plunging into the Skykomish River or Vida waylaid by random kidnappers or Vida falling down an old mine shaft were interrupted by a sight almost as fearsome. At four-forty, Ed Bronsky walked into the newsroom dressed as a pig.

Leo laughed so hard that he almost fell out of his chair; Ginny, close to hysteria, rushed for the bathroom, apparently to stave off a pants-wetting attack; Scott, who had already seen Ed in full porcine regalia, merely grinned. At that moment, Vida entered, glanced at our visitor, shook her head, and sat down without a word.

"Hab anabubby god um mebba cudda?" Ed said through his snout.

Scott's forehead creased. "Have I got the float pictures

back yet? No, Ed, Buddy Bayard said they'd be ready first thing tomorrow morning."

"Bo, bo," Ed said rather loudly, beating his hooves on his chest. "Mebba cudda. Ahm thuk."

Scott looked at me, I looked at Leo, and Leo looked at Ed.

"Sir," Leo said in formal tones, "would you please remove your head?"

Ed's head, with its little pink ears and little pink snout and big blue eyes, moved back and forth in a definite negative response. Then he turned his back—or was it his rump?—toward us and pointed to his little curly tail.

"Buh thippath thuk," he all but shouted.

Ginny, who had just emerged from the rest room, caught Ed's words. "I think," she said with a frown, "he's saying his zipper's stuck."

The pig's head nodded vigorously; Ed again pointed to his curly tail.

"The zipper's attached to the tail," Ginny said, bending down. "Let me see if I can get it loose."

Ed was beginning to pant. The afternoon had grown warm, and I suspected it was hot inside the pig suit. As pig suits go, it was very nice, all baby-bottom pink and sort of fuzzy. But then I didn't have a lot of experience for comparison.

"Hold still," Ginny ordered. "I'm trying to get it loose. Please stop waving your hooves around. And don't wiggle your tail so much. Otherwise, we'll have to find some metal cutters."

"Thath . . . wha . . . I . . . thaid," Ed gasped.

"Scott, can you help hold him still?" Ginny asked in a vexed tone.

But Scott was holding his camera. "Hey, I've got a job here, too," he said, starting to frame his shots.

"I'll help," I volunteered.

But before I could grab Ed, Ginny let out a triumphant

little yelp. "I got it!" she cried as we heard a zipping sound.

"Ooof!" Ed cried, toppling forward. "Whoa!"

Managing to brace myself against Leo's desk, I broke Ed's fall. It was no mean feat, considering that he outweighed me by at least a hundred and fifty pounds.

"Wardrobe will hear about this!" he shouted after pulling off the head. "Do they want to kill the pig that laid the golden egg?"

Vida, who had been observing all the mayhem with a jaundiced eye, finally spoke. "I thought you were a comic book character, Ed. Why do you—of all people—need a pig suit?"

Ed, whose flabby face was bathed in sweat and whose receding hair stood mostly on end, glared at Vida. "I don't. I had the producers FedEx me a pig suit for publicity purposes. I used to be in advertising, you know. And I'm not a comic character, I'm a serious pig. It's called animation."

"A quality, I might add, that you often lacked while working for the *Advocate*," Vida responded.

"C'mon, Vida," Ed said angrily as he tried to free his hands and feet from his trotters, "don't be so mean! Who else has ever put the spotlight on Alpine? You'll see, come the fall, everybody in America will be talking about the pig who came from Skykomish County."

"Some of them might even be able to pronounce Skykomish," Leo murmured. "The ones from Harvard, maybe."

Hands on hips, Vida merely looked at Ed.

"See?" Ed snarled, still struggling with his costume. "You've got no answer for that. I've got the means, the money, the whole deal. You're all just jealous."

"Emma isn't," Vida said quietly. "She's going to marry a very wealthy man."

Ed's head snapped around in my direction. "Huh?"

I couldn't help but smile. "It's true, Ed. Tom Cavanaugh and I are going to be married in the spring."

"Cavanaugh!" Ed's mouth stayed open.

"Tommy's moving to Alpine," Vida went on in that same smug tone. "It will be an adjustment for the community to have such a sophisticated resident, but in the long run Tommy should contribute more than mere money. We're all so happy for Emma."

"Gosh." Ed was gaping at me now. Then, he stumbled a bit and held out his right hoof. "Congratulations. I saw you with him in church Sunday, but I thought he was just visiting. Again. That's really great, Emma. I mean it."

Ed probably did, in his own weird way. He had a good heart, if you could find it under the puffed-up chest. I accepted his felicitations, and even allowed him to kiss my cheek.

As Kip MacDuff joined the group, the mood in the newsroom turned almost jocular. I mentioned that I should have brought champagne to celebrate. Even Vida didn't object to the suggestion. Indeed, everyone seemed full of smiles and goodwill.

Everyone, that is, except Leo.

That evening, Ben and I had a long, satisfying talk. He reminded me that I had never experienced Holy Matrimony, and that it was a sacrament, not a ceremony. I knew this, but he was right to reinforce the concept. Technically, I should attend classes on marriage with Father Kelly, but our pastor would waive his right and allow my brother to tell his sister everything she needed to know about the wedded state. Since neither of them had ever been part of it, some might find such advice unrealistic. But both were practical men, had been raised in stable families, and possessed good sense. Besides, when Ben told me not to put up my usual emotional barriers with Tom, I realized he was speaking from the heart, not the pulpit.

Tuesday meant deadlines, and I couldn't wait much longer for Milo to reveal whatever secrets he was keeping about the O'Neills and their arms cache. Unfortunately, around nine o'clock a serious accident occurred out on the highway by the Deception Falls bridge. It involved a jackknifed semi and at least four other vehicles, and it resulted in two fatalities and a half-dozen injuries. The sheriff, along with the staff at Alpine Hospital, was kept occupied for the entire morning.

As the noon hour approached, Vida suggested that we eat in. "Just us," she said, looking mysterious.

"That's fine," I agreed. "Shall I get something for us from the Burger Barn?"

"So greasy," she murmured as Ginny appeared to refill the coffeepot. "I'm dieting, you know."

Vida was always dieting, an effort—if indeed she actually made it—that never altered her weight one way or the other.

Ginny looked up from the big urn on the table by the far wall. "Did you want me to pick something up? I'm eating in, too. I've got a ton of stuff to finish for the classifieds this week. The first part of June is always heavy."

"Which is good," I remarked.

"What would you like?" Ginny asked, picking up a small pad of paper from Scott's desk.

I stated my preference for an all-white turkey sandwich on white bread with butter and mayo. Vida hemmed and hawed, then requested just a small salad. Ginny started for the door.

"Yoo-hoo," Vida called. "Perhaps I'll have a roll with that. Two rolls. No, make that a tuna-cheese-melt sandwich. And don't let them skimp on the cheese. Sometimes they can be very stingy at the Burger Barn. You might see if they have any of those delicious chocolate chip cookies today. And Roquefort dressing on the salad. Make certain it's a reasonably generous amount. I don't care for dry lettuce and tomatoes. Thank you, Ginny."

I kept a straight face, as did Ginny. Fifteen minutes later, at straight-up twelve o'clock, Vida and I were in my cubbyhole, opening our white paper bags.

"I knew you'd want to hear what I learned from the O'Neill women," Vida said, with a critical eye for her salad. "I didn't get off the phone until almost nine-thirty last night. I was too worn out to call then."

"What did they have to say for themselves?" I inquired, popping a slice of sweet pickle into my mouth.

"Let's start with Kathleen, with whom I lunched yesterday," Vida began.

"That's fine with me," I said. "She's Stubby's daughter by his first wife, right?"

"Precisely," Vida responded, sprinkling salt and pepper on her salad. She kept the shakers in her desk drawer, along with real eating utensils and an eggbeater I'd never seen her use. "Stubby got a high school girl from Sultan in trouble when he was in his twenties. The family insisted that he marry her, and since Mrs. O'Neill was still alive, she wanted her son to do the proper thing. They had Kathleen—Kathy—and then Margaret, or Peggy as she's called. The girls were only a year apart. Stubby's wife, Nancy, was still a teenager when Peggy was born, and one day she simply walked out and never came back. Her parents told Stubby that she'd gotten on a Greyhound bus and headed for Spokane."

"And left the little girls?" I asked, appalled.

"That's right," Vida said. "Grandmother O'Neill took care of them, but four years later, Stubby met Lona when he was logging near Arlington on the north fork of the Stillaguamish. They married, and had Meara. I don't know when the trouble started between Stubby and Lona, but from what Kathy told me at lunch yesterday, he'd been abusing her stepmother for a long time. I have to think that was one of the reasons that the first wife, Nancy, left so abruptly."

"Old habits die hard," I murmured.

"Indeed." Vida paused to take a bite out of her tuna cheese melt sandwich. "I must say Stubby never touched the children. I interviewed Peggy at the mall where she works in the stockroom for Platters in the Sky. She corroborated what her sister had told me. But Peggy, who I think is perhaps the brighter of the two, felt that there was something odd about her father."

The midday sun was slanting through the window over Vida's desk, and I had to move my chair out of the way to keep from being blinded. "Odd in what way?"

Vida frowned. "Peggy found it hard to put into words. He was secretive about where he went, which doesn't sound so mysterious if you consider that Stubby was probably visiting a tavern or a bar. But everyone, including Lona, knew that he and his brothers went drinking quite often. It was the fact that he acted so strangely about his whereabouts that made Peggy suspicious."

"What did she think he was up to?"

"Lona, naturally, thought it was another woman," Vida replied. "The girls weren't so sure. Why would Stubby usually be in the company of his brothers? Not that they couldn't all go to a brothel, but Peggy says it just didn't fit. She believed it had to be something illegal, such as drugs."

"Did Peggy know about those lockers in the basement?" I asked.

"She knew they were there, and she thought it was very peculiar," Vida said, scooping up the dregs of her Roquefort dressing with a large piece of lettuce. "The three girls were warned never, never to go near those lockers."

"How long were the lockers in the basement?" I inquired. "How old were the girls when they first noticed them?"

"Peggy said they'd only been there for the last two or three years," Vida replied, dabbing at her mouth with a paper napkin. "She had no idea what might be in them, unless it was drugs."

The time had come to tell Vida about the weapons cache. I didn't want to break faith with Milo, but it wasn't fair not to confide in her. In fact, I was rather surprised that she hadn't wrested the truth from her nephew Bill Blatt.

Except that she had. "Heavens!" Vida exclaimed, with a windmill wave of her hand. "Billy told me about those rocket launchers or whatever you call them last night. I took him out for ice cream."

Aghast, I leaned back in the visitor's chair. "Why didn't you tell me?"

"Because," Vida said in a reasonable tone, "Billy insisted I keep it to myself until Milo made an official announcement."

Shaking my head, I smiled at Vida. "I should have known. But did Bill tell you where the weapons came from?"

"No," Vida replied, looking irked. "To be honest, I don't think he knew. Indeed, I got the impression that Milo either didn't know or wasn't letting on."

"Going back to Peggy O'Neill," I said, "if she didn't have any other ideas about what her father was involved in, did her stepmother or her sisters make some suggestions?"

"Not Kathleen, though I spoke with her before I interviewed Peggy. Lona was another matter." Vida let out a big sigh. "Lona O'Neill is a bundle of contrasting emotions. The foolish woman must still be in love with

Stubby. How else can you explain her reluctance to divorce him or her apparent grief at the wake?"

"People are very complicated," I remarked, then added, "as you well know, Vida."

"So true." She paused to finish her tuna melt. "Again, Lona insisted she had no idea what was in those lockers in the basement of the house they shared together before the breakup. She thought it might be liquor."

I wrinkled my nose. "Liquor?"

"Contraband, from Ireland," Vida said. "Apparently, Stubby and the rest of the O'Neill males often received parcels and mail from the old country. Cousins, she thought, who'd send Irish whiskey and those fishermen's sweaters and other items that the O'Neills could sell for a profit. They'd receive them as gifts, and thus wouldn't have to pay duty. Lona herself got a very nice cardigan out of it a year or so ago."

I gazed at Vida. "Do you believe Lona?"

"I believe she got the cardigan sweater. I've seen her wear it."

I looked askance at Vida. "Maybe so, but do you really believe Lona?"

Vida scowled. "It's hard to tell. I spoke to her on the phone last night, so I couldn't see her face or watch her eyes. She's a bit naïve, if you ask me. Stubby was a villain one minute, a good husband the next. So typical of women who love the wrong man, always defending him, yet unable to hide the truth."

"We know those lockers at Lona and Stubby's house and the chests up at the O'Neill place weren't full of sweaters," I pointed out. "That's not to say that they couldn't have been selling black market items, though I never heard of such a thing. Did you?"

Vida shook her head. "Not Irish items. Cuban cigars, French perfumes not available in this country—that sort of thing. I believe people smuggle snakeskin shoes and handbags into California."

"I'm talking about Alpine," I said with a slight smile. "The point is, Vida, if anyone happened to be selling hot stuff around this town, you'd know about it."

"Well . . . perhaps," Vida admitted. "The real issue is that none of the O'Neill women seemed to know about the weapons."

Ginny Erlandson poked her head around the corner. "When's Leo due back?" she asked.

I shrugged. "I'm not sure. No later than two, two-thirty. He still has to finish laying out the ads. Why?"

Ginny made a face, then stepped into the newsroom and closed the door. "Dan Peebles is here. It seems Al Driggers wants to pull his standing ad this week."

Vida choked on her hot water. "That's absurd!" she sputtered. "Driggers Funeral Home has advertised in the *Advocate* ever since it was founded seventy years ago! What's wrong with Al? Has he lost his tiny little mind?"

Ginny looked at me and gestured toward the front office. "Do you want to speak to Dan?"

"I guess." The Driggers ad was two inches deep by two columns wide. It always ran on the church page, and had been changed only in the subtlest of ways since I took over the paper. As a standing advertiser, Al got a special discount.

Dan Peebles was down-at-the-mouth when he slunk through the door. "Mr. Driggers wants you to know this isn't anything personal," Dan said, stopping in front of Vida's desk, with his pale blue eyes sliding between the two of us. "It's sort of a political thing."

"What do you mean?" I asked.

"Maybe that's not the right word," Dan replied, clearing his throat. "But Mr. Driggers feels that with all the rumors about getting sued by those Conley people, it might be best if he laid low for a week or two."

"Ridiculous," Vida declared. "It makes no sense."

"Vida's right," I said. "No suit has been filed, so no story about it will appear in the paper. Al and his father and grandfather before him have always run a fine business. He has no reason to be embarrassed. Look," I went on, giving the young man a friendly smile, "I'll call Janet Driggers. We're friends. Let's see if we can work this out."

"If it's the revenue you're worried about—" Dan began.

"No," I interrupted. "It's not that. Removing the ad will cause more talk than leaving it in where our subscribers are used to seeing it every week. I'll call Janet right now." I got up from Vida's visitor's chair and started toward my cubbyhole. "Is she at the funeral home or the travel agency?" I asked over my shoulder.

"The funeral home," Dan replied.

Janet picked up the phone on the first ring. "Driggers Domicile of Doom," she answered.

"Janet—what's wrong?" I asked, alarmed at the unusually somber tone in her voice.

But Janet laughed. "We have caller I.D.," she said. "I knew it was you. We got this gadget on an experimental basis."

Phone upgrades were slow in coming to the hinterlands, such as Alpine. "Then you're not about to seal yourself in a casket?" I inquired.

"Not quite," Janet replied, sounding serious but not morose. "But things could be better. I take it that Dan showed up at your office?"

"He's here now," I replied. "I'm trying to talk him out of canceling the standing ad." I explained my reasoning to Janet, who understood.

"I agree," she said, "but it's Al's idea. He's dying of embarrassment—excuse the expression. Let me see if I can whip some sense into him. Meanwhile, keep the ad.

I'll take responsibility." She paused, then dropped her voice. "Could you meet me for a drink after work? The ski lodge?"

"Why, yes," I replied. "Five-fifteen, five-thirty?"

"Sounds good," Janet said. "As long as nobody croaks between now and then. See you."

I passed the message along to Dan Peebles, who appeared relieved. "Mr. Driggers is really upset," Dan said, backpedaling toward the door. "Nothing like this has ever happened in the four years I've been an undertaker. Mr. Driggers and I can't understand it. Have you heard anything more from the sheriff or out of New York?"

"No," I answered. "I don't expect to hear from New York at all. What should I be hearing from the sheriff?"

Dan paused in the doorway. "Well . . . you know, if somebody found the body. At Sea-Tac, maybe."

I shook my head. "I don't think that's going to happen."

"Gosh." Dan looked dismayed. Without another word, he left.

"Why did you say that?" Vida asked.

"Because," I responded slowly, "I've never heard of such a thing, and I've been in the news business in this area for almost thirty years. Catastrophes like that leak out, even if good taste and advertising threats manage to keep them from becoming public. I'm even dubious about the possibility of losing a corpse in New York."

"Anything's possible in a big city like that," Vida declared.

"Maybe," I said. "By the way, did you tell me everything you learned from the O'Neill women? What about the wife who got away?"

"Nancy? Or Dana?"

"Dana, Rusty's long-gone wife," I said. "I got the impression Nancy was long gone."

"Apparently," Vida replied. "I'm still trying to track

down Dana. She's living with someone, which makes it difficult because the phone isn't listed in her name. Lona really doesn't keep in touch with her, at least since she—Lona—moved to Everett. And I still want to speak with Meara. I'm very curious about the father of her child."

"So am I," I agreed, "even though it probably has nothing to do with rocket launchers."

"Why is it a secret?" Vida demanded. "Meara said the poor fellow was dead."

"Protecting his reputation?" I suggested. "Or maybe she didn't mean literally. He's dead to her and the baby, as in married or living in Sri Lanka."

Vida sighed. "Possibly. But sixteen-year-old girls can be very difficult. Occasionally, even I have trouble talking to them."

That was quite an admission for Vida, and I said so. But there was more to come. She wouldn't have the story on the O'Neill women ready for this week's issue. It was unlikely that she'd be able to speak with Meara before our five o'clock deadline.

I assured Vida there was no rush. We had plenty to fill the paper this week, since we'd written some of the features in advance and we were heavy with photographs.

But there was still one glaring hole. Not having heard from Milo, I headed down Front Street to his office shortly after three o'clock. His Grand Cherokee was parked out front, but Sam Heppner informed me that the sheriff wasn't in.

"Dodge didn't get back from the accident site until almost noon, and then he got a call from Everett," Sam explained. "He just got back about ten minutes ago and went down to the Venison Inn for some lunch."

I returned the way I'd come, past the Sears catalog store, Parker's Pharmacy, the hobby shop, the *Advocate*, on by the dry cleaner's, and finally to the Venison Inn. Milo was nowhere to be seen in the restaurant itself, so I peeked in the bar. Sure enough, he was seated at a small round table, drinking a beer and smoking a cigarette.

"Aren't you on duty?" I asked, pulling up a chair without being invited.

"Yeah," Milo replied, barely looking at me. "So what?"

"You don't usually drink on the job," I said as Oren Rhodes, the bartender, gave me a high sign. "Pepsi," I called back to Oren, who nodded.

"It's been a bad day," Milo said. "That wreck out on the highway was a nasty one. The semi hit the Deception Falls bridge, jackknifed, and smashed into two other cars, totaling them both. Then a car coming the other way hit the semi and got rear-ended. The truck driver died; so did a passenger in one of the cars the semi hit. There were at least two real serious injuries, including a ten-year-old boy. Damn, why don't people use seat belts? It's the law in this state."

"Nobody local?" I asked as Oren brought me my Pepsi along with Milo's bacon burger and fries.

"No," the sheriff replied with a nod to Oren. "The semi was headed for Wenatchee and the rest of the victims were from out of the area. Scott picked up the story."

"Good," I said, though there was nothing good about it in human terms. "What took you to Everett?"

Milo's long face twisted in disgust. "Goddamn those O'Neills," he muttered, and angrily stubbed out his cigarette.

"What have they got to do with Everett?" I asked, surprised by Milo's reaction.

It took the sheriff a moment to answer as he composed himself and picked up his bacon burger. "You wanted to know about that arms cache, right?"

"That's why I'm here," I replied in neutral tones.

"Okay." Aggressively, he took a big bite of the burger and chewed much faster than usual. "I've been waiting to find out where those weapons, especially the rocket launchers, came from. They're not exactly the kind of thing you can order from a catalog. Remember the break-ins over at the naval station in Everett a while back?"

"Vaguely. We didn't use the story because it didn't have a local angle."

Milo's gaze was hard. "Well, it does now. Those rocket launchers were stolen from the navy, apparently by the O'Neills. The weapons in the two old chests we took out of the house on Second Hill were handguns and high-powered rifles. They've been traced to several arms dealers in King, Pierce, and Snohomish Counties."

"Legal arms dealers?" I asked.

Milo nodded. "Several of the handguns were purchased at gun shows. The others were bought privately. So the question is, what the hell did the O'Neills want with all that firepower?"

"To sell for a profit?" I offered.

"Maybe." Milo oversalted his french fries and swore under his breath. "But sell to who? That's the trouble with this mess—the O'Neills are dead, and we'll never know."

I had to agree with the sheriff.

But this time we were both wrong.

Chapter Fifteen

THE ARMS THEFT from the naval station was a tricky story to write. Without proof, the O'Neills couldn't be mentioned as suspects, only as having been in possession of illegal weapons. I didn't want to burden Scott with such a complex article this late in the day, especially since there were some holes that Milo couldn't fill. Consequently I spent over half an hour on the phone, talking to three different people in Everett. When I finished, I didn't have much more than I started with. To say that the military can be discreet is putting it mildly. They're a bunch of damned clams when it comes to security. Maybe that should make me feel more secure, but as a journalist I felt only frustration.

The basic, attainable facts were these: there had been three separate break-ins during the past six months, one in February, one in March, and one in late May. No details of how or who were revealed, nor would my sources tell me if there were any accessories who had conspired with the O'Neills. I knew there were, because Milo had let me know that an investigation of at least one person was under way. Aware that Lona O'Neill worked at the base, I asked if she was a suspect. The query was stonewalled, but Milo had indicated that her relationship with Stubby and the other O'Neills would arouse suspicion. The sheriff also planned to interrogate her Wednesday morning.

"Very odd," Vida declared just as I sent the story to the backshop at five to five. "Lona works for the navy, her husband had the stolen arms in their house, and there were other weapons at the O'Neill house on Second Hill. The only problem is, I don't believe she took the job in Everett until a month or two ago."

"That's not the only problem," I said, trying to get the kinks out of my neck and back. "Can you see Lona involved in something like that? Or imagine Stubby trusting her, especially since they'd been estranged for a year or more?"

Vida was putting on her coat. "Perhaps not, but it's certainly an odd coincidence." She finished the sentence in a rush as her phone rang.

I started for the backshop to check with Kip MacDuff. I'd gotten to the door when Vida put the phone down and gave me a peculiar look.

"That was my daughter Amy," she said in a strange voice. "Meara O'Neill is at her house."

"Meara?" I was taken aback. "At Amy and Ted's house? Why?"

"I've no idea." Vida seemed thunderstruck. "I'd planned to interview her over the phone this evening. There was no mention of her coming to Alpine from Everett, and certainly not of going to Amy and Ted's. I had no idea Meara knew them, except in passing. Goodness."

"Do you want me to go with you?" I asked, forgetting all about my date with Janet Driggers.

"No, certainly not," Vida responded, now purposefully striding toward the door. "I'm not uneasy, I just don't understand the connection."

Vida went out one door, Kip came in the other. "It's looking good," he declared. "Twenty-four pages, plus the summer solstice preview section. Leo managed to get the ads to sustain this big issue. How does he do that with Fleetwood and the radio station here?"

"Hard work and knowing how to entice the local merchants," I said. "Leo's very creative when it comes to putting advertising packages together. By the way, you left the Driggers ad in?"

Kip nodded. "But what if Al doesn't want to pay?"

"Then I won't charge him. Oh!" I exclaimed. "I'm supposed to meet Janet Driggers in five minutes. Thanks for reminding me."

I grabbed my belongings and hurried out of the office. I'd be a couple of minutes late, since the ski lodge was almost a mile from the *Advocate*. When I arrived in the bar with its ersatz northern lights and Nordic gnomes, Janet wasn't there yet. I sat down in a small booth against the wall where I could watch the entrance. To my surprise, Tiffany Eriks came over to take my order.

"When did you start working here?" I inquired, probably sounding more abrupt than I intended.

Tiffany, however, didn't seem to take offense. "I'm just filling in," she replied, brushing her long blonde hair off her forehead. "Dani Erdahl is getting married this weekend."

I glanced around the bar, which wasn't very busy early on a Tuesday evening. "I'll wait to order when my friend gets here. Have you recovered from your terrible shock last week?"

"Shock?" Tiffany's long eyelashes fluttered. "Oh, you mean with that guy's body. Yes, I'm pretty much okay. It was really creepy, though."

I offered Tiffany my most ingenuous smile. "I'll bet that was your idea—the part about Brian looking cold."

"He *was* cold," Tiffany said. "I mean, he'd been up there on the Ridge for so long."

"And," I added dryly, "he was dead."

Tiffany nodded eagerly. "That's right, he'd been dead

for ages. At least that's what Tim told me. He wasn't just stiff from the cold."

I wondered if Tiffany's apparent obtuseness was genuine or a front. I didn't know her well, though I'd become acquainted with some of her family over the years. Certainly her maternal grandfather, Durwood Parker, laid claim to being the worst driver in Skykomish County, but he'd been an excellent pharmacist before his retirement some twelve years earlier. Recklessness might be in the genes, but not necessarily stupidity.

"I was referring to when you and Tim placed Brian's body in the meat locker," I said, trying to steer Tiffany back on course.

"Oh." She blinked at me some more. "That was awful. We panicked."

It was like a recording. Tiffany panicked, Tim panicked, they both panicked. I wasn't getting anywhere. Two well-dressed men who looked as if they might be sales reps entered the bar. Tiffany excused herself and went over to wait on the newcomers.

Sitting in bars, especially alone—which wasn't often—made me want to start smoking again. The cigarette machine was mercifully out of sight, but an older couple in a corner booth had just lighted up. I wriggled around in my seat, wished I hadn't decided to wait for Janet, and wondered if there was any gum in my purse.

I was still squirming when Tiffany returned. "Mrs. Driggers called to say she couldn't make it. She said she was very sorry, but something came up."

Disappointed, I thanked Tiffany and told her I'd be leaving. I put a couple of dollar bills on the table and headed home. For once, I wasn't terribly anxious to arrive at an empty house. Tom's increasingly frequent visits and my contemplation of our future cast a pall over living alone. Maybe, finally, the independence I'd fought for all my life had lost its luster. It occurred to me that it might not have been self-reliance I'd sought, but a hedge against loneliness and a sop for hope. I felt I was already changing, no longer thinking solely of *me* but of *us*. I liked the new concept.

My meandering route took me past The Pines, the upscale development where Amy and Ted Hibbert had moved a year or so before. With nothing better to do, I drove past their house, where I saw Vida's Buick parked out front by the mailbox. I wondered what she'd found out from Meara O'Neill. Then I noticed an older, smaller car parked just a few yards from the Buick. The other car, which looked like a Honda, had an infant seat in the back. Meara's, I figured. She must still be there.

Fidgety, I drove along the winding roads that traversed the sloping area once known as Stump Hill. Maybe if I timed it right I'd go by the Hibbert house just as Vida came out. In a cul-de-sac by Dr. Starr the dentist's home, I stopped and took out my cell phone to call Janet. Maybe she'd gotten sick; maybe Al had had a nervous breakdown.

Janet didn't answer until the fourth ring. "Yes?" she said in a breathless voice.

"It's Emma. Are you okay?"

There was a moment of hesitation. "Emma?" Janet finally echoed. "Yes. Yes, I'm fine. Are you up at the ski lodge?"

I explained that I'd left and was waiting for Vida in The Pines. "I was afraid you might have gotten sick. Or that something had happened to Al. I mean, I know he's been upset lately."

This time the pause was so long that I could hear Janet's breathing. "Emma?"

"Yes, I'm still here."

"I can't find Al."

"What do you mean?"

"I mean," Janet said with the old fire returning to her

voice, "Al's not home, he's not at the funeral parlor, he's not anywhere. I tried his cell phone. He doesn't answer. Do you think I should call the sheriff?"

"Maybe he stopped for a drink after work," I suggested. "You know, to steady his nerves." I had started the car again and was creeping along the road back toward the Hibbert house.

"Al doesn't drink," Janet said flatly. "And he always leaves his cell on in case somebody croaks."

"Have you spoken with Dan Peebles?"

"Yes," Janet replied. "Dan was still at work, but he said he hadn't seen Al since around four. I left about three-fifteen. I had to catch up on my housework. This working two jobs is nuts. Cammy still has spots and doesn't want anyone to see her looking so gruesome. But," she added, her voice suddenly a wail, "where the hell is Al?"

"Janet," I said soothingly, "he's only been missing for less than two hours. If it makes you feel better, call the sheriff. They'll probably find Al in about fifteen minutes."

Janet's voice dropped, becoming more normal. "You're right. It's just that I feel so . . . oh, I don't know . . . these last few days have been pretty damned rugged."

"That's true enough," I said, putting on the brake as I approached the Hibberts' driveway. "Listen, I'll be home in a little while. Call me there and let me know what's going on."

Janet promised she would and rung off. I'd just disconnected my phone when I saw Vida, Roger, and Meara come flying out of the house. Vida was in the lead, but hurrying backwards, with her arms outstretched. Halfway down the drive, Roger stopped abruptly, jammed his hands in the pockets of his baggy jeans, and put his head down.

"Don't you dare run off!" Vida shouted, wildly waving an arm.

"Please, Mother . . ." Amy wailed from the porch. I couldn't catch the rest of her words.

Meara, who was holding the baby, made a couple of quick moves, sidestepping Vida. Just as I got out of the car, Ted appeared in the doorway next to his wife, looking cowed.

I ran over to the Honda, barring the driver's side. "What's going on?" I yelled as Meara came within ten feet of me and stopped.

"I want to go home!" Meara shouted. "Let me alone!"

Having noted my presence, Vida faced Roger, putting an arm around him. The kid made a feeble effort to break loose, but let his grandmother steer him back up the driveway. Halfway to the house, she turned around, shook her fist, and cried, "Hussy!"

I looked into Meara's face; she was pale and frightened.

"Okay," I said, stepping aside. "Can I ride with you? My car broke down."

"What?" Meara stared at me and clutched the baby closer to her breast.

"I need a ride to Cal's Texaco," I said, hurrying around to the Honda's passenger side. "Do you mind? Come on, we'd better get out of here."

Suddenly energized, Meara opened the rear door on my side and put little Cornelius into his infant seat. Her movements were deft. The baby smiled and gurgled at his mother.

"Emma!" Vida cried, frantically waving at me. "Wait!"

The car window didn't have a power function and Meara was already sliding into the driver's seat. "Later!" I shouted at Vida.

She looked irate, seemingly rooted to the spot as we pulled away and lurched down the winding road. The car was old, and probably in need of repair. Either that, or Meara wasn't a very good driver. Then I realized she was only sixteen. Roger's age. I began to wonder.

We didn't speak until we reached Alpine Way, where the Texaco station was located, just a few blocks north. "Meara," I said in my most humble voice, "could I impose on you for a big favor? I left my checkbook at home. Could you turn right up here on Fir Street? It's only a few blocks. I'll run in and get it if you'd be so kind as to wait."

"Jeez!" Meara shifted gears and gritted her teeth. The gears sounded as if they were gritting their teeth, too. But she made the quick turn and a few seconds later I pointed out my log house.

"You'd better be quick," she said, pulling up in front. "I've got to go home to feed Cornelius. He's going to fuss pretty soon, and I have to drive all the way to Everett."

I seized the opportunity. "Have you got a bottle with you or are you breast-feeding?"

"He's a bottle baby," Meara replied. "Why?"

"Do you have a bottle with you?" I repeated.

"Yes." Meara scowled at me. "So what? I can't drive and feed him."

"I thought," I said gently, "you might like to come inside to feed him. It'll be an hour, maybe more this time of night, before you get to Everett. You know how bad the commuter traffic gets between five and seven once you reach Monroe."

Meara stared at me, looked at the baby, then gazed out the car window. "Maybe that's a good idea," she said. "The traffic won't be so bad. I don't like driving Highway Two. I've only had my license for six months."

"Come on in, then," I said, starting to get out of the Honda.

"What about your car?" Meara asked.

"Cal's open late tonight," I lied. "I may have him tow

it into the garage." Cal Vickers, like most Alpine businessmen, didn't believe in working past six o'clock. "If you can't make it in eight, you won't make it in nine" was the local byword.

After Meara got Cornelius out of the infant seat, we trudged into the house.

"This is cute," she said, looking around the snug living room. "Mom and I are stuck in an apartment about the size of a matchbox."

"Do you need to warm the bottle?" I asked, having decided to hold off on inquiring about the scene at the Hibberts' house. I needed to gain Meara's trust; she needed to collect her thoughts. "I can heat some water," I added.

Meara shook her head. "Room temperature is fine."

She sat down on the sofa, kept a firm grip on the baby with one hand, and reached into a diaper bag shaped like an elephant with big ears for pockets.

"Do you think," I asked, "that he looks like you?"

Offering Cornelius the bottle, Meara peered down into his face. He had a thatch of brown hair, blue eyes, and a slightly receding chin.

"I can't see it," she said. "His eyes may change color. So may his hair. At least that's what Mom says."

"It's a shame his father didn't live to see him," I remarked, sitting down in one of the side chairs. "Does Cornelius look like him?"

"Maybe," Meara allowed. "I'd like to think so."

I took a deep breath. "How did his father die?"

Meara looked up sharply. "Why do you want to know?" Her blue-green eyes narrowed in suspicion. "Did you bring me here to ask a bunch of questions for your newspaper? Is this a trick?"

What little I knew of Meara O'Neill indicated that she was smart and spunky. I wouldn't try to fool her. Hedging would be a better approach.

"I'm not interviewing you, if that's what you mean," I

replied calmly. "I'm interested, that's all. Your family has had a triple tragedy, with the deaths of your father and your uncles. On top of that, Cornelius's father is also dead. It seems too much to bear, and yet you're holding up. I admire you for raising your son when you're not much more than a child yourself."

I can't say that Meara seemed placated, but her features softened a bit. "I don't feel like a teenager," she said, holding Cornelius against her shoulder to burp him. "I've felt old all my life. Maybe it was having two older half sisters. They always ganged up on me, so I had to learn to defend myself. Then there was Mom. She needed my support when Dad got out of control. Kathy and Peggy were no help. Even though they never really knew their own mother, Mom was the wicked stepmother as far as they were concerned."

"Would you rather not talk about your baby's father?" I asked.

Meara put the bottle back in Cornelius's mouth. "What's the point? It isn't as if we were going to get married, even if he'd lived. He was older, he had a steady girlfriend." She paused, her eyes flashing. "You think he must have been a creep, right? And I must have been a slut. But it wasn't like that."

"Strange as it may seem," I said quietly, "I believe you. Did you know that my son was born out of wedlock?"

Meara's face registered surprise. "No. I thought you were divorced."

It wasn't the proper time to go into details about my own checkered past. "So," I said, "you can see why I'm not making any snap judgments."

"Right." Meara turned her attention to the baby, who had suddenly decided he didn't want to eat anymore. "Okay, I'm sorry. But I still don't want to talk about it."

"That's fine," I responded, hiding my disappointment.

"Can you tell me what the commotion was at the Hibberts' just now?"

Cornelius flailed his small arms, pushing the bottle away. "That was weird," Meara replied, rocking the baby in an effort to quiet him. "It's that Roger. He's got a big, fat crush on me."

"Roger?" I was aghast. I thought the only thing Roger yearned for was adult videos and a bucket of ice cream.

Meara gave me an ironic glance. "We were in the same grade at Alpine High. He always trailed around after me, a real pest. His grandmother—Mrs. Runkel—wanted to talk to me for some story she's doing for your paper. We were going to do it over the phone, but this afternoon Mrs. Hibbert called, all upset. She said that she and Mr. Hibbert had to see me. They wanted Mom to come, too, but she had an appointment with somebody at the apartment and I got the feeling that she'd rather not have Cornelius and me around. So I said I'd drive over to Alpine and that way I could do the story thing with Mrs. Runkel and find out what was going on with the Hibberts."

Cornelius let out a big squall and Meara stopped speaking. "I think I'd better change him," she said after he refused his pacifier.

"So Vida—Mrs. Runkel—met you at her daughter's house?" I asked as Meara delved into the diaper bag while the baby cried and kicked.

"Yes," Meara said, though not before she'd divested Cornelius of his wet diaper. "Mrs. Hibbert must have called her. Anyway, I guess Roger had been bragging to some of his buddies that he was the one who'd gotten me pregnant. His folks heard about it and had a five-star fit."

"What?" I could hardly believe my ears.

"You heard me," Meara said with an ironic expression.

"That's incredible," I gasped.

"Yes." With a dry diaper in place, Cornelius settled

down. Meara gave him the bottle and he began to suck contentedly. "I wasn't there very long, because Roger was acting like a total creep and insisting that we'd been carrying on for ages," Meara continued. "I don't think his parents believed him, but Mrs. Runkel defended everything he said and blamed me for leading him on. Can you imagine?"

Unfortunately, I could. What I couldn't imagine was that Vida believed Roger's wild claim. Perhaps she had only been trying to help him save face.

Dry pants had increased Cornelius's appetite. He finished the last ounce in the bottle and began to coo.

"We'd better go," Meara said, smiling back at the baby. "Mom should be finished with her meeting or whatever it was. Would you mind if I use your bathroom?"

"Go ahead," I replied. "I'll hold Cornelius." I'd had some practice in the not-too-distant past. A young woman and her illegitimate son had lived with me for several months. I seemed to attract unwed mothers. There was no mystery to that.

Cornelius O'Neill seemed perfectly content in my arms. I made weird clucking noises that amused him. He was a good-looking baby. Not all of them are. Mavis, my old friend and coworker from *The Oregonian*, had a firstborn who was so homely that when I saw him in the hospital I could only blurt out, "How . . . baby!" Happily, he had grown into a very good-looking young man.

Despite what Meara had said about Cornelius, I thought he did resemble her somewhat. I wasn't sure how, and then I realized that none of his features really reminded me of her or any of the O'Neills.

But they were familiar.

I was still puzzling over this when Meara returned from the bathroom.

"Thanks again," she said, taking the baby from me.

"No problem," I replied, gathering up Meara's belongings. "I'll carry them out to your car."

"Thanks," she repeated, then smiled, and I realized for the first time that she was very pretty. Maybe I hadn't noticed before because Meara O'Neill hadn't had much to smile about lately. But the smile still didn't suggest a resemblance to Cornelius.

While Meara fastened Cornelius into the infant seat, I put the diaper bag and purse up front. Then she got behind the wheel and wished me luck with my car.

I'd forgotten about the ruse, and must have looked blank before I caught on. "Oh—yes, I'm sure it's nothing serious. Please don't worry about Roger. Even his grandmother will acknowledge eventually that he's doing some macho bragging."

Meara's face was grave. "Probably. But that's not what worries me."

"Oh?" I hadn't closed the door on the passenger side, so I leaned farther into the car. "What do you mean?"

For a moment, Meara stared out through the windshield. "I told you that little creep has been following me—stalking, really—for ages. He knows who Cornelius's father was. I just hope he keeps his fat mouth shut."

Chapter Sixteen

I WASN'T SURE why, but I felt uneasy walking back to The Pines to collect my car. It was only seven o'clock and the sun hadn't yet begun to set. There was a scent of roses from a nearby garden as I crossed Second Street on that mild Tuesday evening, and chipmunks chattered in a cedar tree at the corner. But as the Burlington-Northern whistled on its passage through town, I was reminded of something less ordinary. I'd only heard the "dead whistle" twice since my arrival in Alpine, but the memory made me shiver. The whistle was sounded at the mill when someone died in the woods or in the mill itself. Fred Engebretsen, father of four, had been killed when he fell from a sixty-foot fir on Windy Mountain; Duane Griswold, only nineteen, had fallen under the wheels of a logging truck near Martin Creek. Vida had once told me how the dead whistle had haunted her while she was growing up. She said you always feared that the whistle signaled the passing of a loved one. And because Alpine was so small, the victim was always someone you knew. Fatalities were more frequent when logging was king—and killer.

Yet Alpine Way looked perfectly normal. Traffic was sparse, a middle-aged couple walked their dog, a young man on a bicycle cruised down the wide street's slope. When I arrived at the Hibberts', all seemed calm. Vida's car was still there, however, so I assumed the family was thrashing its way through Roger's crisis. I got into the Lexus and drove back home.

The feeling of gloom remained. I tried to call Janet Driggers, but there was no answer except a recorded message. It wasn't until almost eight o'clock that I realized I hadn't eaten dinner. Something had spoiled my appetite. I was in the kitchen searching the freezer when Vida arrived at the back door, out of breath and out of temper.

"What's gotten into you, Emma?" Vida raged as she stamped into the kitchen. "Has becoming engaged destroyed your sense of loyalty?"

"I don't know what you're talking about," I said, calmly. "Shall I make tea?"

"No." Vida sat down hard on one of my kitchen chairs. "This isn't a social visit."

"Oh, great!" I exclaimed, dropping into one of the other chairs and holding my head. "What did I supposedly do this time?"

Under the crinkled brim of her green taffeta cloche, Vida looked very stern. "You took sides. You chose Meara O'Neill."

"Oh, Vida." I shook my head. "I did no such thing. I wanted to talk to the girl, just as you did. How was I to know there was some sort of ruckus going on at your daughter's?"

"You might have guessed," Vida retorted.

"Come on, Vida," I said, "you know damned well I had no idea what was going on. I saw your Buick when I drove through The Pines and thought I'd wait for you to find out what Meara had to say for herself and why she was at Amy and Ted's. It occurred to me that we could go to dinner and talk about it."

"Dinner!" Vida waved a hand in front of her face. "Who could possibly eat? And don't swear," she added.

"I'll swear I didn't know what was happening," I declared. "Now I've heard Meara's side of the story. What about Roger's?"

Under her summer coat, Vida's shoulders slumped. "It's most remarkable."

"I imagine."

Vida sighed. "Young people grow up so fast these days."

"What?"

"One day they're tiny tots, the next, they're adults." Vida shrugged. "You blink, and the years have flown by."

Vida was floating on that same pink cloud she ascended whenever she spoke of Tom and me. Now, apparently, she had put Roger—and maybe poor Meara—on a similar puff of romantic gauze.

"Vida," I said firmly, "do you actually believe that Roger got Meara pregnant?"

"Young love, first love," she murmured. "It seems so right when it's so wrong. My, my."

I almost thought a tear glistened in Vida's eye, but it was probably the light reflecting off the dishwasher's rinse button. "You sound like an idiot."

Vida scowled at me. "Mind your tongue, Emma." She paused, and her expression softened. "We're quarreling. That's not right."

"Of course it's not," I agreed. "Tell me why you believe Roger."

Vida was taken aback. "Why, I've always believed him. He's a very truthful boy. Oh, he's told the occasional fib as children do. But he's not a liar by any means."

I doubted that. "Why would Meara deny it, then?"

"Notions," Vida answered promptly. "Meara must have invented a romantic idea as to who fathered her baby. A mysterious older man, now dead. So tragic. And such a lovely fantasy."

In my opinion, Meara could have fantasized Quasimodo as the father of her baby, and he would have been more appealing than Roger. But though I refused to admit it out loud, Vida's rationale wasn't completely unbelievable.

"Meara's Irish, you see," Vida said as I sat there cogitating. "The Irish are so clever with words, they have such wonderfully sentimental music. Sadness and loss seem to be their motif."

But Roger? I wanted to say. There are limits. Instead, I offered Vida a sympathetic look. "Sadness and loss are a prominent cultural theme. It's natural, it's their history."

"Victims," she said. "Perhaps they like being victims, like women who stay with abusive men. And vice versa. Those famines—they lived on an island. Didn't anyone have a fishing rod or a gill net?"

Vida was off on a tangent, perhaps to divert me. "Do Amy and Ted believe Roger?" I asked.

She snatched off her glasses and rubbed her eyes. "Ooooh . . . you never can be sure with them. They want not to believe him, of course. Legal and financial reasons. Responsibility."

"Meara doesn't want to marry Roger," I declared, practically quivering at the very thought.

"Not at present," Vida replied, giving her eyes a final rub. "But down the road, who knows?"

I reached out and grabbed her hand. "Vida," I said, forcing her to look at me straight on, "I don't believe Roger. His parents don't believe him. Meara says he's lying. Why can't you, of all people, see the truth?"

As soon as I'd spoken, I knew the answer. Because nobody else believes him. Someone must have faith in Roger or he will become a lost soul. "Never mind," I blurted before Vida could open her mouth. I let go of her hand and gave it a quick, fond pat. "Al Driggers is missing."

"What?" Vida's gray eyes were huge as she put her

glasses back on. "How can he be? I saw him this morning."

I explained Janet's anxiety, which Vida pooh-poohed. "Janet is a very emotional woman. She's overextended herself, trying to work at the funeral home and the travel agency. Ever since their two daughters moved away she's been at loose ends. What Janet needs is a hobby, not a job. Al makes a very nice income."

It was clear that, for once, Vida had no thought except for her own family problems. And I had no wish to hear her ramble on in defense of Roger.

But there was one thing I had to say. "Meara says Roger knows the identity of her baby's father."

"I should think so," Vida said primly, then wagged a finger in my direction. "Make no mistake, I don't hold with all this promiscuity. But as you of all people know, love can overcome good sense."

"I was twenty-one," I said dryly. "Tom was twenty-eight."

Vida stood up. "Really, Emma, you're being very difficult."

"No, I'm not." I stood up, too, my chair making an annoying scraping sound on the faux wood floor. "I'm trying to be objective about this. I'm a journalist, after all."

Vida started for the back door, but turned to speak over her shoulder. "So am I."

I didn't like parting on unpleasant terms with Vida, but she was being a mule. Halfway through eating a tuna fish sandwich and some sliced tomatoes, I had another visitor. Spencer Fleetwood arrived on my porch with a bouquet of small yellow orchids.

"Peace offering," he said, thrusting the flowers at me before removing his sunglasses. "May I come in?"

"Okay," I said, aware that I didn't sound very welcoming. "Why are you declaring peace?"

Spence gestured toward one of my side chairs. "May I?"

"Go ahead," I said, both apprehensive and curious. I gazed at the orchids in my hand. The stems were encased in a glass tube filled with water. "Let me get a vase." I picked up my half-eaten supper with my free hand and headed for the kitchen, then remembered my manners. "Can I bring you something?"

"Only goodwill," Spence replied in his rich radio voice.

"Okay," I said, returning to the living room and sitting on the sofa. "What's this all about?"

Spence gave me his off-center grin. He had nice white teeth, almost as fine as Scott Chamoud's. He also had a slightly beaklike nose, a long, sharp chin, and shrewd brown eyes that seemed just a little too close together. As usual, he was wearing a cashmere sweater—baby blue—and tailored slacks.

"You have a big advantage over me," he said, the brown eyes glinting.

"Such as?"

"The sheriff." Spence stretched out his long legs and settled back into the chair. Somehow, even on enemy turf he exuded an air that indicated he was in control.

I was annoyed, but tried not to show it. "You mean because I've known him for ten years?"

Spence nodded. "That, and the fact that you're a woman."

Now I didn't try to hide my annoyance. "Are you insinuating that I use my so-called feminine wiles to get information from Milo Dodge?"

"No." He paused for effect. I wondered if Spence had majored not in broadcasting but drama. "It's natural that a woman can get a man to open up. Conversational skills, let's say."

That was better than accusing me of sleeping with the sheriff. And though I had, it had never made Milo reveal any information he hadn't wanted me to know. Indeed, for some time after we broke up, he'd been uncooperative and recalcitrant.

"If you knew Milo just half as well as I do," I said, sounding stilted even to myself, "you'd know that he's very cautious, very deliberate. Milo goes by the book. What do you think I know that you don't?"

Spence threw back his head and laughed. "Could I call you cunning?" he finally said, his brown eyes narrowing slightly.

"I don't think I've ever been called cunning," I replied. "Just about everything else, though."

Spence was now serious. "So have I. It comes with our jobs. Look," he went on, leaning forward with his hands on his knees, "we both know we're operating in a limited market when it comes to advertising. As long as we stay in business, we'll fight and claw each other for every dollar we can get. But it's news I'm talking about, and there's where I have the advantage."

"Of course," I allowed. "So what's your point?"

"We're sitting on the biggest story to ever break in Alpine, right?"

"Maybe," I said. "We've had a few others since I've been here, and I'm sure there were some big ones before I arrived. This isn't the first multiple homicide I've covered."

Spence shook his head. "I'm not talking about the Hartquists knocking off the O'Neills. Not exactly. I'm talking about this weapons thing. Surely you've considered the implications?"

"I'm considering the facts at the moment," I replied with a lift of my chin. "In some ways, I'm like Milo. I don't speculate in public."

Spence gave me that off-center grin. "This isn't public. This is private. Or have you got the house bugged?"

"Of course not," I retorted, wondering if he was actually serious. "But you're a journalist, too. Whatever I say is—"

"Off the record," Spence interrupted. "Come on, Emma," he prodded, using my Christian name for the first time that I could recall, "this story is bigger than both of us. Do you really think Dodge is going to figure it out?"

"He often does," I replied in defense of Milo. "He takes his time, but he usually gets there."

"With, I've heard, a great deal of help from you and Mrs. Runkel," Spence asserted. "I haven't been in Alpine very long, but word gets out. You and that House and Home editor seem to go beyond the call of duty when it comes to crime."

"You can't help but get involved with major stories in a small town," I said. "Look—you're doing it yourself."

"So I am." Spence seemed amused. "Shall we consider the facts?"

I knew he was trying to trick me, but I could play that game, too. "All right. Just the facts. It's your idea, you start."

Again, Spence leaned back in the chair. "The Brothers O'Neill are murdered in apparent gangland style by the Hartquist family."

I held up a hand. "Why gangland?"

"They were all shot at close range," Spence replied. "None of the Hartquists were wounded despite the fact that they claimed to have been shot at first. Wouldn't you say that the Hartquists must have come—probably by stealth—to the O'Neill house on Second Hill, barged in, and started shooting?"

It occurred to me that when Scott and I went through the house, we hadn't noticed any bullet holes. Nor had Milo mentioned them.

"No," I said, aware that Spence's theory was a trap.

"No?" he repeated. "So you're saying that the shooting must have occurred outside."

"That's a fact," I said. "We were speaking only of facts. At least that's what the Hartquists implied at their arraignment."

Spence nodded slowly, the slightly hooked nose reminding me of a bird. A kinder person might have described his profile as eaglelike; I was thinking more of a vulture. But Spence was right. There should have been some trace of bullets in the O'Neill house if the trio had been shot indoors.

"Let's conjecture for just a moment," Spence said amiably. "The Hartquists arrive in their truck. They either fire a couple of shots into the air, or they call the O'Neills out. Maybe they say they just want to talk, consider a truce. In any event, the O'Neills come outside. They're probably armed, but not ready to start shooting."

Spence's deep voice had fallen into its on-air mode, arresting, intimate, confidential. I half expected him to recall an encounter of his own with the neighborhood bully some forty years earlier. I also expected that eventually he could lull me to sleep.

"The Hartquists surprise them," he continued. "I understand that the O'Neills' blood alcohol count was well above the legal limit."

Damn. Milo hadn't mentioned that, and I hadn't thought to ask. Neither, I assumed, had Scott Chamoud. I felt like a bungling amateur. Worse yet, I had to admire Spence's thoroughness.

"The Hartquists get the O'Neills outside, maybe using some kind of ruse," Spence recounted as if he could picture the sorry scene in his mind's eye. "Perhaps Cap and his boys are hiding in the shrubbery. That place on Second Hill isn't exactly a landscaper's delight. The O'Neills are confused, puzzled, and, as I mentioned, drunk. The Hartquists charge them and start shooting at close range. The

O'Neills fall, the Hartquists retrieve their victims' weapons, they load the dead men into their truck, and off they go to Alpine Meats. How am I doing?"

Pretty damned good, I thought, and hoped I was hiding my annoyance. "It's plausible," I conceded. "But why?"

"Why kill them or why cart them off to the meat locker?"

"Both."

Spence gave me a rueful look. "How else can a feud like that end except with annihilation? Hasn't it gone on for years, even across generations?"

"That's true," I said. "It all started with Paddy O'Neill accidentally running over Cap Hartquist's goat. Until then, they'd been close friends."

Spence gave a single nod. "Those things fester, especially in small towns. Macho stuff, family honor, the whole bit. Even in big cities relatives get into it over an inheritance, neighbors go after each other because a dog tore up the petunia bed. You can't isolate these incidents to only small towns."

"I know," I said. "But in cities, the aggrieved usually start by calling their lawyers."

Spence waved a hand, flashing his expensive watch. "You know what I mean. The feud had to end this way. Maybe it'll be a lesson for the younger generation."

"Maybe." As far as I knew, the Hartquist and O'Neill youths had never gone much further than exchanges of nasty words. Then I thought of Mickey O'Neill. He was the only male descendant on either side of the feuding families. That was just as well. "So far there's been no retaliation," I added hopefully. "But why the warehouse?"

Spence shrugged. "Some kind of statement? Dead meat? It's over? I'm not a mind reader. You seem like an intuitive sort of person. What do you think?"

I suppose I should have been flattered. Instead, I became mulish. "I only know what the Hartquists said they did. I don't think any of them are into symbolism. They took the easy way out."

"Why not leave the bodies up on Second Hill? They were bound to be found," Spence pointed out.

"Maybe the Hartquists were almost as drunk as the O'Neills," I said. "Maybe they panicked." For all I knew, the crazy clan might have wanted to put their victims on a summer solstice float.

"Okay." Spence gave me another grin. "Back to the facts. Rocket launchers and other weaponry, the heavy stuff stolen from the Everett naval station. To what purpose?"

"To sell it?" I replied. "What else?"

"To whom?"

"I don't know. Who's buying?"

"It's a hot market out there," Spence said. "Lots of people are buying arms, legally and illegally. The whole Middle East. Africa. Central and South America. You name it."

"I considered the IRA," I confessed, "but haven't they declared a truce?"

Spence shrugged. "It's not holding very well."

"Stupid," I remarked. "The Irish can't get along in the old country; you put a Catholic family and a Protestant family together in Ireland, and too often they want to kill each other. You set them down in Alpine, and they get along just fine."

"It's history, it's oppression, it's in the old sod," Spence responded. "Have you been to Ireland?"

"No," I admitted. "When I was in Europe years ago, I missed Ireland. I'm not Irish."

Spence chuckled, a rich, rolling sound that no doubt endeared him to his listeners. "That often doesn't keep Americans from visiting the Emerald Isle. And may I point out that the Hartquists and the O'Neills seem to have revived an ancient Viking-and-Gael animosity?"

Maybe he had a point. But I was growing anxious for my guest to leave. So far, I'd learned only that the O'Neills were drunk at the time of the shooting. That wasn't news; their enemies probably were, too. Besides, the Hartquists had said at their arraignment that the shooting had taken place outside the O'Neill house. Whether the rest of their story was an exaggeration or even a lie would come out in the trial. As for the arms cache, Spence had merely added a few potential buyers to my mental list.

"One more thing," Spence said as if he could read my mind, "why was Brian Conley's body removed from his casket?"

"Honestly," I replied, "I've no idea."

Spence pointed a finger at me. "Think about it. Why are the Conleys threatening to sue Al Driggers and a bunch of other people?"

"Because they're crazed with grief?" I said. "I don't blame them, they have to focus their sense of loss on something or somebody, since the killer hasn't been identified. Besides, you can't criticize them for being upset over what in effect is a double loss."

"But an intriguing one," Spence remarked, looking rather smug. "For instance—why did the Conleys receive their son's recently issued passport just yesterday?"

I couldn't hide my surprise. "How do you know?"

"Because," he answered easily, "I spoke with Mrs. Conley on the phone. I discovered you'd gotten pretty chummy with her since Brian's body was found. How could I let the *Advocate* get one up on KSKY?"

"She called you?" I demanded.

"I called her. Although she did say she'd tried to reach the radio station a couple of times but couldn't get through to me. She may have dialed wrong." He shrugged.

"So what about a passport?" I asked, still irked. "Has this information been broadcast?"

"No." Spence's expression was still self-satisfied, maybe because he had a scoop, maybe because he enjoyed getting me rattled. "I'm in no rush, since you've already gone to press for the week. The outside media dropped the Conley story within twenty-four hours. Oh, I think one of the metropolitan dailies and maybe a couple of radio and TV stations picked up the bit about the empty coffin. The Hartquist-O'Neill shoot-out didn't get that much coverage, either. But now I hear the big city boys and girls are snooping around the naval station at Everett. The *Herald* over there certainly will be on top of the arms theft."

The Everett *Daily Herald* had run several articles about the break-ins, including a follow-up feature a couple of weeks earlier concerning security at the naval station. We took the *Herald* at work, and there were several other subscribers in Skykomish County. But when it came to timing, I couldn't compete with a daily newspaper, any more than I could with a radio station.

"The passport," I put in. "What about it?"

Spence craned his neck in the direction of the dining alcove and then the kitchen. I figured he was trying to find out where I kept the liquor. Or at least the coffeepot. I, however, remained an ungracious hostess.

"Mrs. Conley told me that yet another upsetting thing had happened to her and her husband," Spence said, giving up on his perusal of the house. "They'd received Brian's passport in the mail. It was dated March thirty-first, and had been sent by the Irish consulate in Seattle."

"That doesn't make sense," I countered. "Brian went missing on Tonga Ridge the last week of March. Did Mrs. Conley say when her son had applied for the passport?"

"She wasn't aware he'd done it," Spence replied. "She and her husband had no idea that their son was planning a trip."

"So they didn't know where he was going," I murmured.

"What do you think?" Spence asked, almost as if he really cared.

I kept my expression blank. "How would I know?"

"Conley worked at the Irish consulate, didn't he?"

"I believe so. Yes, that sounds right."

Spence cocked an eyebrow at me. "Come on, Emma, you know perfectly well that he did. Have you talked to the consul?"

"No." It was the truth, but it was an oversight.

"I have," Spence said, confirming my sudden realization that once again he had been more thorough. "The consul didn't know of any trip planned by Brian until he heard about the passport and sent it on to the Conleys in Penn Yan."

"Interesting," I remarked, though I kept my tone neutral. "Was the consul helpful?"

"As much as he could be," Spence replied. "He's clearly not someone who's comfortable talking to the media."

Spence as the media almost made me want to smile. "Consulates aren't usually in the limelight, unless the country is a trouble spot," I said in an offhand manner.

"So." Spence gave me a conspiratorial grin. "I showed you mine, you show me yours."

"My what?"

"Your bit of information that I don't have which might help us piece this whole thing together."

"We're working as a team? Since when?" I knew I sounded belligerent.

Spence made an expressive gesture with his hands. "Doesn't your newshound's soul demand that you figure all this out? Do you really have that much faith in Milo Dodge?"

"Yes."

"I'm disappointed in you," Spence said, pulling a long face. "You and I are city people. We ought to band together."

"To outwit the local yokels?" I asked wryly.

Spence shrugged. "In a manner of speaking. Small towns move at a slower pace, and so do the brains of the people who live in them. It's perfectly natural."

I didn't dignify his comment with a response. "Where are you from, Spence?" I inquired.

"Boston." He was gazing around the room again, as if he expected a butler to show up with the drinks tray. "Why do you ask?"

"Just curious." I gave him an ironic little smile. "My newshound instincts. You don't sound as if you're from Boston."

"I worked hard to get rid of the accent," he responded. "How well do you think a 'strawr' vote or a speeding 'cahr' would go down in L.A. or Chicago?"

"Good point," I said, and shut up. Maybe Spence would take the hint and go away.

Surprisingly, he did. Or maybe he was merely bored and frustrated. "If you change your mind," he said, standing up, "let me know. You have almost a week before you can print anything again. Unless," he added, offering me a caustic glance over his shoulder, "you put out another special edition."

"I might do that," I said, also getting to my feet.

"I suppose you might." The brown eyes glinted with what could have been amusement. "Good night, Emma."

"Good night, Spence."

I closed the door, but put my eye to the peephole to make certain he was leaving. Sure enough, I saw him head toward his car, which he'd left parked by my mailbox.

Letting out a big sigh of relief, I hurried to the telephone. He'd shown me his, but I hadn't shown him mine. The information he'd given me might pay some dividends.

I dialed directory assistance and asked for the phone number of Gina Ancich in Seattle.

Chapter Seventeen

Apparently Spencer Fleetwood hadn't known that Gina Ancich and Nolan Curry had visited Alpine. Or if he'd heard about it, it had slipped his memory. Such a small incident wouldn't make it onto KSKY's hourly news update.

Gina answered on the second ring. At first she didn't seem to remember me, despite the visit to my house.

"The log cabin," I coaxed, "at the edge of town."

"Oh!" Gina exclaimed. "You're the newspaper person."

"That's right," I replied in an encouraging tone. "Have you spoken with Brian's parents lately?"

"Not since they heard his coffin was empty," Gina said. "Can you imagine how careless people are these days?"

I could, but I was beginning to think that carelessness had nothing to do with it. "It's terrible," I remarked. "Gina, did you know that Brian planned to go abroad?"

Dead silence. When Gina spoke again, her voice had dropped an octave and all the usual flightiness had disappeared. "How do you know that?"

"Because his parents received his passport," I said. "I gather it had been delivered to the Irish consulate, probably at Brian's request. They didn't know what to do with it after he died, so they forwarded it to Mr. and Mrs. Conley."

"I see." Gina's tone had gone stone cold. "If he was planning a trip, I don't know anything about it. But," she added, a bitter note surfacing, "there were lots of things I didn't know about Brian. That's why I was about to break up with him."

"You were? I didn't get that impression when I saw you last week."

I heard Gina sigh. "It would have been inappropriate. Besides, Nolan Curry—Brian's friend—didn't know. He still doesn't. What's the point of telling anybody now?"

"You just told me," I pointed out.

"That's different," Gina declared. "I don't know you. You didn't know Brian."

Her point was apt. I realized that I was dealing with a different person than the one who had called on me earlier. There was nothing vague about Gina now; she was no airhead, no Tiffany Eriks. Whatever the reason for the birdbrain act, Gina had abandoned it in favor of candor.

"Do you have Nolan Curry's phone number?" I inquired.

"At the consulate or at home?"

"At home."

"Why do you want it?" Now it seemed that Gina was interrogating me.

"I want to find out if Nolan knew where Brian was going. On his trip, that is."

With another sigh, Gina gave me Nolan's number. "Look," she said, "I don't mean to be rude, but please don't call me again. I'm trying to work my way through this whole Brian thing. I was just starting to pull myself together when his body was found. Now I feel like I have to start over, and conversations like this don't help."

"I'm sorry," I said. "Really. But it's my job as a newspaper editor to present the entire story, especially when it involves a murder investigation. Alpine isn't like Seattle. Murder—any murder—is big news here."

"Okay, I understand," Gina said a bit testily. "But I still need to heal. This has been going on for way too long."

"Believe me," I assured her, "I know all about loss and heartache. Not quite three months isn't all that much time. Give yourself at least a year."

"A year?" Gina let out a gusty laugh that would have made Janet Driggers proud. "It's been more than that."

The response puzzled me. "But Brian went missing at the end of March. This is the middle of June."

"I don't mean that," Gina said with no sign of mirth, ironic or otherwise, in her voice. "Did you think I was referring to his death or his disappearance?"

"Yes, of course."

"Brian and I were off and on for a year," Gina said with bite. "That's why he went snowboarding alone. He was supposed to figure out if we had a future. I refused to put up with his cheating one more time. When I found out he'd gone up to Tonga Ridge by Alpine, I made up my mind that it was over. I planned to tell him when he got back to town."

My confusion still reigned. "I don't get it. Why was Tonga Ridge the breaking point?"

"Because," Gina said through what sounded like gritted teeth, "Alpine was where he knocked up some high school girl a year or so ago. And it sure wasn't the first time he'd fooled around on me. Brian wasn't exactly Mel Gibson in the looks department, but he had a way with women. And underage girls, I might add."

I took a deep breath. "Underage girls like Meara O'Neill?"

"What?"

"Was the teenager named Meara?"

"Maybe. I don't remember. I don't care. It's over."

It might be for Gina Ancich, but not for the rest of us.

I felt that the call to Nolan Curry would be anticlimactic. Since he didn't answer, it wasn't even that. I left my name and number on his voice messaging, then checked in with Janet Driggers. She didn't answer, either.

Ordinarily, I would have called Vida immediately after the conversation with Gina Ancich. Now I hesitated. My House and Home editor had been so hostile that I thought it was best to let her cool off until morning.

It was well after nine when darkness finally settled in over the mountains. I considered finishing what was left of the tuna sandwich, but still had no appetite. The sense of unease that I'd felt in The Pines returned. Stepping outside for a moment, I took deep breaths of the evergreen-scented air and tried to clear my head. A silver moon was on the rise, peeking through the big cedar tree next door. I could see a trillion stars above the mountains, a thousand lights in the town below. The soft June night and the faraway sound of the river should have been soothing. But they weren't.

The phone rang, summoning me inside. Nolan Curry was on the line, sounding curious. "What's up?" he asked.

"A couple of questions for you regarding Brian Conley," I said. "Did you hear about his passport at the Irish consulate?"

"Sort of," Nolan replied. "I guess it showed up at the office a couple of months ago."

"You knew that at the time?"

"I heard about it later," Nolan said. "The receptionist had it. I don't talk to her unless I have to."

Hit on her, got turned down, I figured. "So it just sat there until the last few days?"

"I guess," Nolan replied. I pictured him tugging at his

red forelock. "I mean, it wasn't like we knew Brian was dead, right?"

Wrong. "Where did you and the other people at the consulate think Brian was?"

"You never know, do you?" Nolan responded.

I suppressed a sigh of impatience. "Did you know where he was planning to go?"

"You mean when he went snowboarding?"

That wasn't the question, but I played along. Gina appeared to have learned of Brian's destination after the fact, which meant someone else must have told her. "Right," I said.

"Yeah, I knew he was going to Tonga Ridge. That's why we called the ranger station up there when Brian didn't get back."

" 'We'?"

"Gina and I called. I mean, she made the actual call after we started to get worried," Nolan explained. "He went up that Sunday just for the day. When he didn't come back that night, Gina started to get upset, so she phoned me to ask if I'd heard from Brian. I'd been gone all day, but he hadn't left either of us a message. That made Gina even more upset."

Maybe Gina had thought that Brian was with Meara. "She thought he'd had an accident?"

"I guess." Brian was sounding vague again. "I figured he'd gotten a late start."

"How come?"

"It was Palm Sunday, and I knew Brian was going to early Mass at the cathedral before he took off," Nolan recalled. "So it seemed that maybe he'd run into some bad weather up around Alpine and had decided to wait a day. But when Brian didn't show up for work Monday, I got worried, too, and told Gina we'd better call the ranger station."

"Where was Brian going on that passport?" I inquired, reverting to my original question.

"Ireland," Nolan replied. "He'd never been there, and he thought that as long as he worked for the consulate, he ought to visit the place."

"When did he plan to leave?"

Nolan hesitated. "I'm not sure. He wanted to have the passport on hand in case one of those real hot deals on airfares came up."

"Have you been to Ireland?" I asked.

"A couple of times," Nolan replied. "Once with my folks when I was a kid. Then right after I got out of college. It's really pretty, all green, with lots of great seacoast."

My queries had run out, and so had my luck. I hadn't learned much from Nolan Curry. I thanked him for his time and rang off. The call had indeed been anticlimactic.

And still I felt apprehensive.

Maybe Vida was the cause. I almost dreaded going in to work that Wednesday morning. But for the first time in recent memory, Vida had phoned Ginny Erlandson to say that Roger was unwell and that only his doting grandmother could nurse him back to health.

"Vida sounded very concerned," Ginny informed Leo and me shortly after my arrival. "Vida's daughter Amy had a dental appointment with Dr. Starr. Ted had to go to work, and Vida wouldn't hear of Roger's being left alone, even for an hour. I gather she'll be in the office by one o'clock."

Roger was no doubt faking, trying to gain the sympathy of his parents as well as his grandmother. Not that he needed to try with Vida—she already had too damned much sympathy for the kid, in my opinion.

After Kip arrived with the morning's confectionery, I grabbed a sugar doughnut to go with my coffee and secluded myself behind a closed door. It wasn't yet eight-thirty, but I figured that, with a baby, Meara O'Neill would be up and about. I dialed Lona's number in Everett and waited through six rings before I got an answer.

"Ms. Lord," Meara said, breathless. "I was just changing Cornelius. He was crying, and I didn't hear the phone at first."

"That's okay," I responded. "Meara, I know who Cornelius's father is."

"You do?" she gasped.

"Yes," I replied. "I hope you're not ashamed of him."

"No," she said slowly, "it's not that. It's more like that . . . we could never be together."

"Brian's parents might like to know about his son," I pointed out.

"Maybe." Meara didn't sound convinced.

"Does the name Gina Ancich mean anything to you?" I asked.

There was a long pause. "Gina does," she said slowly. "I don't know her last name."

"Are you referring to Brian's sometime girlfriend?"

Another, shorter pause. "Yes."

I explained how I'd spoken to Gina the previous evening. "Brian's"—I stopped, searching for the right word—"romance with you came up only because of Gina's jealousy. By the way," I continued, keeping my voice casual, "did you see Brian the weekend that he was in Alpine?"

"No," Meara said, and there was grief in her voice. "I planned to, after he got back from snowboarding. When I didn't hear from him later that day, I figured he'd decided that meeting me was a bad idea. He'd never seen Cornelius, and I felt he should. Until I learned Brian was missing, I thought he'd . . . panicked and gone back to Seattle. To Gina. The two of them always seemed to be having problems."

Something Meara had said distracted me so that the rest of her words went by in something of a blur. "You mentioned you didn't hear from Brian later on in the day. Did he call you when he got to town?"

"No," Meara answered, "he called from Seattle just before nine. He was leaving to come up to Alpine. He said he'd go snowboarding first, while the weather held."

"I see." It was time to change the subject. "How's your mother doing?"

"She's okay, I guess," Meara replied. I could hear Cornelius fussing in the background. "She had to go to Alpine this morning, but I'm not sure why. Maybe it has something to do with the rental house."

I remembered: Milo was interrogating Lona O'Neill today. "Did your mother take the day off?"

"Yes. Excuse me," she apologized. "I have to feed Cornelius. Sometimes it makes me so sad to think that he never got to see his father. You won't tell anyone, will you?"

I couldn't promise. "Don't worry about it. You're doing very well as his mother." It was the least and the most I could say; it was also the truth.

After hanging up, I felt a rush of excitement. Tiny bits and pieces of the puzzle were beginning to show up, if not yet fall into place. It was like doing a jigsaw, with all blank blue coming out of the box first, then the tip of a tree branch or the top of a hill. No real meaning, but at least some guidelines.

My head jerked up as someone knocked on my door. "Come in," I said, feeling a bit guilty, since my staff wasn't accustomed to their boss working in private.

But it wasn't one of my employees who loped into the little room and closed the door behind him.

"Dammit," Milo Dodge breathed. "I don't need more complications in my life right now."

My curiosity climbed. "Such as?"

Milo sighed as he took off his regulation hat and perched it on his knee. "Tara gave me an ultimatum last night."

"What?" I leaned forward in my chair. "But you two haven't gone together that long."

"Six months, since the holidays," Milo said, his expression grim.

"Do you mean she wants to get married?"

Milo nodded, his long chin almost touching his chest. "She doesn't like being a widow, I guess."

Over the years, I'd come to realize that I was the only person in whom Milo confided his personal feelings. The sheriff was a real Lone Ranger, with a few buddies but no real friends. Perhaps because of or maybe in spite of the physical intimacy we'd shared, he trusted me. "How did you react to Tara's ultimatum?" I asked.

Milo grimaced. "You got any of that fancy coffee?"

It wasn't "fancy," though Milo deemed it so, if only because what came out of the sheriff's urn tasted like sludge to the rest of us.

"I'll get you some," I said and scurried out into the editorial office.

Surprisingly, Vida was at her desk. She gave me a narrow-eyed stare as I poured coffee into a Starbucks mug. "What's he doing here so bright and early?" she demanded.

"I'll tell you later," I said, noting that Vida's demeanor was still frosty. I thought I heard her snort as I went back into my cubbyhole and closed the door.

"So," I said, sitting down again. "Tell Mother Emma how Tara's sudden burst of desire for marital bliss really makes you feel."

I don't think I'd ever seen Milo sneer before, but he did now. "Stupid," he replied, never one to go deeply into his inner self.

"I don't think that's quite the proper description," I remarked dryly. "Do you reciprocate the lady's feelings?"

"Not about getting married," the sheriff retorted. "Hell, Emma, even when you and I were dating, we talked about living together, but not about getting married. I was burned pretty bad by Mulehide. I'm still running scared."

"Mulehide" was Milo's name for his ex-wife, Tricia. She was a teacher at the middle school and had had an affair with one of her colleagues. He had left his wife and moved to Bellevue to escape the scandal. Tricia soon followed her lover out of town, taking the three Dodge children with her. That had been over ten years ago, but Milo's heart was like everything else about him—slow, cautious, and difficult to change.

"Are you in love?" Strange, it wasn't an easy question to ask.

Milo grimaced again. "I don't think so."

"But you could be?" I hesitated. "I mean, if you gave it time?"

"Maybe," he allowed after a hesitation of his own. "She's a fine woman, smart, good-looking, a decent cook. I could do worse. If I wanted to get married again."

"What's Tara's rush? I mean, aside from the fact she doesn't like being a widow."

The sheriff took a swig of his coffee. "I don't know. She just sort of sprung it on me last night. I thought we were doing fine just the way things were."

Men always thought that. As long as a woman didn't get hysterical every other day or try to hang herself from a clothes hook in the ceiling, the couple was "doing fine."

A few drops of rain spattered the small and only window in my office. "Be honest with Tara. Tell her you aren't ready for anything permanent."

Milo was silent for several moments, staring at the

rubble on my desk. "Right. That's the truth. Even if she wants to break up, that's the way it has to be."

"Break up?" I echoed. "She threatened you with that?"

"Kind of." Milo winced. "Fish or cut bait, that's how I'd put it."

"That's not fair," I declared. "Not this early in the game. If Tara's unwilling to compromise, maybe you don't need her." I refrained from adding that she sounded selfish.

"You're right." Milo batted his hat against the edge of my desk and stood up. "Thanks for listening, Emma. You've always been pretty good at that."

For Milo, the compliment was extravagant. "Sure, any time. Say, have you heard anything about Al Driggers?"

Milo looked puzzled. "Al? Like what?"

"Janet told me he was missing," I said. "I thought she was going to report it to you."

Milo shook his head. "Nobody's heard anything about it at headquarters. Are you sure Janet wasn't off on some tangent?"

"No," I admitted. "You're probably right. Janet can jump to conclusions."

"Sounds like her," Milo said, his hand on the doorknob. "I have to question Lona O'Neill. She's due in at nine. Thanks for everything."

I asked Milo to let me know if he found out anything from Lona. I also asked him to leave the door open. Apparently preoccupied with his romantic problems, he forgot. After opening the door myself, I dialed Janet Driggers's home number.

"What's going on with Al?" I inquired without preamble. "Did he show up?"

Janet laughed in her raucous manner. "Al's fine," she replied. "He was just running some errands."

I was relieved. "When did he get home?"

"Home?" Janet sounded odd. "Well, he didn't. He

went to Seattle." She cleared her throat. "Business stuff. He'd been too busy with all these funerals to tend to it until now."

"Oh." I frowned into the phone. "Of course. That makes sense."

It didn't, but I didn't say so.

Then, after I hung up the phone, I realized that it did make sense. I felt appreciably enlightened.

I also felt more than apprehension.

I was suddenly afraid.

Chapter Eighteen

CURIOSITY—ALONG WITH her basically good heart—seemed to have cured Vida of her anger toward me. I was still thinking about Al and Janet Driggers when my House and Home editor tromped into my cubbyhole.

"Well now," she said, looming over my desk, "what's all this with closed doors and Milo and goodness knows what else?"

I gave Vida a sardonic look. "When did I stop being a traitor?"

"Mmm." She sat down, a slightly sheepish expression on her face. "I decided you weren't using sense. The engagement, you know. You're muddled by love."

I refrained from saying something like *gack*, and shook my head. "Dubious, but if it means we're not on the outs, I'll take it. I thought you wouldn't be in to the office until later."

Vida waved a hand. "Amy canceled her dental appointment. She had too many other things on her mind. Meanwhile"—Vida glanced over her shoulder and lowered her voice—"Ted went to see Marisa Foxx first thing this morning. Marisa's quite a good attorney, and she informed Ted about Roger's rights and responsibilities with regard to Meara's child. Ted conveyed all of this to Amy, who told Roger, who said he must have made a mistake. He wasn't really certain that he could be the baby's father, and I—I'd already gone over to Amy's—I said no doubt Roger was feverish yesterday when he spoke so out of turn. Coming down with the flu, you see. Sometimes it causes delirium."

"Really." I didn't believe Roger was sick, feverish, or delirious. He'd wanted to boast of his manly prowess. Period. When he heard that a child would involve all sorts of legal and other entanglements, Roger had bowed out.

But I was of two minds about confiding in Vida. Having been begged by Meara not to let on who had fathered her baby, I hadn't revealed Cornelius's paternity to Milo. Not yet. I decided to hold off telling Vida, too.

Vida shot me a skeptical glance, but I feigned innocence. "You wanted to know why Milo was here?"

"Of course," Vida said.

"First of all, Al Driggers isn't missing," I began, "though Milo was never asked to find him. Janet told me this morning that he'd gone to Seattle on business. Apparently she'd forgotten, didn't get the message or whatever." I paused for Vida's reaction.

"Well." Vida's eyes blinked several times behind the big glasses. "I didn't realize Al had seemingly disappeared. Janet is rarely so rattled or so vague."

"True," I agreed. "Which makes me wonder. I've never known Al to go out of town overnight and not take Janet with him."

"Very odd," Vida murmured. "So, what did Milo have to say for himself?"

It wasn't prudent to keep too many secrets from Vida, especially when she'd been so angry with me earlier. "The romance with Tara Peebles isn't going as smoothly as he'd hoped."

"Why not?" Vida pressed.

I hadn't intended to go into details. But Vida knew I was being evasive. "Tara wants to get married. Right away. Milo isn't ready for that yet."

"I should think not," Vida sniffed. "Tara is a virtual stranger around here. What does Milo actually know about her?"

"She seems to have come with a fairly complete résumé," I pointed out. "Banker husband, widowed, mother of two sons, Dan and . . . I forget the name of the one who joined the navy."

I looked at Vida; Vida looked at me.

"Goodness," Vida breathed, "what's wrong with us?"

"I'm going to see Milo," I said, getting up and scooting around the desk.

Vida grimaced. "I'd come, but I told Amy I'd stay by the phone in case she needed me. With Roger. She also promised to call if his temperature went up again."

Again? What had the kid been doing? Spinning himself in the clothes dryer? He couldn't possibly fit, unless it was industrial size.

I was halfway down the street when I saw the big old-fashioned clock that stood on the sidewalk outside the Bank of Alpine. It read fifteen minutes after nine. Milo was probably still questioning Lona O'Neill. Dare I interrupt? Probably not. I'd have to wait until he was finished. Luckily, the morning light rain had stopped, though the skies were still a gloomy gray.

Mayor Baugh was coming out of the bank. He spotted me before I could duck into Parker's Pharmacy.

"Just the little lady I wanted to see," the mayor drawled, crossing Front Street against the light.

"Good morning," I said, trying to exude patience. "I was just going to the drugstore."

Fuzzy looked puzzled. "You were? But Parker's doesn't open until ten."

I struck my head with the palm of my hand. "Of course! What was I thinking of? I got such an early start that it seems later in the day."

The mayor uttered one of his false, hearty chuckles.

"That does happen sometimes, doesn't it? I wanted you to know that the toilets will be installed in time for the parade Saturday. You might want to get a picture of the men at work."

That was a reasonable suggestion. "Sure. I'll send Scott over there in the next day or so. How long will it take?"

"Two days, that's all," Fuzzy replied with pardonable pride. "But the really fine photo you can have for the next issue is the Potty Party Float."

"Oh." I tried to summon up enthusiasm. "Just what will that be?"

"Me," Fuzzy said, all but bursting the buttons on his summer-weight jacket. "Irene will drive our Cadillac convertible and I'll be sitting on a toilet I'm going to borrow from Sky Plumbing. Naturally, I'll have a lot of reading material, including the *Advocate*. What do you think?"

Pants on or pants off? I couldn't tell the mayor what I thought, nor did I want to take the time to find out more. Still, I had to wonder what Irene Baugh made of her husband's latest bit of self-aggrandizement. They had married young, divorced after a few years, then remarried in middle age. Irene must be used to him. Amazingly, the voters were used to him, too. Maybe they enjoyed the comic relief he provided.

By the time I shook off Fuzzy, almost ten minutes had ticked off the bank clock. Toni Andreas was waiting for me behind the curving counter at the sheriff's office.

"He's conducting an interview," Toni replied, "but he shouldn't be long." She jumped as a sharp ring sounded. "911," she whispered.

I pricked up my ears. Toni was frowning as she took the call. "But Ms. Grundle, your cat will probably come back. He always has." She paused and rolled her eyes at me. "Why don't you check back later—say, this evening?

I'm sure Toozle will . . . Doozle? Oh. I'm sure Doozle will be hungry by then."

"Honestly," Toni sighed, hanging up. "Every time one of Ms. Grundle's cats disappears for more than an hour, she calls 911. It's really annoying. The cats always come back, usually the same day."

"How come you're taking 911 calls this morning?" I inquired.

Toni acknowledged Dwight Gould's arrival from somewhere in the rear of the building. I, too, waved. "Because," Toni explained, "Beth Rafferty had to go to the dentist. She broke a tooth Tuesday and Dr. Starr couldn't fit her in until tomorrow, but somebody canceled today so she was able to see him."

The somebody was probably Amy Hibbert. "When is Beth due back?"

"Mmmm . . ." Toni glanced at the big round clock on the wall. "Any minute. I think she went in to the dentist a little after eight."

I told Toni I'd like to talk with Beth. At the vile urn of coffee, Dwight turned around.

"We already did," he said.

"You mean about her brother, Tim?" I asked.

Dwight nodded. "Beth insists that Tim's story didn't vary when he told her about what had happened up on Tonga Ridge. I guess she really reamed him for not calling her—that is, 911."

"That's what he should have done, of course," I said.

"You can trust Beth," Dwight assured me as loud noises erupted from a distance. "Damn!" the deputy exploded, setting down his mug so hard that he spilled coffee on the counter. I half expected the dark liquid to eat away at the fine mahogany grain. "Those Hartquists are at it again! I thought I'd settled their hash. Excuse me." Dwight hurried away to the jail area.

He'd barely disappeared when the door to Milo's office opened. The sheriff and Lona O'Neill appeared, still talking with each other.

"Don't let them pester you too much," Milo said, giving Lona a pat on the shoulder. "Sorry for the inconvenience."

Looking weary, Lona nodded at me and at Toni, then departed. "Hey, Emma, what's up?" the sheriff asked, no doubt surprised to see me again so soon.

"I've got some information," I declared, stretching the truth only slightly. "Do you have a minute?"

"Sure," Milo replied. "Let me refill my coffee mug. You want some?"

"No, thanks." I skirted the urn as if it might explode. "How'd the interview with Lona go?"

Milo eased himself into his big leather swivel chair. "Fine. I'm convinced she doesn't know anything about the arms thefts. I have a feeling naval security believes her, too, though they're damned tight-lipped when it comes to keeping me up to speed."

Before telling Milo what Vida and I suspected, I decided to test the waters. "Are there any other leads?"

Milo lighted a cigarette and scowled. "If there are, the navy's not telling me about them. Not yet. Oh, sure," he went on, exhaling, "they've promised to cooperate with SkyCo, but you know the military—a world of its own."

Even though Milo wasn't going to like what I had to say, I couldn't withhold my theory any longer. "That's why I came to see you," I said as the sheriff's phone rang.

Milo scowled some more, held up a hand, and lifted the receiver. "Dodge here. Can't this wait?" He listened to Toni, presumably, then let out a big sigh. "Okay, put her through."

Trying to become invisible, I busied myself with the latest pamphlet on state hunting and fishing regulations. But of course I was tuned in to the sheriff's every word:

"I'm really busy today. . . . Tonight's no good, I'm

playing poker at Jack Mullins's house. . . . Hey, it'll be late, and it's a weeknight. . . . Because we can't get together on weekends, that's the department's busiest time." Then there was a very long pause on Milo's part. Finally, his face darkening, he spoke again: "If that's the way you feel, so be it. . . . I'm sorry, too. Look, tomorrow night would be fine. Can't it wait that long?" Again, the sheriff didn't speak for almost a full minute, and when he did, his face had softened. "Okay. . . . I know, I feel the same. Bye."

Ringing off, Milo looked almost as if he were blushing. "That was Tara. She's giving me one last chance."

My heart sank, but not because I was jealous. As far as I was concerned, Tara's call couldn't have come at a worse moment. Milo had entrusted his feelings to me. I wouldn't, couldn't hurt him. "Do you want another chance?" I asked in a hollow voice.

Milo winced. "I don't know that I don't want it. I mean, I don't like acting hasty. She's certainly a fine woman. Like I said, I could do worse."

Maybe Milo really was in love. He swore he'd been in love with me. I thought he'd been in love with Jeannie Clay, although I knew it was a rebound romance, and short-lived at that. But until now, it had never occurred to me that he might actually love Tara Peebles.

I stood up. "I'd better leave you to your quandary," I said.

"Hold on," Milo said in surprise. "I thought you had something to tell me."

I gave thim an uncertain smile. "It can wait. I just remembered I've got to send Scott over to Old Mill Park to take pictures of Fuzzy Baugh's toilets."

Milo looked puzzled. "You sure?"

I said I was. Keeping some ugly doubts to myself, I left.

I arrived back at the office to find Grace Grundle shuffling around the newsroom in her carpet slippers. "Now see here, Vida Blatt," she was saying to my House and Home editor, "you've never had animals. You don't know the first thing about them."

"Animals are a nuisance," Vida declared, "and I do wish you'd try to remember that I've been Vida Runkel for going on fifty years."

Leo Walsh appeared to be absorbed in a layout. I didn't much blame him. Scott was on the phone, so I scribbled a note about the toilet photos and tossed it on his desk. He gave me a nod while I skirted around Grace, heading for sanctuary in my cubbyhole.

"Just a moment, young woman," Grace said, holding out an arm to detain me. "Would you please tell Mrs. Runkel here what a comfort cats can be."

"I had cats very briefly," I demurred. "I was sort of cat-sitting for a friend."

"Cats are very sensitive," Grace asserted, looking not at me but at Vida. "They're almost human. Indeed"—she sniffed—"they have more feelings than some humans I could name."

"Oh, bother," Vida muttered.

"Every time there's a death in Alpine, my cats become distraught for days," Grace continued, ignoring Vida's comment. "Doozle in particular. Doozle hasn't been himself for at least a week, and when he's like that, he always runs off. What could you expect with so many deaths all at once?"

"Yes," Vida admitted. "Oscar Nyquist, the O'Neill boys, and of course the discovery of the snowboarder's body. I don't recall such a week in Alpine."

Grace nodded. "Terrible, just terrible. Especially Oscar. Such a fine man. But that doesn't help with Doozle. He's still gone."

"But he always comes back," Vida pointed out with more patience than I would have expected. "You said so yourself. So why are you insisting that we print up circulars advertising his disappearance?"

"Because," Grace retorted, stamping her carpet-slippered foot, "he's been gone longer than usual. What's worse is that I understand you used the item about Doozle getting sick from the awful stench, but nary a word about him running off. Now, when they read your column, everyone will think he's safe at home, when he isn't. I think you should print the circulars for free."

Leo finally looked up. "Sorry, Ms. Grundle, no can do. But we'll give you a discount. How long has the cat been missing?"

"Since last night," Grace replied. "Do you know how much Dr. Medved charges? I had to take Doozle in twice, and it cost over a hundred dollars. How can I afford to pay for circulars? Don't you have a civic duty to your subscribers?"

I stepped between Leo's desk and Grace. "Please, let's wait. Had Doozle recovered from the . . . awful stench?"

"Yes, of course," Grace answered with a firm nod. "He only gets upset when Mr. Driggers runs the crematorium. The wind blows straight up the hill to my house. It's very noxious."

I stared at Grace, whose small, dumpy figure exuded defiance. "What night was that?" I asked, my voice sharp.

Grace jumped a bit. "What? Let me think . . . Tuesday or Wednesday of last week. Tuesday, I think. Yes, I'm sure of it. The milkman comes on Wednesday, and I was afraid I'd run out of heavy cream for Doozle."

I forced a kindly smile. "Yes, I can see why you've been worried. About Doozle, I mean. He sounds very sensitive. Excuse me, I think my phone's ringing."

It wasn't, but I dashed into the office and closed the door, though not before I heard Grace demand, "Now what about my circulars?"

Just as I reached for the phone, it rang. Janet Driggers was on the other end, full of apologies.

"I feel so bad about standing you up at the ski lodge," she said. "How about lunch? Al's supposed to be back from Seattle by then. He just called Dan Peebles at the mortuary to tell him."

"I'll get back to you on that," I hedged. "By the way, what impelled Al to go to Seattle in the first place?"

Janet's tone became conspiratorial. "I'll tell you at lunch. I'm buying, at the ski lodge, to make up for yesterday. Could you go at one so that I don't have to leave before Al gets back?"

I vacillated. But speaking with Janet should prove interesting. "Why not?" I said. Wednesday was always our lightest workday, though not necessarily this week. "But you don't have to treat. See you there."

"Grace!" Vida exclaimed in the doorway as I hung up my phone. "Such a ninny when it comes to those cats."

Along with Grace, Leo and Scott had left on their appointed rounds. Ginny was out front and Kip was somewhere in Skykomish County delivering the *Advocate*. I didn't need to ask Vida to close the door for privacy.

"Maybe," I began as she sat down, "I am a bit muddled by love. Even though the wedding isn't until next spring, I keep having these fantasies of walking down the aisle at St. Mildred's and being on a honeymoon in the south of France and making dinner for Tom every night."

"They aren't fantasies," Vida asserted. "They're your future. But why should you make dinner every night? Indeed, why not work part-time and let Tommy help put out the paper? He certainly has the experience."

I gave Vida an admiring glance. "That's a thought. He'll still have his newspaper empire to run, though."

"Surely it must run mostly on its own," Vida remarked. "That is, he doesn't have to be a hands-on publisher as you do."

"True," I allowed, then folded my hands on the desk and leaned forward. "But that isn't what I wanted to talk about. Maybe I'm jumping to conclusions about the Brian Conley murder and the missing body, but what did you make of Grace's statement that her cat always reacted to a cremation at Driggers's Funeral Home?"

Vida's gray eyes glinted. "Yes. I caught that. I think it's nonsense. I've never noticed a stench from the crematorium. But it did make me wonder. Grace lives on Spruce Street, just three blocks up from the funeral parlor. She could see the smoke, if not smell the . . . well, you know what I mean."

"Grace would imagine that Boozle or whatever the cat's name is was bothered by the smell," I said, growing excited as well as nervous. "And much as I hate to admit it, I do believe that animals can sense things that mere mortals can't. Which makes me wonder if Brian's body never left Alpine."

Vida sat up very straight. "Have you mentioned this to Milo?"

"Not yet," I said. "Little things were beginning to occur to me since last night. And this morning Milo was all worked up about Tara Peebles. Then you and I had the same thought about the naval station. Still, it was mostly guesswork, and while I was in Milo's office, Tara called him. I just couldn't tell him what we suspected."

"He'll have to know," Vida declared, " and the sooner the better. Sentiment can't play a part in this."

"But we could be completely wrong," I argued. "Even with what Grace told us, it's only beginning to come into focus."

"I still say we must tell Milo at once," Vida said, rising to her feet.

I glanced at my watch, which told me it was almost ten-thirty. "I don't know. . . . Maybe I should wait until I see Janet Driggers at lunch."

Vida, however shook her head. "No. Milo must hear this. Even if it's wrong, we should tell him."

"But," I protested, "you know how our sheriff feels about half-baked ideas. He'll look at us as if we're nuts."

Vida wavered. "That's so. He may even think we're fantasizing. Dear me, such a quandary."

"But Janet may be able to tell us something concrete," I pointed out. "Assuming she knows what we suspect."

With a grimace, Vida gave in. "You're right. Two or three hours won't make that much difference."

Yet as Vida went back to her desk, I questioned my judgment. After she left to interview Jean and Lloyd Campbell of Alpine Appliance about their recent trip to Peru, I dialed Milo's number.

Bill Blatt informed me that Milo was out.

"How soon do you expect him back?" I inquired.

"I'm not sure," Vida's nephew replied. "He took some personal time."

I sucked in my breath. "To do what?"

"I don't really know," Bill responded, sounding surprised that I would pry. I suppose only his aunt was allowed to do that. "He didn't say."

The sheriff wasn't required to tell anyone where he was going. But I thought I knew.

The apprehension I'd felt earlier now crystallized into outright fear for Milo.

Chapter Nineteen

BETH RAFFERTY CALLED me on her lunch break. "Toni said you wanted to talk to me. Can we do it over the phone or shall I stop by on my way back from the Burger Barn?"

The Burger Barn was across Front Street, not quite halfway between the sheriff's headquarters and the *Advocate*. My own staff were at lunch, so I asked Beth to see me at my office.

"That's fine," she replied in the perky voice that got shelved when a 911 call came through. "Can I pick up anything for you?"

I thanked her but said I was taking a late lunch. Fifteen minutes later, Beth showed up, carrying the ubiquitous white bag marked with two big red B's and a drawing of a sizzling hamburger patty on top of a barn. Just looking at the logo made me realize I was hungry.

Beth Rafferty was Tim's older sister, close to forty, with short blonde hair and intelligent hazel eyes. She was tall, almost six feet, and painfully thin. For years I'd wondered if she was anorexic, but Vida had told me that Beth had always been just plain skinny. Vida had also informed me that Beth had married a young man from Index when they were both still in their teens. The union had lasted less than two years, and after the divorce, Beth had taken back her maiden name.

"I'm on a wild-goose chase," I admitted. "As you've

probably figured out over the years, journalists like to play detective. It comes with the job description. We dig into stories, the way scientists and historians research their areas of expertise."

Beth gave me an uneven smile, a reminder that she'd been to the dentist and that the Novocain probably hadn't worn off yet. "Digging just like detectives," she put in.

"Exactly." I returned the smile. "I know the sheriff questioned you about your brother Tim. I also know that you said Tim's story was consistent—what he read over the air and what he told you. But was there anything he left out? Some detail, something so minor that he wouldn't feel it was worth mentioning?"

Looking up from her deep-fried mushrooms, Beth frowned. "Didn't you also talk to Tim?"

I nodded. "And Tiffany as well."

Beth sniffed. "Tiffany. Why my brother stays with her, I'll never know. She's the original bimbo."

"The point is," I explained, "I learned very little from either of them. But you see quite a bit of Tim, right?"

"Not as much as you'd expect," Beth replied with a wry expression. "In fact, there are times when I think Tim and Tiffany deserve each other. Our last heart-to-heart talk was when our dad died a few months ago. In fact, we had sort of a falling-out, though we made up later."

I couldn't believe that I'd forgotten about Liam Rafferty. He had requested that his earthly remains be buried in Ireland. Stunned by my lapse, I was silent for a few moments. Beth, eating her mushrooms and green salad, didn't seem to notice.

I took a deep breath and assumed what I hoped was a casual air. "The quarrel wasn't serious, I hope."

"Not really." Beth sipped her Coke before speaking again. "It was that crazy idea my dad had about being buried in the old sod. Or at least Tim insisted that was what he wanted. Our mom didn't know anything about it, but frankly, she has symptoms of Alzheimer's. Anyway, I couldn't find dad's so-called request written down anywhere. He didn't even have a will, but then there wasn't much to leave, and in this state, everything's community property, so it goes to Mom as the surviving spouse."

"Yet your brother insisted that your father wanted to be interred in Ireland?"

Beth nodded. "I couldn't really argue. But it was a big expense, and it seemed odd to Mom—when she remembers—that Dad didn't want to be laid to rest next to her at the cemetery here. Dad was born in Ireland, but Mom is from Skykomish. She isn't Irish, she's German. It hurt her—hurts her still, when she thinks of it. They'd had their problems over the years, but they loved each other. I know they did." Beth's eyes grew misty.

"When did your father die?" I asked.

"April fifteenth," Beth replied. "I'm not likely to forget the date, but of course it was also income tax time."

April. That fit. "Where's Tim right now?"

"What?" It appeared that Beth was still dwelling on her parents. "At the radio station. He fills in quite a bit on Saturdays before he tends bar in the evening."

"Thanks, Beth," I said. "You may not know it, but you've been a real help. I'm sorry I inconvenienced you on your lunch hour."

Beth shrugged. "No big deal, but I'd better get back to work. It took longer than I'd planned at the Burger Barn. They were really busy."

I didn't try to detain her. It was almost twelve-thirty, and with luck, I'd just have time to call on her brother at KSKY. The station wasn't too far off my route to the ski lodge where I was meeting Janet Driggers.

When Spencer Fleetwood formally went on the air almost a year ago, I was suffering from pique and refused to attend his open house. I'd sent Scott Chamoud instead, and of course Vida went, too. A stampeding herd of water buffalo wouldn't have kept my House and Home editor away.

The building that housed KSKY stood in a clearing just off the fish hatchery road. Several yards away was the radio tower. I couldn't guess its height, but it seemed to soar halfway to heaven. If it hadn't, the station's signal wouldn't have gone beyond the first crags of Tonga Ridge.

I didn't recognize the young woman at the desk in the tiny front office. Indeed, her wide, unflawed face indicated she wasn't more than eighteen. I assumed she was a college student and was startled by the deep voice that emanated from her flat chest.

"May I help you?" she inquired.

I told her I'd like to speak with Tim Rafferty. Ms. Deep Throat said he was on the air. I said I'd wait until he played the usual six-pack between commercials.

"He eats lunch then," she said, glancing through the big window behind her where Tim was hunched over a large computer console. "This is the last trio of ads before he has his break."

"Then I'll join him," I responded, and marched into the studio.

"Hey!" The young woman thrust out an arm to stop me, but she was too late. I was already inside where a startled Tim Rafferty pressed a final key and stared at me with his mouth open.

"What the hell . . . ?" he began.

"You're not on the air now?" I whispered, just in case the mike was still open.

"No." He gulped. "What is this?"

"Just a couple of questions, Tim. Relax." I sat down in

the only vacant chair, presumably reserved for interview subjects. Then I threw out my wild guess: "When did the O'Neills tell you about their weapons stash?"

Tim drew back in his swivel chair. "They didn't. What're you talking about?"

"You knew they had illegal arms," I said. "What did they do, ask you to help sell them?"

"No!" Tim was gripping the armrests on his chair so hard that his knuckles turned white. "I never got mixed up in that stuff! And they didn't ask me to!"

"But you knew about it," I said softly. "That makes you part of the conspiracy to sell stolen and illegal guns. How do you think Sheriff Dodge is going to react to your complicity? You could end up in a federal penitentiary."

Tim pounded his fists. "No! I swear, it's not like that!"

"Then why don't you explain it to me?" I suggested. "I can plead your case to the sheriff."

Tim shot a quick glance at the console, then picked up his headphones, apparently to make sure the broadcast was being sent without mishap.

"Look," he said, finally starting to simmer down, "the only thing I know is that the O'Neills were up to something involving guns. I didn't know what, I didn't know where they got them, I didn't want anything to do with it because they were a bunch of nuts, in my opinion."

"Nuts or fanatics?" I prompted.

Tim grimaced. "Fanatics, now that you mention it. You know, like obsessed."

"That's usually the case with fanatics," I remarked. "But the O'Neills got drunk one night and bragged about their big coup, right?"

Tim looked flabbergasted. "How'd you know?"

"I guessed," I admitted. "But I couldn't imagine that the O'Neills could keep a secret forever, not with all the drinking they did. At some point, they had to let something slip. Or do a little bragging. When was it?"

Tim rubbed at his forehead. "Late March, I think," Tim said. "It was when my dad was dying of cancer, and he died in mid-April. Paddy O'Neill—the old man, they called him—had died a couple of months earlier, and we got to talking about our dads. The next thing I knew, the three O'Neills were poking each other in the ribs and laughing their heads off. I couldn't figure it out, except they were pretty drunk."

"That's when they started talking about guns?"

"Not exactly," Tim replied, looking bemused. "I was busy, so I only caught a few words. You know, a phrase here and there. It was a Saturday, and the bar was really loud. But Rusty—or maybe it was Dusty—I never could keep those guys apart except for Stubby. I could always pick him out, because he had those missing fingers from the logging accident. Anyway, they started talking among each other about 'firepower' and how they'd sent dear old Da'—they called Paddy Da'—on his way, and then one of them said you wouldn't think you'd have to use a rocket launcher for the old man's send-off."

Tim paused, his eye on the clock. It was twelve forty-six. "Then one of them asked for another refill, and I had to cut them off. That always made them mad, so just to make conversation and show my interest, I asked what they meant by a rocket launcher. The three of them started poking each other in the ribs and laughing again. 'Wouldn't you like to know?' Stubby said. I knew it was Stubby because of the missing fingers. Anyway, I asked something else, but they just shook their fingers—that is, Rusty and Dusty did—and told me not to get snoopy, or I'd be in big trouble. That was it."

The story was credible. When Milo discovered the arms cache, Tim had put two and two together. But he hadn't come up with a perfect answer as far as I was concerned. My instincts told me he was holding something back.

"Who else was in the bar that night?" I asked. "Who might have overheard the O'Neills besides you?"

"Sheesh." Tim leaned back in the chair and shook his head. "I don't remember. Some of the regulars. You know—a couple of Petersons, a Gustavson, maybe Trout and Skunk Nordby."

They didn't seem like the type I'd had in mind. "One more question and I'll be on my way," I said, then lowered my voice. "Who approached you about having your father buried in Ireland?"

Tim's face paled. "What are you saying?"

"You heard me. It wasn't really your father's idea, was it?"

"No." Tim looked frightened, and I didn't blame him.

"Whose idea was it?"

"Dan Peebles," Tim said in a wavering voice. "But he told me it was the O'Neills' idea because of their dad being buried in the old country. My dad had been born there, too, and Dan thought it was something that he—Dad—might have wanted but never told us."

"Who paid for the extra expense?" I pressed on. "Who paid you off to do it?"

"Christ!" Tim exploded, a hand over his eyes. "Nobody paid me off. That is, Dan promised all the funeral expenses, including the shipping of the body, would be free." The hand dropped to his side. "I couldn't figure out why, but Dan insisted it would all be taken care of by somebody. Look," he went on earnestly, "it didn't make much sense, but Mom wasn't able to make decisions, and I thought that if we could get a free funeral out of it, so what? I never told Beth—she was mad at me about the whole idea anyway. But it seemed like a good deal. You don't have much time when someone dies to think things through. You know what I'm saying?"

"I do," I said with a sigh. When our parents had been killed in a car wreck right after Ben's ordination, neither of us was capable of making well-thought-out decisions. We'd merely let the undertaker guide us through those four horrible days between death and burial.

"Thanks, Tim," I said, getting up from the chair. "You've been a big help."

"Hey," he called after me. "Does this go in the paper? Are you going to tell Sheriff Dodge?"

"Don't worry about it," I replied with what I hoped was a reassuring smile. "I don't see that you've done anything illegal or even anything to be ashamed of. Except with Beth. You should tell your sister the truth. It's bound to come out."

Janet Driggers pulled into the ski lodge parking lot right behind me. I scampered over to her car and motioned for her to roll down the window.

"My turn to bail out," I said. "Look, Janet, I can't explain everything now, but where's Al?"

"At Doc Dewey's clinic," she replied grimly. "I drove up here to tell you I couldn't do lunch, either."

"What's wrong?" I asked in alarm.

"Al's having chest pains." Janet gave a violent shake of her head. "Damn! What's going on around here? Why are all these horrible things happening to us?"

I couldn't take time to explain that I knew what had been going on at the funeral home. Instead, I posed a question: "Al went to Seattle to check on Dan Peebles, right?"

Janet was wide-eyed. "How did you know?"

"I've been trying to put the puzzle together," I responded, speaking far too fast. "Do you know where Dan is now?"

"No." Janet chewed on her lower lip. "Nobody answered at the funeral home when I called to tell him about Al. Poor Al, if this mess is what we think it is, the scandal could ruin him. No wonder he's having chest pains! He hasn't felt this bad since he flunked sexual bondage."

I'd never wanted to hear details of the Driggerses' sex life, and certainly didn't want to now. "Don't worry about the business. You're the only game in town, and none of this is your fault." I stepped away from Janet's car. "How did Al manage to drive all the way to Alpine?"

"He didn't, quite. He had to pull off by the ranger station at Skykomish. They sent for Milo." Janet turned the ignition back on. "Talk to you soon."

Milo. Maybe he was safe after all. But the fears persisted. I followed Janet away from the ski lodge and down Tonga Road. Janet was driving like a demon, and so was I. The Lexus hit seventy-five just before we slowed at the arterial onto Alpine Way. Maybe we'd both get arrested. With any luck, it'd be by the sheriff.

Janet turned right onto Pine Street, where the medical clinic was located. I kept going, heading for Front Street. To my vast relief, Milo's Grand Cherokee was parked out front in his usual reserved spot.

"Milo!" I cried, seeing him behind the desk chewing on a toothpick. "Where have you been? Besides rescuing Al Driggers?"

"Organizing a manhunt," he said, his face as grim as I'd ever seen it. "Don't pester me, Emma. I've got too much on my plate to talk to you."

"Please," I begged. "I have some really important things to tell you."

"No can do." He handed some forms to Bill Blatt. "Maybe around three or so."

"But Milo—"

The sheriff swung through the opening in the counter, all but pushing me out of the way. "Later, damn it. I'm off."

I followed him out to the Grand Cherokee, and before

he noticed, I'd jumped into the passenger seat. "I'm going with you," I said, buckling myself in.

Milo swore long and loud. "You can't! This is serious stuff! Get the hell out!"

"I won't," I retorted, arms folded across my chest. "Let's go."

I knew Milo wouldn't take time to argue or even to remove me bodily from the Cherokee. He swore some more as he pulled out of the parking place and headed down Front Street.

"Where are we going?" I asked, suddenly assuming a meekness I felt Milo might appreciate.

"To search the Peebles house," Milo barked. "The state police have already set up roadblocks, but it may be too late."

"So you know about Dan and Don Peebles?" I said, still meek. "What happened with Tara?"

"She never showed." A muscle twitched near Milo's right eye. He seemed to be holding himself in, trying to control the anger and resentment he felt for his ladylove. "Tara wanted me to meet her at the Number Three Stove in Old Mill Park. It was a ruse, to keep me away from her place."

I was silent for a few moments as we headed into the Icicle Creek development, where Milo lived. Apparently Tara lived there, too, though her modest bungalow was closer to the golf course.

I put a hand on Milo's arm. "You know that Dan was in league with the O'Neills?"

"I need proof," Milo growled.

"The O'Neills got the weaponry through Dan's brother, Don, right? I mean, he's stationed at the naval base in Everett."

"The navy's working on that angle."

"Dan cremated the bodies that were supposed to be

sent to Ireland. Then he filled the caskets with illegal arms. Paddy O'Neill, Liam Rafferty, Brian Conley. Had Dan done it before? Is that what Al Driggers found out in Seattle?"

"Not exactly," Milo replied, "but he was close. Come on, Emma, get out of the damned vehicle. I've got work to do."

I complied. "Was Dan ever employed at the same funeral home as Gina Ancich?"

"No," Milo answered tersely as we made our way along the flagstones in the beautifully tended garden. Tara Peebles definitely had a green thumb, though the rest of her fingers may have been bloodstained. "But," the sheriff went on after a brief lull, "Dan did work for a Seattle mortuary. Before moving up here."

The next question almost stuck in my throat. "Was Tara in on it?"

Milo didn't look at me. "I'm not sure."

"Peebles," I murmured. "That's not an Irish name, is it?"

Milo didn't respond.

I had to ask. "Do you know what Tara's maiden name was?"

Milo swore under his breath. "Yes." He hesitated. "She was Tara O'Hara."

"Oh, dear," I said, very softly, and changed the subject. "Why was Brian's casket found empty in New York?" I asked as Milo opened the front door with what I assumed was his own key.

"I don't know," he mumbled. "Maybe somebody was onto the scheme. Maybe somebody stole the weapons out of Brian's casket."

The sheriff stopped in the middle of the living room. It was rather sparsely, if tastefully, furnished. I had the feeling that Tara traveled light. But Milo didn't move for what seemed like minutes. No doubt he was remembering the happy times. I hoped he wouldn't burst into tears when we got to the bedroom.

"As long as you're here," he said in a curt voice, "you might as well help. I've got a warrant, and we're going to haul out anything that might look like evidence."

"You mean file cabinets, boxes, that sort of thing?"

"There are no file cabinets," Milo replied, going through a trio of drawers in an end table by the sofa. "Frankly, I don't expect to find much."

We didn't. It took less than half an hour to search the main floor and the basement. Indeed, what we didn't find was more incriminating: most of Tara's clothes, as well as some of Dan's, had been removed. Nor did I notice any items of real value. Mother and son were apparently on the lam.

"Am I deputized?" I asked as we carried out a cardboard box and a couple of garbage bags full of what appeared to be sales receipts, carbon copies of checks, and other innocent-looking items.

"I guess," Milo sighed. "Jeez, how do I get into these messes?"

I assumed he meant with women. Before we had begun our romantic relationship, Milo had been involved with a woman from Startup. That affair had also ended badly. The sheriff was indeed unlucky in love. I counted my blessings, and tried to comfort him.

"Maybe she's not criminally culpable," I suggested as we got back into the Cherokee. "After all, any mother would try to help her children no matter what kind of trouble they got into."

"That's still aiding and abetting," Milo muttered. "I'll never go out with another woman as long as I live."

I didn't comment, except for the growling of my stomach. It was two o'clock, and I hadn't eaten anything since breakfast. Maybe I could nip into the Upper Crust across the street from the sheriff's office.

But even as we pulled into Milo's parking space, his beeper went off. "Damn," he said. "I'll get that inside."

As he hurried into headquarters, I grabbed the two garbage bags and followed him. An excited Bill Blatt was relaying the latest news to Milo as I staggered through the door.

". . . outside the naval base," Bill said. "Mrs. Peebles and Dan had beaten the roadblocks by just a few minutes, but the navy was waiting for them when they came to pick up Don."

"Of course." Vida spoke from behind the counter. She was sitting down, and at first all I could see were the artificial roses on her pink straw hat. "They were on the alert, they acted. I'm proud of our brave fighting men."

Milo, however, wasn't looking happy. "That means they've got jurisdiction, at least with Don. The military can't arrest civilians, but the Everett police are detaining Dan and . . . his mother. SkyCo's out of the loop. Goddamn it!" He pounded his fist on the mahogany counter.

"Now, now, Milo," Vida reprimanded. "Mind your language. You'll have your day in court."

Milo expelled a heavy sigh. "I guess. But it still pisses me off."

"Milo"—Vida gave the sheriff her eagle eye—"please."

"So," Dustin Fong intervened, "Don Peebles stole a bunch of those rocket launchers and maybe some other weapons, then sold them to the O'Neills, right?"

The sheriff gave a halfhearted nod.

"Where did the O'Neills get the money?" Bill Blatt asked.

"If, in fact," Milo said in a weary voice, "they were shipping the arms to the IRA in cahoots with Dan Peebles through the funeral home, somebody else was the money man. But not all those weapons we found came from the naval base. I have a feeling the O'Neills had been gathering other items, especially legal handguns, all along. They were probably involved up to their chins."

"I agree," Vida said, standing up and tugging her dress down over the hem of her white slip. "Paddy, too. There was probably some connection between the O'Neills and Dan Peebles even before he came to Alpine. Indeed, I wonder if that's why he came in the first place. His brother was stationed in Everett, there was a job opening with Al Driggers, the O'Neills were already in place."

"Maybe things got too hot for them in Seattle," Bill suggested. "A small town like Alpine might seem like an ideal spot to settle down for a while."

Toni Andreas sat back down in the chair Vida had usurped. "Wouldn't it be easier to find them here?" Toni asked. "I mean, there aren't that many people in the whole county."

"The authorities would have to have a reason to look for them in the first place," Dustin responded. "It isn't like they changed their names."

"Or did they?" Vida asked.

Milo shot Vida a sharp glance. "I don't think so."

"I suppose you ought to know," Vida said with a touch of acrimony, then assumed a more cordial manner. "I do wish we could find out who removed the weapons from poor Brian's coffin. Have you heard anything from New York, Milo?"

"Not yet," the sheriff replied. "But I think somebody got wise. They'll probably figure it out back east. New York might be one big jungle of a city, but they've got the resources and manpower to conduct a thorough investigation."

"Wow," Dustin breathed. "This has really been some kind of case."

"It sure has," Bill agreed. "But at least it's over."

I hadn't uttered a word for the last five minutes. Suddenly I felt compelled to speak my mind.

"It's not over," I said through lips that had gone dry. "We still don't know who killed Brian Conley."

Chapter Twenty

MILO THOUGHT I was wrong. "It'll all tie in," he asserted. "Dan must have murdered Brian. I've sworn out a warrant for his arrest on the homicide charge. Hell, I can't do anything until the navy and the Everett police finish their investigations."

"You could check Dan's alibi for the weekend that Brian disappeared," Vida put in.

"I can't do that until I talk to him," Milo retorted, fingering a copy of the SkyCo phone directory. Suddenly, he slammed it down on the counter. Bill, Dustin, and Toni all gave a start. "Let's move on. We've got other work to do around here."

Vida, who is never easily dismissed, came from behind the counter and headed for the double doors. "Milo's right," she said with a pleasant smile. "We're in limbo at the moment. Let's be on our way, Emma."

We went, though I managed to run across the street and purchase a big gooey cinnamon roll with a pat of butter. This late in the day, the Upper Crust Bakery was out of doughnuts.

Leo and Scott were at their desks; Ginny and Kip joined us from their respective posts. Vida and I regaled the staff with the latest turn of events.

"The IRA's just a bunch of thugs," Scott declared, "like those terrorists from the Middle East. I don't know how Irish-Americans can get sucked into that game. I'm of Lebanese descent, and I wouldn't shell out a dime to help any of those Middle East factions."

"You're basically right," Leo replied. "But it's different with the Irish. For one thing, we've got a special love for the old sod—even if we've never been there. For another, the Irish have always had the short end of the stick, especially the Irish Catholics. They've suffered and starved and died for centuries just because of their race and faith. Hatred and resentment don't fade easily for us micks."

Scott looked vaguely chastened. "But you wouldn't send rocket launchers to Ireland, would you?"

Leo uttered a wry laugh. "No, but that doesn't mean that after I hear how some British soldiers shot a bunch of women and children, I wouldn't feel a touch of satisfaction when a bomb went off in London. Hey," he said sharply, "don't get me wrong. I wouldn't dream of doing anything like that. I don't advocate violence, but you can't help how you feel. Call them thugs, call them gangsters, call them nutcases—but don't forget, in the beginning, the IRA was made up mostly of idealists. And call them the Provisionals. It's what they call themselves."

Scott held up his hands in surrender and grinned at Leo. "IRA, Provisionals, terrorists. I'll take your word for it."

"Leo's right," Kip said, looking uncharacteristically serious. "My great-uncle in Edinburgh worked hard all his life to bring back a Scottish parliament. Some amount of independence is very important to the Scots. It's too bad Uncle Ian didn't live to see the Scottish parliament open."

Ginny seemed befuddled. "Was Oscar Nyquist part of the plan? I mean, how could a Norwegian wanting to be buried in the old country fit into all this?"

"He didn't," Vida said. "Anyway, Oscar ended up being buried here where he belonged."

I took the cinnamon roll into my cubbyhole and devoured it like a member of Ed's pig family. Scott came in as I was licking my fingers.

"Hey," he said, keeping his voice down, "did I make Leo mad?"

I shook my head. "Forget it. Leo had to state the Irish case."

Scott looked relieved. "One other thing—I got this crazy idea while I was working on the summer solstice articles this afternoon. I found out that KSKY is having a float. Why not us?"

"Ah." I'd been too busy interrogating Tim Rafferty to notice any float activity at the radio station. "Do you know what they're doing?"

Scott nodded. "It's a flatbed truck they borrowed from Kenworth. I talked to Spence about it when I ran into him at Harvey's Hardware on my lunch hour. As a matter of fact," Scott added with a sly glance, "Spence wondered if we'd like to share. An all-Alpine media float, as it were. Or could be."

It wasn't a bad idea. Except that Spence had gotten it before I did. All the years that there had been Loggeramma or summer solstice festivities, *The Alpine Advocate* had been merely—and typically—an observer. But we had competition now, and the enemy seemed to be declaring a weekend truce. I suspected Spence's motives. Or maybe he wanted us to share the flatbed rental charge.

Scott saw me waver and leaped into the silence. "Ginny and Kip have some ideas for what we could do. Like take front pages of special, even historical, editions, blow them up, and mount them on the flatbed."

"Not bad," I admitted.

"And what about those old linotype and monotype machines out back?" Scott said, enthusiasm sparkling in his dark eyes. "Wouldn't it be cool to put them on the float, too?"

"Not bad," I repeated.

"Kip could wear an old-fashioned typesetter's outfit—you know, with the big apron and the visor, and . . ."

Vida had come up behind Scott. "I think it's a splendid idea," she said, "but Emma and Tommy should ride on the flatbed. It would be like an engagement party. I'll host a table at the postparade picnic in Old Mill Park."

"Oh, Vida," I protested, "I'd feel like a fool. And Tom would be embarrassed."

"Nonsense," she retorted. "It's perfect. I don't know why we didn't think of this before."

"Vida—"

She gave a definite shake of her head. "This is one time that you need to come out from behind the *Advocate*'s pages. Everyone loves lovers. You might even increase circulation."

After a decade, I still often felt like an outsider. Maybe this would prove I was part of Alpine. While I still had reservations about Tom and me sitting on the float like a pair of idiots, this was an opportunity to promote the newspaper. "Make a fool of yourself for Christ," Ben often quoted. I supposed I could make a fool of myself for the *Advocate*.

Thursday and Friday flew by. There were the float preparations, the special edition covering the summer solstice, and the flurry of activity throughout the town. There was not, however, much news from the sheriff. He was still glum, and not just about being temporarily unable to pursue the county's part of the case against the Peebles brothers. I tried to comfort him about his broken romance, but my euphoria over Tom's return made me sound like a big phony.

Still, a sense of apprehension persisted even as I got ready to leave the office Friday. Maybe I was worried about Milo, afraid that he might actually withdraw into a shell and give up on women.

The entire staff was in the newsroom as I headed out into the mild June evening. Scott, Ginny and Kip were planning the final touches for the float we'd share with KSKY. Leo was helping with a blowup of an old grocery ad from the 1940s, when you could fill up a bag for five dollars, including meat.

Vida was heading for dinner with Amy, Ted, and a completely recovered, if not rehabilitated, Roger.

"Do give Tommy my best," she gushed. "I can't wait to see him in the parade tomorrow. He'll look so handsome."

"You'll both look great," Scott declared.

"Remember to be at the staging area on Railroad Avenue by ten-thirty," Ginny reminded me.

"Bring some rain gear just in case," Kip cautioned. "Around here you never know what to expect in June."

"And do have a wonderful evening with Tommy," Vida added. "We're all so happy for both of you."

I acknowledged the advice and good wishes as I went to the door.

And still Leo said nothing.

Tom didn't arrive until after eleven. Fog had delayed his flight out of San Francisco. I thought he looked tired, and I said so.

"I am," he confessed, his arms around me. "For a while there, I wasn't sure we'd get out at all tonight."

"Since you're beat, let's go to bed," I said. "Unless you want a drink first."

He grinned at me and squeezed my waist. "I'm too beat to have a drink, but not too tired to go to bed."

Later, after we'd made love and Tom had fallen asleep, I lay in the circle of his arms. I could see the stars through the window and hear the soft spring breeze in the evergreens. There hadn't been much time to talk, but the few words we'd spoken had been about our future. In the darkness, I felt optimistic and secure. It was a feeling I'd never thought I would have. Sometimes the reality of it, confirmed by Tom's embrace, was difficult to grasp. But I was more ready to get used to being happy.

Over breakfast, I broke the news about the *Advocate* float. At first Tom was appalled.

"Why me?" he asked, though not without humor. "I'm not an official resident yet."

"Vida thought it would be a good idea," I said, though I sympathized with Tom. In fact, I sympathized with me. I still wasn't keen on riding in the parade. "You don't want to get off on the wrong foot by offending Vida, do you?"

Tom laughed and shook his head. "No, never that. Besides, I like her. She has a good head and a good heart."

"We don't have to be in costume," I pointed out. "I'm going to put on something I'd wear to work. For you, that crimson cashmere sweater with the gray shirt and dark slacks you had on last night would do just fine."

Tom sighed. "If I must, I must. Good God, what an introduction to Alpine!" Thankfully, he laughed.

Over a third cup of coffee and while we got dressed for the big event, I related everything that had happened in the Brian Conley and O'Neill cases since Tom had been out of town. Tom rarely interrupted. I'd concluded my recital by the time we left the house.

"So the Conley killing isn't officially solved," Tom remarked, taking over behind the wheel of my Lexus. "Isn't Milo upset?"

"I think he's more upset about Tara," I replied. "Besides, he seems sure that Dan murdered Brian. It turns out that Al found what he presumed was Brian's ashes, stashed somewhere at the funeral home. I spoke with Milo yesterday on the phone, and he said that since Brian worked for the Irish consulate he'd have been able to make the arrangements for the coffin shipments. Obviously, he was in on the whole scheme. He never dreamed that he might be paving the way for his own casket."

"Poor Milo." Tom shook his head, then backed out of the driveway. "He's had a rough time of it lately."

I knew Tom genuinely liked the sheriff. Oddly enough, while Milo might still harbor some jealousy, he never showed it. I took comfort in that, and tried to relax as Tom and I headed for the parade staging area between the railroad tracks and the Toyota dealership.

All was in chaos when we arrived. Musicians practiced on their instruments, organizers ran around in circles shouting orders, cars and trucks tested their engines to make sure they'd start, and the Rainbow Girls' Drill Team marched in one last formation under the old railroad water tank. The air was filled with odors of hay, gasoline fumes, and leavings from the Dithers sisters' horses. We watched the floats line up, with the high school band first, then Fuzzy on his toilet. Sure enough, he was already seated—pants on, thank God. Irene was at the wheel of the Baughs' ten-year-old Cadillac convertible. A banner displayed the winning name for the mayor's innovation: FUZZY'S WHIZZIES. Tom thought it was funny. Maybe he'd fit in after all.

Somewhere in the middle, between the 4-H float and the Masons, were the Bronskys, all seven of them dressed as quite credible pigs. Even their dog, Carhop, was wearing a pig snout. The float's bucolic backdrop looked professionally done.

Karl Freeman, the grand marshal and high school principal, was climbing up on the backseat of a new Corvette loaned by the Nordby Brothers GM dealership. Kip MacDuff was standing by the *Advocate* float, looking pleased with himself.

Tom admired my staff's handiwork. The blowups of

old-time front pages and long-ago ads had turned out well. The typesetting machines, especially the ancient monotype, however, looked dilapidated, as well they might. Spencer Fleetwood came over to greet us. I introduced him to Tom. If Spence was impressed, he didn't show it. KSKY's half of the float looked good enough; it was a reasonably accurate mock-up of a broadcast booth, with music blaring.

At precisely eleven o'clock, the parade began with the high school band whistling, tootling, and oompahing away. We were behind the Masons and in front of the Elks. As we turned onto Front Street, I felt very self-conscious.

"Tom," I said in a hushed voice, "is this too awful for you?"

Tom grinned. "No. I think it's kind of sweet. Old-fashioned, nostalgic. You know what I mean."

I did, though I still felt silly. But as we moved slowly past the onlookers who were gathered two and three deep on both sides of the street, I saw so many friendly faces that my spirits rose. Some waved and cheered; several called my name. Even Spencer Fleetwood turned around from his place on the other half of the flatbed and smiled at me.

We cruised past the Tall Timber Inn, the public utility district office, McDonald's golden arches, and Francine's Fine Apparel. The Alpine Buckers' band was up ahead three blocks, blaring out a Sousa march. Above us, the sky had cleared. We were in sunlight on a perfect June day.

Passing the Venison Inn on our right and the Whistling Marmot Movie Theatre on our left, I could see the *Advocate* office just ahead. Ginny had found some red-white-and-blue bunting to put over the main door and the two front windows. In the crowd at the corner I spotted Ginny with her husband, Rick, and their two small children. Scott was taking pictures; when he saw our float he let out a war whoop. Vida, of course, would be at Old Mill Park, readying our picnic lunch. There was no sign of Leo, but he was probably helping Vida. I felt proud of my staff, proud of the paper, most of all proud of being with Tom. I turned to him as we passed the *Advocate* on one side and the Alpine Building on the other.

"I don't feel so foolish anymore," I said with a big smile. "In fact, I don't know when I've felt so happy."

The last word still hung in the air when the shots rang out. I jumped, then looked at Tom. He was staring at me, his mouth open as if to speak. Before I could do or say anything, he pitched forward, knocking me to the hard floor of the flatbed.

People were screaming, shouting. I could hear what sounded like running footsteps and cries of "Get down! Get down!"

I was already down, with Tom's weight shielding me. It was difficult to breathe. The cab of the truck had jerked to a stop. Whoever had fired the gun had stopped shooting, thank God. But the paradegoers were still making ear-wrenching noises. It sounded like a full-fledged riot had broken out on Front Street.

"What's happening?" I finally managed to whisper to Tom.

Tom didn't reply.

Tom didn't move.

I gave him a poke with my finger. "Tom?"

Nothing.

I managed to move just enough to look at his face. He was still staring at me with those wonderful blue eyes.

"Tom!"

His name was wrenched out of me as if by physical force. I was frantic, panicked, half crazed.

Somebody, several somebodies were on the flatbed, moving Tom away from me. I rolled over on my side, just in time to see where the crimson of his cashmere sweater had turned dark. And wet.

"Oh, God!" I screamed. "God, God, God!"

"Get her out of here." It was Jack Mullins's voice, shaken but in command. "Move!"

"No!" I cried, fighting off the arms that took charge of my helpless body. "No!"

"Emma, please." It was Kip MacDuff, his face drained of all color.

"Kip," I said stupidly, then gripped his upper arms. "Tom—is he . . . ?" I couldn't say the words.

Neither could he. I saw Kip swallow hard, his expression anguished. My head turned in the direction of Tom and the men who had moved him off to one side. The ambulance siren suddenly wailed from close by. I reached out toward Tom, but he was too far away.

And then the blue sky with its drifting white clouds turned black. It was as if Emma Lord had ceased to exist.

And in a way, she had.

I woke up on a gurney in the hospital with Spencer Fleetwood standing over me. He was the last person I wanted to see. Maybe I'd died and gone to hell.

"Emma?" His radio voice was soothing, though it gave no comfort.

"Tom," I said in a voice that sounded very queer to me. "Please tell me . . ."

Spence took my hand. "I'm sorry, Emma. He died instantly."

I should have become hysterical. But I just lay there, staring at the ceiling of the emergency room. Later I would learn that the IV in my left hand was delivering Valium.

Doc Dewey came in, sympathetic and kind, as his father had been before him. "Dear Emma," he murmured as Spence stepped aside. "No words can express how sorry I feel for you."

"No," I said in that same queer voice. "What happened?"

"Milo can tell you," Doc replied, gently squeezing my shoulder. "You'll be going to sleep very soon. It's the best thing right now."

There was nothing that was "best" right now. Or maybe ever again. But Doc was right about one thing: I was losing focus. And then I thought of Adam.

"My son," I whispered to Doc. "I must call . . . to tell him . . . his father is . . ." The rest of the words wouldn't come out. I felt dull-witted, depleted, helpless.

Doc looked around the examining room, but Spence had tiptoed away. "I'll speak to Vida. She's in the waiting room."

That was the last thing I remembered until I woke up in a private room on the second floor. The venetian blinds were drawn, but I could tell it was still broad daylight. Vida was sitting by the bed. Her eyes were bloodshot and her face was haggard. The stalwart shoulders drooped and her impressive bosom sagged, making her look like an imitation of herself.

"Emma," she whispered. "You poor, poor darling. I'm sick at heart."

The IV was still running, which must have explained my lassitude. "What happened?" I asked in a lifeless voice.

Vida glanced up at the ceiling. Maybe she saw something there that was invisible to me. Maybe it was strength.

"Tom was shot from a second-story window in the Alpine Building. Two shots, actually. One hit him in the back and the other went into the monotype machine." Her voice had none of its usual zest. Vida sounded like a faltering newscaster who was reading from cue cards.

"Milo was two places behind our float with the sheriff's posse. He immediately figured where the shots had come from and, along with the other deputies, dismounted in pursuit of the shooter." She paused, removed a crumpled handkerchief from her sleeve, and blew her nose.

"Milo and Dustin cornered the culprit a block away, behind the Baptist church. He opened fire on them, and one of the bullets grazed Dustin's thigh. Fortunately, Milo managed to shoot the killer in the shoulder before he could do further damage. He's in the recovery room with Dwight Gould and Sam Heppner guarding him."

I felt as if I were listening to an account of an event that had nothing to do with me. Vida could have been reading news out of Seattle over KSKY. But in a dull voice I said, "I see." I saw nothing, except my empty future.

"I spoke with Adam," Vida said, her voice regaining some of its usual briskness. "He's flying from the Twin Cities tonight. He should get into Alpine very early in the morning."

"Oh." My son's name made some kind of dent in my stupor. "Thank you, Vida."

"I also called Ben," Vida went on. "Ben can't get here until late tomorrow night."

Of course not. He had to say Mass for his flock this evening and Sunday morning. He'd remember Tom in his prayers. And me.

"I don't have any numbers of who to call in San Francisco," Vida went on, "but Tom's children must be notified as soon as possible. Do you know where they can be reached?"

I didn't. "Call his office. The number's in my purse, in my little address book. Even on Saturday, someone should be there. They always keep some staff on hand in case one of his dailies runs into a problem."

"I'll do that," Vida promised. She looked at me closely,

her eyes very grave. "Emma, don't you want to know who did this horrible thing?"

I blinked at Vida. "Do I? What does it matter? Knowing won't bring Tom back."

Vida reached for the hand that didn't have the IV attached. She gave my fingers a firm squeeze. "But you must know who—and why. It matters. If not now, it will later."

I sighed. "Okay, tell me."

"The man who shot Tom was the same one who stabbed Brian Conley," Vida said. "Milo's certain of it. You see, after the culprit was wounded, he became . . . not precisely demented, but irrational. He kept shouting 'Erin Go Bragh.' Milo told me he wanted to . . . brag." She flinched at the word. "A fanatic, you see."

Vida had finally captured my attention. Maybe the Valium was wearing off. "Who was it?"

"Nolan Curry," Vida said. "Brian's best friend and coworker at the Irish consulate."

Leo Walsh was the one who told me the details. He came to see me in the hospital that evening right after Father Kelly had stopped by. Doc Dewey had checked on me earlier, insisting that I spend the night. I'd told him I couldn't possibly do that; Adam was arriving in the wee small hours. Doc, who is wise beyond the practice of medicine, told me that it might be better if I came home to Adam—instead of to an empty house.

And then Leo showed up, looking tired and sad. "You never guessed about Tom, I take it," he said. "You never knew he was involved with the Irish cause."

"No."

"I thought not," Leo said. "I found out by accident when I worked for Tom on one of his papers in Orange County."

I stared at my ad manager. "You knew all these years and never told me?"

Leo let out a little grunt that might have been part laugh. "I couldn't. I wasn't supposed to know. Too dangerous." He gave me one of his quirky little smiles. "Seven, eight years ago when I found out, I confronted Tom. He tried to make me understand his motives. I suppose I did, in a way. But I had to swear to secrecy."

"Why did he get involved?" I asked, surprised at the anger in my voice.

"You knew his father had an artificial leg?"

I nodded. "Tom mentioned it."

"That was courtesy of a British soldier," Leo explained. "His dad was born just before the turn of the last century in Ireland. Do you know about the Easter Rebellion in 1914?"

"Sort of," I said. "I know it was triggered by the outbreak of the First World War. Didn't Britain put the independence movement on hold? The Irish—mainly the Catholics—rebelled and tried to take over Dublin."

"You're close enough," Leo said with a pat on my arm. "Anyway, Aidan Cavanaugh was a teenage hothead. He wanted a piece of the action, and unfortunately he got it after the Brits sent reinforcements. Fighting in the streets broke out all over Dublin. Aidan was behind a barricade not far from the post office that the rebels had seized. The British soldiers overran the barricade, and Aidan was severely wounded and left for dead. Eventually he crawled away and got medical help, but the leg had to be amputated. The uprising was over, and the insurgents were being arrested. Aidan managed to hide out until—I think it was almost six months later—he took ship to America. He was only fifteen."

I was silent for some time. "It's ironic," I murmured. "I always blamed Sandra for holding Tom hostage with her inherited wealth. I never dreamed that Tom's own father had passed on an equally fatal legacy." Again, I was quiet for a few moments. Then I looked at Leo. "But why did Nolan Curry shoot him?" There. I'd said it out loud.

Leo grimaced. "Remember last Saturday?"

I did. Tom had been working in the yard, hauling debris to the dump. I'd been so happy. I thought he was, too.

"Tom stopped by my apartment to see me for a few minutes," Leo went on. "He wanted to explain himself to me. Tom was very perceptive about people. He always sensed that because I knew he was involved in helping the Irish, I not only didn't approve, but I wouldn't want to see you get mixed up in it in any way. To my surprise, he agreed. He confided that he'd been trying to make a clean break. But since he was the money man, it would be difficult. It's rare that anybody abandons the cause, at least if his associates are zealots. Tom had been a major West Coast financial supporter. Nolan Curry and Brian Conley were both involved, mainly through their work at the Irish consulate. Not that the consul or any of the others knew—but Nolan and Brian had gotten caught up in the thing as teenagers. It was romantic, it was an adventure, they felt like heroes."

"Gangsters," I muttered. "No different from other gangs, really. A sense of belonging, empowerment—and needless violence."

"My feelings exactly," Leo said, "at least for the younger generation, both in Ireland and North America. Ironically, Brian Conley wanted to get out, too. Unlike Nolan, Brian believed that the recent truce in Northern Ireland should be given a chance. I gather that's why he wanted to go to Ireland, to see for himself what was happening. Last March, Brian used snowboarding as an excuse to come to Alpine. He knew Tom was in town visiting you and he wanted to see him, get his take on what was happening overseas."

I gaped at Leo. "Tom knew Brian Conley?"

Leo nodded once. "Tom was known to the other Irish sympathizers as T. C."

T. C. Nolan Curry had mentioned the name—the initials—in reference to somebody or something. My fuzzy brain couldn't quite recall. I closed my eyes and tried to think.

"My house," I said slowly. "Nolan and Gina Ancich stopped by. They mentioned a man called T. C. who'd taught somebody—maybe Brian—how to snowboard at Lake Tahoe."

"Is that right?" Leo gave a shake of his head. "Tom told me he'd known Brian, but he couldn't imagine who'd killed him."

"He didn't suspect Nolan?" I responded in a flabbergasted voice.

"No," Leo said. "He thought Brian and Nolan were best friends. Face it, Tom's connection with what I'd call the foot soldiers was remote. Remember all those dinner engagements Tom had in Seattle on his way up here? Maybe they were with the middlemen. Anyway, I think he was ignorant of the Alpine connection until the O'Neills' arms cache was found. Brian never came down from Tonga Ridge that Sunday. Tom told me he never heard from him. If anything, Tom may have believed that the O'Neills killed Brian."

"So," I said after another pause, "Tom was going to end his association. I suppose he wanted to see how the truce worked out, too."

"That was part of it," Leo agreed, then put his hand back on my arm. "But not the main reason. He was getting out because of you."

"Me?" I stared again at Leo.

He nodded. "I've always felt that was one of the reasons he put off marrying you after Sandra died. Tom was rethinking his support for the cause. But even if he still believed in it at some level, he couldn't put you in danger. In marrying you, he wanted a fresh start, a clean slate. Unfortunately, one of the extremists didn't see things that way."

"Nolan Curry," I said, barely able to speak his name. "You mean it wasn't all political?"

"Not from what Nolan told Milo in his ranting and raving," Leo replied. "Brian didn't tell Nolan about his decision to quit until they were up on the Ridge. Still, Milo thinks Nolan had an inkling of what was to come. Maybe that's why only Brian signed in at the ranger station. I gather Nolan went off his nut when Brian said he was finished with the cause. That was his death warrant. But it was different with Tom."

It was hard to bear, but I had to hear why Tom—and my dreams—had died. "How so?"

Leo gave me a grim little smile. "What did you think of Nolan Curry when you met him?"

I thought back to the get-together in my living room. "He seemed like a dork. Vague, not too bright, nobody you'd pay much attention to."

Leo nodded. "That, according to Milo, is how Gina Ancich felt about him. But Nolan wanted attention. Being an Irish sympathizer gave him an identity, like being in any gang. A successful, sophisticated financial backer like Tom who never got involved in the dirty work angered Nolan. He saw Tom as having it easy, sliding through life on his money and prestige. Tom got in, Tom could get out. That was anathema to Nolan. He considered Tom not just a traitor, but a personal affront."

"My God." I held my head. "Jealousy? I can't believe it."

Leo gave me another pat. "It wouldn't be the first time. Hey, for all I know, maybe he was jealous of Brian and Gina, too. Nolan Curry is probably mental."

I knew there were sparks in my eyes. "He won't get off on an insanity plea."

"No," Leo agreed. "He won't. Milo will see to that."

Ben and Father Kelly offered a memorial Mass for Tom Monday morning. Adam assisted, and, somewhat to my surprise, Leo gave the eulogy. St. Mildred's was almost full, though due to the lack of prior publicity, the Wailers were mercifully absent.

I managed to get through it with the help of my menfolk and two Valium. The following day, Ben, Adam, and I flew to San Francisco with Tom's body. Al Driggers, on his feet again, but still extremely upset, had offered to take care of everything for free. I appreciated the gesture, and promised I would make sure that Scott Chamoud's articles absolved him of any blame. The burden of reporting on Tom's death would fall mostly on Scott. I couldn't have written a single word without falling apart.

The funeral Mass was held Thursday in the new marble and glass cathedral, which I found impressive but lacking in warmth. When the white pall was placed over Tom's casket, Adam leaned down and kissed it. I rarely cry, but the tears flowed freely until we were out of the church. They began afresh when a trio of Irish bagpipers played at the graveside.

I was too distraught to feel awkward in the presence of Tom's children. They seemed polite, if curious. I couldn't blame them. To Kelsey and Graham Cavanaugh, I was the Other Woman.

The hard part was acknowledging that Tom would be buried next to Sandra in the cemetery of her ancestors. But, as Ben counseled me, Tom had never belonged to Alpine, only to me. That was one reason we didn't attend the funeral reception. I didn't want to see Tom's home in Pacific Heights. I'd never been a part of his life in the Bay Area. I needed no reminders of Tom with Sandra, of Tom with his other children. I had my own memories of him, if ever I dared to bring them back into the open.

Ben flew from San Francisco to Flagstaff and on to Tuba City. Adam returned with me to Alpine, where he planned to stay for a few days. We'd come home Thursday night, and I resisted my son's urgings to take Friday off. There was the Hartquist murder trial under way, the arraignment of Nolan Curry, and the Everett police had turned Dan Peebles over to SkyCo. Tara had already been charged by the Everett police as a co-conspirator with her sons. Her fate and Don's were out of Milo's hands. He was bitter, of course, since she had tried to manipulate him into marriage as part of some lamebrained scheme to avoid prosecution.

That Friday morning, the sheriff filled me in on the gaps in the Curry case. Nolan had come with Brian to Tonga Ridge. I'd figured that much out from talking to Gina Ancich—Nolan had lied about Brian going to early Mass at St. James Cathedral in Seattle. Meara O'Neill had heard from Brian shortly after nine o'clock that morning. He was already in Alpine. With Nolan Curry.

As Leo had related, when the two young men got up on the Ridge, Brian announced that he wanted out. Nolan had stabbed him to death and hidden his body. He bragged about it, considering himself a martyr to the cause, comparing himself to the Irish patriot Bobby Sands, who went on a hunger strike and died in prison many years ago. Milo figured that Nolan's martyr complex was why he'd shot Tom so boldly and so publicly. Nolan was making a statement. For Ireland. As if most Irish men and women on either side of the ocean cared.

But I cared. I cared so much that I couldn't have borne going home from work that night if Adam hadn't been waiting for me.

But he was. When I pulled up in the driveway, I saw him standing in the front yard, looking at some of the new plantings I'd put in to fill the spaces Tom had cleared.

The Lexus drives so smoothly that my son didn't hear my arrival. For a moment, I watched him, his back to me, and looking so like his father at that same age. My heart filled up with longing. No wonder I had felt such apprehension. I'd mistaken it as worry for Milo. How odd that we often can't read our own feelings.

Odd, too, that we don't ever really know another person. In the past couple of weeks, I'd misjudged a number of people: Gina Ancich, Dan Peebles, Nolan Curry, and maybe—just maybe—Spencer Fleetwood. They'd hidden their true selves from me. But we all do that, and Tom had good reason to keep his secret.

There were so many questions that would never get asked. The future I'd glimpsed so briefly had withered, like spring buds in a killing frost.

Adam was still studying the garden, still reminding me of Tom. For almost thirty years, ever since I met Tom, he had rarely been at my side. But Adam had been with me always, from the womb.

Getting out of the car, I called his name. He turned to look at me with Tom's blue eyes. The last time I'd seen Tom's face, he'd looked at me with those same eyes. I didn't know it then, but they were the eyes of the dead.

Adam was still alive.

Maybe I was, too.

Afterword

ALPINE, WASHINGTON WAS a real town, a company town, and as such, it was doomed from the start.

In the early twentieth century, Carl Clemans and two partners went into the timber business, first in eastern Washington, and later in the Cascades, a mile off the Stevens Pass Highway. The site they chose was a whistle stop called Nippon on the Great Northern Railroad. Carl Clemans rechristened the town-to-be as Alpine. He built a mill and began logging operations.

A benevolent man, Clemans was both boss and father figure to the men and the families who moved to Alpine. From 1915 until 1921, my grandfather and my great-uncle were among the workers he employed. My mother and her five siblings were raised in the town, which could be reached only by railroad or by climbing a mile up the mountainside.

The family returned to Seattle after my mother graduated from high school. But that was not her last look at Alpine. In 1926, she married my father, who took a job at Carl Clemans's sawmill. My parents remained there for almost two years, but saw the handwriting on the clear-cut slopes. By 1929, Clemans's parcel of land had been logged out. There was no other reason for the town's existence, so it was shut down and burned. Such was the fate of many company towns that had outlived their reason for being.

But memories lingered on and were possibly gilded. From my earliest days, I listened to my parents and grandparents and other relatives speak of Alpine with great fondness and good humor. Geographically isolated, snowbound six months of the year, these hardy souls formed a bond that endured through the rest of the century.

That sense of community and continuity for a tiny town that had been erased from the map inspired me to make Alpine come alive again in my series of mystery novels. I suppose it was inevitable. I never saw Alpine, but it has been with me since the beginning. It lives again, at least in my imagination.

—Mary Daheim